Praise for *The Gentleman Sp*

"Schwarz launches her *Gentleman Spy Mysteries* series with an intimate and suspenseful Regency romance. The magnetic love scenes and enticing mystery will have readers eagerly anticipating the next installment."

— *Publishers Weekly*

"I love Eliza and Allen together—not only do they lead interesting Regency-era spy lives, but their friends-to-lovers arc is based all the way on healing, trust, humor, and pleasure. A charming read!"

— Molly Ringle, author of *Lava Red Feather Blue*

"*The Innkeeper's Daughter* is a sumptuous, sensual Regency romance that teases the senses and recalls the golden age of romance novels."

— *Foreword Reviews*

"A gritty, steamy series opener full of dark twists and hot trysts."

— Grace Burrowes, *New York Times* bestselling author

"*The Memory of Her* enfolded me once again in a richly detailed world of spies and traitors, of lovers and friends, all set against the backdrop of Regency England, and all framing two characters we've already come to know and care about—a woman with gumption and heart, and a man with a heart full of love for her."

— Amanda Linsmeier, author of *Starlings*

"*The Gentleman's Daughter* is an escapist romance novel whose pleasures and terrors culminate in a hopeful restorative ending."

— *Foreword Reviews*

"Historically well-researched with enthralling characters and excellent storytelling. Absolutely wonderful."

— C. H. Armstrong, author of *The Edge of Nowhere*

"The chemistry between the charming Sir Henry and independent Isabella is delectable, and the intrigue is woven in perfectly to round out a thoroughly enthralling historic romantic mystery."

— Kelly Cain, author of *An Acquired Taste*

The Gentleman Spy Mysteries

THE GENTLEMAN SPY MYSTERIES

THE SPY'S DAUGHTER

BIANCA M. SCHWARZ

central
avenue
PUBLISHING

2023

Content Warning: This book contains scenes of and references to assault, kidnapping, and explicit sexual activity.

Published by Central Avenue Publishing, an imprint of Central Avenue Marketing Ltd.
www.centralavenuepublishing.com

Published in Canada
Printed in United States of America

1. FICTION / Mystery & Detective/Historical 2. FICTION / Romance/Historical

THE SPY'S DAUGHTER

Trade Paperback: 978-1-77168-352-4
Ebook: 978-1-77168-353-1

1 3 5 7 9 10 8 6 4 2

Keep up with Central Avenue

To my son, in the hope that he too will find his way
in the world.

SETTING: LONDON AND BRIGHTON

YEAR: 1826

CAST OF CHARACTERS (IN ORDER OF APPEARANCE)

EMILY MARCH (SIR HENRY MARCH'S ILLEGITIMATE DAUGHTER)

SUZIE (EMILY'S MAID)

BARON OSTLEY (ONE OF THE KNIGHTS; HUSBAND OF EMILY'S MOTHER)

CHARLES OSTLEY (BARON OSTLEY'S SON; EMILY'S HALF-BROTHER)

BOB (BARON OSTLEY'S SERVANT)

MAXIMILIAN WARTHON, LORD DIDCOMB (THE EARL OF WARTHON'S GRANDSON/HEIR)

ELIZA STRATHEM (AGENT TO THE CROWN; FRIEND OF THE MARCH FAMILY)

THOMAS (EMILY'S FAVORITE FOOTMAN)

SIR HENRY MARCH (AGENT TO THE CROWN; EMILY'S FATHER)

ISABELLA, LADY MARCH (PAINTER AND EMILY'S STEPMOTHER)

DANNY (EMILY'S BROTHER, SIR HENRY AND ISABELLA'S SON)

DOROTHEA (EMILY'S SISTER, SIR HENRY AND ISABELLA'S DAUGHTER)

MRS. TIBBIT (HENRY'S HOUSEKEEPER)

WILLIAM (HENRY'S FOOTMAN)

BERTIE REDWICK (EMILY'S COUSIN AND BEST FRIEND)

RUTH REDWICK, DOWAGER DUCHESS OF AVON (GROSSMAMA, EMILY'S GREAT-GRANDMOTHER)

CONSTANCE WARTHON (MAX'S MOTHER)

COUNTESS OF WELD (CONSTANCE WARTHON'S COUSIN AND NEIGHBOR, JANE'S MOTHER)

EARL OF WELD (ONE OF THE KNIGHTS, THE EARL OF WARTHON'S CONFIDANT)

LADY MELCHIOR (SOCIALITE, NEIGHBOR OF HENRY AND ISABELLA)

MR. BROMLEY (SOCIALITE AND PIANIST)

BEN SEDON (LORD DIDCOMB'S PARTNER AND FRIEND)

JANE SEDON (FORMER LADY JANE, BEN'S WIFE)

EDGAR (JANE AND BEN SEDON'S SON)

EARL OF WARTHON (MAX'S GRANDFATHER, HEAD OF THE KNIGHTS)

ALLEN STRATHEM (AGENT TO THE CROWN, ELIZA'S HUSBAND, FRIEND OF THE MARCH FAMILY)

MR. SPENCER (BERTIE'S FRIEND FROM OXFORD)

MR. SEDON SENIOR (BEN SEDON'S FATHER, OSTLER AT WARTHON CASTLE)

ROBERT PEMBERTON, VISCOUNT FAIRLY (HENRY'S FRIEND)

STEPHANIE PEMBERTON (ROBERT'S WIFE)

MENTON (MAX'S SERVANT)

LORD BERESFORD (MEMBER OF THE KNIGHTS)

LORD JENNINGS (CURRENT DUNGEON MASTER FOR THE KNIGHTS)

SINCLAIR (MEMBER OF THE KNIGHTS)

MRS. BENNETT (HOUSEKEEPER AT CHARMELY)

MARY (EMPLOYEE AT THE KNIGHTS' CLUB IN LONDON)

THE SPY'S DAUGHTER

PROLOGUE

HYDE PARK, OCTOBER 1825

THE MORNING SUN SET THE TREES AROUND THE Serpentine alight in shades of yellow, orange, and red, and reflected them in the mirror-smooth surface of the lake. Bending to pick up another horse chestnut, Emily March decided she had more than enough to teach her two-year-old brother, Danny, how to play conkers. Slipping the chestnut into the pocket of her powder-blue walking dress, she picked up her skirts so she could move faster. The path narrowed among the fall-colored trees. Emily rushed ahead, eager to get to the bridge across the Serpentine, where she was to meet with her friend Eliza for a morning walk.

Emily was almost at the far edge of the wood, the road already in sight, when she was lifted off the ground by a strong arm seizing her around her waist and pinning one of her hands to her side. Just as she let out a surprised shriek, she heard a similar shout from behind her and felt her heart sink. Her maid, Suzie, must have been similarly accosted. Had Emily been at Avon, she would have assumed her cousins were intent on scaring her witless, but this wasn't her uncle's estate, and it was unlikely one or more of her cousins had made their way to the capital. Emily realized, just as a rough leather-clad hand clamped over her mouth, that she was once again in trouble. And then she saw the black coach and knew someone was intent on kidnapping her. Truly frightened now, Emily thrashed wildly in hopes of dislodging herself, or at least the hand over her mouth, so she could scream.

"Did you think I would let that arrogant ass rob me of my revenge?"

Emily recognized the Baron Ostley's voice instantly, a nightmare come to life on this lovely autumn day. She pulled frantically on the gloved hand over her mouth. Not him, not again. Her eyes darted around, hoping to find someone who could help her, but there was no one in sight.

"And did you know his grandfather also has an axe to grind with your father? He has very interesting plans for you." The words, accompanied as they were by a nasty cackle and the stench of his breath wafting against her skin, made Emily nearly faint with nausea. She kicked with all her might against his shin, which earned her a slap across the face. It stung, but the nasty baron's hand was off her mouth, so she screamed as loud as she could until the hand stopped her once again.

"Warthon will have fun with you, you bloody wildcat!" Ostley panted with the thrashing girl in his arms. They were out of the stand of trees now and perhaps forty paces from the coach. "Open the door, Charles. And you better hold on to her until I can climb in. Looks like you're going to have to earn your turn with her."

Emily was busy pulling, scratching, and making herself as difficult to carry as she could, so when Ostley barked the command over her head, it took her a moment to comprehend the meaning of what he had said. The realization that there were two of them this time made her redouble her efforts.

An angelic-looking blond boy in his mid-teens opened the door to the coach and jumped down. His eyes were wide with horror. "I don't think she wants to come, Papa. We should go before we attract even more attention." He pointed toward a nursemaid clasping a crying child to her bosom and running as fast as she could toward Rotten Row, where a few gentlemen were on their morning ride.

Ostley seemed unperturbed by the prospect of a bigger audience and kept dragging Emily toward the vehicle. "Nonsense, no one is going to believe a maid's word against mine. Get in the coach and hold the door open."

Emily's predicament was frightening enough, but the arrogance with which Ostley assumed he would get away with kidnapping her was truly terrifying. And she had only herself to blame. She had been just as arrogant to think she was safe, that she could leave behind Thomas, the guard her father had imposed. She had been a fifteen-year-old fool the first time Ostley had assaulted her, and she was still a fool. After Ostley had been foiled two years ago at the inn by Lord Didcomb, Emily had assumed the baron would simply go back home and leave her be. And he had, for two years. But apparently he had been waiting for the right moment all the while. Emily's skin crawled as she realized he must have been watching her.

Pulling Emily's head against his shoulder, Ostley breathed into her ear. "I'm going to let him fuck you before I tell him who you are. We will see what he thinks of his precious mother then. She's a whore just like you are."

The words cut through Emily like a knife. Her mother, Lady Ostley, had loved her father; she was not a whore. Tears of frustration gathered behind her eyes. Then it dawned on Emily who the boy was. The monster was going to make her have relations with her brother. Fury burned within her at the injustice of it. How dare this monster make her the instrument with which to punish her mother. Emily wasn't sure she wanted to meet the woman who had given her up at birth, but she would rather have died than meet her like this.

As the door to her doom loomed closer and closer despite her constant kicking and scratching, the panic engulfing Emily sent blood rushing in her ears, so she didn't hear the horse approaching until it was almost upon them. But she saw the look of panic on the face of the boy—her brother Charles. Then she was jerked around violently as Ostley turned and shouted, "Take the bint, Charles." Then louder: "Bob, drop the maid and help the boy."

Emily was now facing backwards but still being dragged toward the coach. They were followed by a burly brute, who grinned a gap-toothed grin and had the writhing Suzie flung over his shoulder. At his master's command, he dropped the maid, but before he could carry out the second command, he was mowed down by the approaching horse. Behind the wild tangle of horse's hooves and the fallen man, Emily could just make out Suzie struggling to her feet and running for the trees.

Emily's golden god, Lord Didcomb, Max, the man who had come to her rescue two years prior, jumped off the still-moving horse and landed not ten paces from her and her captor, his riding crop raised high and ready to strike. "Didn't I tell you never to come near Miss March again? Let her go this instant!" His green eyes flicked to Emily's for a moment, making her knees weak for an entirely different reason.

Even in her present predicament, Emily had to admire the young lord's stormy countenance. The scowl on his face suited her romantic hero image of him perfectly, but behind her she could feel Ostley tremble, and she didn't think it was with fear. "Charles, grab her hair and yank on it hard if she doesn't do as you say. I must deal with this upstart."

"Charles, I would advise you not to lay a hand on your sister." As soon as Max said it and saw the shock on the boy's face, he knew Charles hadn't known who his father was kidnapping, and he began to feel just the tiniest bit sorry for the younger Ostley. Max knew all too well how a cruel relative could bend a boy to his will. Only a few short years ago, his grandfather had had Max so far under his control, Max had wanted to hurt Emily March himself.

Lord Didcomb's voice was icy cold and menacing, making Emily feel sorry for the boy gasping behind her. But she had no time to worry about him. Though Ostley literally vibrated with rage, his voice was oddly calm. "And now you've gone and ruined my surprise." He grabbed Emily by the hair himself so he could free up his right hand.

Out of the corner of her eye, Emily caught sight of a pistol, and panic flooded her once again.

"Gun!" was all she could get out before the shot ripped through the morning air.

At the same time, Emily saw a pistol glint in Didcomb's hands, and then another shot rang out. The baron fell back, pulling her to the ground with him. He let out a strange little gurgling sound and then went completely limp and still, while a stench worse than his body odor hit Emily's nose. Realizing Ostley no longer held on to her, she scrambled away as fast as she could. Didcomb was next to her in three long strides and lifted her to her feet.

Emily, shuddering with disgust, stepped into Maximilian Warthon's arms for the second time in her life. "God, he stinks."

Max folded his arms protectively around Emily March and thanked the gods he once again had reached her in time. "My father was a soldier and used to say the worst thing about death was the smell."

Emily chanced a glance at the man on the ground. "Is he dead?"

"Yes, I got him square in the chest."

"Good." Emily sighed gratefully and rested against his broad shoulder once more, but then abruptly looked up as a thought struck her. "Did he shoot you?"

Max grinned, which put a dimple in his left cheek, making him look boyishly young. "Luckily the late Baron Ostley was a very bad shot and at eight paces only managed to ruin my jacket." He nodded to his right shoulder, where the bullet had ripped a powder-burned hole.

Emily stuck her finger in the hole, making sure there was no blood despite Max's soft laughter at her fussing. She loved the velvety sound and smiled up at him, completely captivated by the man in front of her. He was just as tall, his face as perfectly manly and his blond curls as impossibly golden, as she remembered. His arms around her felt like heaven.

And in this perfect moment, she heard the click of a gun being cocked, and then Charles's voice.

"Step aside, miss. I don't wish to hurt you, especially if you are indeed my sister."

Emily froze and then slowly turned around. She was calm enough, but all the blood had apparently drained from her brain. She couldn't, for the life of her, think of a way to save her rescuer without getting herself shot by the shaking, wide-eyed boy in front of her. And then the second fortunate event of the morning occurred. From around the side of the coach stepped none other than Eliza, the friend Emily had planned to meet today, with a small pistol clasped in both hands. Her gun and her determined dark eyes were trained on the brand-new baron intent on avenging his father.

"Charles Ostley, lower the blunderbuss. Your mother will never forgive you if you harm Emily."

Charles shot Eliza a surprised look. "Mrs. Strathem, what are you doing here?"

Max used the moment of inattention to pull Emily behind himself, but Emily would have none of it and stepped back in front of Max. Luckily it was of no consequence. Eliza was now close enough to Charles to put her hand on the barrel of the gun and force it lower.

"Stopping you from making a huge mistake, apparently."

The boy looked stricken and very young. His voice was unsteady. "But this man just killed my father. A gentleman can't leave that unavenged."

Max, impatient with Emily's insistence to position herself in the line of fire, wrapped both arms around her, but before he could swing her around and shield Emily with his body, Eliza took the gun out of the boy's shaking hands.

"There is nothing to avenge, Charles. You know better than anyone what kind of husband your father was to your mother. You saw what he just tried to do to your sister. Everyone is better off without him."

The boy leaned into Eliza and began to sob. "What am I to do?"

Eliza handed the heavy shotgun to Max, who had stepped closer, slipped her own gun into a pocket in her burgundy walking dress, and pulled Charles into a warm embrace. "I think we should load your father into the coach and take him to Oxfordshire so your mother can arrange for his funeral." She then turned to the coachman who had watched the whole scene unfold, doing his best to keep the nervous horses under control. "What do you say, Coachy? Will you help us convey your late master back to his estate?"

The coachman nodded. "Yes, ma'am. And I think we should get the young sir away from here before the law arrives. But"—he pointed to the burly ruffian on the ground—"I'd rather not take him back, he's a nasty piece of work."

Eliza nodded and turned to Max. "Can I leave you to deal with Ostley's man? I think paying him off will be sufficient."

Max regarded her for a moment, a look of quiet admiration in his eyes, then bowed. "Thank you for your timely intervention, Mrs. Strathem. You may depend on me. I will also convey Miss Emily safely back to her father." He then bent to help the coachman pick up the late baron and carry him to the coach, where Charles held a somber watch over the proceedings.

At last, Eliza turned to Emily and pulled her into a tight embrace. "I was worried about you when you weren't on the bridge at the appointed time. Are you well, poppet? It seems you found yourself a reliable champion."

Emily gratefully returned her friend's embrace and sighed her relief. "My golden god, you mean? Yes, he has proven himself twice over now." Considering her friend, she asked, "You are in contact with my mother, are you not?"

Eliza kissed both her cheeks. "Yes, poppet, I'm acquainted with your mother. Your father couldn't contact her for fear of bringing Ostley's wrath down on her, but I struck up a friendship with your grandmother some years ago. She timed her visits during Ostley's absences whenever possible and took me along on a few of them with me posing as her companion. That's how I got to know your brother, too. Let me take him home and get the baron under the ground, and then, if you wish, we can arrange for you to meet your mother."

Emily couldn't help feeling conflicted at the prospect of meeting the mother who had condemned her to the life of a bastard, to never quite belong. It had been done to protect her, but still. She was glad Eliza was there to wipe away the tears rolling down her cheeks unbidden. These weren't the kind of tears she wanted to shed in front of a near stranger, no matter how beautiful he was, or how safe his arms felt. By the time Max had caught his horse and was striding toward her, Emily had herself under control again. At the same time, Emily's footman, Thomas, leaning heavily on Suzie, emerged from the edge of the wood, and her landau arrived, convincing Emily that she was finally safe. She urged Eliza into the coach, to take Charles away from the gathering crowd of onlookers. Then she went to help Thomas to the landau, while Max dealt with the deceased baron's now conscious servant.

Before Emily stepped into her conveyance to make her way home, she sent Max a relieved smile. "Thank you, my lord."

Max nodded his acknowledgment. "You are most welcome, Miss March." He held her gaze just long enough to make her blush, then returned to dealing with the bruised brute.

Before long, they were on their way across the bridge. Leaning back into the comfort of the carriage seats and surrounded by people she could trust, Emily had to admit even her taste for adventure was satisfied for some time to come.

CHAPTER ONE

"BUT PAPA, WE SIMPLY MUST INVITE HIM. HE saved me twice!" Emily, a flush of annoyance staining her porcelain cheeks, stood in the middle of the back parlor, facing her father, who held up the envelope she had neatly addressed to Lord Didcomb.

Sir Henry frowned at his eldest daughter. "I told you repeatedly, I expressed my gratitude to the man at the time, so there is no need for you to associate with him on any level. He knows my feelings on the matter and doesn't expect an invitation."

The light of battle sparked in Emily's deep blue eyes, eyes that were so much like her father's. "My dearest papa, you may know how to keep me safe, but when it comes to social graces, an eligible bachelor I owe a depth of gratitude to should most definitely receive an invitation to my ball. Just ask Grossmama."

Invoking Grossmama's authority was a valid point since Emily's come-out ball was to take place in the ducal palace on St. James's Square. Henry found his wife's blue-green eyes across the room, seeking her counsel.

Isabella smiled, serenely dandling their baby daughter on her knee. "Darling, Didcomb never attends balls for fear of matchmaking mamas, so I really don't see the harm. Emily is right, it would be rude not to send him an invitation."

Knowing they were both right, and aware resistance would be futile when his wife took his daughter's side, Henry sighed and put the invitation back on the mantel with the other addressed envelopes. "Let's hope he stays true to form."

Henry had managed to keep his daughter away from Lord Didcomb for three years, but she was now eighteen, more beautiful than ever, and about to be brought out into society. If he was letting her into the lion's den of fashionable London, perhaps it was time to trust her to make good choices without his dictating to her.

Isabella lifted the baby high above her head, which made young Dorothea squeal with delight. Beaming up at the baby, she gently chided her husband, "You worry too much."

Perhaps he did. Henry crossed the room and kissed the baby, then his lovely wife. "Speaking of worry, where is Danny?"

"In the garden, with his nurse," supplied his wife, her ivory cheek dimpling, and offered her lips for another kiss.

Emily, her blond head bent over the next invitation, added, "He is decapitating daffodils. For a two-year-old he is pretty good with that wooden sword."

Henry obliged Isabella with another kiss. "I suppose I better erect a training dummy away from anything that blooms."

"If we are to enjoy any flowers this summer, that might be wise. Your son is singularly focused on smiting them all." Isabella gently extricated her dark curls from the baby's grip and held her up so her father would take her.

Chuckling, Henry settled Dorothea on his hip. Not too long ago he had carried Emily like this; now she was seeking a husband. Time marched on relentlessly. He inhaled the baby's soft scent. "Come on, sunshine, let's see if the ground is dry enough for you to crawl in the grass." Holding out his free hand to help Isabella up, he led her to the open French door. "I suppose that is why we had daffodil blossoms floating in a bowl on the dinner table instead of a bouquet last night."

"No point in letting them all go to waste." Turning to Emily, Isabella inquired, "Do you have much more to do, dearest?"

"I just finished the R's. Maybe another hour, then I'm done." Emily smiled at her stepmother, then returned her focus to the invitations as Henry and Isabella stepped out onto the terrace to survey the damage to the spring flowers.

Emily worked to the sound of her brother and sister squealing with delight as their parents played with them in the sunshine. This was what she wanted for herself, a husband who loved her like her father loved Isabella, and a family of her own. It was worth braving the ton for.

Once Emily had set the last invitation on the mantel, she rifled through to find Lord Didcomb's envelope. Smiling to herself, she took it to the piano by the tall windows overlooking the garden, set it on the ledge right above the keys, and paused for a moment. Having settled on the right piece of music in her mind, she placed her hands on the piano and closed her eyes to let the music flow from her heart into her hands. She put all the longing she felt into the simple succession of notes forming Beethoven's *Für Elise* and let the music drift through the air. When the last note had shimmered away, she opened her eyes, brought the envelope to her lips, and kissed it. "You will come to my ball; I know you will."

Emily took the envelope back to the mantelpiece and arranged all the invitations on a silver tray. Then she rang for William, their majordomo, and charged him with delivering them. "Make haste, William, my grandmother is most anxious they should reach everyone before they can make other plans for the appointed day."

It was more than three weeks until the day of her ball, and half of the ton had not even officially arrived in town, but William was aware how important Miss Emily's come-out was to his master and the Dowager Duchess of Avon, and so he promised all eighty-seven missives would be delivered before nightfall.

Satisfied that her father couldn't change his mind again about inviting Lord Didcomb, Emily took herself to her room on the second floor
of the house, opened the windows so she could hear her father's young
family playing below, and flung herself on her bed to daydream about the
love she hoped she would soon find.

And why shouldn't the object of those dreams be Lord Didcomb?
He had proven himself twice over, had he not? The first time he had
come to her rescue had been almost three years ago, at a small inn along
the Brighton Road. She had run away from her father's house, thinking
herself the obstacle to her father's happiness with Isabella. Ostley had
tricked her into accompanying him to a private room, and the cretin had
tried to do unspeakable things to her. Isabella had come after her and
done her best to fight off the fiend, but it had been Didcomb who had
rescued them both. Add to that all the young lord had done for her in
Hyde Park the previous October, and Emily failed to understand her father's objections to the man.

Her father might not like it, but she intended to get to know Lord
Didcomb over the course of this season, and should he not be ready to
wed by summer, she would wait for him. But having made that decision, she also intended to enjoy every moment of her season. Her favorite
horse was in the stable so she could ride out at the fashionable hour, tick-
ets to concerts and the theatre had already been purchased, and invitations fluttered into the house every day. Despite her illegitimate birth, it
seemed high society was eager to look her over, and she had her grandmother and her stepmother to thank for that. Both women had talked
about her beauty and her talent for the past two years and expressed their
regret when her come-out had to be postponed because of her stepmother's difficult second pregnancy. The fact that she was an heiress added to
her appeal, but she knew society wouldn't have deemed that sufficient if
her father had not married in time and if her stepmother had not been

so universally liked.

Emily was going to have the most wonderful ball in her ducal uncle's ballroom, and she would play at recitals, where she would outshine even her father. All the while, Maximilian Warthon, Lord Didcomb, would be at her side and have eyes only for her. She would dance with him at every ball, and he would escort her out onto cool moonlit terraces, where he would pull her gently behind columns or topiaries and kiss her passionately. Oh, she couldn't wait. Her life was about to begin, and she was more than ready for it.

WHILE EMILY DREAMT OF HER adventure-and-romance-filled future, a servant presented a courier-delivered missive to Lord Didcomb. His Lordship was blessed with intelligent green eyes in a handsome face surrounded by golden-blond curls and anchored by a strong chin. His tall, athletic frame marked him as a sportsman, but he was more interested in his various business ventures than in hunting anything.

Comfortably established in his favorite armchair in his study, Didcomb took what looked like an invitation off the presented tray and turned it a couple of times. The back bore Avon's crest, but a female hand had addressed the envelope. Sudden anticipation made him break the seal and pull out the card. The cardstock was embossed with a rose and printed. Obviously, no expense had been spared. But below the cordial invitation to Miss Emily March's ball to be held at her uncle, the Duke of Avon's, mansion on Friday the seventh of April, there were three handwritten words in the same hand as the address on the envelope.

They said: "Please come. Emily."

Max had the fanciful notion he could hear music and smiled. Emily March had sent him an invitation over the objections of her father, who had made it abundantly clear that he wanted his daughter to have as little as possible to do with him. Max had known she was to have her season this year and that she had arrived in town. He always knew where she was, was always ready to come to her aid. He had promised Emily and Sir Henry she would be safe from the Baron Ostley, and he had kept his word; the baron was now dead. But Max still needed to keep Emily safe from his grandfather. He knew firsthand what cruelty the Earl of Warthon was capable of, and that he held a grudge against Sir Henry. Max knew the earl would use Emily to extract his revenge, given half a chance.

But that was not the only reason he was keeping an eye on Emily. Miss March was impulsive to the point of recklessness, but she was also the only female Max had ever encountered who set his heart racing. Standing the invitation on the marble mantel above the fireplace, Max moved to the desk to mark the occasion on his calendar. Pulling out an elegant card, he wrote his acceptance of the invitation, but then thought better of it. He would send the acceptance at the very last minute and directly to Avon. He had no wish to give Sir Henry a chance to uninvite him out of concern for his daughter. Best not to move in her circle until then either.

THE FOLLOWING THREE WEEKS WERE spent shopping for Emily's and Isabella's wardrobe and preparing for the ball, the official starting point of Emily's season. Madame Clarise was charged with creating the majority of Emily's wardrobe, but Isabella, an artist who liked to design her own gowns, had found an Italian seamstress in a little side street off Piccadilly. The relatively unknown dressmaker stocked the loveliest fabrics and was happy to make Isabella's designs to her exacting specifications. Naturally, on hearing about the woman's existence, Emily insisted Isabella should design her gown for the ball, and they spent several afternoons getting the design just right.

Emily and Isabella attended a few early dinners and dances designed to give the debutantes a chance to get used to being in society. Most of Emily's cousins had come to town to be present at her come-out ball, so she had friendly faces at every gathering. The young men of the ton flocked to her because of her beauty, and the matrons admired her skill at the piano, but they were still cautious to keep their daughters away just in case a friendship with Sir Henry's illegitimate daughter should harm their charges' chances of catching a husband. While Isabella; Henry's godmother, Lady Greyson; and the dowager duchess worked hard to overcome this social hurdle, Emily was unconcerned. She never lacked for a dance partner or an invitation to ride out, and that was all she required to enjoy herself.

The only discordant note, as far as Emily was concerned, came in the form of a letter from Lady Ostley, Emily's mother. Cecilia, as she had asked Emily to call her on the first of their two visits, wished her a happy come-out and a most successful season, but begged her to understand her absence. Emily's mother and brother were still officially in mourning, so attending the ball would have been unseemly. Ostley's death had been ruled a tragic accident, and all involved were cleared of wrongdoing. Sir Henry had succeeded in keeping Emily's name out of the affair, but the late baron's friends were still suspicious, hence the caution. Lady Ostley also feared her presence might remind the ton too forcefully of Emily's illegitimacy, so they would opt to remain in the country. It was a nice letter, but all it did was remind Emily of the many places she didn't belong. Evidently, she didn't belong with the woman who had birthed her either.

Emily handed the letter wordlessly to Isabella.

Her stepmother read the missive and finally nodded. "I agree with her, her presence would stir gossip. Are you sad?"

"No, not really. I like my mother well enough, but I don't know her well. It's you I want at my side." She leaned her head on Isabella's shoulder. "And it's Grossmama who has been there for me from the beginning and always."

Isabella pulled Emily into a tight hug. "Of course, darling."

Returning the embrace, Emily confided, "No one was ever unkind to me at Avon, and I always had Grossmama and Bertie, but the duchess went out of her way to make it clear at every turn that I didn't belong, could never have the same expectations as my cousins, and should be grateful for her tolerance of me."

"I'm so sorry you were not happy there." Isabella's hand stroked soothing circles on Emily's back.

"Oh, it's not that I was unhappy." Emily lifted her head, a little smile on her face. "That's not what I wanted to say." Her brows drew together as she rallied her thoughts. "These last three years, living here with you and Papa, have been wonderful. You can't know how lovely it is to have siblings of my own and to be made to feel as if I belong."

Isabella brushed a loose strand of hair out of Emily's face and tucked it behind her ear. "You do belong here with us."

Smiling, Emily reached for her stepmother's hand and held it. "I know, but it's a temporary kind of belonging. What I mean to say is, now I know what it feels like, and that is what I want when I marry. When I have a loving husband and my own children, that's when I will truly belong."

Isabella smiled and squeezed Emily's hand. "That's what I want for you, what your father wants for you too."

THE PREPARATIONS FOR HER BALL continued. At last count, more than three hundred guests had accepted their invitation, and Grossmama was quietly optimistic the child would be a success despite the society matrons' reluctance to encourage their daughters to befriend Emily.

Meanwhile, Emily spent many hours being fitted for the most marvelous gowns and daydreaming about the look in Lord Didcomb's eyes when he saw her in them. She knew he had not yet confirmed his attendance with either her parents or Grossmama, casting a shadow over the preparations. Perhaps she had mistaken his gallantry in rescuing her for interest in her person, but no matter how disappointed she would be by his absence, this was still her ball and the prospect of being introduced into society was exciting.

In this fashion, time flew by, and before they all knew it, it was time to move to Avon House on St. James's Square for the day and night of the ball.

CHAPTER TWO

IT WAS AN EXTRAORDINARY FEELING, EMILY thought, to stand at the entrance to the most opulent venue imaginable, between her uncle, the Duke of Avon, and her father, greeting guests who had come specifically to watch her make her first public appearance. Below, the brightly illuminated ballroom, decorated with garlands of pink and white roses, was beginning to fill. The orchestra was hidden behind a veritable forest of potted trees, and the crystals on the three chandeliers and countless wall sconces sparked rainbows all over the polished parquet dance floor.

Emily curtsied to guest after guest, the names and titles jumbling in her brain. Whether all these people had come out of respect for her uncle or curiosity about her, Emily did not know, but they were here, and she would enjoy her moment. How could she not? She was wearing the most beautifully shimmering cream-colored satin dress, embellished with the sheerest organza, overlaid onto the bodice and the deliciously puffed sleeves and peeking from beneath the hem of the gown. The broad waistband was embroidered with seed pearl roses, and seed pearls decorated her dancing slippers. Lustrous pearls shone from around her neck and in her shiny hair, where they held three pale pink roses in place, and the most marvelous three-tiered pearl bracelet was clasped around her wrist over her elbow-length cream satin gloves. Papa had presented her with the pearls in honor of her come-out, and they complemented her outfit beautifully.

Her father looked handsome, standing next to her in a white satin waistcoat and dark blue velvet suit, and her cousin Bertie supplied scandalous gossip about the young bucks falling over themselves to kiss her gloved hand. The overblown efforts of those young men to get their names onto her dance card made her giggle, but she had no more dances to give. She was keeping the supper waltz open. She couldn't very well tell Lord Didcomb she had forgotten about him when he came to claim his dance, and she hoped fervently he would come.

MAXIMILIAN WARTHON, LORD DIDCOMB, STOPPED in the shadows under the Doric columns separating the foyer from the mezzanine with its broad staircase, and took in the picture before him. Emily March stood by the railing next to the stairs into the ballroom. She was flanked on one side by her uncle, the Duke of Avon, on the other by her father, and listened to something evidently amusing Bertie Redwick was whispering into her ear. A bolt of jealousy shot through Max. He wanted to be the one whispering secrets to her.

Most guests had already arrived and descended into the great room below, so the receiving line had thinned considerably. The orchestra was in the process of retuning their instruments, and soon Emily's father would lead her down for the opening quadrille, but for now Max could drink in the sight of her. Someone very clever had dressed Emily head to toe in softly shimmering cream satin and organza, bringing out her stunning ocean-blue eyes and blond tresses to best advantage. The gown's neckline was modest, as befitted a debutant, but that somehow made her all the more alluring. Emily March had been lovely at fifteen, and beautiful when he had rescued her from Ostley the second time last October, but now she took his breath away. Her eyes sparkled with excitement, and her hair shone like spun gold. Her skin was pale and luminous with just the right amount of color in her cheeks, and her previously lanky frame had filled out into perfect curves. She was slender without being thin and had the most beautiful bosom he had ever seen: high and proud, and he was willing to bet firm. When he caught himself speculating on the color of her nipples, he called himself to order and stepped forward to make his bow.

EMILY SAW MAX THE MOMENT he handed the footmen his cloak and hat and came walking toward her. Her heart leapt in her chest at the sight of his sheer masculine allure. He moved with strength and grace, and his height was accentuated by his perfectly tailored charcoal-gray evening attire. The cravat expertly tied around his neck in a complicated pattern was snowy white and brought out his slight tan. In contrast, his golden-blond curls were just a touch too long for current fashion and ever so slightly mussed. His green eyes were fixed on her despite the fact he was about to make his bow to the Duke and Duchess of Avon. Emily blushed and lowered her gaze. It felt like her destiny had just arrived, but given her father's attitude toward Lord Didcomb, she hoped he wouldn't notice her reaction.

Evidently Max, Lord Didcomb, had remembered himself sufficiently, because when she looked up again, he was greeting her aunt and uncle with due respect. Moments later she was formally introduced, sank into a curtsy, and granted him her hand in greeting.

Max brought her gloved hand to his lips and bowed very properly, but his voice was low and smooth and just for her. "Miss March, I hope I find you well. May I have the honor of a dance with you later?"

Emily smiled with all the joy she felt at seeing him. "I'm very well indeed," she murmured, and despite her father's put-upon sigh, she handed Max her dance card. He filled his name in the last space available, the supper dance she had saved for him.

Realizing the dance was a waltz, Max held on to the card as he asked, "Do you have permission to waltz?"

"Yes, my grandmother secured it for me." She indicated the ballroom below, where the Dowager Duchess of Avon held court, comfortably established on a sofa along the far wall, with Henry's godmother, Lady Greyson, by her side.

Max handed the card back with a bow. "I'll be sure to express my gratitude." He turned to Henry and Isabella. "Your servant, Sir Henry. Lady March."

They both eyed him warily but greeted him with all the civility called for. Henry shook Didcomb's offered hand. "Welcome, my lord." And Isabella added a polite, "We are so glad you are able to attend."

Bending over Isabella's hand, Max lifted his startlingly green eyes to her. "But of course. I couldn't miss Miss March's grand party." He then waited for the footman in charge to announce his name and title to the assembled guests and made his way downstairs without a backward glance, just as he ought.

Once Lord Didcomb was out of earshot, Henry let out a frustrated huff and mocked, "'But of course.' Mark my words, Emily's ball will be the only one he attends all season, singling her out by his mere attendance, the crafty bugger."

Isabella didn't quite know what Henry had against a future earl singling his daughter out. Lord Didcomb's attention could only help with finding Emily a suitable match. But then she saw the way Emily's gaze lingered on Lord Didcomb's perfectly proportioned back as he gracefully descended the stairs into the ballroom. Emily was still watching when he made his bow to the dowager duchess, and Isabella started to foresee a whole host of complications herself. It would not do for Emily to set her cap exclusively at Lord Didcomb, whose grandfather was not likely to favor a match with Henry's daughter. They never had found out why the Earl of Warthon felt such animosity toward Henry, but neither Henry nor Isabella doubted that he did.

But no matter, this was Emily's night, and the musicians were done tuning their instruments for the opening quadrille. Isabella gently nudged her husband. "Time to lead Emily out." When he still grumbled, she whispered, "Don't worry Emily's head about it. This is her night. Let her enjoy it."

Henry favored his beloved wife with a reluctant smile. "You are right, tomorrow will be soon enough to worry about what Didcomb's game is." He brought both Isabella's hands to his lips and kissed them one by one, holding her gaze. "The first waltz is mine." With that he kissed her cheek for good measure, then took Emily's hand to lead her down to the dance floor.

Emily knew her father had objections to her golden god, but Lord Didcomb had come, and that made her happy. She laid her hand on her father's arm and smiled up at him as they descended the stairs to the first strains of the music. Father and daughter took their place on the dance floor, and moments later other couples lined up behind them. When all were in place, Henry led Emily into the first formation, starting the quadrille and thereby the ball. Emily was an excellent dancer and confident enough to truly enjoy herself. It didn't take long for Henry to be convinced she was more interested in dancing than in Lord Didcomb, so he relaxed and enjoyed his dance with her. They acquitted themselves with skill and flair, and before they knew it, they had performed their last formal bow and curtsy of the dance. Henry had barely led Emily to the edge of the dance floor when a young man came up to claim her for the country dance which followed the quadrille, and the enthusiasm with which Emily followed the puppy back to the dance floor convinced Henry further that he had nothing to worry about.

Bertie partnered Emily for the first waltz, then it was her cousin Julian's turn. Emily danced every dance, talked to all her partners, and seemed to have an equally good time with each. The assembled guests concluded that Emily March was not only a graceful dancer, but also a happy, good-natured sort. That she was beautiful was plain enough to see.

By the time the supper waltz was announced, Henry, Isabella, and Grossmama had every reason to believe Emily's come-out to be an unmitigated success. Several matrons had promised the dowager invites to their balls, and Isabella was being congratulated on how naturally her stepdaughter took to society.

In short, everything was going to plan until Lord Didcomb, who had created quite a stir when he had first descended into the ballroom, reappeared from the cardroom and bowed over Emily's hand. As the heir to an earldom, Didcomb was the highest-ranking bachelor on the premises, if one discounted Julian Redwick, who had eyes only for his fiancée. As such, every mama present had noted his entrance, then rolled her eyes as he made his way to the cardroom as soon as the dancing started. But here he was, leading Sir Henry's illegitimate daughter out for the supper waltz. Few knew what to make of it.

EMILY HAD JUST CURTSIED TO her last dance partner when she felt him at her elbow.

With the lightest of touches to her arm, Lord Didcomb bent close and whispered, "Are you ready for our dance, fair Emily?"

She pirouetted toward him, her eyes sparkling with pure joy. "I've been looking forward to it all night."

Max was stunned for a moment. Apparently, it didn't occur to Emily to hide her enthusiasm for his company, and it charmed Max in a way not even her beauty had. It seemed Emily March never prevaricated; she said what she felt, and amongst the ton, that made her rarer than an orchid. He bent over her hand, then offered her his arm.

Emily walked out onto the dance floor with him. She had dreamed of this moment for three long years, and still she was unprepared when his arm encircled her rib cage. He felt both forbidden and safe, sinful and utterly right. Emily had no idea where this would lead, but she knew she would never tire of the feeling. His hand was warm and strong in the center of her back as he swung her into the first turn of the waltz, followed by many more as he danced her down the length of the ballroom. The feeling of him matching her every movement and the music flowing through them both was too precious to spoil with words, so she locked eyes with his and leaned into his arms with a smile.

Max had held Emily on two occasions before this day, so he had some notion of how it might affect him. And still, he was unprepared for the sheer pleasure. Emily moved like a dream and smiled at him like he was the only man in the world, and all he could do was smile back and keep holding her. Max had known Emily's eyes were blue, but he had never before realized the depth of the color in them. They reminded him of the ocean three days out to sea, when you looked straight down into a thousand-league depth on a sunny day. Like the ocean, her eyes sparkled and shimmered in a hundred different shades. He didn't find his tongue until the last strains of the waltz had rung out and he was forced to let her go or make a scene in Avon's ballroom. All he could do was to step back, bow, and give her a moment to catch herself. Emily did wake from her happy trance, curtsied, and gushed, "That was lovely. You are an amazing dancer. Do you play any musical instruments?"

Again, not a hint of pretense or any attempt to check her enthusiasm. It was utterly charming. With her hand on his arm, he led her toward the supper room and told her something he had never told another soul. "My mother insisted on piano lessons before I moved to Warthon Castle, but I always preferred to feel the music and move to it rather than making it myself. Do you play?"

"I do indeed. My grandmother is rather famous for her skill on the pianoforte. She taught me."

Having had the pleasure of hearing the dowager play on several occasions, Max was impressed. "In that case, I very much look forward to hearing you play."

"You could have that pleasure tomorrow at Lady Melchior's musical. Both Grossmama and I have been asked to perform."

Max looked down into her eyes once again and discovered there were golden specks collected around the inner edges of her irises. "I will have to find a way to get myself invited, then."

They had reached the room adjacent to the ballroom where supper was readied. Four long tables covered with pristine white tablecloths and decorated with arrangements of pink and white roses awaited the guests, while the food was laid out buffet style on a table pushed against the wall. All around, men were trying to find appropriate seating for the lady in their charge, and those who had already found their lady a seat were busy selecting food to bring back to their partner. Max pointed across the room. "There are still several seats at the third table."

Emily had a better idea. She led Max along the length of the first table to a row of windows half hidden by potted palms. "The seats by the windows are the best seats in this room."

Max followed her without hesitation. The first window was already occupied by Julian and his Miss Brockhurst, but the second window seat was free. "This is marvelous. So much more comfortable than the tables."

Emily grinned up at him. "I know all the best places in this house. I lived here with my uncle and grandmother until my father's marriage three years ago."

Max chuckled. "Of course you do. Shall I fetch us a tray? What would you like?"

"Just a little roast beef with creamed horseradish for me. And I'm partial to eclairs."

"Champagne or punch?"

"Definitely champagne. And I would like a glass of water."

Max sketched her a small bow. "Water it is, my lady."

Giggling at the "my lady," Emily watched Max as he weaved his way around the diners in the room to select food from the buffet. He was more fascinating than even she had thought. He liked music, and she knew he sat his horse well. Was there a more perfect man for her in all of England?

He returned with a selection of meats and sauces, tiny crab cakes, strawberries and cream, the requested eclairs, and the glass of water. He then took two flutes of champagne from the footman who had followed him and handed her one. "May I make a toast to finally meeting you without having to rescue you?"

She laughed out loud. "To not needing to be rescued."

They clinked their glasses together and sipped their champagne. The alcove allowed for them to sit catty-corner and rather close together, so unless they raised their voices, they would not be overheard by the people sitting at the long tables in the center of the room. Max filled Emily's plate with roast beef and creamed horseradish. "So, we established earlier that you are a marvelous dancer, and you play the piano. What else do you like to do?"

Emily was very proud of herself that she remembered to chew and swallow before she answered. "Horses. I love horses and adore riding. And all sorts of other animals too."

Max smiled at her enthusiasm. It was refreshing to talk to someone so unabashedly enamored with life. "I'm fond of animals myself. They are often better company than humans."

She screwed up her mouth in an adorable pout. "You keep company with the wrong humans."

Max couldn't help it, he laughed. "You might be right."

She smiled. "So, what do you like to do, besides dancing?"

"Oh, many things. I like talking to you."

She rolled her eyes. "That's not what I meant. I told you what I like."

Max shot her an assessing glance. She may have been young and inexperienced in the way of the world, but she was genuine and knew when she was being held at bay. He would have to remember that. Evidently Emily March was not just a pretty face. "I like finding new inventions and ventures to invest in. And I like being in charge."

She gave him a "that's better" smile. "Inventions? Like the steam engine?"

"Precisely. I invest in several railroads, and I have three ships that go back and forth between here and India. I import tea and spices, mostly, but also silks and precious woods."

They drank and ate and thoroughly enjoyed themselves until it was time to return to the ballroom. On their way there, Max suddenly couldn't bear the idea of not seeing her till the next evening, so he asked: "Would you ride in the park with me tomorrow morning?"

"I'm sorry, my cousin Bertie is already taking me tomorrow, but I see no reason why you can't join us. We will set out from here at ten."

Her smile was so open and guileless, it convinced Max that Bertie was not a rival. He gently squeezed her hand on his arm. "I will be here."

As soon as they entered the ballroom, Emily was claimed for the next dance. Max bent over her hand in adieu, already feeling her absence, and not two minutes later he took his leave from the hostess.

EVERYONE WHO HAD SEEN THEM together that evening agreed that Emily March and Maximilian Warthon made a lovely couple. He so tall, muscular, and Greek-profiled, she slender and fair, as beautiful and delicate as a fairy. But no matter how perfectly they danced together, no matter the way they looked at each other or laughed at each other's jokes, future earls did not marry illegitimate misses, not even well-connected ones, so the assembled company felt almost sorry for the girl.

Emily and Max's display on the dance floor sparked a competitive spirit among the mamas present, and it was generally decided that if inviting Emily March would afford the hostess hope Lord Didcomb might attend her party and thereby give her daughter a chance to show up Emily, that would be a risk worth taking. And if Emily March bestowed her fortune on a lesser member of society in the process, so be it. An earl was well worth the attempt, and there were plenty of bachelors who needed Miss March's money; everyone could appreciate that.

CHAPTER THREE

AT TEN O'CLOCK THE NEXT MORNING, MAX RODE up to the Duke of Avon's town residence on St. James's Square, where two saddled horses were being walked by a mounted groom while a footman held the front portal open. The white Palladian facade of Avon House contrasted nicely with the black wrought-iron fence around the square, where nursemaids walked their highborn charges amongst the daffodils and the trimmed hedges in the morning sun. Blossoming trees around the perimeter of the square spread a carpet of white petals over the cobblestone pavement and added a sweet fragrance to the usually foul London air.

One of the horses waiting outside Avon House was a dappled gray Arabian mare Max assumed to be Emily's mount. The mare was just the right size for her, but she danced rather nervously and threw up her head in warning when Max's chestnut hunter got too close. He hoped Emily knew how to handle her or they would have to shout at each other over a distance. The other horse was a big-boned bay gelding who whinnied as soon as Bertie Redwick emerged from the building. Evidently Bertie was a horseman who inspired loyalty in his mount.

Emily's cousin, two years older than her, halted on the top step and threw over his shoulder, "Come on, Em, your beau is here."

Max could hear Emily's shriek of despair.

"Bertie, you beast."

A look of pure boyish mischief on his face, Bertie bounded down the front steps and greeted Max with a nod, "Didcomb."

"Redwick." Grinning at Bertie, who swung himself into the saddle,

Max dismounted so he could play the gallant and help Emily mount.

Emily came rushing out of the house clad in a lilac riding habit with a jaunty little matching hat. Her face blushed a deep red when she realized there was no way Max had *not* heard Bertie's remark, or hers.

Her eyes shooting daggers at Bertie, Emily curtsied. "Good morning, my lord. Please don't mind Bertie, he was raised by wolves."

The idea that the very correct Duke of Avon's offspring had been raised by wolves was so charmingly outrageous, Max burst out laughing. Bowing, he offered, "I shall bear that in mind. Good morning, Miss March."

"Ha, you were raised by the same wolves." Bertie chuckled from atop his big gelding.

Emily wanted to kill him. With her bare hands. He knew this was her golden god, that she wanted to make a favorable impression. How dare he ruin this for her? But she couldn't make matters worse by rising to her cousin's bait and acting unladylike, so she squared her shoulders, smiled at Lord Didcomb, and allowed him to help her into the saddle. She took up the reins and thanked him prettily, and while he was busy getting back onto his horse, she let her mare, Addy, dance forward until she was right next to Bertie, took her foot out of her stirrup, and kicked his shin. Bertie yelped and inadvertently tightened his legs around his horse's belly, which sent the gelding lurching forward.

While he was busy getting his steed back under control, Emily turned to Max with the sweetest of smiles. "It is such a lovely morning for a ride, don't you think?"

Max had no doubt that Emily had intentionally caused Bertie's horse to misbehave. The two of them acted in all things like siblings, and that was good as far as Max was concerned. Her cousin had embarrassed her, trying to get a reaction from her, and he had almost succeeded. Steam had risen from Emily's head and fire had leapt from her eyes, but she had controlled herself admirably, and then, when she thought Max too busy to notice, she had exacted her revenge. Emily March had a temper and wasn't above doing her own dirty work. Max liked her all the better for it. There was something wild and unexpected about her.

Schooling his features into a pleasant smile, Max agreed, "It is indeed. Where do you intend to ride this morning?"

Emily shrugged. "Hyde Park? But let's cut through Green Park. It's not as busy, so we can let the horses stretch their legs. What do you think, Bertie?"

"Capital idea." Evidently Bertie didn't hold grudges, but that didn't mean he was about to behave. "I do want to see Didcomb's face when he realizes what you mean by 'letting the horses stretch their legs.'"

"What's wrong with a good gallop?" Emily asked.

"Nothing as far as I'm concerned," Max offered diplomatically.

Bertie just laughed and led the way down to Pall Mall, while Emily shrugged. This might be London and it was spring, but when it came to her morning ride, she wasn't about to bow to her aunt's dictates. Walking her horse sedately around the Serpentine wasn't exercise for her or her horse, and Emily needed exercise; it was the only thing that could ever completely calm her. She pulled Addy next to Lord Didcomb's big chestnut and patted her horse's neck. She could feel her wanting to run and felt the same excitement.

Emily assessed Max's mount. "He looks like he could do with a run too."

Glad to observe that Emily was more than capable of controlling her nervous little mare, Max smiled at her. "He is indeed a little fresh, so it seems we are all eager to stretch our legs."

"Well, what are we waiting for, then?" They had just turned into Pall Mall where the cobbles ended and a broad, dirt-packed, poplar-lined riding path began. Emily kicked Addy into a trot and had caught up to Bertie before Max could even react. He scrambled to catch up to her, and as soon as Max and Bertie appeared on either side of her, she let the mare lengthen her stride. They flew down Pall Mall, enjoying their moment of freedom in the middle of London.

Before long they came up to a carriage and had to rein the horses in, but then it was time to veer right into Green Park. This park was a large triangular expanse of grass with a tree-lined pond in the middle and a hill overlooking Hyde Park Corner. The path grew narrower as soon as they entered, so they couldn't ride side by side, but there was no one else around for as far as they could see.

Emily urged Addy into a gallop with a joyous yelp. "Race you to the lookout!"

Bertie was only a split second behind her, obviously used to Emily's antics, but Max didn't need much encouragement either. The more Max saw of Emily, the better he liked her. She was a force of nature, and seeing her bent low over her galloping horse's neck, escaped tendrils of her blond tresses fluttering behind her, was a sight to behold. Looking over her shoulder to see how far ahead she was, she raced up the hill, one with her horse and exuberant in her enjoyment.

In truth, Constitution Hill was more of an incline than an actual hill, but it was perfect for a fast gallop. Max managed to pull past Bertie and next to Emily, who took one look, laughed, and bent lower over Addy's neck. A clack of Emily's tongue sent the mare surging forward, and although Max dug in his heels and did his best to keep up, Emily won the race handily by half a horse's length. Reining in her little Arabian mare on top of the hill, she turned to her two companions with triumph sparkling in her deep blue eyes.

Max brought his mount to a halt next to her and sketched her a little half bow to acknowledge her win. "Well done, Miss March. You are an accomplished rider indeed."

Bertie pulled alongside the two of them and shook his head. "Don't take it to heart, Didcomb. Addy is wickedly fast."

"Ha, *you* can't make her run like this." Emily just couldn't resist.

"Of course not, I weigh twice as much."

"That's not why. She loves me."

Max had to laugh; the two cousins' constant squabbling was entertaining, but he bet they would do just about anything for each other. It was nice to see their bond, and a relief to see Emily had someone else who would look out for her, since her father was busy with his new family. "You beat us both fair and square. But I'm curious: Addy seems a rather prosaic name for such a magnificent creature."

Bertie grinned wickedly. "Yes, Em, do tell us why your purebred Arabian has a servant's name."

"Oh, shut up, Bertie." Emily blushed furiously, then turned to Max and explained, "Addy was my twelfth birthday present. She was my every dream come true. From her velvet-soft fur and her flaring nostrils to her soulful eyes and perfect proportions—she was magnificent. She still is, as you can see. To me she was the personification of beauty, so I named her Adonis, after the Greek god of beauty. It never occurred to me the ancient Greeks could possibly be so perverse as to choose a man to represent beauty. Then Bertie over here started to tease Addy for her name, so I had to shorten it into something female." She threw Bertie another dirty look, then took up the reins again and set off toward Hyde Park Corner and the crossing into Hyde Park. Bertie, conscious he had teased Emily into a snit, decided to let her have some time with Max and stayed a few horses' lengths behind them.

Catching up to Emily, Max trotted alongside her and continued their conversation. "You could have renamed her Aphrodite."

Emily shot him an amused look. "That's what I named her daughter. She is completely white with a gray mane." Growing thoughtful, she added, "In truth, I like the name Adonis for Addy. It suits her and I never wanted to change it. I still call her Adonis when we are alone."

"Which isn't often here in London, I bet."

Emily's face spread into a beatific smile. "Oh no, I see her in my father's stable all the time. I like taking care of her."

It was very unusual for a female of their class to take care of her own horse, but Max liked her dedication. "Where is Aphrodite now?"

"She is at Avon. I ride her when I'm visiting there, but she just had a foal of her own and he looks like he might be another one headed for the racetrack. He has the longest legs you have ever seen."

"Wait, did you say you have a horse on the racetracks?"

Emily turned to him and grinned. "Addy's son Hero has won Ascot twice."

Max's mouth literally dropped open. He had watched Hero win his second trophy. "Hero is Addy's son? And you own him?"

Still grinning, she nodded. "Officially he belongs to an investment group, but my father and I are the only investors." She sobered a little, seeing Max's stunned face. "I know it's not very ladylike to breed horses, talk about stud fees and bloodlines, but I'm good at it. I'm good with horses." Shrugging, she gave him the shyest smile he had seen on her so far. "I love it."

That much was evident in the way she interacted with her mare. Something else to like about Emily March. Turning toward her as far as sitting on a horse allowed, he smiled. "I think it's marvelous."

Emily saw the sparkle in his spring-green eyes and it made him look so much younger than the austere expression he usually sported. She worshipped her gallant rescuer and had fancied herself in love with him for the last three years. But Max, the young man who thought it marvelous she bred horses that won races in Ascot—that was someone she might come to love in truth, not just in fancy.

ON A WALKING PATH ALONGSIDE Rotten Row, the Earl of Weld nudged his countess with his elbow and nodded toward Warthon's heir. "What the devil is Didcomb up to?"

The countess only shrugged. "Dashed if I know, but I'm glad Jane doesn't have to deal with bringing out the March girl."

The earl turned a mottled shade of red. "Good God, woman. She married the son of an ostler."

Lady Weld patted her husband's arm. "Calm down, dear, I'm just focusing on the bright side. Besides, Ben Sedon is the very rich son of an ostler, who happens to be the next Earl of Warthon's best friend. And you can't deny that little Edgar is a darling."

The earl relaxed a fraction at the mention of his grandson. But nothing would ever reconcile him to the fact that Lady Jane was now a mere Mrs. Sedon. Not to mention his daughter's antics and eventual choice of a husband had created a rift between him and Warthon, but perhaps he could mend that rift by keeping the earl informed of his heir's dealings with Emily March. Apparently, the boy had attended Miss March's come-out ball the night before, and now here he was, riding out with her. Even if Didcomb planned to deliver the girl to his grandfather so he could take his revenge at long last, Warthon would want to know.

Not that it looked like young Didcomb was anything but smitten with the March girl. By Jove, but the girl was pretty, and she could ride too. Her little Arabian danced nervously under her, but it didn't seem to bother her one bit. She controlled the horse effortlessly and kept right on flirting with the Earl of Warthon's grandson as if she had been courted by him for months and didn't have a care in the world.

He turned to his wife and inquired, "Are we going to the Melchior musical tonight?"

"Of course, dear. The dowager is playing. I'm sure I told you."

The Earl of Weld just nodded and sent one last assessing look after

Didcomb and his fair companion.

BY THE TIME THEY DEPARTED Rotten Row and headed over the Serpentine bridge to the less populated areas of Hyde Park, Bertie and Emily were back to arguing over trivialities. Unable to keep up with the banter, Max just hung back and observed. Emily was as comfortable in the saddle as she was in the ballroom. She was no longer a damsel in distress needing rescue, leaving Max free to just enjoy her company.

CHAPTER FOUR

EMILY NEEDED TO PRACTICE. HER YOUNG SIB-
lings playing in the garden called to her, but she planned to offer
Beethoven's Piano Sonata no. 8 at the Melchior musical. It was full of
drama and passion and was wickedly fast in some places. The perfect
piece to show off her ability, as long as she didn't make any mistakes. She
worked for more than two hours, but when she had played the piece for
the fifth time without a stumble, she allowed Isabella to persuade her to
rest for a spell before dinner.

The Melchiors' townhouse was on the west side of Cavendish Square,
so, since it was a warm spring evening, Henry led his wife and daughter
across the square on foot. Isabella was lovely in a straw-colored silk with
sea-blue velvet trim around her neck and hem. The dress brought out her
eyes beautifully, and her dark curls were held together with blue-green ribbons in a loose Grecian style. Henry wore an elegant midnight-blue suit
that complemented his wife's outfit perfectly, while Emily had chosen a pale
pink satin gown for the night. She particularly liked the gossamer overlaid
puffed sleeves embroidered with silver stars, and the matching shawl, also
embroidered with silver stars. She imagined the shawl would look marvelous, carelessly slung over the piano bench beside her while she performed.
Her hair was devoid of any ringlets and twisted into a simple knot at the
back of her head, held together with several crystal pins, continuing the
star theme. Small diamond stars dangled from her earlobes, and a matching pendant graced her modest décolletage. Her arms were covered to the
elbows in silver satin gloves, which she would take off for her performance.

They reached the brightly lit venue for the musical and were greeted with neighborly warmth. Emily was immediately ushered to the group of young people getting ready to perform, leaving Henry to find his wife a comfortable seat on a green damask-covered sofa.

The instruments were grouped in front of the green velvet curtains covering the windows in the Melchiors' large drawing room, and the performers were seated in a half circle behind the instruments. All in all, there were about a dozen performers, mostly young women eager to show off their musical accomplishments, but also several men. The Dowager Duchess of Avon had not yet arrived, but would no doubt be seated on the most comfortable chair in the front row of the audience. She was, after all, the star performer of the evening.

This was to be Emily's first official performance for the ton. Nervous, she gratefully accepted a glass of champagne from one of the male performers. She had seen the young man somewhere before but couldn't remember his name.

Luckily, he introduced himself as Mr. Bromley and inquired, "You are Miss March, are you not?" When Emily answered in the affirmative, he continued, "What instrument will you be playing tonight? Or will you offer a song?"

Emily smiled politely. Evidently all he knew about her was her name. "I play the piano."

His eyes lit up. "Me too. May I turn the pages of your music for you?"

"That won't be necessary, Mr. Bromley. I have the piece memorized. I find the music flows better when I just concentrate on playing. But I'll turn yours if you want."

Mr. Bromley looked impressed. "That would be much appreciated. I'm not brave enough to play for an audience without my music in front of me."

"That's settled then." Emily smiled. "Do you know the order in which we will perform?"

Indicating Lady Melchior, who was weaving her way through the crowd, Mr. Bromley's mouth hitched up in a becoming half-smile. "I believe we are about to find out."

Lady Melchior was indeed approaching their group with a broad smile on her face. She was middle-aged, tall, and very fashionably attired in blue watered silk. She was known for her deep appreciation of music. She also made it her business to know her performers' level of proficiency before they performed in her salon. Once she reached Emily's little group of performers, she pulled a sheet of paper from under the pile of sheet music on the piano and motioned for them to gather around her.

"I took the liberty of writing out the order in which you will be performing. Miss Wesley and Miss Allis, you will begin with your charming duet. Lord Estes will follow on the piano and then Lady Carolina on the harp. The three Misses Bingly will sing and play their offering, followed by Mr. Right, then Miss Wuster and Miss Dole on the harp. Mr. Bromley, you and Miss March are about evenly matched in skill, so I leave it up to you who goes first. Then Lord Melchior on the violin and the Dowager Duchess of Avon for the finale. How does that sound?"

There were eager nods all around and a smattering of applause from the front row where people had overheard. Lady Melchior smiled brightly. "Wonderful, that's settled, then." She tapped her index finger on the piece of paper. "I'm leaving the order of performances right here so you can refer to it."

Just then, a commotion by the entrance to the brightly illuminated salon heralded the arrival of the Dowager Duchess of Avon. The rest of the guests filed in to find their seats behind her. Lady Melchior clapped her hands together excitedly. "There is our guest of honor." Turning to the young performers, she added, "We will begin once Her Grace is seated." With that she rushed off to greet her venerable guest.

Across the room, Emily met her great-grandmother's eyes, and when the old lady winked, Emily smiled, some of her nerves dissipating. But she still inquired of Mr. Bromley, "Do you mind if I go first, Mr. Bromley? This is my first time playing in public, so I'm a little nervous."

Mr. Bromley bowed graciously. "Whatever makes you feel most comfortable, Miss March."

It took a few minutes for Grossmama to settle into her seat of honor. During the commotion, Max slipped into the room. Finding most seats occupied, he opted for a space along the back wall from where he had an unobstructed view of the performers.

Emily felt him before she saw him amongst the other young bucks standing along the back wall, and a whole new wave of nerves took hold of her. They had become friends over the past twenty-four hours. She had shared confidences with him, told him things the rest of society would neither understand nor condone. She had danced with him and raced him through Green Park, and somewhere along the way, the golden god had been replaced with a flesh-and-blood man, and Emily cared what Maximilian Warthon thought of her. Their eyes met across the heads of a hundred of London's wellborn music lovers, and both felt it like a physical thing. Max declined his head in greeting, while Emily smiled, feeling shy for perhaps the first time in her life.

Mr. Bromley, oblivious to the exchange, lightly touched Emily's elbow to guide her to the seats for the performers, set up along the wall next to the makeshift stage. Emily instantly collected herself and took her seat. Mr. Bromley settled next to her, a circumstance which elicited a dark look from Max.

Something primal stirred within Max's chest. Emily March didn't belong to him, and if he wanted his grandfather to stay out of his affairs, she couldn't, but he couldn't stand the thought of another man with her.

Emily remained unaware of Max's displeasure as the concert commenced with a lively duet, followed by passable performances on the piano and the harp. The skill level of the performers gradually increased, along with the length of the offered pieces. Mr. Right had a lovely singing voice, marking the beginning of the more proficient performances, and when the two young women took their places to play a piece for two harps, an expectant hush fell over the room. The two ladies were skilled and perfectly matched, playing Handel with sensitivity and skill, taking the listener on a lyrical journey. Loving music above all else, Emily was utterly charmed, but since she was to play next, she was also grateful for the extended applause following the harpists' performance. She let the applause ring out, then took her seat at the piano.

Removing her gloves, Emily let her shawl fall around her like she had envisioned, then laid her hands on the keyboard to collect herself. Something strange happened to her whenever she prepared to play: the music seemed to gather around her, in her, lived through her. By the time she struck the first chord of Beethoven's Piano Sonata no. 8 in C Minor, the room crackled with anticipation. From the first tension-filled, slow opening chords and single notes drifting through the air like passing clouds, it was clear to every person in the room that they were witnessing something special. Emily played with her whole being, her eyes closed, passion moving through her body as her fingers flew across the keyboard like a storm across the land, taking her audience on a musical adventure. Through it all, Emily felt Max's eyes on her like a caress, and it imbued her music with an emotionality she had never achieved before.

Max watched and listened as if thunderstruck. How could one small female move a whole room full of people? How could she be so utterly skilled at two things as different as riding and playing the piano? Then again, she did seem to do both things with the same all-consuming passion. What would it be like to be loved by her? Max wanted that passion directed at him, almost as much as he wanted her to continue playing. Emily March was unexpectedly and utterly beguiling.

Alternating between slow, intense passages and the fast movements played with the skill of a virtuoso, Emily held her audience enthralled from the first note to the last and made even the strictest matron forget that Beethoven wasn't considered suitable for young ladies to play. In short, she was a revelation, and the applause that erupted once the last note had drifted away was nothing short of thunderous. She heard it first as a distant noise, breaking the spell of the music and dragging her back to Lady Melchior's music room. She kept her eyes closed for a moment, savoring the appreciation of her audience. A smile spread across her face as she opened her eyes. Playing for people felt even better than she had imagined.

The first thing she saw was Max's admiring eyes, but Mr. Bromley's beaming face broke their connection. "That was simply marvelous, Miss March. I have never heard this sonata played with such control or with as much passion. It almost seems impossible to achieve, yet I just witnessed you do it. Simply marvelous." He held out his hand to help her up so she could make her curtsy to the audience. "I feel ill-equipped to follow such a performance." With that he bowed to her and stood aside. Emily smiled at the still-applauding audience and watched her great-grandmother wipe away tears of pride. There was no doubt, her first official concert was a triumph. Eventually she turned to Mr. Bromley and indicated for him to take the seat at the pianoforte. Clapping for him, Emily stepped next to the young man to turn the pages of his music.

Against the back wall, Max had to force himself not to move. Every cell in his body wanted to go to her, and, more importantly, take her away from the young man who so easily claimed her attention.

Mr. Bromley turned out to be a gifted pianist in his own right. He played Bach with great skill, but rather too much reserve. Luckily technicality and reserve suited Bach, but it wasn't enough to truly impress Emily. Nevertheless, her father smiled broadly at her, no doubt not just because of her performance, but also because she was turning pages for the perfectly harmless and acceptable Mr. Bromley. Little did he know, Lord Didcomb's very presence sent prickles of awareness up and down her spine. Best not to look at the young lord and leave her father in the dark for now.

Mr. Bromley finished to steady applause and was followed by a stirring performance on the violin by Lord Melchior. Finally, Grossmama closed out the concert with Mozart. Her fingers may not have flown across the keyboard quite as nimbly as they once had, but there was no doubt in anyone's mind that her talent shone the brightest. Her touch was so light she made the music itself dance, to the delight of her appreciative audience. When the last note had resounded, she graciously received the accolades bestowed upon her, but the moment the applause came to an end, she directed her attention to Emily.

Grossmama squeezed both of Emily's hands. "You were wonderful, *mein Liebchen*. You held the tension of the slow movements beautifully."

Emily almost cried with relief. For her great-grandmother and teacher to be satisfied with her performance was the greatest of compliments imaginable. "I was so nervous, Grossmama, but it felt right."

"It didn't show, darling. *Es war wunderbar.*"

As the audience came to their feet, starting to seek the refreshment tables in the adjoining rooms, a circle of admirers formed around Emily, this time including matrons and young misses her own age. Emily March was not just beautiful and had powerful relatives, she was magnificently talented, and that would be an asset in any home. Society was beginning to forget about her regrettable birth.

From the back of the room, Max watched the play of emotions on Emily's lovely face and noted with an odd sense of pride how quickly society took to her. He wasn't ready to examine the strange mix of emotions tightening his chest; all he was willing to acknowledge was that he wanted to steal her away from that circle of admirers and find a deserted salon to have her all to himself. But since that was not possible, he settled for joining the circle around her, and when it was his turn to bow over her hand, he murmured so only she would hear, "I can't decide if you are more beautiful galloping through Green Park or playing the pianoforte. May I escort you to the refreshment table?"

Emily blushed and forgot to thank him for his compliment but managed to curtsy. "I do admit to being parched."

Behind Emily, Sir Henry was about to step in when his wife laid a calming hand on his arm and whispered, "Leave her be, he is actually helping her entrance into society. No matron will exclude her from an entertainment if her presence might persuade Didcomb to attend. Besides, the more you object, the more she will dig her heels in."

Henry sighed deeply and watched the young lord lead his daughter out of the room. "You better not let her out of your sight."

Isabella gently urged him to follow in the couple's wake. "I don't plan to, dear."

CHAPTER FIVE

SUNDAY MORNING BROUGHT RAIN. EMILY WAS not fond of rain, mostly because no one wanted to go riding in inclement weather, and that meant she had to take a groom with her. Who wanted to be saddled with a surly servant? Even Bertie, who loved the land and farming, was remarkably intolerant to getting wet. When the rain didn't let up all during breakfast, Emily began to worry. Not only would it be a soggy ride, but it would also be muddy and slippery for Addy, and Emily always considered her horse's comfort.

Frustrated and in need of exercise, Emily decided to walk to St. George's for Sunday mass. Her father and stepmother were sporadic churchgoers and had already settled into the upstairs sitting room to play rainy day games with the young children, but Grossmama would be at church. Still, Emily needed an escort, so she skipped up the stairs to don her pelisse and give Suzie the bad news. Suzie, used to her mistress's disregard for weather, kept her groans to a minimum and helped Emily into a rose-pink silk pelisse with rope trimming and epaulets like a military uniform. The matching hat was secured with two long hatpins before Suzie saw to her own hat and coat. She also equipped herself with an oversized umbrella. The thing was hazardous on the busy sidewalks of London, but thankfully only to the other pedestrians.

Emily laughed when Suzie came downstairs with the umbrella. "It's a good thing it's Sunday, we do have to cross Oxford Street."

Suzie leaned the umbrella against the hall table under the mirror before she stepped behind her mistress and checked Emily's hat was secure. "Yes, miss, but I'm not going out there without it."

"You better share then, Suz."

Suzie's lips twitched the merest bit. "Of course, miss."

At that moment there was a knock on the door. Thomas, Emily's favorite footman, opened the door to see who would call on such an inhospitable day. But before the visitor had time to leave his card, Emily peeked around the door. "Lord Didcomb, you are visiting early."

Noting Emily's pleased smile, Thomas stepped back to let Lord Didcomb out of the rain and into the foyer, where the young lord bowed over Emily's gloved hand in greeting.

"You are about to brave the elements, Miss March?"

Emily indicated Suzie and the umbrella. "We are on our way to church."

"May I offer my carriage, Miss March? I'm on my way to St. Martin's myself and stopped to offer my services. The boys' choir is singing Handel for the service today."

Emily's eyes lit up, and so did Suzie's—Emily's because hearing Handel with Lord Didcomb would be much more exciting than walking to St. George's, and Suzie's because taking the carriage would be far better than traipsing through the rain.

Emily was already heading for the door. "Do you know which mass they are singing?"

"As I understand it, they are performing a number of his Psalms, and one of their own is performing the solos." Spying the umbrella in Suzie's hand, he reached for it. "May I?" Then he offered Emily his arm and led her out. As soon as they crossed the threshold, he opened the umbrella and held it over Emily. His carriage was right outside, and his footman opened the door while Max held the umbrella aloft, first for Emily, then for Suzie, who followed.

Thomas, meanwhile, closed the front door and took it upon himself to go tell his master where and with whom his daughter was going to church. Servant and master agreed that an outing with Lord Didcomb was less than ideal, but since they were going to church and Suzie was with Emily, there was not much anyone could say against it.

THE ST. MARTIN-IN-THE-FIELDS BOYS' CHOIR was the best of its kind in the country, except for perhaps the boys' choir at Canterbury, where the English archbishop resided. Emily had persuaded her father to make the trip to St. Martin's to hear them on several occasions, but attending with Lord Didcomb felt special. They entered just as the first note of the first psalm soared into the rafters. She loved the pure voices of the boys in their white robes and marveled at the acoustics in the church as they paused in the vestibule. Max found Emily a seat in the back row but had to wait for an attendant to bring him a portable prayer bench before he could sit. Apparently, the choir attracted quite a crowd.

It was remarkable how pleasurable a Sunday service could be if spent in the right company. The choir was splendid, but if it had not been for Emily, Max would not have noticed. In fact, he would not have come. He did attend Sunday services when he was at Warthon, or with his mother in Suffolk, but it had never occurred to him to drag himself to church on a Sunday after an entertainment in London. He also had not anticipated that his attendance with Emily March would attract attention.

There was no room for anything more than an exchange of smiles during a church service, but the few members of the ton who attended services at St. Martin's that Sunday did note that Emily and Max attended together. One of those worshippers was the Earl of Weld. The earl had endured the musical the night before and had gone home reassured that the March girl was just as happy interacting with the pianist Mr. Bromley than with Didcomb, but for Didcomb to bring her to church was worrisome. The older man carefully watched the young couple's interactions, the smiles, the girl's blushes, the sharing of a prayer book, and decided it all warranted a letter to the Earl of Warthon.

Max saw his grandfather's former confidant and noticed the man's interest but thought it best to ignore it. Surely Weld wasn't going to run to the old man just because Max went to church with a female. Besides, he couldn't quite bring himself to divert any attention away from the fascinating woman beside him. Emily was so much more than he had ever thought any member of her sex could be. He glanced at her out of the corner of his eye, admiring the delicate lines of her profile as she sang a hymn bent over her prayer book. The next moment she glanced up and smiled into his eyes before she held her book closer so he could share it. It was such a simple moment, but it touched Max's heart in a way nothing else ever had. So far, Max's interest in women had been restricted to the pleasure they could give him, but he had always assumed that if he should marry, he would marry for love like his parents had done. Was Emily the one? And if she was, could he make an illegitimate girl his future countess?

And then Max's mood darkened as the specter of the Earl of Warthon rose between them. His grandfather would be furious—more than furious, livid and possibly murderous. Warthon hated Sir Henry with an enduring passion no one could fully explain or comprehend. He had even had plans once to use Emily to exact revenge for the murder of Lord Astor. Lord Astor had been the dungeon master of the ancient brotherhood, the Knights, of which Max and his grandfather were prominent members. Unfortunately, Astor had also been a spy for the French with some harebrained plan to unite all of Europe and widen the sphere of influence for the Knights. These days the Knights were an economic alliance, and a very successful one, thanks to Max, but his grandfather still held that grudge and he was still the head of the Knights.

Max felt the warmth of Emily's body next to him and decided it was time to figure out if he truly had feelings for Emily March. And if he did, it would be best to marry her fast, before his grandfather found a way to separate them. He smiled down at Emily and gently touched his elbow to hers. She lowered her eyes as a blush colored her cheek, but she returned the pressure. When she looked back up to him again, they sparkled with pure mischief. Max's whole body heated at the sight of it.

Suzie stood in the back with the rest of the servants, but she made sure never to let her young mistress out of her sight. She had been there when Lord Didcomb had rescued her mistress that horrible day by the Serpentine, but she knew the whispers that followed Emily March due to her illegitimate birth. Suzie liked her lively mistress very much and wanted her to marry well, so she took it upon herself to keep watch and make sure no harm would come to her. That is how she came to be aware of the older gentleman in the pews near the altar on the other side of the church who kept staring at Emily and Lord Didcomb. She had never seen him before but made careful note of his person and which servant belonged to him. As it turned out, the red, yellow, and silver livery was rather distinctive.

Emily remained unaware of being watched and felt uplifted by the pure voices of the choir as she walked out on Lord Didcomb's arm and halted under the portcullis overlooking Trafalgar Square. "That was lovely. Thank you so much for taking me."

"My pleasure entirely, Miss March. I saw last night how you feel the music, so I had to make sure you didn't miss today's service."

With the rain still pouring, they waited for Lord Didcomb's carriage to make it to the head of the line of vehicles picking up worshippers. Suzie had appeared at Emily's side by the time the first person stopped to greet Emily, meeting all requirements for respectability. All seemed well, but when Max's eyes met the Earl of Weld's calculating gaze, he felt as if he was running out of time.

The feeling stayed with him as he handed Emily up into his carriage.

Weld wouldn't pass up such an opportunity to get back into his grandfather's inner circle. Max could foresee a whole host of scenarios his grandfather might spin out of the knowledge that Max was friendly with Sir Henry's daughter. None of them appealed in the slightest.

Taking his seat next to his fair companion, Max's apprehension finally dissipated when Emily smiled at him as if he had gifted her with a star. "It is lovely to have someone who seems to understand my twin obsessions of horses and music. I truly thank you."

Her praise warmed him, and it seemed suddenly very important to be honest with her. "I admit I'm far more familiar with horses and therefore more able to share that interest, but I do appreciate music and am in awe of talent such as yours."

"But that is just the thing," Emily explained. "It's less about you sharing my interest and more about you understanding and taking the time to take me to an event I will enjoy. I would like to find out more about your investments. Are there any innovations you are investing in you could show me?"

Max was so pleased, he didn't know what to say for a moment. Even his investors were only interested in the money they made from the opportunities he found. "I would be honored. Have you heard of the Stockton and Darlington Railway?"

Emily's brow furrowed in concentration, then cleared. "Oh, my father was very impressed when it opened last year. It's the first steam engine on rails, correct?"

Nodding enthusiastically, his eyes now keen with interest, Max leaned forward a little. "It is indeed. The railroad is up north, so I can't take you there, but I've invested with George Stephenson, who built the steam engine. He is currently building one he calls an *active* for a passenger railroad between Liverpool and Manchester, which I have also invested in. I would love to show you where I think we will be building the first London railroad."

"Here in London? Will there be room for the iron rails?"

It was a fair question, one he and the builders struggled with. "We believe the railroads will be the way we all travel soon, so we will just have to make room for the rails and stations. The first one will go to Greenwich. Let me set something up, perhaps your family would like to come, and we can make a day's outing of it?"

Emily literally bounced up and down with excitement. "We could ride to Greenwich and go to the observatory, have a picnic on the lawn there. I'm sure my stepmother would like to go." She smiled at him with the sort of confidence that made him want to never leave her side. "I can't wait for the day you will be able to take me on a railway behind one of those actives."

Max realized something as he looked at her and contemplated the significance of their interaction: Emily March had become that rare thing one might call a woman of substance. She had passion, talent, and integrity. She was someone he was proud to call his friend.

They reached Emily's home much too soon for Max's liking. He stepped out of the carriage to help Emily and Suzie down but had not planned to come into the house. However, when the front door opened, a somber-faced Sir Henry stepped out to wave him up the stairs into the foyer. "Come in, Didcomb, I've been meaning to have a word with you."

Max knew Sir Henry was not enthusiastic about his daughter's acquaintance with him, so he was apprehensive about this interview, but it had long been his wish to be on better terms with his grandfather's foe. The animosity Warthon held against Sir Henry was puzzling as well as troubling, and perhaps Sir Henry would be able to shed some light on it. Max schooled his features into a neutral expression and nodded.

Emily threw her father a weary glance but curtsied prettily to Didcomb's bow and went looking for Isabella to find out what her father wanted with Max and to persuade her to agree to the outing to Greenwich. To that purpose she asked, "Thomas, could you bring us a tea tray, please? And add some of those plum tarts Mrs. Tibbit made, the ones my stepmother likes so much."

Sir Henry eyed his daughter with some suspicion but called after Thomas, "You better bring us a pot of tea as well." Then turning to Max, he continued, "Unless you prefer a brandy."

Shaking his head once, Max smiled tentatively. "Tea will be perfect."

Henry ushered his guest into the library and tried to think of a kind way to say what he needed to say, but as they settled into the leather armchairs by the front window, he decided to come right to the point. "Didcomb, I'm in your debt, as you know, but I just can't let my daughter run around London with you unsupervised. Seeing you at entertainments is inevitable, but if you single her out again the way you did today, she may well end up in the earl's crosshairs, and I can't allow that."

Having just been at the receiving end of Lord Weld's arctic gaze, Max could only agree with Sir Henry. But Max liked Emily. He liked her very much, in fact. And it irked him that Emily's father thought he might endanger her. "I assure you, Sir Henry, no harm will come to your daughter in my company. I know my grandfather has some long-held grudge against you, but he is far away in Brighton and not likely to interfere."

At least Max hoped his grandfather wouldn't interfere. He could see the doubt in Sir Henry's eyes and remembered the murderous look in the earl's whenever Sir Henry was mentioned, and that gave him an idea. "It occurs to me that you might be able to help me find out what this grudge is and why my grandfather holds on to it. I know he was furious when Lord Astor's carelessness exposed the Knights, but that doesn't explain his dislike of you. In any case, it's high time we put it behind us, whatever it is. I don't like that our families are not on good terms when I can't help but feel drawn to your daughter."

So, the young lord was *drawn* to Emily. That fact wasn't lost on Henry, but for Max to ask for his help in working out why the Earl of Warthon held such a grudge against him certainly got his attention. "I admit I have a vested interest in finding out why Warthon hates me. I know it has something to do with the Knights, but you don't share his opinion of me, so there must be something more to it. Surely, he was not aligned with Lord Astor. As soon as it became clear that Astor was a traitor, even his father didn't press for vengeance or even justice."

Max shook his head. "I know Astor was a frequent visitor at the castle, and he was a dungeon master after my grandfather's taste, I'm afraid."

Henry nodded. Warthon's inner circle had tormented many women in the past, including his own wife Isabella—something Henry couldn't forgive.

Max continued, "I always thought that was why the earl liked Astor so much. I was young then and not in my grandfather's confidence, but I do know that many a maid departed hastily after one of Astor's visits. It's all rather distasteful, so I stay away as much as I can. The earl and I do not see eye to eye on many things. Not his sexual escapades, his politics, nor anything concerning the function and future of the Knights. The Knights were founded as an economic alliance of mutual support for the founding Norman Knights in a conquered land."

"What is the function of the Knights now, if I may ask?" Henry was genuinely interested.

"We are still relevant as an economic alliance. We pool our funds and invest in ventures that will benefit the country and us." Didcomb smiled. "As a matter of fact, I just invited your daughter on an outing to Greenwich to show her where the first rail line from London will go. I do hope you and your lovely wife will join us."

Henry had been aware that Didcomb was investing funds for the Knights, but to have him explain the venture as the main objective of the

Knights made clear how much power he had already wrested from his grandfather. Henry knew enough of the history of the Knights to know there was more to it, but there was nothing in that history that might explain the old earl's animosity toward him. Perhaps getting closer to Didcomb and allowing this outing to Greenwich was a good idea, but it was certain to get the earl's attention, and Henry didn't want to expose Emily to his ire. "I'm very much interested in the new railroads and have invested in the Liverpool and Manchester Company. I would love to see where you intend to lay tracks from London to Greenwich, but could we turn it into a picnic with a few more interested people invited? I do have to think of my daughter's safety."

The young man graciously inclined his head. "I'm happy to arrange for a larger party, but a bigger outing is more likely to be reported to the earl."

"Yes, but it will look less as if you are courting my daughter." Henry settled penetrating eyes on Didcomb. "Are you courting my daughter, Lord Didcomb?"

Max felt his face heat under Sir Henry's scrutiny. The man was certainly direct. What were his intentions? Had it only taken three encounters with the fascinating Emily to bring him to this question? Apparently yes. Max shook his head in disbelief at himself and smiled as he looked back up at Henry. "I suppose I am."

Henry had to admire the man's candor. It would be an absolute scandal if Emily married the heir to an ancient earldom, and he didn't really want that sort of attention on her or on himself, but it was always better to know where one stood.

"Wait, Ben." Max hailed his friend and confidant on Charlotte Street.

Ben Sedon turned to wait and smiled. "You have a spring in your step this morning. I take it the numbers are good?" They continued walking together, both on their way to the same meeting of their investors at the Knights' clubhouse.

"Very good," Max affirmed. "The carpets we acquired from the Turkish trader in Bombay fetched almost twice what we expected."

"Excellent, and we don't have to go all the way to India to get more."

Max nodded but laid a hand on Ben's arm. "A word, please."

They paused in their progress toward the unassuming house in the middle of the quiet residential street.

"What can I do for you, Max?"

"I need to step back from my duties with the ladies at the club."

Ben faced Max more fully. "Oh, what brought that on?"

"I intent to court Emily March, and it doesn't feel right to keep managing the girls." Max's smile was almost shy.

Ben was astonished, but also pleased for his friend. "About time, my friend. Leave it to me, I'll find someone decent who will treat them as you would."

"I knew you would understand. Thank you."

There was no time for any further intimacies as the door to the townhouse opened and the two men made their way inside. After divesting themselves of their hats and coats, they proceeded to the meeting room at the back of the house, where the seventeen members of the Knights who were also investors in Ben and Max's company were already assembled. Greetings were exchanged, and once the footman serving tea and coffee departed, closing the door behind himself, Max cleared his throat.

"Fellow Knights, we have several points of business to discuss today. The first being the purchase of our fourth Indiaman. If we are all agreed, then we should discuss how much each of you will invest in the new ship. Mr. Sedon and I will be responsible for fifty-one percent as usual." Max took a stack of papers out of a leather folder and handed them around the table to the men assembled.

"This is the quarterly report and breakdown of our profits. Please note that the *Estelle* is out of the dry docks and ready for her trip to Turkey. Carpets fetch a great price at present. Mr. Bingly will make the trip to ensure the quality and has already made contact with the merchants."

There was a general murmur of gratitude for the young man who declined his head to the group. "I'm glad to be of service."

Max acknowledged Mr. Bingly with a nod, then addressed himself to the whole room again. "Gentlemen, before we move on, I have an announcement to make. I will not be taking part in any future displays for the Knights and am looking to replace myself. Is anyone here interested in taking on my duties alongside Lord Jennings?"

The men around the table looked at each other, considering, assessing. One hand went up while most demurred, then a second man raised his hand.

Max waited for another beat, then nodded to the two men. "Beresford, Marlow, I will tell Lord Jennings and my grandfather of your interest, and Jennings will decide who he will train. Thank you."

There was a hum of excitement in the room. But soon the men returned to their business concerns.

CHAPTER SIX

THE RAIN PERSISTED FOR THE NEXT FEW DAYS. Despite that fact, the March salon was always busy during the morning visiting hours. On Wednesday, the day of the Audley ball, it was still chilly, but the sun had finally come out, and Emily received a note at breakfast saying Bertie would pick her up for a ride at ten. Happy to do something more exciting than traipse around in the rain, Emily was in the foyer in her moss-green velvet habit with a charming matching hunter's hat, checking her appearance in the hall mirror, when the most beautiful bouquet of dusky pink roses arrived. Thomas handed them straight to her with the accompanying card bearing Didcomb's coat of arms.

It wasn't the first bouquet of roses Emily had received. In fact, every side table in the house now held a vase with flowers she had received since her come-out ball, but these roses were just the right shade to bring out her eyes. She held them close to her face to admire the effect in the mirror and wondered if Isabella would allow her to order a dress in this dark dusky pink, or if she would have to wait until she was engaged, or, God forbid, in her second season.

As Emily stood there dreaming of grown-up dresses, the sound of hooves on cobbles announced Bertie's arrival and prompted Emily to stuff the note in her sleeve before she handed the bouquet to Thomas. "Put them in my room, please."

She was already out on the front step when she realized it was just her groom with Addy and no sign of Bertie yet. She greeted her horse with a pet on the neck and a nose rub, but instead of letting the groom help her into the saddle, she pulled the envelope out of her sleeve. The note read:

For the most fascinating woman I have ever danced with.
Save the supper waltz for me, please?
Max

Emily blushed deeply and pressed the note to her bosom, hiding her flaming face in the horse's neck until she was reasonably sure it was a normal color again. Glad she hadn't opened it in the foyer where she would have been seen, she stowed the note in the concealed pocket in her skirt and mounted her horse. There was a lightness in her heart she had never felt before, a quiet understanding that Max felt for her what she felt for him. It was a floaty kind of feeling, like the moment of suspension when you jumped a fence.

Bertie chose this moment to canter into the square. "Hallo, Em. Let's go."

Emily didn't need to be told twice; she had cantered past Bertie by the time he turned his gelding in the direction of the park. They didn't speak as they navigated the traffic on Oxford Street and then picked their way through a crowd gathered around an animatedly orating fellow on Speakers' Corner. But once they were inside the park and there was no one close enough to overhear, Emily asked: "What did you think of Lord Didcomb?"

Bertie shot her an inquiring look, and what he saw evidently persuaded him not to tease her. "After all your hero worship and calling him your 'golden god,' I expected him to be either an insufferable bore or a conceited fribble, but he is neither. I like him. He is the kind of man you want at your side when you are in a scrape."

Emily's smile was pure relief. "I'm glad you like him. I might need your help with my father. He thinks Max is not good for me for some reason only he is privy to."

Bertie laughed out loud. "I knew there was a catch." Sobering a little, he added, "But seriously, Em. If you think you can get around Uncle Henry, you are crazy."

Grinning from ear to ear, Emily stated what Bertie hadn't said. "But you will help."

He only shrugged and urged his gelding into a gallop. Of course, he would help. Emily was not only his favorite cousin and his near-constant companion for fifteen years of his life, she was also his very best friend. It was strange to say that about a girl, but it was true. He had made some friends in Oxford over the past two years, but there was no one he was closer to, not even his brothers. If Emily wanted Didcomb, and Bertie had little doubt that Didcomb wanted Emily, then Bertie would help. At twenty years of age, Bertie Redwick, third son of the Duke of Avon, had just enough experience with the opposite sex to know that love was rare and therefore important.

They reined their horses in when they got to the Kensington side of the park and cantered down to the Serpentine from there. When they slowed to a walk along the lake, where it was much busier, Emily asked, "How long are you staying?"

Bertie lifted a questioning brow. "Till next week, why?"

Emily rolled her eyes. "I thought you were staying longer. Didn't you take time off?"

"I have a paper on crop rotation due."

"Ah." That explained it. Bertie didn't give two figs about the classics or any other academic subject; growing things on the land was his passion. "But you are coming back to London."

This time it was Bertie rolling his eyes. "Don't worry, I'll be here if you need me."

"You better. Dance the first waltz with me tonight?"

That surprised Bertie. "Don't you want to keep your waltzes for Didcomb?"

She looked thoughtful. "Not all of them. He asked for the supper dance, and until I know how to handle Papa, I don't want to be too obvious."

"He already asked for the supper dance? When?" Bertie was incredulous.

A happy little giggle escaped Emily. "He sent me the most beautiful roses."

"And the roses came with a note," Bertie finished for her.

Well, Emily certainly hadn't lost any time. He had seen the way the two of them looked at each other on their ride the previous week, but private notes were a big step from a morning ride. "I suppose I better stay close to Uncle Henry tonight and see how he reacts to you dancing with Didcomb." He shook his head and looked at Emily with awe. "Goodness, Em. You might end up a countess."

Emily stuck her nose in the air and gave her best impression of her aunt, Bertie's mother, the duchess. "You will have to call me *Your Ladyship*." She offered him her hand in the most condescending way possible, and as he bent over it in mock fealty, they both dissolved into laughter.

THAT EVENING, IN THE AUDLEYS' lavishly appointed wood-paneled ballroom, Emily was enjoying the first waltz of the evening when she spotted Max. He had halted on the step separating the entrance hall from the ballroom and surveyed the crowd. Emily smiled to herself watching him stand there. His hair shone like burnished gold in the candlelight, and his tanned skin contrasted beautifully with his snowy neckcloth. The olive green of his tailcoat made his eyes shimmer like peridot. He was simply beautiful. Their eyes met across the room, and the world stilled for a moment. Everything suddenly felt right. Not that Emily had thought anything amiss the moment before, but now, with Max present and his eyes on her, everything was right. Max's lips curved up slightly in a private acknowledgment, and then another couple moved between them, but even with the eye contact broken, the feeling remained.

"Em, where the devil did your mind just wander off to?"

Bertie's voice broke into Emily's thoughts, and she blinked up at him. "Didcomb just arrived."

"Oh, is that why I now have crushed toes?" Bertie grumbled. "If you ask me to dance with you, the least you can do is keep your feet in order."

Emily just laughed. "Oh, stop fussing. I'm not heavy enough to crush your toes, even if I had stepped on them, which I didn't."

Shrugging, Bertie swung her into a turn. "A man doesn't like to be ignored by his dance partner."

Emily sighed dreamily. "I couldn't help it. He stood there, all handsome and tall, looking at me like I'm the only person in the room…"

Bertie grinned at her antics, but there was a hint of concern in his brown eyes. "I suppose I better have a talk with the chap, make sure he is worthy of you." He watched Max turn to greet an acquaintance and wondered if he was doing more harm than good by encouraging his friend.

They twirled down the line, and Emily could feel Max's eyes on her the entire time. "Just talk to Papa, please."

As they slowed to the last strains of the waltz, Bertie squeezed her hand. "I will, Em. I know this is important to you. But be careful."

Seeing the concern in her friend's eyes, she nodded. "I know, I can't expect anything. He is the heir to an earldom, and there is bad blood between his grandfather and Papa for some reason."

What remained unsaid was the difficulty Emily's illegitimacy would pose in gaining the approval of the earl, but they both knew that. Bertie offered Emily his arm to lead her back to her stepmother, who stood chatting to Mr. Bromley.

Isabella turned as they approached. "Hello, Bertie." Then to Emily, she continued, "Dearest, you of course know Mr. Bromley from Saturday last, but he asked me to introduce him formally, so: Emily, may I introduce you to Mr. Bromley?" She winked at Emily, then turned to Mr. Bromley. "Mr. Bromley, please meet my stepdaughter, Miss Emily March."

Emily curtsied with a friendly smile. "It's very nice to see you again, Mr. Bromley."

Mr. Bromley bent over her hand with all the ceremony of a proper suitor. "And you, Miss March."

"I suppose now you can officially ask me to dance." Mischief twinkled in Emily's eyes as she said it, and Mr. Bromley smiled in response, his eyes lingering on her admiringly.

"You are laughing at me, but that was exactly my purpose. May I have the next dance?"

Emily pulled up her dance card, but before she could answer, Max's voice came from behind her. "The next dance is mine, I believe."

Tingles went up and down Emily's spine. She pretended to consult her dance card and did her best not to blush as she turned toward Max. "Lord Didcomb, good evening." And finding his pleading eyes, she continued, "This dance is indeed yours."

Turning back to Mr. Bromley, she smiled apologetically. "I'm sorry to disappoint you. I have the country dance following this quadrille free."

Mr. Bromley apparently knew that he had been outmatched. He bowed. "I shall look forward to the country dance then." With that he retreated.

Max's bow over Isabella's hand was perfectly proper, but when he turned back to Emily, he beamed at her as he led her out toward the dance floor, their heads leaning close. Max and Emily had eyes only for each other, but they drew attention from almost everyone else in the room. The silvery blond fairy and the golden lord made a striking couple, and if that wasn't enough to interest the gossips, the way they looked at each other certainly was. The romantics smiled and likened them to Cinderella and her prince, while the cynics speculated on the apoplectic fit Warthon would surely have over his heir courting Sir Henry's by-blow.

IN THE BACK OF THE room, the Earl of Weld turned to his countess. "I will be traveling to Brighton tomorrow, early. This Didcomb situation needs to be made known to Warthon."

Lady Weld raised an eyebrow. "Whatever for? The boy must marry sometime and they look marvelous together."

Weld growled impatiently. "The girl is illegitimate."

"Yes, but her mother is a baroness, her father a rich knight, and the girl is incredibly well connected. That must count for something. No one I know would even think to give her the cut."

The color was starting to rise in Weld's round face. "That's not how you talked about her when Sir Henry was courting Jane. She would be married to him right now if you had been so charitable toward the girl back then. Warthon will not allow the connection, you can be sure of that."

The countess had to admit that her husband had a point. Several, in fact. "I'll make our excuses to the hostess."

Weld nodded. "Good. You might want to pen a note to your cousin. Mrs. Warthon might be able to talk some sense into her son." Looking back at the dancing couple, he added, "I just wish I knew what Didcomb is up to. Surely he knows Warthon will have his head if he offers for the March chit."

THE COUPLE IN QUESTION WAS oblivious to the attention they

attracted. They were too consumed with each other. As they took their positions on the dance floor to the first strains of music, Max bent close to Emily's ear. "Thank you for not exposing my lie. I didn't think I could wait till the supper waltz to be close to you."

Blushing, Emily's eyes found his. "Me neither."

She held his gaze and smiled as she placed her left hand in his, let her right arm float up into the beginning position, and pointed her foot out. Max felt his breath hitch as the raising of her arm pushed up her bosom. The baby-pink gown she wore brought out the blue of her eyes and made her skin luminous. She was delicate, sensual, and full of strength all at the same time, and there was no place on this green earth Max would rather have been than by her side.

He held her gaze, smiling into her eyes, and bowed over her hand. She curtsied, her lips curving in an answering smile as they matched their steps to the other dancers. It was a stately dance that allowed for intermittent conversation, but for the moment they just enjoyed the sensuality of moving in unison. Max was a wonderful dancer, his movements fluid and confident, and his gestures expressive. He was fully in his body and felt the music, but also had the necessary precision for the courtly pace. Emily admired his ability greatly. Being one with the music came naturally to her, but she was less comfortable with the constraints of the formal dance. Normally she preferred the waltz where you had more room to improvise, but it seemed everything she did with Maximilian Warthon was wonderful. Dancing, riding, going to church in the rain; it wasn't about what they did, it was the fact that they did it together.

ON THE OTHER SIDE OF the ballroom, Henry stepped next to his wife. "He is serious about her, you know."

Isabella leaned into him. "I can see that. How do you feel about it?"

"I don't suppose we can interest her in Mr. Bromley?" A self-depreciative smirk accompanied the question. He could see well enough there was no hope of that.

"That would be unkind to the poor boy," his wife admonished. "You should have seen his face when Didcomb claimed her for the quadrille. He would never be able to keep up with her."

Henry sighed. "I better find out what old Warthon has against me."

Her eyes on the dancing couple, Isabella observed: "That night in his chapel, you had just forced Warthon to shoot one of his friends when he gave you that icy look. Is it possible his annoyance with you is related to that incident only?"

Taken aback, Henry contemplated the question. Could it be? Could it have been only Ostley seeking revenge three years ago when he attacked Emily at the inn, only hours before the incident with Isabella in the chapel? Every instinct in Henry told him Ostley and Warthon had colluded back then. Besides, Ridgeworth, Isabella's kidnapper, had taken Isabella to Warthon Castle, and the earl must have known what he intended and that Henry had been courting Isabella. On the other hand, Isabella had reported that it took quite some time for the earl to rouse himself, so perhaps he had not been all that keen to be involved in the whole kidnapping plot. But then why would Didcomb mention the animosity? No, he had seen the pure hate in Warthon's eyes; he was not mistaken about this. And that look had accrued before the shooting, if he remembered correctly. Warthon's animosity toward Henry predated the first incident involving his daughter, and also predated Isabella's kidnapping by her abuser.

Henry shook his head. "No, there is more to it. Didcomb even asked for my assistance in working out why his grandfather is so adamant to punish me."

"You see? It will all work out. You are already working to remove the obstacles to your daughter's happiness. You will find out what has the earl so upset and deal with the problem." She patted his arm encouragingly and smiled, her face full of confidence in him.

Bertie stood nearby and overheard the exchange. Then Didcomb led Emily back to her parents and exchanged a cordial handshake with Henry. It seemed Emily had nothing to worry about as far as her father not accepting Didcomb was concerned.

While Emily danced with Mr. Bromley, she observed Papa in a friendly conversation with Didcomb and Bertie. Her father's attitude toward the young lord was markedly improved, allowing her to relax. Mr. Bromley was a good dancer and just as pleasant to talk to as he had been at the Melchior musical. They chatted easily about music, the weather, and spring flowers in the park, until Mr. Bromley asked her if she would come for a walk with him and she answered that she preferred to ride.

Mr. Bromley looked rather worried and asked, "Are you not afraid to fall off?"

Emily laughed. "I can't count how many times I have fallen off. You just dust yourself off and get back on."

The man's eyes grew round with horror. "Aren't you afraid to injure your hands?"

Cocking her head to the side, Emily studied Mr. Bromley. "Are you afraid of horses?"

Embarrassed, Mr. Bromley looked anywhere but at her, then nodded.

Emily smiled kindly. "It's actually quite common. My cousin Julia is afraid of them too."

Mr. Bromley was grateful she understood, but also quite certain he had bungled any chance he might have had with this beautiful, talented woman. In some way it was a relief. Now he could simply enjoy her company without feeling the need to make it something more.

CHAPTER SEVEN

WALTZING WITH MAX WAS SIMPLY MARVELOUS. Emily could no longer think of him as Lord anything; she didn't even feel like referring to him as the golden god anymore. This new intimacy, this wonderful feeling of closeness, of perfect accord with him, demanded the familiarity of his Christian name. She leaned into his strong arm around her upper back and let herself swing into the next turn. His hold tightened a little in response as he secured her body closer to himself. It was just what she had needed without knowing she needed it. Now she could feel the warmth of his body all along the front of her torso. The smolder in his eyes told her he felt it too.

"May I call you Emily, please?"

She smiled at the synchronicity of their thoughts. "Please do. I'm already calling you Max in my head." A little shrug accompanied her admission.

Max laughed at her unaffected honesty, and there was such pure joy in it, she joined in. It was so easy and natural to be with him, so utterly right.

Her fingers tightened around his hand. "Do tell me if you prefer Maximilian."

"No one I love has ever called me Maximilian. Max is perfect."

Emily wanted to lean into him. Was she someone he loved? His fingers on her back stroked gently in tiny individual circles. The flush in her cheeks intensified as their eyes locked again in a heated gaze. Both inwardly wished they were somewhere private so they could close the gap between them. They seemed to no longer need words. Touch would be so much more eloquent; at least that was what Emily's instinct told her.

With an effort, she dragged her attention back to the room. "When are you taking me to Greenwich to see where your steam engine will go?"

Reluctantly, Max widened the space between them a couple of inches. "Not right away, I'm afraid. Your father suggested to make it a bigger party so as not to feed the gossipmongers too much material."

Emily growled in the back of her throat, as much because of the loss of Max's warmth as her father's interference. "Of course he did. He would rather I didn't see you at all." Her brow knit and her eyes flashed to match the growl.

She looked like a fierce kitten, and Max's groin tightened at the sight of her fire. It was a shame to have to douse it. "Actually, I agree with him. My grandfather is a powerful man, and I would rather not put you in his crosshairs. Ostley could have acted alone both times he tried to abduct you, but I doubt it. I think Warthon was at least a part of it, and it has to do with this grudge he holds against your father. But we will get to the bottom of my grandfather's animosity, so don't be alarmed."

And there he was again, her golden god. "I know you will keep me safe."

Her confidence in him made Max feel ten feet tall. He knew his grandfather was wily and could be underhanded, but Max wouldn't let him come between them; he would find a way to appease Warthon and make him accept her.

The waltz came to an end, and Max led Emily to supper, but this time there was no cozy alcove. They supped seated next to each other at one of two enormous tables set up in Lady Audley's orangery. The orange trees in their terra-cotta pots had been moved out onto the terrace, and lanterns hid in their foliage. The French doors to the terrace stood open to create ventilation as well as a charming passage from the ballroom into supper. It was lovely, an Italianesque midnight picnic illuminated by a hundred flickering lights, but there was no privacy. They ate and spent a lighthearted hour talking to Bertie, who had joined them. Max evidently liked Bertie and asked the younger man about his studies, which led to some reminiscences of his own days at Oxford. Max had read classics, as was expected of an heir to an earldom, but had spent more time seeking out new inventions than sitting in lecture halls. From there the conversation led to the steam engine and the future of the railroad. Bertie declared himself intrigued by the notion of a steam engine carrying passengers and was promptly invited to the Greenwich outing. Emily's cousin promised to come back from Oxford for the occasion. It was further decided Max would be the one taking Emily riding in the park in Bertie's absence, which suited everyone.

EMILY ARRIVED BACK AT CAVENDISH Square in the small hours of the morning and barely managed to stay awake long enough for Suzie to peel her out of her gown before she fell into a deep, dreamless sleep. She was in love, and the object of her affections returned them. Nothing disturbed her slumber.

Max, on the other hand, was not so lucky. A note from Ben Sedon awaited him, and the contents of it had him tossing and turning until dawn broke outside his heavily curtained windows. Ben warned that his father-in-law, the Earl of Weld, was to depart for Brighton in the morning to apprise Max's grandfather of his keeping company with Emily March. Ben also related that the countess would be writing to Max's mother, Constance Warthon.

Max had no doubt his mother would welcome whomever he chose for his bride, especially if he followed her advice and married for love. But his mother was a gentle, sensitive creature, and burdening her with any of the trouble that was sure to come if he defied his grandfather and married Emily was not to his liking. No doubt the countess would pressure her cousin, Max's mother, to travel to the capital, stay with her, and use her influence to bring Max to heel. What the Countess of Weld didn't know was that it had been his mother and his friend Ben who had saved Max from becoming the coldhearted bastard the Earl of Warthon had raised him to be. Without their kindness, he wouldn't have a heart to love with.

Max resolved to write to his mother, tell her about Emily, and invite her to come to London so they could meet. This way, if she chose to come to town, she would be staying with him and away from the pressure to call him to heel. As to Weld and his grandfather, Max decided to simply wait for the earl's summons and enjoy his time with Emily.

Most of fashionable London slept the majority of their days away, emerging in the afternoon to receive callers at appointed times. Emily, however, could not remain abed when the sun was shining, and her mare needed exercise. She woke at ten, rubbed the sleep out of her eyes, donned her favorite dark blue superfine riding habit with a fall of white lace down the front, and was at breakfast before anyone else. While she heaped eggs and mushrooms onto her plate, she informed Thomas, her favorite amongst the footmen, that she wished him to accompany her on her ride this morning. It wouldn't do to ride with Max by herself, no matter how much she wished for privacy. It wasn't the fashionable hour, but there would still be too many people out riding for her to flout propriety. Besides, she knew how much Thomas enjoyed a ride.

Max had been skeptical when Emily suggested eleven o'clock for their outing in the park, but when he arrived at the appointed hour, a footman was already walking her mare and a second horse up and down in front of the house. He handed the man his reins as well and took the front steps two at a time. The door was opened immediately by another footman and revealed Emily standing at the ready, pulling on her riding gloves.

"Good morning, Miss March." Max bowed over her hand, then placed his under her elbow to lead her outside. "Shall we?"

Her deep blue eyes sparkled. "Good morning, my lord. By all means." She halted on the top step to admire the black stallion dancing sideways next to Addy. "Oh, he is beautiful! Is this the same horse you rode the day you rescued me?"

Max's heart skipped a beat at the memory of that day, and he instinctively pulled her a little closer. "It is." Leading her down the steps, he continued, "Meet Caesar, he is a little temperamental, so I don't like to ride him if there is a crowd, but it's early today."

Addy nickered in welcome as they descended the steps, so Emily took a moment to rub her horse's nose before she turned so Max could boost her up. She put her hands on his shoulders to steady herself, but when his hands closed around her waist, she could feel their warmth all the way through the soft blue wool of her habit and riding corset. Heat suffused her cheeks.

With his hands around her slender waist, Max was overcome by longing, but when she blushed and lowered her gaze, he boosted her into the saddle before he could kiss her right in the middle of Cavendish Square.

She wrapped her right knee around the pommel, murmured, "Thank you," and gathered her reins while he guided her foot into her stirrup. Bertie and a number of other men had boosted her into the saddle, but never had she been thus affected, never had it felt like an intimacy. Emily looked down at Max and saw the heat in his eyes. Seeing him equally affected turned the moment into something wonderful, a shared secret, a promise of more to come. She smiled and nodded, indicating that she was ready.

Max saw the smile and knew he would kiss her today. He took the reins and mounted his steed, and they set off out of the square, followed by the footman. They headed down Piccadilly and entered the park by

Marble Arch. There were some riders and foot traffic on the wider paths leading down to Rotten Row and the Serpentine, but the bridle path leading diagonally through the park to the trees flanking the Long Water, which separated Hyde Park from Kensington Gardens, looked clear for a gallop. Emily saw it, grinned at Max, and challenged, "First to the woods gets to choose what we do next."

Several possibilities flashed through Max's mind, starting with a walk through those woods. "On your mark, whenever you are ready."

The silver bells of her laugh sounded, and she threw over her shoulder, "Try to keep up, Thomas."

The footman answered with a respectful "Yes, miss." But Max saw the grin forming on his face. The man evidently looked forward to a good gallop.

They halted at the turn into the dirt path. There was no one on it all the way to the stand of trees that was to be their finish line. To their left, an allée of trees separated them from the main path down to the Serpentine, but they would still be a spectacle. It didn't matter to either of them. The anticipation of a contest hummed in both Max's and Emily's blood. She raised her arm. "Three, two, one—go."

She dropped her arm at the same moment she gave Addy her head and dug her heel in. All three riders shot ahead. It only took a couple of yards for them to fly into a full gallop and for Max and Emily to pull ahead of Thomas. From there the two of them were neck and neck, Emily sometimes moving marginally ahead, then Max, but eventually Max eked out a solid lead of a half-length. There was just enough room to swerve away from the trees.

"Do you concede?"

Emily laughed, turning left just as Max did the same, and reined Addy into a canter along the stand of trees. "You win, this time. Your stallion is magnificent."

Joining in her laughter, Max slowed his mount gradually. "Your mare inspired him. I think he likes her."

Studying Max's horse, Emily turned thoughtful. "He has marvelous hindquarters, and he is fast. It might be worth a pairing."

Behind them Thomas reined in his horse but kept a respectful distance as they cantered around the little wood and on to the west. There was another stand of trees there that led to a lake.

Slowing to a trot, Max asked, "Will you walk with me?"

"Your boon for winning?" she quipped, but seeing the heat in his eyes, Emily knew he sought the privacy they might gain among the trees. She held his gaze and nodded, anticipation humming through her.

Turning to Thomas, she commanded, "Hold our horses. We will take a stroll to the pond."

"Certainly, miss."

If Thomas had any notion why his mistress wanted to walk to the pond, he gave no sign of it. He swung down from his horse, held Addy so Emily could slide out of the saddle, and took Max's reins from him to lead the horses along the edge of the trees.

Max and Emily raced ahead, laughing at something Max had said. Entering the woods along a tiny winding footpath not wide enough for them to walk side by side, Max reached his bare hand out to Emily. She took it and they headed through the cool woods toward the water shimmering on the other side of the trees. As they walked through the spring-green stand of trees, with patches of yellow and purple crocus on either side of the path, their laughter faded and turned to a silence pregnant with anticipation. With only a few steps remaining to the Long Water's shore, where they would be visible from the other side, Max pulled Emily behind the trunk of an enormous oak, dropped his beaver hat to the ground, and brought both her hands up to pull her gloves off.

"Emily."

Her breath hitched as he kissed first one hand, then the other, then searched her face.

"Max." She drew nearer still, giving her silent consent, her eyes full of expectation, and when Max placed her hands on his chest, she slid them up to his shoulders with a hint of a smile. He needed no further encouragement. Ever so gently, he cupped her face with both hands, stroking her cheeks with his thumbs, and bent to touch his lips to hers in a feather-light kiss. Her eyes fluttered shut as she melted closer to him, and when his lips left hers, she made a little distressed sound in the back of her throat.

The kiss had been lovely. Lovelier even than her girlish imaginings, but it was over far too soon. Emily wanted, needed more. She had dreamed about this for three long years, it couldn't be over so soon, so she pushed herself up onto her tiptoes and offered him her lips again.

All Max's good intentions not to frighten her with his passion floated away on the spring breeze. He kissed her again, brushing his lips from one delectable corner of her mouth to the other. When she opened her lips to sigh in bliss, Max drank in her breath, then fused his mouth to hers and deepened the kiss. At first, he used his lips only, stroking, massaging, and gently sucking. The plush pillows of her lovely lips were as soft and succulent as they looked, her breath sweet and her sighs even sweeter. Max was utterly smitten. One of his hands found its way to her nape and from there caressed down her back to bring her flush with his body. He had wanted to do just that when they had danced the night before, and her soft, feminine curves felt as wonderful against him as he had imagined.

The feeling of Max's body against her front was a revelation. She fit so perfectly against his masculine planes. Then she felt his member swelling against her belly, and it was a source of feminine pride to know how much she affected him. His tongue flicked out to lick the inside of her top lip, and the strange little caress ushered in a new phase of their kiss. She experimentally licked him back, and when he growled deep in his throat, she did it again and he touched his tongue to hers. It was a singular experience to be sure, and Emily reveled in it.

Emboldened, Max gently sucked on her tongue, and when she opened her mouth wider, he let his tongue slide all the way against hers into her mouth. It was a challenging kiss, but she didn't shrink from it; on the contrary, she returned his tongue's caress. Pressing herself against him, she matched him in every way, and it made him feel like a king.

Innocent as Emily was, her responses were passionate beyond Max's wildest dreams, and had they not been in a spring-bright stand of trees where half of London might stumble upon them, he would have continued. But birds sang all around them, and then a twig cracked somewhere to the left. As the world intruded on their intimate moment, Max reluctantly ended the kiss. He withdrew slowly after one last whisper-soft brush across her lips and opened his eyes. The sight that greeted him was almost as delectable as the kiss had been. Emily's eyes were still shut, a dreamy smile playing around her slightly swollen lips, a flush of color suffusing her beautiful face. Dappled sunlight breaking through the oak's canopy put golden highlights in her silvery blond hair, and a few strands had come loose from her chignon. Her blue hat had slipped to the side. She was a well-kissed, gorgeous mess.

"Mmmmh, that was even better than I dreamed it would be."

Max brushed another kiss to her lips and tucked one of the escaped strands of hair behind her ear. "Indeed."

Emily opened her eyes while Max swept hair out of her face. There was so much tenderness in his touch and his smile, she was mesmerized. "Can we stay here forever?"

Max pulled her into a close embrace and chuckled. "I wish we could, but someone is bound to come upon us, and your groom seems loyal. He will come check on his mistress before long."

She laughed. "He is. Thomas is a good man." Sobering a little, she continued, "And he would have to answer to my father if he failed to keep an eye on me." Still in his arms, she straightened, lifted her arms, and started the process of putting her hair to rights.

Max let his hands brush down her back and around her waist as he stepped back. But seeing her struggle to smooth her hair around her hat, he pulled the hatpin out and lifted the tiny sapphire-blue silk beaver away to make fixing her hair easier. Smiling her thanks, Emily pulled out the hairpins keeping the chignon in place and stored them between her lips. The hair uncoiled and she leaned her head back, smoothing all the loose strands around her face into a luscious, shimmering mane falling to her waist. Gathering it in her hands, she twisted the long ponytail into a heavy coil at her nape, pulled the end bit under the outermost layer of the coil and around until the coil held by itself, then secured it with the hairpins held between her lips.

Max watched her with rapt attention. "How did you do that? It looks perfect and you don't even have a mirror."

Grinning, Emily took the hat and hatpin out of his hands. "Bertie is utterly useless at fixing hair, so I had to learn how to do it myself or draw my aunt's ire. She is not terribly fond of me, due to my unfortunate birth, mostly, I think." She waved a dismissive hand. "In any case, she thinks me most unladylike."

Irritation on her behalf flashed across Max's face. "I'm glad you don't live with her any longer. You are beautiful and a lady through and through." He bent to kiss her cheek, then took her hand. "Let's take a quick look at the lake and then go back."

"Let's, I do want to see if there are any violets blooming."

They strolled to the water's edge, leaning into each other, their fingers entwined, but when Max spotted a rider on the other side of the lake, he stepped back. Emily mourned the end of their closeness but was soon distracted by a cluster of violets in the short grass between the trees and the water's edge. She crouched to pick the three fully open blossoms, then found another cluster. Seeing her enthusiasm for the tiny deeply violet flowers, Max picked a few himself, and when she came back to him to place a few into the buttonhole on his lapel, he placed his little bouquet into the second button of her riding jacket and pulled them secure. All the while they were smiling into each other's eyes, the world around them receding, all other considerations melting into the background. It was a moment every bit as intimate as their kiss had been, until it was interrupted by Thomas leading their horses to the water's edge a few yards south of them.

"Begging your pardon, miss, I found a wider path through the trees."

Max reluctantly stepped back from Emily and murmured, "I knew he would be coming to check on you."

Emily shrugged and smiled, then turned toward Thomas and the horses. "Thank you, Thomas."

CHAPTER EIGHT

MAX RODE WITH EMILY ALMOST EVERY MORN-
ing, and every morning he found a way to kiss her. Sometimes during a
stroll on a secluded little path, sometimes finding a moment while in the
saddle; and if they couldn't, Max would help put Addy up in her stall after
the ride. They reveled in the intimacy of those moments alone with each
other, and then, at night, they would dance at one of the society events. It
was a fairy-tale courtship, and come May not even the most conservative
matron could deny that a love match between Emily March and Lord
Didcomb was inevitable. No gentleman courted any woman this openly
without following through, and it had to be acknowledged that Emily,
accomplished musician, heiress, and beloved member of the Avon family,
would make the future Earl of Warthon a beautiful, if not entirely suitable, countess.

Unbeknownst to Emily, Max had received no less than five angry letters from his grandfather, demanding to know what kind of game Max
was playing. Max shared the contents of these letters with Sir Henry in
the hopes they might find the reason for the earl's antipathy, but all
that could be confirmed was that Warthon did still hate Sir Henry and
extended that dislike to his daughter. It was also evident the animosity
had started after the death of Lord Astor in his dungeon more than six
years prior. The only other thing Max could confirm to Sir Henry was
Warthon's presence that long-ago night, watching from a room behind a
mirror as Astor and his pimp associate had tortured their female victim.

It had been a horrible night. Acting in his capacity as agent for the
crown, Sir Henry had interrupted Lord Astor in his dungeon and killed

the pimp. During the confusion that followed, Henry's friend Viscount Fairly had put a bullet in Astor's brain. At the time, Henry and his men had not known about the existence of the room behind the mirror, or the group called the Knights. Those facts had come to light later.

Max recalled the old man had been furious. However, Max had always assumed he had been angry about Astor's carelessness in allowing himself to be caught and thereby foiling the scheme to discredit the Duke of Avon, whose illegitimate daughter had been the torture victim Henry and his agents had saved that night. The Earl of Warthon's particular hatred toward Sir Henry, however, continued to be a mystery.

All the while, Max's and Emily's feelings for each other intensified, and Sir Henry resigned himself to having to confront the earl in order to ensure the couple's future happiness. But how he could achieve such a feat, when the earl never left his estate and Henry had no plausible reason to visit him, required further reflection.

Amongst these considerations, on a beautiful spring day, the Greenwich party assembled for breakfast at Lord Didcomb's townhouse in Burton Street. Number 5 was a modest red brick building with large, six-paned white sash windows and a black lacquered front door. There were no flowers on the windowsills, marking it as the bachelor residence it was, but two potted boxwood trees sculpted into perfect spheres framed the main entrance. Emily was immediately charmed, willing to love anything connected to Max.

Emily, Sir Henry, Isabella carrying baby Dorothea, and two-year-old Danny were ushered into a spacious library where the map of the proposed railway was spread on a table in the center of the room. Bertie and his friend from Oxford, a Mr. Spencer who studied engineering and was known to the March family, were already studying the map, but at the sound of the new arrivals, Max stepped forward.

"Good morning, Lady March, Sir Henry, Miss March. Welcome to my home."

Danny put his hands on his hips and inquired, "Where is the other boy?"

"Danny, we talked about not speaking until you are spoken to, and certainly not before you are introduced," Isabella admonished gently.

Max only smiled. "We have met in the stables." He then offered his hand to Danny. "Good morning, Master Danny. My friend Ben Sedon and his family will be here any moment. Would you like to have a look at the map and the locomotive?"

"You have a locomotive?" Danny asked with round eyes.

"Just a drawing and the schematics for now, but would you like to see?"

Danny nodded and let Max lift him so he could see the papers spread over the table. Emily joined her brother and let her hand rest right next to Max's strong hand, bracketing Danny sitting on the table. Max instantly knew she was there, crossed his pinky finger over hers, and smiled into her eyes in a private greeting. He used his other hand to show both Emily and her brother where they would go on their outing this day, and where the railway would go.

Sir Henry established his wife and daughter on a nearby sofa before he, too, had a look at the plans. The map was impressive, but Henry had questions. "Are you really proposing a station right next to London Bridge? That is a very busy intersection."

"All the more reason to have the station right there. It's central to the City of London and connects with several stage lines. I envision that there will be more than one train station in London connecting us to all four corners of the country."

Sir Henry nodded. "You really believe the railway will be the way to travel in the future?"

"I do. Just imagine, one locomotive pulling twenty cars, and every one of those carrying as many passengers and luggage as a stagecoach, and more. There will be no stopping to change horses, consistent speeds of thirty miles an hour, and no muddy roads to contend with."

"Sounds like a dream to me." Bertie nudged his friend. "Imagine being able to get on the train in Oxford in the morning and arrive in London only two hours later, come rain or shine."

Mr. Spencer looked impressed. "That does sound rather good. You could be in Glasgow in a day."

Danny wiggled to be let back down on the floor, having spotted the model of a three-masted schooner on Max's desk in the corner of the room. "I like ships better."

Max lifted the boy to the ground, but before Danny could go inspect the ship, Mr. and Mrs. Sedon entered with their son between them.

Danny drew in a surprised breath and, pointing, beamed at the little boy. "It's you!"

The other boy was dark-haired and brown-eyed like his father. A little shorter than Danny but about the same age, he smiled broadly. "Danny!" Then, turning to their host, he asked, "Can I show Danny your ship, Uncle Max?"

Mrs. Sedon, brown-haired with intelligent gray eyes, crouched next to her son. "Why don't you introduce us to your friend first?"

Just then Isabella asked from the sofa, "Who is your friend, Danny?"

Across the room the mothers smiled at each other. If there had been any awkwardness concerning a meeting between Sir Henry and his former almost-fiancée, Lady Jane, it was behind them now.

Danny stepped forward. "Mama, Papa, this is Edgar. He helps me sail my boat in the pond at the park."

Edgar executed a very credible bow, but rather than introduce his friend, he asked Max, "Can we see the ship now?"

Max grinned from ear to ear. "Everyone, this is Master Edgar Sedon, and this here is Master Daniel March." Then he nodded to the boys. "The *Angelica* is on my desk."

Edgar grabbed Danny's hand and headed across the room. "That's the name of the ship. Come on."

Max made the remaining introductions, then they walked through a sliding door into a sun-filled morning room where a lavish buffet-style breakfast awaited them on the sideboard.

An hour later, the parade of four open carriages departed Burton Street and turned south into Bond Street toward Piccadilly. From there they took Haymarket to Charing Cross down to the Strand and wound their way through the city until they reached London Bridge, where they briefly stopped to let the boys look at the big sailing ships on the lower Thames. It was a considerable undertaking to follow the proposed route of the railway from London Bridge all the way to Greenwich, but therein lay the fun. They would drive to Greenwich, picnic in the park, and return via river barge to give the three youngest members of the group a chance to rest.

The sun was strong enough for the ladies to employ their lace-trimmed umbrellas, and the men made sure their hats shaded their eyes. Max took the lead in his curricle with Emily by his side as they continued south of the river. Their route led them down Tooley Street, then Fair Street through south London.

From her high perch, Emily looked at the busy streets around them. "Where are you going to lay tracks for a railroad? There are houses and streets everywhere."

"That is the biggest problem in trying to build a railroad in a major metropolis. No one wants to make way for progress, but progress will have to be made. I think we may have to build the railway on a viaduct for at least part of the way so the common land we build on can continue to be used by the residents. It will make the project more expensive, but since the railway will go through several parishes, it might be the best solution."

Still confused, Emily inquired, "But what of people's houses?"

"We won't build right on the high street but further toward the river, where there is more room. We may have to pull down a few houses, but think of the work the people around here will have from building the railroad and then later from working the stations and running the trains. Besides, most of the land is owned by big landowners, and we will compensate them and any individual affected."

Emily craned her neck to look between the houses toward the river, but still could only see houses and, farther down, warehouses. "It seems an impossible undertaking."

Max laughed. "I like impossible undertakings. I view them as a set of problems to be solved, and once you solve them, everything falls into place. I'm successful in my investments because I pledge my support, then solve the problems the projects face before I invest the money."

"That seems a good way to go about things. But do most people not simply want a return on their investment?"

"They do indeed. That's why they like to invest with me. The projects I work on usually make a profit, given time."

"Ah." Emily smiled in understanding. "I'm beginning to grasp why my father has invested with you. You do for investments what an impresario does in the theatre and music world."

Max sketched her a sitting bow, then returned his attention to the horses. "My grandfather derisively calls it being in trade, but I like your analogy much better."

They had reached the end of Hickman's Folly and were about to turn north into Georges Row when Max pointed to the south. "Here the railroad will be built through those common lands. That part has already been approved. But there is no road to the Grand Surrey Canal through there, so we will take Rotherhithe Wall."

They made their way along the river to the delighted squeals of the two little boys. Emily grinned broadly when her brother Danny started pointing out every ship to the Sedons' boy, Edgar, shouting from one carriage to the other. Once on the bridge over the Grand Surrey Canal, both demanded loudly they should stop and watch the funny flat boats. While halted to appease the boys, Sir Henry took the opportunity to invite Edgar Sedon to ride in his landau so the boys wouldn't need to shout over their parents' heads. Edgar was lifted into the Marches' vehicle by a grateful Ben Sedon, and they continued their journey in a much more peaceful fashion along Queen Street toward Deptford, where the landscape became more rural and picturesque as they neared Greenwich.

Greenwich itself was a lovely old town with a long naval tradition and a famed observatory. Max stopped at the pie shop on the corner of Church Street and Nelson Road, handing Emily the ribbons. "What kind of pie would you like?"

Fully occupied with the swell of pride in her heart that Max would trust her with his team, Emily shrugged. "There is really no need to buy pies, our housekeeper packed enough food for an army."

"Ah, but this is the best pie shop along the Thames, so it would be a crime not to sample them."

Sir Henry's landau pulled alongside them to the excited cries of the boys who had spotted the pie shop's window display.

"May we have apple pie?" Edgar enquired.

Danny sat a fist on his hip. "I like the little custard pies best."

Sir Henry tried to intervene, but Max jumped down and executed a credible salute. "Aye, aye, captains! Apple and custard pies it is." Then turning to Sir Henry, he asked, "Steak and cheese pie for you? Or would you like to come in and choose for yourself?"

"Just get a selection. Thank you, Didcomb. They do smell tempting."

Max disappeared into the shop while the other vehicles drove past, and when he re-emerged with a heavy wicker basket on his arm and climbed back into the curricle, he peeled back the white serviette covering the contents to show Emily his bounty.

She laughed at his eager face. "I'm not sure who wants those pies more, you or the boys." But she did lean closer to have a look. "Goodness, they look as good as they smell."

Max lifted a small round custard pie out of the basket and held it to her mouth. "Take a bite. I know you are partial to eclairs, but these are scrumptious."

Emily, her eyes sparkling and her hands full with the horses, took a bite before anyone could scold her for such unladylike behavior. "Mmmm, these are good." The buttery crust had just a touch of sweetness, and the filling was smooth and rich with a sprinkle of sugar caramelized on top. The combination was delectable. Turning her attention back to the horses, she urged them into a trot and directed them toward the park, licking crumbs and custard off her lips. "I'm glad Danny demanded custard pies."

Parking behind the other vehicles, and with the rest of the party already in the park, Emily leaned into Max to be fed another morsel. Making sure his groom was busy with the horses, Max obliged her with another bite, then shoved the rest of the pie in his mouth. Both grinning naughtily around mouthfuls of sweet goodness, Max lifted her out of the curricle, and they walked into the park holding the pie basket between them.

Isabella and Jane Sedon decreed they should climb the hill to midway so the boys would be able to see over the rooftops of Trinity Hospital to the river. They hoped watching the ships go past on the Thames would keep them entertained long enough for everyone to eat in peace. But the hill itself proved too steep for a comfortable picnic, so they climbed all the way to the top, where they found a lovely spot under an oak tree to the right of the observatory. A veritable feast was laid out, and the pies, in particular, were devoured with gusto.

After the meal, both Isabella and Jane encouraged their offspring to nap, while Henry conversed with Ben Sedon about the proposed railway, and Max asked leave to take Emily for a walk. Bertie and his pal had already made their way to the observatory in hopes of seeing the telescope.

Taking the opposite direction, Max and Emily walked a winding path under the oak trees covering the top of the hill and admired the view. Past Greenwich below, the river flowed at a stately pace, studded with ships, barges, and smaller watercraft going in every direction. The ferry crossed in the foreground, and the Isle of Dogs, verdant and green, drew the eye on the other side of the Thames. In the distance the masts of big ships could be seen, looking as if they sailed an ocean of green meadows.

"Where are all those ships? I thought the ocean was far to the right." Emily pointed to the masts in the distance.

"They are most likely in the Collier Docks. There are two huge wet docks and numerous canals in the marches," Max explained.

Emily shielded her eyes with her hand, pushing her creamy breast up into the rounded neckline of her seafoam-green day dress. Max caught his breath. But charming as the view was, their vantage point offered no privacy from the watchful gazes of Emily's parents, so he proposed to look at the view from the other side of the hill.

Emily turned to him with little devils dancing in her eyes. "You mean you want to find a nice, secluded spot to kiss me."

Max barked a laugh, but his pupils widened with desire. "Kiss you, devour you, ravish you." His gaze dropped from her eyes to her breasts, and Emily swallowed, her pulse quickening at his intensity. But she didn't demur. She threaded her arm through his and let him lead her through the trees. They walked, arm in arm, their bodies strumming with anticipation, until Max found a cluster of smaller trees offering cover from inquisitive eyes and pulled Emily into the thicket. A quick glance around assured him no one was near, so he pulled her close and crushed her lips in a searing kiss.

Arms snaking around his neck, Emily melted into the embrace and opened her lips to him. She welcomed his stroking tongue and gave it a little playful bite, making him growl and whisper against her lips, "Careful, sweeting. I have a good mind to lay you down on the soft new grass and make you mine."

Instead of being frightened, Emily sealed her lips to his and challenged his tongue to a duel. For a long while the kiss was all that mattered, the closeness, the feel of each other's skin, the desire it stirred. When the kiss finally ended, Max let his lips trail open-mouthed to kiss down her neck until he reached the tops of her breasts and lavished kisses there. Emily bent back in his arms, giving him full access, abandoned to the pleasure of his mouth on her. Was there anything more wonderful than this?

Eventually Max lifted his head to look at her. "Emily, my love. I want you more than I have ever wanted anyone or anything. Will you marry me?"

Straightening in his arms, her eyes dark with passion, Emily stroked her hand down the side of his face and smiled, happy beyond all measure. "Of course."

Framing her face with his large hands, he kissed her eyes, then her nose and finally her mouth with exquisite care before he pulled her head to his chest and hugged her close. "I must travel to Brighton to see my grandfather."

She leaned up and buried her face in his neck. "Must you?"

"He is demanding my presence, but I will return within the week, and then I will speak to your father."

"I think he is finally ready to accept you." She nodded into his neck. "I shall miss you." Being with Max was like breathing, natural and essential all at once.

"I will be back as quick as I can."

CHAPTER NINE

IN THE MOST RECENT OF WARTHON'S LETTERS to Max, the demands for a visit to Warthon Castle had turned into the threat for Warthon to come to the capital himself to put a stop to his grandson's unsuitable and utterly vexing courtship. At that, Max finally decided to go see the old man and tell him in person. Emily was the woman he loved and would marry, and nothing could deter him from his cause. But Warthon was formidable when he was angry, so Max enlisted Ben to ride down to Brighton with him. Having family on the Warthon estate, Ben readily agreed.

As soon as the two friends had left the noise and bustle of London behind them, Ben said, "I know the earl is furious, if my father-in-law is to be believed. What is your plan?"

Max slowed his horse to a trot so he wouldn't have to shout. "I don't really have a plan, since I still don't know why my grandfather hates Sir Henry so much. I think my only hope is to convince him of the unfairness of visiting the sins of the father on his daughter. I will marry Emily, and if he wants to be part of my life and the family I hope to have, he needs to accept her."

Ben emitted a low whistle. "So, you mean to deliver an ultimatum?"

"If it comes to that. I hope he will understand once I tell him how much I love her." Max knew his grandfather was a hard man and had nothing but contempt for women, but surely he had to have some concern for his grandson's happiness.

Ben had no such illusions about the old man, but his best friend was in love and wanted to believe the best about all the people in his life, so he swallowed the derisive words about to spill from his lips. "I will help in any way I can. Just watch your back. You know how he can get."

A harsh laugh escaped Max. "All too well, but I'm not a boy anymore and he is not as strong as he was."

"Nor quite as powerful," Ben agreed, but he was still wary.

With the sun shining and the road wide open in front of them, Max urged his stallion into a gallop, bringing their conversation to an end. The two friends enjoyed the companionable travel and made good time. The sun sent its last rays horizontally across the landscape when they reached the gatehouse, reined in their horses, and entered the Warthon estate.

It was then Max turned to Ben with apprehension in his eyes. "You will stay close, won't you?"

Ben met his gaze and nodded. "I'll be in the tunnel leading to the back of the fireplace. You are talking to him in the great hall?"

"I assume that is where he will be. Thank you, you know him almost as well as I do. You can tell me what you make of his reaction." This was precisely why Max had brought Ben. Ben could listen impartially to the conversation with his grandfather; just a shame he wouldn't be able to see the old man's expression. Max would have to watch for any sign of deceit there himself.

Riding out of the stand of trees shielding the estate from the road, they rode into the afternoon sun toward the medieval-looking pile. Warthon Castle was an imposing square structure, complete with turrets, battlements, and a moat, but both men knew it had been constructed during the Tudor period, when the first earl had built himself an imitation of a medieval castle. The Tudor influence was visible from the outside in the large, beveled glass windows and became more and more prominent as the two men rode across the moat bridge, left their mounts in the courtyard, and walked into the entrance hall. Here, dark oak paneling covered the walls right up to the coffered ceiling carved out of dark wood.

The wooden staircase, carved from the same dark oak, led to the upper level from the center of the entrance hall, and halfway up it split into separate flights leading to the left wing and the right wing. It was an impressive staircase, beautifully worked, but neither of the young men took any notice. Ben took the servants' corridor toward the kitchens, and Max impatiently tapped his foot as he waited for the ancient butler. When the old retainer finally huffed up the few steps from the servants' quarters, he had to walk right up to Didcomb before he recognized him, but when he did, his wrinkled face split into a wide smile.

"Lord Didcomb, welcome home. Are you looking for the earl?"

"Indeed I am. How is the old man?"

"You will find him in the great hall in front of the fire. The gout seems to be troubling him less today, so he insisted on a brandy before dinner. I presume you will be joining him?"

"For dinner, yes. I'm staying the night."

"Very good, your room is ready as always."

The ancient retainer turned to take Max to the great hall, and Max followed, knowing his grandfather would refrain from hurling abuse at him while his butler was present. Max hoped that would give him a chance to explain himself. However, he was disabused of that notion almost immediately upon entering the great hall.

The butler had barely finished announcing Max's name when the earl flung his brandy glass into the enormous fireplace, where the spirits made the log burning there hiss and spit, not unlike the earl himself.

"About time you showed your faithless self around here! What the devil are you playing at, prancing around London with Sir Henry's bastard on your arm?" With his lips twisted in derision, the Earl of Warthon banged his carved ivory walking stick on the flagstones for emphasis. "You of all people should know she is destined to be the instrument of our revenge on the cretin, and now you have raised expectations that will brand you less than a gentleman if you make her your whore. What the hell are you thinking, boy?"

Ruthlessly holding on to his temper and keeping his facial expression neutral, Max bowed to his grandfather with all the respect he could muster. "Good evening, sir. Allow me to explain."

Hoping for the earl's ire to dissipate a little, he went to pour himself a drink. But it seemed there was no appeasing the old man. His ice-blue eyes followed Max, full of suspicion and malice. "It can't be good if you need Dutch courage to tell me."

Max sipped his brandy and took a seat on the other side of the hearth, facing the earl. He kept his tone even, trying to let the facts speak for themselves. "Emily March is not only beautiful and talented, but she is also the beloved niece of a duke, beloved great-grandchild of the dowager duchess, and newest darling of the ton. There is no way you can exact your belated, and may I add misguided, revenge on her without bringing the wrath of the crown upon your head and damaging our organization. I can't let you do that. Besides, I plan to marry her."

"Misguided?" the earl exploded. "Belated revenge? The rotter is responsible for getting Astor killed and it is our duty to avenge him."

And that was the crux of it. Why was revenge more important than the Knights? Or Max's happiness, for that matter? Max could feel the heat rising in his face in his effort to keep calm. "No, Grandfather. It is our duty to keep the Knights out of the limelight when the existence of our organization could be construed as less than patriotic."

The earl's eyes were blazing, his age-lined face hard like carved oak. "Poppycock, we have rules, and those rules outweigh all other considerations. Bring me the girl and I'll show you."

"Absolutely not." Cold sweat gathered on Max's brow at the mere thought of it.

"You are not marrying March's bastard! Do you hear me?"

Max's jaw tightened, and his eyes were hard as steel. "There is nothing wrong with my hearing, sir. Nevertheless, I will marry Emily March."

"Then get out of my house. I have a good mind to disinherit you."

White-hot anger overruled Max's common sense. He let his glass fly in the same direction his grandfather had flung his earlier and stormed out, muttering under his breath, "No, you won't. Letting the title revert to the crown would irk you more than seeing me married to a beautiful bastard."

Behind him the earl raged on. "Come back here, you ungrateful whoreson. I will teach you to talk back to me!"

Max knew the ivory cane would be raised to strike him and almost wished his old tormentor would disinherit him so he would be free of all further obligation. He strode out of the hall and through the foyer to the front door without a backwards glance, then crossed the yard to the stables. His gelding was already unsaddled and happily munching oats in his stall, so Max had another horse saddled, and mounted as soon as the stable hand brought the horse out to him.

"Tell Ben I will be at the Waterfront Hotel for the night."

Still furious, he rode out of the castle's courtyard, possibly to never return.

IN THE SECRET PASSAGE LEADING to the enormous fireplace in the hall, Ben held his breath. The meeting between his friend and the old earl had gone about as badly as it could have, and the earl had gone deathly quiet. So quiet, Ben was starting to get worried for the old curmudgeon. But just when he was about to peek around the side of the fireplace to check on the earl, the old man banged his walking stick on the ground with a vicious thud.

"I'll teach you to defy me. If it's the last thing I do, I'll teach you."

A cold shiver ran down Ben's back. He knew what cruelties the earl

93

was capable of and had no doubt he still had the power to be a danger to the lovely Miss March. Max best marry her posthaste so they could protect her. Retreating as quietly as possible, Ben let himself out of the secret door in the forgotten pantry and made his way to his father's apartment above the stable.

Mr. Sedon Senior had been in the earl's employ since his boyhood and had worked himself to the position of ostler. He was a kind, hard-working man who was immensely proud of his only son's success but wouldn't have loved him any less if he had remained a stable hand. His weathered face split into a broad smile when his son entered. "Ben, I wasn't expecting you."

The younger man leaned in for a one-armed embrace. "I came with Max, but he had a disagreement with the earl and has already left, so I don't have much time."

"That's a shame. Do you have time for tea, at least?" Mr. Sedon turned to the stove in the corner of the room where a teapot and a covered plate were kept warm. "The girl just brought them up from the kitchen."

"Go on then, I suppose I can stay for a cup."

Mr. Sedon brought the teapot to the table, then took cups and a loaf of bread from the sideboard and the butter dish from the windowsill. "Sit down, my boy, and tell me about my rascal of a grandson."

Ben chuckled. "Rascal is right. Max invited us for an outing to see the proposed train route to Greenwich, but he and Sir Henry's son are obsessed with sail ships, so that's pretty much all we heard about all day."

The older man shook his head, smiling. "I wish I had seen it."

"You could have. Come live with us. There is no need for you to work any longer." This was an ongoing argument between them, but at this moment Ben was glad his father still had influence in the earl's household, so he added, "Well, soon anyhow."

"Ah, so what was Lord Didcomb quarreling with the earl about?"

Ben took a steaming cup of tea from his father and sipped. "Do you remember how angry the earl was three years ago when Sir Henry March come to the chapel to rescue his lady friend?"

Mr. Sedon wrapped his rough hands around his cup to warm them. "Aye, he was hopping mad about having to shoot the vicar who'd become a viscount. The two of them had been close."

"Yes, that's the one. It turns out Warthon has some older quarrel with Sir Henry, and that incident just intensified the hatred. Max has fallen in love with the man's illegitimate daughter."

The older Sedon blew out a silent whistle. "Does Sir Henry acknowledge the girl? Is the earl worried Didcomb will ruin her?"

A harsh laugh escaped Ben. "The earl wouldn't care if Max put her to work in the club. No, it's worse. Miss March is acknowledged by her father, who has given her his name, and she was brought up in the Duke of Avon's household. Miss Emily March is lovely in every way and exactly what Max needs. Father, you should see how much in love he is, it's a thing of beauty to behold."

Assessing his son, Mr. Sedon put two and two together. "But you are worried."

"I am indeed. Max just told the earl that he intends to marry Miss March, and the earl is planning mischief, I just know it."

"So, you want me to keep an eye out and let you know who he meets with, who comes to visit, and who he sends private messages to?"

"Exactly."

Ben's father winked at his only son and smiled. "See, that's why I'm still here. As long as the old earl is still alive, he can make trouble for you and your friend."

"Thank you, Dad. You make a good point. But when Max is married and settled, you'll come and stay with us for a spell at least?"

The older Sedon reached across the table and squeezed Ben's hand. "I would like that. Edgar will be ready for his first pony soon."

Ben smiled and shook his head. "If you ask him, he is ready right now."

They both chuckled, familiar with Edgar's antics, and drank their tea in companionable silence.

"WHAT ARE YOU GOING TO do?" Ben had related the earl's last comment to Max, who was staring out at a tumultuous sea.

Stroking a weary hand down his face, Max sighed. "Tell Sir Henry there might be trouble and marry Emily as soon as the banns can be read."

"I suppose she has already said yes?" Ben's only answer was a sideways glance, so he asked the next question. "Wouldn't a special license be better?"

"No, that would give Grandfather fuel. I want no undue haste to overshadow our nuptials and give the ton reason to gossip. We will marry in church, Emily will have time to order a wedding dress, and her family will send out invitations to the wedding breakfast." Turning his back on the drama outside, Max continued, "Even Warthon will be invited, and he can show his displeasure by declining to attend. Maybe being rude to my bride will appease him some." Max dropped into an armchair by the fire. "Thank you."

"For what?" Ben was genuinely puzzled.

"Always being there for me, you dolt."

"Ah. Well, you are the golden goose." That earned Ben a laugh, and when he indicated the carafe of brandy on a nearby table, Max nodded.

"Just a small one. I intend to rise early tomorrow."

CHAPTER TEN

AS BEN AND MAX SHARED A DRINK IN BRIGHton, Emily was summoned to the library. She loved the book room at this time of day, when the early evening sun bathed everything in golden light, making the ocher drapes and Persian rugs glow with warmth. Emily was still in her pale orange day dress. Her hair was brushed off her face and styled into several small braids, which were then twisted into a chignon at the nape of her neck, a hairstyle she favored over the obligatory corkscrew curls at the temples. Her hair was naturally straight, so the tight curls were hard to achieve and even harder to maintain. The chignon made her feel elegant and grown-up.

Emily dipped a curtsy to her father, who stood at the back fireplace. "You called for me?"

"I did, poppet, sit down. Would you like a sherry?"

"Oho, you are offering me alcohol. This sounds ominous." She grinned at her father, hoping to lighten the mood.

Henry's lips twitched, but he remained serious and went to pour them both a drink, sherry for Emily and brandy for himself. "I don't know about ominous, but what I want to discuss with you is serious."

Emily took the sherry from him and sat on the leather sofa. "Is it about Lord Didcomb coming to talk to you when he returns from Brighton?"

Nodding, Henry sat in the other corner of the sofa and angled his body toward his daughter. "Am I right in the assumption that you already have an understanding with him?"

Emily blushed, but her whole posture was defiant. "Yes, Max asked me to marry him and told me he would come talk to you after he returns."

"And you said yes?" Henry searched her face.

"I did."

"I thought as much." He continued to study her as he took a sip of his brandy. "Well, before we have the banns read, I need to tell you a few things about your Maximilian, and I suggest you ask him a few pointed questions before you give him your final answer."

A fold appeared between the perfect arches of Emily's eyebrows. "That does sound ominous. Are you trying to talk me out of marrying Max?"

"No, poppet, I'm not blind, I know you are in love with him, and he with you. But there are things about him you need to know."

"You are being very dramatic, Papa. Please just tell me whatever it is."

"All right, poppet." Henry sighed deeply and proceeded, choosing his words carefully. "You know that Max is at odds with his grandfather and that some of that tension has to do with me. Six years ago, I investigated a case of treason. During the course of the investigation, we killed the traitor, and I somehow crossed the Earl of Warthon. Neither Didcomb nor I can figure out precisely why Warthon hates me, but he does, and he extends that hatred to my family. The first thing I need you to understand is that you cannot trust the earl."

Emily nodded. "From all I have heard, he is a thoroughly disagreeable person, so I can promise to keep my distance."

"Good." Henry fortified himself with a swig of brandy. "The next thing I need to tell you is not the sort of thing a father ever should have to speak to his daughter about, but I love you too much to let you walk into marriage with Didcomb blindly. I know this will come as a shock, but if I say no without an explanation, you will just run off with him."

Knowing her father was right, Emily had the good grace to blush. "I can't help it, I love him."

"I see that. That's why I'm telling you this so you can either work things out with him or decide against marrying him yourself." Henry paused again to steady himself, while Emily looked at him quizzically.

"Max is heavily involved with a secret society called the Knights. This society is very old and very powerful, and the Earl of Warthon is still the leader. However, Max has worked very hard to make this organization relevant today, and apart from making the members rich with his investments, he runs a clubhouse for them." Henry struggled to continue, but from whichever angle he looked at it, Emily had to know. "This is no ordinary gentleman's club, poppet. You can't just become a member there. You must be born into a family belonging to the Knights or be invited to become a member. This club is a way to make sure members can't simply leave the Knights once they have joined, a way to gain leverage over them."

The frown on Emily's beautiful face was getting deeper. "What do they do in this club?"

"Well, they talk, gamble, and drink, as in most gentleman's clubs. But there are also women there. Women hired to entertain the members, to give them whatever they want, no matter how depraved."

Emily's eyes snapped to her father's as the blood drained out of her face. "He keeps prostitutes at this club? You must be mistaken. No gentleman would do that."

It was excruciating to have to shatter Emily's innocence and her trust in her beloved like this, but Henry believed it to be the only way. "You are right, it is not very genteel of him, but so-called gentlemen have done far worse."

"Papa, I know him. He wouldn't do such a thing. He saved me from a truly depraved man."

"Yes, he did, poppet. But human beings are complex. They do things for all sorts of reasons, and honorable men can sometimes do less-than-honorable things. Max hires and keeps women at the club for the pleasure of the members."

Emily was close to tears now. "And possibly his own."

Henry reached to take her hand. "I don't know if he partakes. All I know is that he hires them, they live there, and, to his credit, he is good to them. Allen managed to sneak into the club and found out that much."

She barked a desperate sort of laugh. "Well, at least he is good to them." Tears were streaming down her cheeks unchecked.

Mortified for her, Henry pulled her into his arms. "I'm so sorry I had to tell you about this. Please know that this doesn't mean Max is not a good man. In fact, I believe he is. It also doesn't mean his love for you isn't real. Lots of men frequent ladies of the night. You know that I had a mistress before I married Isabella."

Balling her fist against his chest, Emily straightened. "Eliza was never a prostitute, and you didn't run a house of ill repute." Anger was beginning to course through her. "How could he?"

Henry could only sigh and try to explain. "In his defense, he started the club to keep members away from his grandfather, who was part of a group who did even more objectionable things." When her round eyes looked at him expectantly, he held up his hands. "Do not ask me to explain that further. I have already told you more than any decent man should tell his daughter."

She crumpled against him again, and he held her for a while until she asked, "Why are men so vile?"

Sighing, Henry kissed the top of her head. "Men have urges. But good men are faithful once they marry the woman they love."

Emily sat up, took the handkerchief her father offered, and dried her face. "The way you are. I suppose I need to ask Max what he intends to do with the club now we are to get married." She blew her nose noisily.

"That would be my first question too." Henry nodded.

"And maybe he could promise me not to see those ladies again."

Henry was glad Emily could be practical about this situation. "I knew you would see a way to handle this."

She, however, shot her father a dark look. "I'm not ready to forgive you for telling me all this, but I know you mean to ensure my happiness. I still can't quite believe this is real. I shall go and ask Allen. I believe he and Eliza are in residence in Chelsea."

A smile played around Henry's lips. His daughter was a skeptic and a realist, and if her love for Max survived this, it was truly love and he would give his blessing gladly.

"I just had a note from Allen. They will be in Chelsea till the end of July."

Emily swallowed the last of her sherry, handed her father her glass and his wet handkerchief, and stood. "I want to go by myself and speak to Allen before I see Max next. Can I take the carriage tomorrow morning?"

"Yes. Take Thomas with you."

She nodded and left the room with her head held high.

EMILY MAINTAINED HER COMPOSURE UNTIL she reached her room, but once the door clicked shut behind her, she stomped her foot with all her might and let out a screech of frustration. Of course, her father would know all Max's secrets and tell her rather than let her make a mistake. But he had another think coming if he thought this would deter her. Max would just have to find someone else to run his stupid club; she was not going to let him ruin both their lives with a house of ill repute. And here she had worried marrying her might blemish *his* reputation! Ha, he would have some explaining to do when he returned. And the gall of his grandfather to look down on her. She may be illegitimate, but at least she didn't run a whorehouse. Another stomp left a dent in the polished parquet floor.

Oh Lord, where was Bertie when he was needed? She kicked off her slippers and rang for Suzie so she could help her out of her day dress and into her dinner ensemble already laid out on her bed. Thank God there was no entertainment to attend; Emily didn't think she could plaster on a fake smile for an entire night. Dinner was going to be bad enough.

Emily was still trampling the flowers in her aqua, pink, and beige Persian rug when Suzie knocked.

"Yes, yes. Come in."

Suzie quietly pulled the door shut, but on seeing her mistress her jaw dropped. "What is it, miss? You look like a storm cloud."

"Oh Suz, why are men such idiots?" Some of the fight went out of Emily, and she let herself drop onto the chaise longue in dramatic fashion. At least she didn't have to pretend with her maid. "Lord Didcomb is doing something he shouldn't be, and of course my father found out and told me. Now I want to strangle His Lordship."

Moving her mistress slightly so she could start unbuttoning her, Suzie attempted to soothe, "Don't worry, miss, wanting to strangle the person you are in love with is part of being in love. Men do the strangest things, and we can't do nothing about it."

Emily stood to let the dress slip to the floor and stepped out of it. "Well, I intend to do something about this situation. We are going to Chelsea tomorrow, by the way. Tell Thomas he is to come with us to see Mr. Strathem."

Taking the orange dress to the armoire, Suzie mused, "That will be a nice drive. It should be sunny tomorrow."

Growling, Emily splashed water into her face in the hope it might settle her. "I just wish he had told me about it instead of me having to hear it from my father. I thought I might die of mortification."

"Being thoughtless is another thing men are good at. His Lordship probably hoped you wouldn't find out." Suzie nodded wisely.

"How do you know so much about men, Suz?"

The maid laughed. "I have five brothers and each one is worse than the next, and then there is Thomas."

"Ah, so you and Thomas are walking out together now?"

Suzie blushed and smiled dreamily. "We are, miss."

Emily nodded. "Thomas is a good man and will make something of himself."

"That he is, and handsome. But it doesn't stop him from being infuriating at times, especially when he is trying to spare my feelings about something."

Emily let that sink in. "So, you think His Lordship didn't tell me because he wanted to spare my feelings?"

With Emily's hands and face washed, Suzie held out the aqua silk dinner dress for her mistress to step into. "It's plain to see His Lordship cares about you; it makes sense, don't it?"

Threading her arms into the puffed half-sleeves, Emily thought for a moment. She shrugged into the dress and turned so Suzie could do up the buttons in the back. "It does make sense, but he should know me better than that, and he should have known my father would find out and tell me."

Suzie smoothed the fabric over Emily's shoulders. "I don't know what His Lordship is doing, and Sir Henry is unusual in the way he tells you and Her Ladyship things. You should give Lord Didcomb a chance to explain."

"Yes, he will most definitely have to explain." Emily gave her reflection in the vanity mirror a dark look as she sat down. "The hair still looks fine, and I like it. Just hand me the diamond earrings with the teardrop pearls." She hooked the glittering gems into her earlobes and checked her refection. But when Suzie offered her the matching necklace, she shook her head. "No, just my charm bracelet."

The bracelet had been a Christmas present from her father when she was twelve but was still a favorite. Tonight, she felt in need of the talisman. It was a reminder of all the things she loved: horses, music, and her family. Those things would always be there for her.

Emily stood and checked her whole appearance in the cheval glass, turning this way and then the other. "I like the aqua very much. It looks marvelous with my hair."

"Yes, it's lovely, miss. You will be able to wear it out if you get engaged."

Grinning, Emily headed for the door. "That's a very good argument for forgiving His Lordship for not telling me all he ought to."

The lighthearted moment was short-lived, however. As Emily descended the stairs to join her family in the drawing room, her thoughts returned to the conversation she would have to have with Max when he returned from visiting his grandfather.

CHAPTER ELEVEN

THE OPPORTUNITY FOR THIS CONVERSATION came sooner than Emily had anticipated. Allen had sent word he would see her in the afternoon, so Emily had just called for her horse and was halfway up the stairs to change into her riding habit when Max was admitted into the foyer. She turned toward him with one eyebrow raised. "I thought you were visiting your grandfather?"

Max smiled up at her, so very glad to see her. But when she didn't smile back and just stood there looking down on him, he knew all wasn't as it should be. "I saw him. He was very disagreeable, and here I am, at your service." That damnable eyebrow of hers was still raised. Max stepped closer and whispered, "What's wrong?"

Emily's face fell. In a fraction of a second her haughty mask of disdain transformed into utter misery. Her lower lip trembled, and her eyes swam with unshed tears. "We have to talk." She hiccuped on the last word, ran down the few steps, and dragged him by his sleeve to the breakfast room, the one room in the house she knew would be empty at this time of day. Pulling him in, she shut the door and let go of him.

He tried to embrace her, but she quickly moved to the other side of the table. Now truly worried, Max pulled out a chair for her. "Emily, please sit and tell me what's troubling you."

She ignored his gesture and sat on the opposite side of the table, indicating for him to take the chair he had pulled out. Smoothing her hands over the cherrywood, she tried to find a way to say what needed to be said. But where to begin? In the end she just blurted out: "My father knows about your secret society club with the loose women, and he told me."

All color drained from Max's face.

He looked so guilty; it was infuriating.

"How could you let me find out such a thing from my father, for heaven's sake?"

"Bloody hell!" He stared at her in open-mouthed astonishment, unaware even that he had used profanity in her presence. When he finally collected himself enough to answer her question, even he knew his answer was lame. "I didn't know he knew about the club."

It was her turn to be astonished. "Max, my father investigated you the moment our paths crossed for the first time three years ago. Finding out other people's secrets is what he does. I thought you knew." Her voice sounded brittle, and she looked utterly miserable. "You should have told me yourself."

Max was slowly recovering from his shock. "I do know it's what he does, and thinking about it now, I should have realized he would know about the club. I even expected him to ask me about it. But Emily, it would never have occurred to me he would tell you about it."

Again, anger sparked in her deep blue eyes. "And that is supposed to make me feel better? I should thank my father for insisting I don't go blindly into an engagement with you. So, explain yourself, what do you have to do with the women there?"

Max was relieved to see the anger. It was better than the hurt. And when she focused on the women, he realized she didn't care about the secret club or the secret society, she was worried about the women there. "Darling…"

"Don't you darling me!" Emily's eyes flashed with fury, the fiery emotion making her even more beautiful. But she continued and the words cut straight through Max. "The thought of you with those—those harlots." She balled her hands in front of her on the table. "How could you?"

Max tried to reach across the table for her hands, but she pulled them out of his reach. "Emily, please, let me explain."

"You'd better."

"I haven't been to the club since the Monday after your come-out ball, and only for business. From our first dance I knew you were the woman I wanted, and no other would do."

She softened slightly. "But you still run the place."

"Actually, I don't. I hired a manager a while ago."

"So why is it your club and why were you ever involved in the running of it?"

"That has to do with an ancient society my grandfather and I belong to. My grandfather is the leader and very much enjoys the power he gains through it. You see, the Knights date back to William the Conqueror, and the society was formed to advance and protect the political interests of its members. However, we are not living in the Dark Ages, and I have long thought we should be more of an economic alliance. When I suggested as much about five years ago, my grandfather and his cronies laughed. Knowing my grandfather, I didn't bother suggesting it again and got together with some of the younger members instead. But we needed a place to meet away from the old guard, so I created the club. It's immensely popular with all the members by now and has allowed me to influence the organization and lead it away from the useless political maneuvering. I invest and make money for a large portion of the membership."

Emily, her brow furrowed, tried to make sense of Max's story. "I know you invest for people, and Papa told me about the secret society and that you are doing good work there, but Max, why the women?"

Max looked extremely uncomfortable. "Oh Lord, I never thought I would have to explain any of this to a female, let alone the woman I wish to marry."

Getting impatient, Emily demanded, "Just tell me, Max."

"They keep the members entertained and away from my grandfather and his archaic ideas." Max did not want to say any more. In fact, he had never planned on saying anything at all about the club or the society, but he knew he had to explain himself to Emily. There was a real, tangible reason for the women's presence at the club, one that had nothing to do with what they did for the men there. He heaved a sigh and relented. "Most of the girls there are perfectly nice country girls either my grandfather or one of his cronies corrupted. They couldn't stay where they were, all of them either cast out by their families or worried about shaming them. My grandfather had no plans to do anything for them, so I offered them employment in the club, where they are well cared for and well paid."

Max studied his hands, not ready to look Emily in the eye after this last admission. "You see, my grandfather uses his power to behave however he pleases. I'm trying to do better, but I know how feeble my attempts must look to you."

Emily's tone finally softened. "So, you do your best to clean up after your grandfather. That, at least, is commendable. The earl sounds like a thoroughly unpleasant individual, but I'm not about to be engaged to him. Will you be attending this club in the future?" Her eyes bored into him.

Finally meeting her gaze, Max hated to disappoint her, but knew he had to be honest, or she would never trust him again. "Yes, I will continue to have meetings with members there because that is the purpose of the club, and it would affect my standing amongst the members if I didn't."

He could see the hurt and anger return to her eyes, so he leaned forward to cover her hand with his and continued, "But I can promise you I will not engage the services of any of the women there."

Biting her bottom lip to stop it from trembling, Emily stared at Max's hand on hers and shook her head. "How would I ever know?"

"Emily, look at me." Max's voice was rough with the fear of losing her. When she lifted her eyes to his he breathed a sigh of relief. "I will not touch any of them. The only woman I want is you." Searching her face, he caressed the back of her hand. "If you need proof, you can ask Ben. He is almost always present at the meetings."

Two fat tears rolled down Emily's face when she finally nodded. "I will ask Mr. Sedon. But first of all, I have to speak with my father's associate. Will you come back tomorrow, please?"

"I will, my darling." He stood and walked around the table so he could kiss her hand. "I'm glad there won't be any secrets between us."

Emily would have preferred he had no secrets to share in the first place, but she gave him a watery smile and allowed him her hand. Once he had departed, she wiped her tears with one of the napkins on the sideboard, then made her way up the back stairs to don her riding habit. Emily had never needed a gallop as much as she needed it now.

In the May sun the drive to Chelsea was rather pleasant, despite Emily's gloomy mood. The broad, tree-lined streets of Belgravia with their tall white mansions and the busy streets around the Emporium in Knightsbridge gave her plenty to look at. Suzie kept up a steady stream of chatter Emily largely ignored, but it was nice not to be alone. When they got stuck in traffic on Kings Road, however, the slow pace tested Emily's patience.

Sitting back, Emily sighed. She would have preferred to walk that last mile, but it most likely would take longer than crawling around the accident. In the end, the traffic resolved itself quicker than expected and soon they turned into Smith Street where they drove through green fields until they came to the little lane leading to the gates of Eliza's small mansion. Emily loved the house surrounded by mature trees and flowering rhododendron bushes. It was an oasis of calm and beauty in the middle of the hectic metropolis. Coming here always felt like a reprieve from the world. Even with all the questions she had to ask about Max weighing on her, Emily looked forward to the visit. The gates were opened for them, and by the time the carriage reached the house, both Allen and Eliza were on the front steps to greet her. Thomas swung out of the saddle and opened the door for Emily, but Allen was already there to help her out.

As soon as Emily's feet were on the ground, she threw herself into Allen's arms and burst into tears. "Oh, Uncle Allen, what am I to do?"

"There, there, sweet pea. Let's get you into the house where we can discuss it all." Allen patted her shoulder and turned them toward the house. Henry had told him Emily would need information about the club from him, but Allen hadn't quite anticipated the level of drama it would involve. Thankfully, Eliza came to his aid.

"Emily, darling, we will sort this out. There is tea in the drawing room, or we could have it outside, if you prefer."

Emily shook her head. "I would rather be in private for this."

Eliza and Allen exchanged a look. "Indeed." Evidently Emily cared a great deal about this matter.

After telling Suzie she wouldn't be needed for a while, Emily followed Eliza into the spacious drawing room, where she was urged onto the walnut-and-cream-brocade love seat. Eliza poured her a cup of tea, then handed one to Allen and sat down next to him on the sofa opposite. "Now, Emily, tell us what this is all about and how we can help."

Emily took a fortifying sip of her tea, set the cup on the low inlaid table next to her, and took a deep breath. "I presume Papa informed you that he told me about Lord Didcomb's club."

Allen nodded, so Emily continued, "I originally wanted to ask you what His Lordship's role is in the club and what contact he has with the loose women there, but His Lordship came to visit me this morning, so I have already talked to him. He says he hired a man to manage the club and has not been involved since right after my come-out, when he realized he wanted to court me." Staring down at her hands, she dragged a shuddering breath into her lungs, trying to control her emotions. Talking about this with her friends was even harder than talking to Max had been.

"Allen, can you find out if he truly did? I need to know if I can trust him, if what he said is true, if he really isn't fraternizing with those women." Emily finally looked up at Eliza, her eyes swimming with tears. She was barely holding on to her composure. "I love him, and not just a girlish kind of love. It is my dearest wish to marry him and spend my life with him, and he feels the same about me." She paused, wringing her hands in her lap. "He tells me he only wants me, but I know men have strange ideas about such things. How can I trust him when he has such easy access to these girls in the club?"

Exchanging a worried look with Allen, Eliza rose to join Emily on the love seat. She gently put her hand over Emily's. "Darling, I'm so sorry. This is quite the predicament. It seems love is never completely smooth sailing, but are you sure you want to marry a man in whose fidelity you may not be able to trust?"

A tear made its way down Emily's cheek. "Oh, Eliza. I don't think I'm like you or Papa, I will not find another love. This is it for me. I know he is the love of my life and as long as he lives there will be no other for me. But what if I'm not the only one in his bed? I'm not sure I could bear it." She was sobbing now.

Eliza pulled her into the shelter of her arms and soothed, "Let Allen investigate and find out if he told you the truth. If he did, then maybe you can trust him."

From the sofa opposite, Allen added, "From what I heard from the ladies in the club three years ago, at the very least he was a good employer. He engaged them, took care of their needs, and dealt with difficult customers for them. I still have a contact in the house, so I can verify whether a new manager has been engaged. Would that help?"

Emily nodded into Eliza's neck. "Yes, please."

Rocking her back and forth, Eliza continued the joint effort to calm her. "Just think, he has never pursued an eligible female before, so being in love and having to be responsible for his actions is new to him. Maybe you need to give him a chance to do the right thing."

Allen chimed in, "If he did hire a manager for the club, I would consider that doing the right thing. By all accounts, the club is important to him."

Emily brightened a little. "He did say so. But he also declared he couldn't promise not to go to the club because he has business meetings there." Another wave of misery overtook her. "Who does business deals in clubs?"

"Everyone," Allen promptly supplied. "That is one of the major functions of gentlemen's clubs."

Both Emily and Eliza stared at him open-mouthed. "Most gentlemen's clubs don't employ prostitutes," Eliza finally managed.

"Of course, but it's still essentially a club with a dining room and rooms for socializing and reading. The girls are upstairs in their separate drawing room. From what I observed, there are normal club amenities on the ground and first floor, and the second floor is the girls' domain. Max could easily have meetings there without ever seeing any of the light-skirts."

Having it explained like that did make Emily feel better. "So, you think I should trust him."

Allen smiled at Emily's hopeful expression. "Let me find out a little more, but I think he may be on the level."

Allen's confidence in Max cheered Emily considerably. She sat up, dried her tears, and plucked a macaroon from the platter of sweets on the tea tray. Taking a plate from Eliza and adding a second macaroon, she asked, "When do you think you might be able to confirm the presence of a new manager at the club?"

"By tomorrow, I should think." Heaping his own plate full of macaroons and lemon pound cake, he smiled at his wife. "You don't need me for anything tonight, do you, love?"

"Indeed, I don't, but you better not stay out too late, dear."

There was a secret little smile on Eliza's lips that prompted Emily to study her friend a little closer. Eliza was slender and beautiful as always, but there was a certain glow to her. This glow prompted Emily to later remark to her stepmother she believed their friend to be with child.

CHAPTER TWELVE

THE FAMILY WAS STILL AT BREAKFAST THE NEXT morning when Allen called. He was promptly invited to share their meal, which elicited excited shrieks from Danny as he threw himself into Allen's arms.

"Uncle Allen, can we have a sword fight?"

Henry intervened on his friend's behalf. "Danny, let the man eat his breakfast first."

"And what of the food left on your plate?" his mother added, pointing for Danny to return to his place.

Laughing, Allen carried the boy back to his chair and promised, "How about we eat breakfast, I have a word with your sister, and then I shall meet you in the garden for swordplay and a piggyback ride."

"Yes." Danny pumped a triumphant fist into the air, then settled down to eat his eggs.

Having dealt with the youngest March present, Allen turned to Emily, who eyed him with a mixture of trepidation and hope. He gifted her with a reassuring smile and a nod before dedicating himself to his food.

"I see you still eat for three." Henry chuckled, which earned him a grin from his friend.

"It's a long ride from Chelsea, and Eliza had business in Kensington, so we rose early."

"How is Eliza?" Isabella inquired.

"She is well. Although…" Allen hesitated for a moment, then confided, "Her stomach seems fragile of late."

Exchanging a look with her stepdaughter, Isabella asked carefully,

"Does this occur at a specific time of the day?"

"Yes, she goes green at the sight of food in the morning but seems right as rain by midday." Allen stopped to contemplate what he had just said and met Isabella's eyes across the table. "You don't mean—could she be in a delicate condition?"

Isabella smiled. "She might well be."

"But why didn't she tell me?"

"Perhaps she is waiting to be sure?"

Suddenly agitated but with sparkling eyes, Allen pushed his chair out and stood. "Emily, Didcomb told the truth. If you will excuse me, I must go see my wife."

Isabella grinned and waved him away.

"Uncle Allen! You promised to play swords!" Danny was clearly outraged.

Going down on one knee next to the boy's chair, Allen held both his hands. "I know, Danny. I'm very sorry, but I just realized I must ask Eliza something very important. What do you say I come back tomorrow, and we play then?"

Danny didn't look convinced. "What do you have to ask her?"

Allen lowered his voice conspiratorially. "I need to ask her if she is having a baby."

Cocking his head to the side, Danny considered, then pulled a face. "I suppose we can play tomorrow. But tell her to have a boy, girls are boring."

Laughing, Allen hugged the boy, then kissed Emily's and Isabella's cheeks and made his way to the foyer, where Henry had already called for his horse and stood ready to embrace his friend. "I hope congratulations are indeed in order. Bring Eliza tomorrow, we will make a day of it."

EMILY WAS ALMOST AS DISMAYED at Allen's rushed departure as her little brother but took heart in the fact Allen had confirmed Max's truthfulness. Consequently, she donned her riding habit, and when Max called at the appointed hour, she was ready and waiting for him in the foyer, while Thomas walked Addy outside, ready for their morning ride.

Beyond relieved to see the mare on the doorstep, Max handed Thomas his reins and hurried up the stairs and through the open door.

"Good morning, my angel." He bowed and kissed both her hands. "Will you ride with me?"

Emily was close to tears just seeing him, knowing he had told her the truth. She nodded.

Max had spent the worst night of his life, tossing and turning, questioning his every life choice and in mortal dread of losing Emily. Now he stood with her hands pressed to his heart, drowning in her deep blue eyes. "Thank you."

Leading her outside, Max lifted Emily into the saddle before swinging himself onto his own horse. He didn't care how she had confirmed the truth of what he had told her the previous day, he was simply glad she was willing to give him a chance, such was his need and love for her.

Gathering her reins, Emily watched Max climb into the saddle and knew she would marry him, no matter what he had done in the past. What should it signify if he employed loose women? It did not stop her from loving him, wanting him, even trusting him. Perhaps that was the lesson to be had from this interlude: she loved him, and nothing could break that.

They rode through the streets of London in silence, but once less-populated parts of the park opened up in front of them, Thomas fell several lengths back so the couple could talk.

Max was the first to speak. "Emily, I am so very sorry for my past behavior and the way you had to find out about it. I should have told you; I know that now."

Taking a deep breath, Emily met his eyes. They were sincere and full of love. "Thank you. I do understand you hoped I would never have to know." Turning to look straight ahead, she continued, "I now know you spoke the truth yesterday. I was even informed it is possible to have meetings at your club without ever encountering the women there, and that gentlemen indeed have meetings in their clubs. But Max—"

Emily could no longer bear the distance between them and reached out her hand. He took it and nodded for her to continue. "I need a solemn promise you will not fraternize with them, that you will be faithful to me." Trying to swallow the emotion threatening to overwhelm her, she whispered, "You see, I love you, but I don't think I could forgive you such a trespass."

"Oh, my darling. Of course, I promise." He meant it. It was an easy promise to make. Emily truly was the only woman he wanted. If she became his, he would be hers, forever.

The vise grip of worry around Emily's heart finally eased. If he was willing to promise, she was willing to trust. She squeezed his hand, and he brought their intertwined hands up to kiss hers.

They had reached the spot where the footpath cut through the woods to the Long Water. The trees were green now and would afford them privacy. Smiling into her eyes, Max reined in his steed, swung down, and moved around to lift Emily down. "Walk with me."

Returning his smile, Emily took Max's arm, leaving Thomas to take charge of the mounts. Max led her to a spot between two old oak trees where they would be shielded from view, and there, amongst the bluebells in the dappled sunlight with robins chirping overhead, Max went down on one knee in front of the woman he loved. "Emily March, I love you like I never thought I could love another. Marry me, please, for in my mind you are already my wife, my love, my everything. I swear I will not touch another until death do us part—and beyond."

Smiling through tears of joy, Emily framed his face with her hands and bent to kiss him tenderly on the mouth. "Yes."

Max stood and lifted her in one movement. Both laughing and crying all at once, he spun them in circles until she bent to kiss him again,
and he let her slide down his body slowly, kissing her back, inhaling her
scent, tasting the salt on her cheeks and kissing the tears away. "You make
me so happy. I promise, nothing will ever come between us again."

Her eyes shining brightly with happiness, Emily took in the man
who was to be her husband, her lover, her mate for life. In this moment
truly everything was right with her world. She knew Max's family, especially the earl, would need convincing, but she felt equal to that task too.
Had she not charmed the whole of the ton? Had she not won the love
of her golden god? All she needed was a meeting with the earl and she
would clear up this misunderstanding he had with her father and make
the old man like her. She could do anything as long as she had Max's love.

The couple lingered for some time in the May-bright oak grove,
strolling along the water and making plans for their life together. The
sun had climbed past its zenith by the time they rode back to Cavendish
Square so Max could officially ask for Emily's hand in marriage.

Sir Henry gave his consent, having had reassurance from Allen concerning the club and Didcomb's involvement. He was still uneasy
about the earl and his dislike of anything to do with the March name but
reasoned even the earl wouldn't do anything to his grandson's wife.

Max agreed the banns should be read at St. George's in Mayfair rather than at the Warthon chapel. St. George's was Emily and Max's parish
since his personal residence also fell within its borders, and Max had no
plans to live at the castle. In fact, he stated his intent to remain in London
and move his household from Burton Street to a bigger residence. These
were all factors which further reconciled Henry to his daughter's choice,
but it soon became apparent the reading of the banns would involve the

Earl of Warthon. It was the bishop himself who insisted the banns also be read in Hove, the official parish for the Warthon earldom. That then necessitated the earl to be told before the invitation to the nuptials were sent out, a task which Max undertook with no small amount of trepidation.

The reply came swiftly.

Didcomb,
If you think I will sanction this farce, you do not know me.
Warthon

It was exactly what Max had expected, but it still upset him, even sent a shiver of foreboding down his spine. Consequently, he thought it necessary to tell Emily and warn Sir Henry. Emily, he now knew, hated to be kept in the dark, and although he would endeavor to keep her well away from his grandfather, he would have to introduce her at some point. It was best she should know Warthon was not to be trusted.

THE DUKE OF AVON'S DRAWING room was teeming with Redwicks and Marches in celebration of their engagement, making Max feel the absence of his family. His mother was to arrive in town the next day, and her side of the family had already accepted the invitation to the wedding, but he still felt the lack. How would Emily feel about his grandfather's rejection? Even realizing Emily would be better off never meeting the man, his grandfather's refusal to attend their wedding was troubling.

But when she looked up as Max was announced and smiled at him across the room, everything else ceased to matter. They would live far away from his monster of a grandfather and concentrate on loving each other, surrounded by her bustling family, and it would be enough. Max made his bow to the dowager and the duke, kissed the duchess's hand,

and waved at Bertie before he finally stood in front of his beloved. He raised both her hands to his lips. "I've been counting the minutes."

A delighted peal of laughter was his reward. "Ever since our morning ride? That must be a good two hundred then."

"Two hundred and seventeen." He grinned. "Will you come and introduce me to the rest of your cousins? I only know Bertie. Julian I met at Eton, before my grandfather insisted on educating me at Warthon, but that was a long time ago, and there seem to be a lot more." The recollection of his childhood dimmed his mood and reminded him of the note in his pocket. He lowered his voice. "My mother is to arrive tomorrow, but the earl is refusing to attend, I'm afraid."

Emily took his arm and patted it. "We knew he might. Does it bother you very much?"

"What bothers me is that he is being rude to you."

She thought she knew why the earl was against the match, and it saddened her that her illegitimacy should intrude on their day in this way, but she didn't want Max to feel bad about it, so she made light of it. "We will have a duke, a duchess, a dowager duchess, and two viscounts in attendance. I think we can spare an earl." Her little speech had the desired effect of taking the worry out of his eyes. She twined her arm around his with a conspiratorial wink and led him across the room to meet her female cousins.

"So, who are the two viscounts?"

"Papa's friend Viscount Fairly, and my cousin Julia's husband."

"Oh right, Bedford. I'd forgotten he is part of your family." The poor fellow was all too easy to forget, but he had money and an eye for investments, which was how his path had crossed Max's.

Emily threw him a quizzical glance. "Don't tell me he invests with you."

"He owns a stake in my shipping company."

A giggle escaped Emily. She could never remember the bland viscount either. "Well, don't talk shop within my great-grandmother's hearing, she will have both your heads."

Squeezing her arm, Max smiled. "You have my word on that."

They strolled around the room and Emily introduced him to all her relatives. Once the task was completed and they were about to join her father and Robert, Viscount Fairly, by the far window, her mind returned to the earl. "Are you concerned about your grandfather not attending?"

"We will most likely enjoy our day more without him present, but his acceptance of you is important to me."

Max bowed to Sir Henry and his companion while Emily kissed the viscount's cheek and introduced him.

"Uncle Robert, meet my fiancé, Lord Didcomb. Max, this is Viscount Fairly, one of my father's best friends."

"I'm delighted to make your acquaintance." Max bowed.

"Likewise. I hope you both will be very happy." The viscount smiled at the couple.

Max shook hands with both men, then turned to Henry. "I have a matter I would like to bring to your attention, sir."

Henry exchanged a look with Robert. "That sounds ominous. I hope not bad news from Warthon?"

"I'm afraid the earl will not be attending the wedding."

Henry could see the young lord had more to say but hesitated to do so, either because of Robert or Emily. "Emily, why don't you and Robert get us some tea, I see the duchess is pouring."

Robert grinned and took Emily's arm. "Come, poppet, we are being dismissed."

"Well, I want to have a word with Grossmama anyway." She giggled, a plan forming in her head.

CHAPTER THIRTEEN

AS EMILY AND ROBERT WALKED TOWARD THE other side of the cavernous room where tea was being served, Max handed his grandfather's missive to Henry. "I admit to being uneasy about this."

Henry scanned the message and handed it back. "What do you think he might do? The banns are being very properly read. He could write to the bishop and voice his objection, but that will not achieve anything since you are of age and Emily is accepted by me and her ducal family."

"He could start gossip by his mere absence."

"He could, but Emily is no stranger to gossip, and we are all united in our support for her."

"I know that and I'm grateful." Max swallowed. He would not let his pride get in the way of keeping Emily safe. "What if I can't protect her from him?"

It was excruciating to know that the earl's animosity toward Emily was his fault, but heartened by Didcomb's concern for his daughter, Henry patted the young man's shoulder reassuringly. "It seems their paths are not to cross in the foreseeable future, and I do have resources should they become necessary. So please, if there is ever a time you do not feel equal to the task of protecting her, come to me for help."

"Thank you, I will bear that in mind," Max replied, comforted by Henry's offer. "I want to make her happy."

"I know you do, or I would not have given my consent. But since we are talking about this and there is a possibility your grandfather may meddle to get back at me, please promise me you will let me know the moment anything untoward occurs."

"You have my solemn promise."

WHILE HER FATHER AND MAX conferred in the corner, and Robert got drawn into a conversation with Avon, Emily sat down next to Grossmama and asked quietly, "You know the Earl of Warthon, don't you?"

"I do indeed, *Liebchen*. Is the old curmudgeon making trouble?"

"He is refusing to come to the wedding, and Max worries over it."

Grossmama could well imagine what the ton would say if the earl did not attend his heir's wedding. "I could write to him. He once was friendly with my Charles. At the very least he will then know he is crossing me and the Duke of Avon with his absence."

Emily hugged her great-grandmother. "I knew you would know what to do, Grossmama. Thank you."

The rest of the grand family tea party was used to plan out the wedding breakfast and discuss the decorations for the church. Since it was a June wedding and the duke's estate boasted ample rose gardens, Grossmama offered to supply the yellow and white blooms necessary to make garlands and bouquets for St. George's and Henry's terrace, where the breakfast would be served. Having spent many happy hours in Avon's gardens, Emily was delighted with the idea, but the duchess clearly hated for her flowers to be depleted, so Henry stepped in. He argued it would be far better to employ a florist and let the city merchants have the benefit of the wedding account. After an extended back-and-forth, it was agreed only Emily's bridal bouquet would be coming from the ducal gardens.

Once the flowers had been decided on, Lady Greyson and Isabella started on the dishes to be served, but since Emily had already been consulted on the food and Mrs. Tibbit was already planning to make eclairs, she had little interest. What was far more important to her was to discover where she would spend her first night as Lady Didcomb. Max had not even mentioned the new house on York Terrace yet. It was utterly frustrating. She wanted to walk through it and plan, be part of making it her home. But all she had been able to squeeze out of her father was that it overlooked Regent's Park, and since she didn't know the street number, she couldn't figure out whether it was the one with the rounded bay windows or the one with the Palladian portico, or one of the simple facades. No matter what she tried, Max remained tight-lipped, wanting the house to be a surprise.

Nevertheless, the teasing about the new house amongst the cousins proved entertaining. York Terrace was a very grand address, and they speculated on how many rooms she would have and how many servants it would take to clean it. Bertie even went as far as to joke his mother would turn green with envy when she discovered Emily's house was bigger than the ducal palace.

All in all, it was a lovely betrothal party.

THE NEXT MORNING, EMILY SAT on the Aubusson carpet in the center of her stepmother's sun-filled drawing room, rolling a ball to her baby sister, when William announced Lord Didcomb and Mrs. Warthon. Emily had only just time to rise to her knees when Max walked in with his mother on his arm.

"William, the tea tray, please." Scrambling to her feet, Emily curtsied to her visitors, but had to immediately chase after Dorothea, who had decided to speed-crawl toward the open veranda door.

"No, Thea. You are to remain here with me." She lifted the squealing babe and settled her on her hip. "You are getting to be far too much trouble." Her sister smiled a beatific, one-toothed smile, charming the middle-aged lady with the lovely green eyes on Max's arm.

"Who is this delightful little lady?" Max's mother, Mrs. Warthon, stretched out her hands to take Dorothea out of Emily's arms, and since Thea had no objections, Emily let her.

"This is Dorothea March, my little sister."

Mrs. Warthon cuddled Dorothea to her bosom and beamed at Emily. "You must be Max's Miss March. You are every bit as beautiful as he said you were."

Emily blushed and curtsied again. "Call me Emily, please."

"Very well, Emily. And you must call me Constance." She smiled at Dorothea, who was beginning to squirm to get back to the floor. "You are intent on your freedom, aren't you, sweet Dorothea."

"She is taking after her brother." Emily settled her sister back on her hip, while Max bent to kiss Emily's cheek.

"Where is our resident knight this morning?"

"Papa took him to meet Edgar Sedon in the park."

"Would that be Jane's boy?" Constance Warthon asked with interest. "He is charming."

Max nodded to his mother and explained to Emily, "Edgar's mother, the former Lady Jane, is our cousin. Mama's home in Suffolk is right next to the Earl of Weld's estate, and Jane and Edgar are frequent visitors there."

Emily was about to comment when William entered with the tea tray and set it on a low table close to the hearth while murmuring to Emily, "Polly is on her way." Then he retreated.

Breathing a sigh of relief, Emily settled Dorothea on the sofa and handed her one of the oatcakes she had spotted on the tray, then urged her future mother-in-law to take a seat before she checked the tea had sufficiently steeped. She smiled at Max. "Ah, that's why you and Mrs. Sedon are like brother and sister." Turning to his mother, she continued, "Milk and sugar, Mrs. Warthon?" Emily blushed again. "Constance."

Constance smiled. "Just milk, please, dear."

Emily handed Constance her tea and tucked a serviette in the lap of the relentlessly drooling Dorothea. "When did you arrive in town, Constance? Do help yourself to strawberry tarts."

"Oh, no thank you, we just broke our fast. I arrived late last night, so everything got delayed." Turning to the baby, she continued, "You are teething, aren't you? Where is your nursemaid with the ice chips?"

Grinning, Emily wiped some of the drool off Dorothea's chin. "This little monster cut a tooth last night and used up all the ice. Since I was the only one who got any sleep, I encouraged my stepmother to take a nap, then sent the girl out for more ice."

"Well done, my dear. Your stepmother must be very glad to have such a capable helper." Max's mother sent her son a covert nod. Evidently she approved of his choice of bride.

Max could not have been more pleased. He was painfully aware the Countess of Weld had done her best to prejudice his mother so she might influence him away from Emily. He had appreciated his mother's confidence in him when she had refused to rush to town to intervene in his affairs, but now she was here. And Emily had won her over in less than half an hour, all while taking care of her infant sister. Emily March was cool under pressure. She was going to be a marvelous wife and a formidable countess. Max had known he loved Emily for some time now, but this was the first time he was truly proud of her. Maybe she could even win over his grandfather, if only Warthon would unbend enough to meet her.

As Max contemplated his fiancée's ability to charm people, the Earl of Warthon took delivery of a letter bearing the Avon seal. He had little to do with the current duke, but the previous duke had once been a friend. Curious, he lifted his aching feet onto a footstool set in front of his wing chair for the purpose and settled back to read. But when he unfolded the single sheet, he found it filled with the feminine script unique to the dowager duchess.

My dear Warthon,

I know we have not had much occasion to communicate since the tragic passing of our beloved friend, so soon followed by my Charles's death, but I must speak to you on a matter close to my heart. My great-granddaughter, Emily, is to marry your grandson and heir. The two are marvelously in love and entirely suited to each other, but I have been made aware of the fact you refused the invitation to their wedding. I must urge you to attend, if not for their sake, then for mine and the friendship you once shared with my husband.

Emily is so much like Charles, and so dear to me, I cannot bear to see her happiness on her wedding day marred by your absence. It would mean so much to the children; please join us.

In friendship,

Ruth Redwick

The earl made a strangled noise somewhat akin to a sob as he passed his index finger over the words "beloved friend." No one, except perhaps the Dowager Duchess of Avon, knew how much he had suffered at Eugenia's death, but even she didn't know the whole of it. He let the letter sink to his lap and sat lost in thought for a long time. The boy was defying him, and he didn't like it one bit.

Warthon was still ruminating over the letter in his lap when the Earl of Weld was announced. Part of him wanted to know what kind of a spell the March chit had put Max under, but that still wasn't a good enough reason to sanction the union by attending the wedding.

"What news, Weld?"

"Your daughter-in-law has arrived in town, but she won't be any help. She only cares to ensure Max's happiness, and it won't take her two minutes to see the March girl does just that."

"To hell with his happiness, she is a bastard."

"Yes, but a bastard with bloodlines as old as the kingdom flowing through her veins. Her mother is of good stock too."

"What are you saying? That I should give them my blessing?" Warthon grumbled.

"There is something to be said for saving face. Had to do it myself, you know. The banns are read, and the wedding planned. The only person who can stop it now is the girl herself."

Warthon threw his old friend and confidant a sharp look. Weld was right, only the girl could stop it now. He couldn't stop the wedding, but perhaps he could get the girl to annul the marriage after the fact. He looked down at the letter still in his hand and felt a prickle of excitement as a plan started to form in his head. Grunting, he folded the missive and slipped it in his pocket. "Perhaps you are right. Best I attend this wedding after all."

CHAPTER FOURTEEN

TWO DAYS LATER, MAX AND EMILY RETURNED from their morning ride to find the dowager in the drawing room taking tea with Isabella. Grossmama was so gratified to be able to tell Emily and her betrothed that the Earl of Warthon would be attending the wedding, she barely waited for them to come through the door. Waving the earl's letter, she trilled, "He promises to be present at St. George's, at least."

"The earl?" Emily, overjoyed, rushed to embrace her. "Oh Grossmama, I knew he would come if you asked." Turning to Max, she explained, "I asked Grossmama to write to Warthon."

Not having been notified by the earl, Max was skeptical but unwilling to contradict the grand old lady. He knew how much his grandfather's approval meant to Emily and the social standing of their union. If the Earl of Warthon was seen to approve of the match, then society would approve. He was still a powerful man. But why change his mind? Why would he come now?

Meanwhile Grossmama returned Emily's embrace. "Your great-grandfather and the earl were once friends. I simply reminded him of that." She turned to Max and added, "I hope you will forgive my interference."

Max bent over her hand. "We are in your debt, Your Grace." He had never heard of the friendship between the two men, but that didn't mean it had not been a powerful bond; it just proved how little Max knew about his grandfather. Or rather, how little his grandfather had allowed Max to know about him.

Isabella motioned for the couple to sit. "We will have to work on him to accept the invitation to the wedding breakfast, but at least he will be at the public event."

Pouring herself a cup of tea, Emily asked, "Does Papa know?"

"Yes, *Liebchen*. He took the children for a turn in the garden, but he is pleased for you and Max." She patted her great-granddaughter's knee.

Max glanced over the letter the dowager had handed him. It seemed his grandfather truly planned to attend the church wedding; why else would he write to the old lady? She was not a woman to be trifled with. He bowed again, this time to the assembled ladies. "Would you excuse me, please? I would like a word with Sir Henry."

"Of course." The dowager waved him away.

He nodded to Isabella and Emily and strode out of the room. By now Henry's house was familiar to Max, so he had no trouble finding the French doors leading from the music room to the terrace and down to the garden. He cut across the lawn to where Henry was engaged in a sword fight with Danny, holding his infant daughter high against his left shoulder to keep her out of the fray.

"Didcomb, did you hear your grandfather is to attend the wedding?"

"I did indeed." Taking the wooden sword out of Henry's hand to give his future father-in-law a break, Max saluted Danny. "En garde."

Young Master March lost no time throwing himself into a spirited attack, while Henry breathed a sigh of relief and settled Dorothea more comfortably in his arms.

"Her Grace just told us. What are your thoughts on his attendance?"

Twirling his watch on its chain for his daughter's entertainment, Henry met Max's eyes for a moment. "You are uneasy about his change of mind?"

Max sighed but had to refocus on his pint-sized opponent and block a strike to his nether region. "I'm happy for Emily and the social standing his presence will give our union, but I wonder what changed his mind."

He neatly sidestepped another of Danny's attacks. "You saw his previous missive to me; I fear he has some ulterior motive."

Henry made his daughter giggle by lifting her high above his head. "Do you think he may try to interfere in the wedding itself?"

"No, he wouldn't have announced himself if he did. Besides, he hates anything that draws attention to him and the Knights. He prefers to operate in secret, but…" Max thought of all the times his grandfather had forced him to his will and couldn't help the sense of foreboding. "We will just have to keep an eye on him and make sure he doesn't ruin the wedding breakfast."

Henry showed Dorothea the white roses climbing over a freestanding arch. "With any luck he won't want to come to my house anyhow." Catching the babe's hand before she pricked her fingers on the thorns, he added, "I admit to not relishing the thought of hosting him here. I well remember the hatred in his eyes and am still no closer to finding out its origin." Henry paused, then turned to fully face the man who was to be Emily's husband. "You better keep Emily safe from him."

Max disarmed Danny with a twist of his wrist and caught the sword in mid-air, prompting a dismayed but admiring gasp from the boy. He handed the sword back to Danny but did not get back into fencing posture. "She will be safe at the new house. The earl doesn't know about it and I intend to keep it that way."

"Good." There was such relief in that one word, Max didn't know if he should smile or be insulted, but then decided the mere thought was petty. He didn't begrudge Emily her protective father. He fervently wished he still had his own by his side.

Both men watched Danny trying to execute the twist of the wrist Max had used to disarm him. Nodding toward his son, Henry chuckled. "I hope you know he will not rest until you show him how it's done."

A LETTER FROM HIS GRANDFATHER awaited Max on his return to Burton Street. It contained only one sentence and answered none of Max's questions as to the earl's about-face.

Didcomb,
I will attend the church ceremony to avoid gossip.
Warthon

Avoiding gossip was a legitimate reason to go along with the marriage for most members of society, but it didn't seem enough for the man Max knew his grandfather to be. Perhaps the earl did relent due to his friendship with the previous Duke of Avon like the dowager had said. It was possible. In the end, Max decided to stop looking this gift horse in the mouth and concentrate on getting his new house ready for his bride. He would keep his Burton Street address and keep receiving his mail there, just to be on the safe side.

There were only ten days left before the nuptials, so Max threw himself into the building work on the house on York Terrace. It was to be a surprise for Emily, but due to his grandfather's anticipated attendance at the wedding, Max decided to show her his wedding gift early. Surprises on his wedding day no longer held the same charm.

Accordingly, once Max heard all building work on the house was completed and only decorating and furnishing remained, he called on Emily on the Thursday before their big day.

As soon as Emily saw him drive up unannounced, anticipation built in her. By the time she heard him tell William to send Suzie to get Emily's shawl, she was giddy with excitement. Surely the only reason for the impromptu outing was to show her the house she was meant to know nothing about. It took all her self-control to greet him calmly when he entered the drawing room.

"Max! There are several hours still before this evening's entertainment."

He took both her hands and kissed one after the other. "Suzie has gone to fetch your shawl; I have something to show you."

"Oh Max, and it's too big to bring with you?" She was bouncing on her toes with excitement now. "Our house?"

Max mock-scowled at her. "You are not meant to know about the new house."

Laughing, Emily pulled him out of the room. "Come on, I can't wait to see it. Papa told me precious little."

"And there I was thinking your father could be trusted with a secret," Max jokingly groused while Emily giggled and dragged him through the corridor.

"I am my father's daughter and know how to unearth one."

As they reached the foyer, Suzie appeared with the requested shawl as well as Emily's hat, gloves, and reticule. Evidently Suzie was as excited about the new house as her mistress; after all, she was to move there with Emily. A few minutes later, Max handed Emily into his landau while Suzie climbed onto the seat next to the driver, and they departed toward Regent's Park.

The new house was indeed on York Terrace, but Max ordered the driver to go through the gate into the park, then turn left along the carriageway. The uniform brick facades on York Terrace were deceiving. Out to the park the houses were white stucco and as individual as their owners. There was the one with the rounded bay window, several with simple rows of large sash windows, and one with a greenhouse that took up a third of the garden. There were flowering trees, rose gardens, and boxwood hedges. They stopped by the garden gate of the third house, and Emily immediately realized why. The house had its own brand new stable, accessible from the back door of the house through a charming garden, and with direct access to the park. Emily would be able to go for a gallop before breakfast as she was wont to do when living in the country.

"Oh, this is marvelous! How many stalls are there?"

"Just four for our riding horses. The mews and carriage house are at the end of the terrace, but I thought since we will be living here year-round, having our mounts close would be to your liking."

Emily's eyes shone. "Oh, it is. Especially if Addy is to foal again." Emily rushed through the wooden double doors tall enough for a rider to go through and proceeded to inspect her horse's new home. Max took great pleasure in seeing her so excited.

She stood in the open space where a rider would mount and the horses could be tied to be groomed. There were windows on both sides for plenty of light, and to the right, steps led up to a mezzanine where big bales of hay had already been stored, and a door led to the groom's quarters. Below the mezzanine were the four generously sized wooden stalls for the horses, two on each side. A flagstone-paved walkway led to the tack room on the other side of the stalls, and beyond that was the door to the garden. The half doors into the stalls revealed small windows high enough in the wall so the horses couldn't break them and hurt themselves on the glass but letting in enough light to support their natural rhythms. The whole building smelled pleasantly of hay and the straw covering the floor of the stalls.

Over one of the stall's half doors hung a nameplate with Addy's name carved into it. Emily opened the door and stepped into the cozy space. Letting her fingers run along the wooden walls, she mused, "This already feels like home." Then, on a whim, she added, "If ever we are separated, this is where you will find me."

It was an odd thought, but Max found it comforting. Leaning over the half door, he beamed. "I hoped having your horse close would bring you joy. If it can also provide solace, so much the better." He stepped back to hold the door open for her. "Do you like it?"

"It's wonderful. Thank you, Max." Emily smiled dreamily, stood on tiptoes to kiss his cheek, and let him capture her lips. But before he could deepen the kiss, she spun away, skipping through the door into the garden, and called over her shoulder, "Come along and show me the house."

Utterly captivated, he rushed after her. "To the right, darling. The French doors into the drawing room should be open."

Five steps led up to a little landing before the French doors, and once they got close, a dip in the lawn close to the house revealed a row of half windows on the ground floor. Emily pointed. "I suppose that's where the service rooms are."

"The kitchen and storerooms, as well as the housekeeper's and butler's quarters. The other staff bedrooms are on the top floor."

Emily nodded. "That makes sense. It is a rather big house, have you hired staff yet?"

"My housekeeper and butler from Burton Street are already settling in and are hiring more maids and footmen. I take it you want to keep Suzie on, and your father suggested Thomas as your personal footman, so you have servants you trust."

"I would like that very much. Thomas is good with horses too."

Max chuckled. It was just like Emily to think it more important for a footman to be good with horses than good at his job.

That wasn't the whole of it, though; for Emily, being good with horses was synonymous with being trustworthy. She tilted her head up to take in the entirety of this marvelously big house virtually in Regent's Park. It would be good to have someone with her she could trust implicitly. Of course, she could rely on Suzie, but this was a man's world and Thomas knew how to navigate it. Emily had expected a reaction from Suzie at the news of Thomas joining them, but the maid was standing a few steps behind her, staring open-mouthed at the size of the house.

The house was not only large and in a lovely location, it was an architectural marvel. There were four stories above ground and the half-subterranean service level. The level they were about to enter through the double French door had ten-foot-tall floor-length windows, with a half-circle window on top. The windows on the next level were shorter rectangular sash windows, but they were still taller than a man. The next level up had normal six-paneled sash windows, and the top level, smaller ones still. The play with proportion made the facade seem to go on forever, but unlike the rather austere street side of York Terrace, this side of the house had a rather whimsical two-story-high turret-like bay window toward the right corner of the house, obscuring the small gap between this and the next terrace house.

Following the direction of Emily's eyeline, Max explained, "That's the book room, and I thought you might want to have your private sitting room on the level above."

"I would indeed. It's charming." Raising her skirts so she could climb the steps, Emily headed for the door Max held open for her, then abruptly stopped on the threshold. "Oh, my goodness, look at that ceiling!"

"Magnificent, isn't it?"

The ceiling was partially vaulted and decorated with two large, recessed stucco roses; from the center of each a chandelier was suspended. The whole room was white with ornate stucco rectangles decorating the walls. Two black marble fireplaces faced each other in the center of the walls on either side of the bank of windows into the garden, and the parquet floor was a highly polished herringbone pattern. No paintings adorned the walls yet, but the windows were draped in silvery-blue silk, the same color the cherrywood furniture grouped around the right-hand fireplace was upholstered in. On the other side of the room, close to the windows, a grand piano had been placed. Emily headed straight to it. The room reminded her of her father's formal drawing room, only much grander, and the piano was a lovely surprise.

"Your great-grandmother helped me choose an instrument worthy of your talent." Max smiled. Emily was already running her fingers over the keys. "I hope you like it."

She played a few chords and let the notes ring out, marveling at the acoustics of the room. "It's magnificent. Thank you."

"The rest of the room still needs work, but I was hoping you might enjoy furnishing it yourself."

Emily stepped into his arms and stretched up to kiss his cheek once more. "I will ask Isabella to help me. She has impeccable taste."

"She does indeed." He turned her toward the door and wound his arm around her. "We will leave upstairs for our wedding day." Lowering his voice, he added, "I took it upon myself to furnish one bedroom but didn't know if you wanted your own."

She leaned closer, and blushing, whispered, "I was hoping we would sleep in the same bed."

Max nuzzled her temple, breathing her in. "It's settled, then. I'm counting the minutes until I can finally make you mine."

Her sapphire-blue eyes darkened with passion. "Two more days."

"Two more days."

They made their way into the corridor, followed by Suzie, who kept a discreet distance. The corridor opened into a light-filled foyer, the front door straight ahead and two large windows looking out to York Terrace on either side of it. To the right of the entrance was a small square room where visitors not known to the household could be received, then a wide staircase leading to the second-floor mezzanine. From there the stairs continued to the third floor on the other side of the foyer walls. To the left of the entrance, a more modest staircase led to the subterranean level. An enormous chandelier hung from the domed ceiling three floors up and reflected in the white marble floor.

Emily turned in a slow circle in the center of the magnificent space. "Max, this isn't a house, it's a palace."

"A mansion, my darling. It's no grander than the townhome entailed to the Earls of Warthon. You will wear the countess's coronet one day, after all."

As if summoned by magic, the butler appeared by the door and opened it for Max to lead Emily through so he could hand her into the waiting carriage.

CHAPTER FIFTEEN

EMILY'S WEDDING DAY DAWNED BALMY AND
crystal clear, an errant beam of sunlight prying her from sleep. Ordinarily
she was no slug-a-bed, but her whole life was about to change, and the
excitement of it all had kept her awake into the small hours of the morning. Covering her eyes, Emily moaned, "Close the curtains."

"I let you sleep as long as I could, darling, but it's eight o'clock and we
are expected at St. George's at ten."

"Isabella?" Why was her stepmother waking her? Emily sat up with a
jolt. "Good God, did I sleep through my own wedding?"

Isabella, already fully dressed for the occasion in a stunningly simple,
seafoam-green silk gown, laughed. "We were beginning to fear that may
come to pass." Sitting down next to Emily, Isabella handed her a slice of
toast and a cup of tea. "You have two hours, but we do have to get on. Suzie has your bath ready, and Mrs. Rosen awaits outside with your dress."

Emily took a sip of her tea and sighed with relief. "That sounds man-
ageable. Did she make the alteration around the bust?"

"She did and it looks very pretty."

Smiling around a big bite of toast, Emily put her cup on her bedside cabinet and slipped out of bed. "Thank you for designing the dress
for me. It makes me feel like a princess." Looking around the room, she
asked, "Did the flowers arrive?" Then she shoved the last of her toast in
her mouth and disappeared around the privacy screen, where her bath
waited for her.

"Suzie is making your crown right now. And you are most welcome,
darling." Isabella was about to leave to see to the next thing on her list of

preparations but halted. "By the way, your mother sent word she and your brother will meet us at the church."

"Oh, I'm glad she will be there." There was a pause while the sound of water sloshing indicated Emily was getting into the tub. "Isabella, I know she is my mother, but you are the one I truly want to be there. I'm so glad you are my stepmother."

Her hand already on the door handle, Isabella stopped. Emotion resonated in her voice. "Oh darling, I'm so happy you feel this way. It's been a pleasure having you with us."

More splashing came from behind the screen. "This is a very happy house with you in it. I hope mine and Max's house will be as blessed."

Isabella smiled. It was good to know Emily had matured from her hero worship for the golden god. "You two love each other, so I'm sure it will be." The door opened from the other side. "Ah, here is Suzie with the flower crown. I'll send in Mrs. Rosen too."

Suzie bustled into the room as Isabella left. "I'll be right there to help you with your bath."

"Actually, I'm done, Suzie. Could you hand me a towel?"

Suzie took the silver circlet with baby's breath and orange blossoms wound around it to form a flower crown and hung it over a corner of the vanity mirror. Then she picked up a fluffy towel from a stool and stepped behind the screen. "Here, miss. Oh good, you kept your hair dry."

Emily grinned at her maid. "That was good thinking to wash it yesterday." She stood and stepped out of the bath, letting Suzie wrap the towel around her and rub her shoulders and back dry. Emily had only just smoothed her new white silk chemise down her front and was helping Suzie get her white satin corset over her hips when the seamstress entered with the dress.

AN HOUR LATER EMILY DESCENDED the stairs, clad in eggshell

satin and snowy white organza. Her veil was hemmed with the most delicate lace and folded back over her flower crown so she could see her way down the stairs. Suzie carried her train behind her. Emily's hair was held back from her face with several artful braids but allowed to flow down her back in luxurious waves covered by her veil. The blue of her eyes and the rosy color of her lips and cheeks was enhanced by the white of her bridal ensemble, making her look like a medieval fairy princess.

A collective appreciative gasp rose from the assembled household in the foyer, but all fell quiet as Henry stepped forward and lifted her hands to his lips before he offered her his arm. "You look absolutely beautiful, poppet."

Emily smiled and let her eyes wander over her father, stepmother, siblings, and the assembled staff. "You all look splendid. Papa, I like the gray and silver of your suit, and Isabella looks stunning in the seafoam green."

Offering his free arm to his wife and indicating for Danny and the nurse with the baby to precede them to the open carriage waiting outside, Henry nodded. "She does indeed. Let's get you to George Street. Charlie will tell us when everyone is settled, and Max is in place."

"Thank you, Papa." Emily beamed up at him, the slight tremble of her lip the only indication she was nervous. "I can't wait to be Lady Didcomb."

"Not long now, poppet," Henry managed to say around the lump in his throat.

MAX WAITED AT THE ALTAR of the pretty white-and-gold church, decorated throughout with white and yellow roses. The vicar stood ready for the ceremony, the vaulted ceiling arching above, and his grandfather's sharp blue eyes bored into him. The old man occupied one end of a pew on the groom's side of the church, Max's mother being the only other occupant. The Earl of Weld and his family, including Lady Jane and Edgar, were on the first bench, and behind them sat the vast array of cousins, aunts, and uncles he only ever saw at weddings and funerals.

On the bride's side, the Duke of Avon, the duchess, and the dowager were in the side pew and had left room for Sir Henry and his family. On the church benches on the bride's side was Emily's large extended family, including her birth mother and her half-brother. Other guests of rank filled the rest of the pews, and the mezzanine on both sides of the church was filled with onlookers and well-wishers. This was clearly the wedding of the season, and no one wanted to miss the moment the heir to an earldom took to wife the most beautiful illegitimate girl the ton had ever welcomed to its ranks. It was a real-life fairy tale.

But to Max the presence of all these people only added to his wedding-day nerves. He worried Emily had changed her mind. He worried his grandfather would be rude to his mother. And then he worried the earl had come to interfere with rather than witness their nuptials. Only the steadying presence of Ben, his best man, by his side stopped him from running to the door to make sure Emily had not suffered some calamity. The church doors were wide open to the portico and the street beyond, so he was the first to see the open barouche drive up and Sir Henry alight to help his family out. Lady March made her way to the front pew with little Dorothea in her arms, and once she was seated, signaled the musicians to begin. Schubert's *Ave Maria* filled St. George's as Henry led his daughter down the aisle toward Max. Danny preceded them with all the dignity of a knight, and a flower girl spread rose petals before the bride. But Max didn't see any of that, heard none of the music. He saw only Emily, all in white, her face veiled by the most delicate lace, a diamond winking from the flower crown on her head but shining nowhere near as brightly as her impossibly blue eyes. She smiled behind the veil, and he answered with his own. And just like that all his nerves were gone, and so was the crowd in the church. Nothing mattered except the gorgeous woman coming toward him to join herself to him for life.

The bridal procession reached the black-and-white-checked marble floor before the altar, where Danny and the flower girl were redirected to join Isabella. Henry led Emily the rest of the way to the altar, where he lifted her veil before placing her hand into the hand of her husband-to-be.

Max's breath caught at the sight of her, her lush pink lips slightly parted, her eyes sparkling with tears and happiness all at once as his fingers closed around hers. She was lovely beyond imagining. His fairy princess.

The Earl of Warthon watched his grandson look at Sir Henry's undeniably beautiful daughter and knew he wouldn't be able to sway him away from her. At least pretending to be charmed by the girl wouldn't be too hard.

Emily held on tight; Max's hand was her lifeline. His green eyes, sparkling like peridot in the sun streaming through the high windows, were her focus. She did notice how marvelously his shiny blond curls and the golden-brown velvet of his jacket framed his lightly bronze skin. His beige waistcoat featured some fancy embroidery, but Emily couldn't bear to tear her eyes from her beloved's face.

She repeated whatever the vicar said whenever Max squeezed her hand, and apparently she said all the right lines since no one called off the proceedings and hauled her out of the church as an imposter. Max kept smiling at her as he said his vows and slipped his ring on her finger. All the while Emily could barely breathe, until he kissed her. His lips on hers made it real. The collective sigh from the onlookers made it real. She was his. Lady Didcomb, Max's wife, and he was her husband. Her dearest wish had come true. She had wished this day would come from the first time she had looked into his eyes, back at that mean little inn, and it had come to pass. Their lives were irrevocably entwined, and she could not have been happier.

Joy coursed through her as they signed their names in the register, cementing their union in legality. Emily took Max's arm and together they walked back down the aisle, the approving faces of their friends and families all around them. Even the Earl of Warthon had come and smiled kindly at her. She so hoped he could be persuaded to attend the wedding breakfast, but there was no way for her to do anything about it. She was to keep walking to the steps at the front of the church, where they would receive the well-wishes of those not invited to the festivities. Hopefully, the earl would at least speak to them. Max said he didn't care what his grandfather said or thought of her, but surely it did matter.

They made it to the portico at the front of the church, where a sizable line had already formed. They stood close, and one by one people stepped forward to congratulate them, while her parents' servants hurried home to get everything ready for the arrival of their guests. Emily stood as if in a dream, smiling at acquaintances, leaning on her husband's arm. Her husband! She couldn't wait to call him that.

In the end he beat her to using their respective official new titles. Once everyone had bowed and curtsied past, Max turned to her and asked, "Shall we join the festivities at home, wife?"

But before Emily could answer, the Earl of Warthon stepped out of the church, leaning heavily on his carved ivory cane.

He addressed Max. "My felicitations, my boy."

Emily could feel Max stiffen, but he smiled pleasantly enough. "Grandfather, thank you for attending. May I introduce my wife."

The earl sketched an almost bow. "It's a pleasure to make your acquaintance, Lady Didcomb."

Emily sank into a deep curtsy, as his rank dictated, then extended her hand and smiled. "Please call me Emily, my lord." She held her breath, hoping he would accept.

After an almost imperceptible hesitation, he clasped her hand and bestowed a rare smile on her. "As you wish, my dear." And turning to Max, he continued, "Your wife is a true beauty."

Max, who had been watching his grandfather closely, softened. "She is. Will you be joining us for the wedding breakfast, sir?"

The old man shook his head in regret. "I'm afraid the journey to London was arduous and the ceremony long. I need to elevate my leg. But would you and your charming wife call on me for tea tomorrow afternoon at Warthon House? I would like to get to know your bride a little better."

Max couldn't help feeling his grandfather may have ulterior motives, but on the doorstep of a church only ten minutes after his wedding was not the time to be suspicious of an olive branch. "We will be happy to come for tea, Grandfather."

Emily curtsied again and blushed prettily, very pleased at the prospect of a reconciliation. "Yes, we will be delighted."

The old man nodded sharply and hobbled down the steps to his carriage.

Emily watched him and asked Max quietly, "How long has he suffered from the gout?"

"The past five years. It has drained much of his vitality from him, but he is still capable of treachery, so beware."

She hugged his arm and smiled up at him, unable to see anything negative on a day such as this. "He came, Max. I think he wants to reconcile with you. Let's go celebrate, and tomorrow we will have tea with him."

It was impossible for Max to be entirely easy about his grandfather's presence in town, but this was their wedding day, and Emily was right: it was time to celebrate.

FOR THE WEDDING BREAKFAST, SIR Henry's back garden was festooned with yellow and white flower garlands on every windowsill and winding around the terrace balustrade. Even the backs of chairs were decorated. The company was seated around three long tables arranged in a horseshoe, covered in white linen and decorated with roses. Delectable jellies, roasts, casseroles, baked goods, and fruit pies were served, and the traditional rolls and eggs were placed in baskets on each table. Once everyone had eaten their fill, four footmen brought out the enormous white icing-covered cake in the shape of a heart and placed it in front of the bride and groom. It was intricately decorated with icing flowers and garlands, a veritable masterpiece of baking.

To the cheers of their friends and family, Emily and Max together clasped the large cutting knife, and with much giggling and theatrics, cut the first piece. Breaking off smaller pieces of the fruitcake within, they fed each other to the delight of the company.

Everyone toasted their health and celebrated until it was time for the couple to say their goodbyes. The time had come for Max to take Emily to their new house and consummate their love.

CHAPTER SIXTEEN

DURING THE RIDE TO YORK TERRACE IN THE
open carriage, they couldn't do more than hold hands and stare deep
into each other's eyes. But as they alighted outside their new house, Max
swung Emily into his arms and carried her straight past the assembled
servants across the threshold and up the imposing staircase.

"Max, what will they think of me?" Emily laughed and wound her
arms around his neck. She was full of playful mischief, but her eyes
brimmed with love.

"That your husband is in love with you and impatient to have you
all to himself." He halted briefly on the landing, where the stairs made a
right angle along the wall, and kissed her with tender passion. Then he
took the rest of the steps two at a time, carrying her all the way.

Their room was halfway down a broad corridor on the second floor.
The ceilings were not quite as high on this level, but they were still decorated with stucco roses at regular intervals where lanterns extended from
the ceiling. The walls were kept in simple white, and the wooden floor
was in another elegant herringbone pattern. There were wall sconces to
the left and right of each door, and at the other end of the corridor a large
portrait of a dappled gray horse in a landscape dominated the wall and
created a focal point.

"Oh, my goodness, you had Addy painted," Emily exclaimed. "Let
me down so I can see."

Chuckling, Max used his elbow to depress the door handle to their
bedroom, carried her through, kicked the door shut behind them, and
then finally let her down, but not out of his arms. "Later, my darling. We

have more important things to attend to at present."

Emily giggled and stretched up to kiss him, but they weren't alone. Suzie stood in the doorway to Emily's dressing room, blushing and curtsying deeply.

Max kept his eyes locked to Emily's. "Suzie, you may go. I will do for your mistress today."

Suzie bobbed another curtsy. "Very good, sir." She fled through the dressing room.

Still looking into Emily's eyes, entwined in her arms, Max brought his mouth down on Emily's in a searing hot kiss that took her breath away and buckled her knees. Letting his hand caress down her back to her bottom, he pressed her to himself, letting her know the state of his desire, and whispered, "Are you ready to give yourself to me, my love?"

All thought of Addy's portrait fled Emily's brain at the feel of the magnificent man pressed to her. Tingling all over and breathless with passion, she nodded. "Yes, husband, take me to bed. I've waited long enough." As she spoke, she pulled the circlet off her head and let the veil flutter to the plush carpet under her feet, then kicked off her heeled satin slippers.

Max stayed her hands and put them back around his neck, where her fingers promptly twined into his hair. "Let me do that, love."

"Oh, we shall undress each other. Is that it?"

Smiling, he captured her lips again. "I would like that very much."

His words tickled her lips, creating magical tingles all over her. She spoke into his lips, hoping it would have the same effect on him. "Do that again, please."

"With pleasure, my darling." But he didn't leave it at letting his breath caress her lips; he kissed his way across her cheek to her ear and let his breath caress there. "Do you like this?"

Her whole body curved into his. "Oh yes, that's marvelous."

Max ran his tongue lightly around the shell of her ear, then briefly dipped it inside. "And this?"

"Oh Lord, I'm going to die of pleasure." She squirmed against him, pressing her pelvis into his erection, guided by instinct.

He groaned. "I'm counting on it, but only a little bit."

"Whatever are you talking about?" she asked, only vaguely interested in an answer.

He tried to create a little space between them to slow things down. This was his wife, a virgin; he couldn't just lift her skirts and take her. "The French call the pleasure you feel during the marital act *la petite mort*, and I very much hope you will experience that."

"*The little death.*" Her smile was dreamy but also adorably cheeky. "If it feels anything like you kissing my ear, then let's get to it." She undid the buttons of his coat as she spoke and pushed the garment off his shoulders, then started on his waistcoat.

He shook both garments to the ground behind him. "Turn around so I can undo your dress."

She turned to give him access. Brushing her hair over her shoulder as he undid her buttons, he nibbled on her earlobe and whispered, "I can't wait to see you naked at last, to touch every part of you, kiss every part of you, and finally bury myself in your soft flesh."

Emily shivered at his words, and he let his tongue trace the shell of her ear again, finally sliding his tongue into it. She melted helplessly against him, sighing with pleasure. Employing his tongue and lips equally, he kissed his way along her nape and neck as he peeled off her dress and undid her petticoats. He let his hands wander over the swell of her breasts, then took her hands and placed them on the bedpost. "Hold on while I undo your laces, love."

Emily did as she was told; partly because she needed to hold on to something, her legs were so wobbly; and partly because she enjoyed him telling her what to do—in this instance, anyway. All her nerves from earlier in the day had melted away, now that it was just her and Max.

Finding where the laces had been tucked in, Max untied them and pulled them loose, admiring the elegant curve of her back and the delectable roundness of her bottom under her silky chemise. Emily March, now Lady Didcomb, was even more beautiful than he had imagined. He pushed the corset over her hips and let it slide to the floor. She stepped out of it and turned toward him so he could lift the chemise over her head. His breath caught. Emily stood before him naked except for her stockings and garters. The afternoon sun made her hair shine like spun gold, and her eyes were like liquid sapphires brimming with desire. Her breasts were high and pert, and the dusky rose of her nipples was the exact same shade as her lips. Max's eyes drifted down her body to the blond curls covering her sex and he was suddenly desperate to find out if her nether lips also matched.

But before he could lift her onto the large bed, Emily started to pull his shirt out of his waistband. "I want to see you too."

He kicked off his shoes while she pulled his shirt over his head, and together they undid the buttons on his placket and pushed his pants and smallclothes down. Stepping out of his garments, he undid his garters and pulled his stockings off in one swift movement, then lifted Emily onto their bed. Taking her left foot into his hand, he hooked it over his shoulder. This way he had his hands free to caress the leg up to her garter and untie it slowly before he rolled down her stocking. He repeated the procedure with the other leg and then let his hand slide down the inside of her thighs to her center, where he gently parted her pubic hair and confirmed the dusky pink of her nether lips indeed matched her nipples and her mouth, now slightly parted in rapt anticipation.

"Good God, you are beautiful." She was everything he had ever wanted in a woman, and he loved her. Disciplining himself not to make love to her before the wedding had been one of the most difficult things he had ever done. But showing her that respect had been worth every agonizing moment. To see her revealed for the first time and do so through the lens of his love was priceless.

Emily saw the expression in Max's eyes and melted a little more. Being with him like this, free and uninhibited, being able to be his in every way imaginable, had been worth the wait. He kissed his way down her left leg, and she let her legs fall open. Realizing he would need more room to join her, she shifted farther onto the bed as he knelt between her legs. He had called her beautiful, but she, in turn, was so in awe of his physique, she couldn't even say the words. She had known he was tall and broadshouldered, but the play of his muscles was fascinating, the smoothness of his skin enticing, and his sheer maleness startlingly erotic. However, the most arousing thing about him was the way he looked at her with both love and desire so clearly written in his face. Emily was utterly beguiled. She wanted to touch him and be touched, do all the naughty things with him she had heard her cousins whisper about.

Max kissed his way across her stomach and then down to her right thigh, and Emily was beginning to wonder if it would be too forward to lift her hips so he would kiss her there, between her thighs, where she ached to be touched and kissed. Thankfully he seemed to read her mind and licked the seam between her thighs. Emily bucked and cried out at the sheer pleasure of his tongue sliding over the little sensitive nub in front of her sex. He promptly wound his arms around her hips to keep her still while he kissed and licked and suckled there until she lost her mind in the throbbing desire and let out a long keening scream as her whole being dissolved into liquid pleasure.

Max felt her come, stroked his tongue over her clitoris one last time, and slid up her body, suckling her nipples along the way before he captured her lips. "Are you ready, my love?"

"Yes," she breathed, still languid from her orgasm, and instinctively pulled up her knees so he could line himself up.

Max pushed into her with as much care as his highly aroused state allowed, but with a sharp intake of breath, Emily's eyes flew open at the intrusion. A moment later she winced when he broke through her barrier. He immediately stilled and watched her until she caught her breath, soothed by his hands caressing her hair and shoulders. "I'm sorry, love. Tell me when you are ready."

Their gazes locked. Finally she nodded, and he pulled back slowly, then pushed in further, and when there was no hint of pain in her lovely sweat-drenched face, he kissed her deeply once more. Holding her, caressing her, kissing her, he loved her with everything he had to give.

The first intrusion into her body had been a shock, but now the physical connection built an emotional connection between them, stronger than anything Emily had ever imagined possible between two human beings. She felt him everywhere; him inside her, her skin against his, his tongue exploring the inside of her mouth, her fingers exploring every part of him. She heard his heartbeat speed up and the blood rush through his veins and knew she had done that to him. They moved at a counterpoint, but as one. Their mouths and sexes fused together, and everything in between connected and entwined, sliding against each other, creating friction where friction was needed. Finding the rhythm to move herself against Max was a little like riding a horse, only so much more intimate, so much more pleasurable, so very loving. And then that wave of tingling intensity built again, not at the apex of her legs this time, but deeper inside. She needed more of Max, so she instinctively grabbed hold of his backside and pushed herself harder onto him while she threw her head back to get more air.

Max, panting in his effort to hold back, realized his error and chuckled. "You want more?"

"Oh God, yes. Hurry." She had no idea how to achieve what she needed but hoped he would.

Max rose above her slightly and took her hands one by one so as not to crush her, placed them against the headboard, and wrapped her legs around his waist. "Brace yourself against the bed, my love, and tell me if it's too much."

She nodded and straightened her arms, her hands flat against the headboard. Immediately realizing how this change in position created a deeper stroke for him, she smiled. "I like it."

"Good. Hold on." He plunged into her to the hilt, drew back, and immediately repeated the move.

Emily cried out but pushed herself into him even harder. Encouraged, Max took her on a wild ride, bracing himself over her, slipping one hand between their slick bodies and rubbing her clitoris with his thumb. She keened and writhed under him like an erotic goddess and eventually screamed out her orgasm just as he could no longer hold back and plunged forward one last time, then held himself inside her as he climaxed like he never had before.

His little virginal wife had undone him. He was hers, body and soul.

CHAPTER SEVENTEEN

MAX COLLAPSED ON TOP OF HER, AND SHE HELD him through the aftershocks. It was a singular experience to be so devastated and so fulfilled all at the same time. They calmed each other with loving, slow caresses while they caught their breath. Once the blood had stopped rushing in his ears, Max asked, "Am I crushing you?"

"No, I like having you close like this. But I wish the window was open."

He lifted his head and kissed her cheek. "Oh, indeed. I'll be right back." Climbing out of bed, he threw the closest window wide open, then filled a tumbler with water from a pitcher on a nearby table, swallowed half, filled it again, and brought it to Emily. She took it gratefully and drank while Max climbed back into bed. As soon as she had finished her drink, he gathered her in his arms. "Are you well, my love?"

Emily grinned. "Never better, but I'm hungry."

He laughed. "Making love can have that effect." Kissing her, he continued, "I'll have them bring us a tray while Suzie gets a bath ready for you."

"That sounds wonderful, but I want to have a look at Addy's portrait first." She handed him the empty glass and climbed over him and out of bed. "How on earth did you manage having her painted without me knowing about it?"

"Your stepmother. She recommended the young painter specializing in horse and hound portraits and organized for him to paint Addy in the mews at times you were unlikely to need her or visit there."

"Isabella is a marvel. And sneaky when needed." Not at all bothered by her nakedness, she threw a cheeky grin over her shoulder and skipped to her dressing room. "I wonder if Suzie has unpacked my Japanese dressing gown." She disappeared inside the other room, and Max could hear her rummage through an armoire. "Ah, there it is. I can steal down the corridor in this. All the servants will be downstairs anyway, Suzie will have seen to that."

"You have great faith in your maid."

"I do, she is a treasure and understands things better than most other people." It appeared she was looking for something else. "Where is your valet, by the way? I don't think I have ever met him."

Max got out of bed and put on his shirt and breeches in anticipation of their trip down the hall. "He is keeping up appearances in Burton Street, but once we have had tea with Grandfather tomorrow, I suppose he can join me here."

There was an audible intake of breath from deep inside the dressing room. "Oh my, we have an actual bathroom! Max, come here."

Grinning from ear to ear, Max followed her voice. "I guess you found your second wedding present."

"Oh Max, it's marvelous, but how on earth will anyone empty the water out?"

Max found Emily dressed in a turquoise silk dressing gown with cherry blossoms artfully embroidered on it. It had a little Asian collar and a row of silk-covered buttons down the front. Silk mules were on her feet, and her hair flowed freely down her shoulders as she bent over the enormous copper tub built into a wooden platform by the window. The whole section could be separated from the rest of the room with a drape now held back by hooks on each wall. There was another drape that could be pulled over the window, and the fireplace was close enough to make bathing comfortable in winter. The room was furnished with a sofa and an armchair, and a chest of drawers presumably held towels. On the other side of the fireplace was a stand with a water pitcher and basin, and close to the door out into the corridor was a wooden enclosure Emily assumed would contain the commode. It was all very modern and beautiful, but she was still focused on the tub. "There is a wooden plug on the bottom, is there a pipe that takes the used water outside?"

"That's exactly it. The drain here is connected to the drainage from the roof and is collected in a stone trough in the garden where it can be used to water plants."

"That's very clever and saves the servants a lot of work, but is the soapy water good for plants?" She straightened to face him and sat on the curved rim of the bathtub.

"The gardener tells me it's actually useful to control certain pests." He stepped close to her and leaned over the tub to look down into the garden.

Emily took his hand and kissed his palm. "I love my wedding present."

Smiling down at her, he stroked his thumb down her cheek. "I'm so glad. Let's go look at Addy's portrait, this door leads out into the corridor." He took her hand to lead her out. "I haven't had a chance to see it properly myself, it only got hung this morning."

"So, the paint is still wet, as they say."

"Better not touch it then." He winked.

She laughed. "Oh Max, I hope being married will always be this much fun."

He twirled her into his arms and waltzed them down to the end of the corridor. "Me too, darling."

"I suppose it's up to us to make it fun."

"And exciting." He swung her to a halt in front of the painting. "Voilà, madame."

She blushed and turned a little shy. "You are exciting."

He took her into his arms once again and kissed her tenderly. "As are you. Now what do you think of Addy's likeness?"

Emily snuggled her back into his chest to have a good look at the painting. It was truly marvelous. The painter had caught the elegant turn of Addy's head, her muscles, and even the delicate lines of her face. But most importantly, he had painted her sweet nature. "Oh, Max, he captured her perfectly. And the landscape behind her is the Avon Springs area close to my uncle's estate where I spent most of my childhood." She stretched up and kissed his jaw. "I adore it. Thank you. But now I really do need something to eat."

They both laughed and danced their way back to the bedroom, where Max rang the bell and Emily dove back under the covers.

Max eyed her for a moment, then grinned slowly. "My lady, I believe you are asking for trouble."

She sat up to lean against the headboard and pulled a sheet up over her breasts, shooting him a seductive look from under her lashes. "I just think we should eat in bed."

He laughed and joined her on top of the blanket to wait for the servant.

TWENTY MINUTES LATER THEY WERE feasting on ham sandwiches and warm scones with clotted cream and raspberry jam, washed down with sweet milky tea, while Suzie readied a bath in the enormous copper tub. It took five footmen seven trips to fill it, and even then, it only looked half full. When the bath was ready, Max dismissed the servants once more. He stripped off his shirt and breeches, tugged the sheet and dressing gown off Emily, lifted her in his arms, and carried her to the tub. Stepping into the steaming water, he sat down with Emily still in his arms.

"Now I understand why they didn't fill it to the top." Emily grinned.

"This is simply marvelous. We can have baths together all the time."

"I don't think it was intentional, but after the effort it took to fill it up, we better make the most of it." Max chuckled while he settled her between his legs.

Emily's hair reached all the way down her back, but before it could get wet, she rose up on her knees and gathered her hair on top of her head. Twisting it into a coil, she pulled the damp ends through the loop it made, then she wound the remaining strands around the bun and threaded the ends through again. Miraculously it held.

Mesmerized by Emily's movements, Max watched her until she sat back into the water. Suzie had pulled a stool beside the bathtub and stocked it with everything that might be needed. The water itself smelled of lavender, lovely and soothing. Max picked up a bar of soap from the stool, worked up a lather, and started to soap Emily's neck and back. Proceeding to wash her meticulously, he directed her to lift one arm at a time so he could tend to them. Next came her legs, and Emily hummed her pleasure when Max gently washed between them too, soothing away the residual soreness there. From there his soapy hands traveled up her belly and to her breasts, tending to them most tenderly. Eventually, he cupped water in his hands and sloshed it over her to remove the soap.

Max's ministrations were wonderful. Emily had never enjoyed a bath more, and hummed her contentment, moving her limbs to give him access to all of her. It was lovely to be so open and free with him; it matched and exceeded all her girlish dreams of physical love. Once he was done washing her, she took the soap from him and began to reciprocate. Earlier, when they had made love for the first time, she had been so overwhelmed by all the erotic feelings assaulting her, she had mostly kept her eyes closed, but now she admired as she washed. Her husband was beautiful. Not just the pleasing whole, but all the little details of his body. She admired the hollow at the base of his neck between his collarbones and the play of the muscles in his arms. Emily delighted in a tuft of blond hair right in the middle of his chest and a birthmark in the shape of a chestnut on his right hip. But most of all she studied his member. The member which grew as she soaped it, caressed it, and stroked up and down to wash it.

Max rested against the rounded lip of the tub and watched his wife taking a good look at his genitals. He loved her hands on him, her eyes on him. He loved the way her eyes lit up when his member moved in her hand, the way her lips twitched with amusement. She was so uninhibited, and yet so innocent; she didn't know how much this all aroused him. But when she looked up, he could see arousal in her eyes too. Her pupils were huge and dark, her rosy lips parted. Without another thought, he pulled her close to kiss those gorgeous lips, and guided her legs to straddle him. "Make love to me."

She framed his face with both her hands and kissed him back, then whispered against his lips, "Show me how."

Nodding, he caressed one hand down her back to her bottom and pulled her directly over his erect manhood. With his other hand he made sure she was coated in her silky-smooth moisture before he guided himself to her opening. "Take me inside you and then move up and down." He kept his gaze locked with hers as she slowly sank down on him. When she smiled while she rose halfway up again, he felt like a king.

When she sank down on him the second time, she took him further, and gaining confidence on the next few strokes, allowed herself to feel. Her eyes rolling up in her head, she exhaled on the downstroke until she was full of him. Her lips parted, her head thrown back, she moved up and down on him, finding her own rhythm, making him glad he was sitting because he felt weak at the knees watching her take him this way, abandoned to her own pleasure.

He let his hands roam over her torso, teasing her pebbled nipples, caressing her sides and eventually holding a buttock in each hand to help her speed up her movement and give her the friction she sought. Water sloshed all around them, the element in as much turmoil as their bodies. While holding her steady, Max reached around to caress her clitoris, eliciting a soul-deep moan from Emily. Together, they climbed to the peak of desire and crashed headlong into a joined orgasm. Stars seemed to explode into supernovas all around them. Eventually, Emily collapsed on Max's chest, feeling utterly boneless and gasping for breath. Max held her there, his chest heaving with exertion, wondering how he had lived this long without ever experiencing satisfaction of this magnitude. This was what he had been looking for all this time, and as he lay there, he realized that it was the alignment of both love and passion that allowed him to feel like this, and how lucky he was to have found both in Emily.

They rested there for a long while, the sun setting over the treetops of Regent's Park. Max idly caressed the lone strand that had escaped from Emily's masterful makeshift chignon as she hummed her contentment. They felt each other's breath slow to normal, and Emily giggled when Max's member softened and slipped out of her.

Kissing the top of her head, Max chuckled. "You wore me out."

Lifting her head, Emily rested her chin on his chest. "That didn't take much."

Max barked a laugh and swatted her wet behind. "You will learn that it doesn't take much to make it rise again either."

"Oh good," she quipped, unfazed by the swat. They both dissolved into laughter. Emily rolled off Max and washed between her legs once more. Strange how even the soreness felt good. "Can we explore some more of the house, or is it already time for dinner?"

"More like supper time. Shall we act like Lord and Lady Didcomb and eat in the dining room, separated by twenty feet of silver and porcelain centerpieces we must crane our necks around to see each other?" Max climbed out of the tub and slung a bath towel around his hips.

"That sounds like fun."

"Anything I do with you is fun. Did I ever tell you that?" He unfolded another towel and wrapped Emily in it.

She nodded. "It is remarkable, isn't it?"

"I love you."

Smiling, she reached up to caress his jaw. "I suppose that does make all the difference, doesn't it?"

CHAPTER EIGHTEEN

THEY DIDN'T RISE TILL NOON THE NEXT DAY, then lingered, eating their breakfast in bed. In fact, the only reason Emily finally washed and dressed was to take Addy for a ride in the park, and of course Max joined her.

"What time does your grandfather expect us for tea?"

"He gets hungry around four and orders a tray with whatever baked goods are on hand that day. All his friends know and drop by around that time. He will expect us then."

Emily pinned a jaunty riding hat to her hair. "That sounds like my great-grandmother. Only she orders soup around five and only joins the family for dinner on special occasions."

Buttoning his waistcoat, Max bent to kiss her neck. "Oh, he will still eat a full dinner, he just gets peckish in the afternoon. Come to think of it, eating earlier and less might do his gout some good, but he is not likely to listen to advice on this."

"Yes, Jane Sedon warned me that any attempt to advise the earl would only anger him."

Their eyes met in the mirror, and Max's were deadly serious all of a sudden. "That was excellent advice. Never forget that my grandfather is a dangerous man, no matter how much of an invalid he looks."

Emily saw the worry in Max's eyes and nodded once. "I won't. But that doesn't mean we can't be on civil terms." She thought for a moment. "We should also visit with your mother. I like her very much. And she is staying with Jane's parents, who are special friends of the earl. They seemed pleased your grandfather came."

He smiled. "Of course, my mother would love to get to know you better. And it can't hurt for the Welds to know you better either." Had this not been their honeymoon, Max would have asked his mother to stay with them.

Emily kissed the hand he had placed on her shoulder. "I'm glad. Shall we visit tomorrow morning?"

"I'll send a message around, but let's go for this ride. I can hear Addy whinnying."

A horse could indeed be heard in the stable below. Emily looked guilty. "Yes, let's go. Addy must be worried; I've not seen her since she was moved to the new stable."

Each pocketed a horsey treat off the breakfast tray, then they took the servant stairs to the back door and stepped out into the garden. From there they took the pebble path to the new stable, where Addy greeted her mistress with soft snorts and head rubs. Emily kissed Addy's velvety soft nose and murmured sweet nothings into her ears. "Goodness, I missed you so much. How do you like your new home? It's grand, isn't it? I like it too." The horse delicately plucked the lump of sugar Emily offered from her hand. "Good girl. Are they treating you well here? Has Thomas been to see you? He lives with us too."

Max greeted his stallion in the stall diagonally opposite Addy's but kept listening to Emily. He fed Caesar a slice of apple and scratched between his ears. The horse blew appreciatively into his face, then turned his attention to Addy and her mistress. "I know I'm not as interesting as the ladies, but you don't have to be quite as obvious about it." He could hear Emily giggle from Addy's stall as he offered his horse the bit and threaded his ears through the bridle.

Winding the reins around his hand below the horse's chin, he called to Emily, "Do you have her haltered? I'm about to lead Caesar past."

"Go right ahead, we are fine."

Max could have saved himself the worry. When he led Caesar out to the staging area, the two horses just blew at each other in greeting, then Emily led Addy out behind them.

Two grooms busied themselves with saddling the horses, who stood amiably side by side.

"Looks like they are both happy with their new lodgings." Emily smiled.

Max bent low to murmur in her ear, "And their new stable mate." The look that accompanied the comment was filled with heat and a promise of carnal pleasures to come. Emily shuddered with anticipation. They had flirted like this before, but now the knowledge of where all that flirting would lead made Emily blush crimson. She was still flustered when Max boosted her into the saddle, grinning broadly.

"You fiend. You did that on purpose," Emily mock-complained, gradually returning to a more becoming shade of pink.

Max only shrugged, still grinning, and mounted his horse. They rode through the tall gate into the open landscape of the park. In the country this was a regular occurrence, but in town it was an unheard-of luxury, and Emily enjoyed every second of it. Side by side, they rode north along the central path, the rose garden to their right and the lake to the left. There was a menagerie planned at the northern end of the park, but for now it was just a grove of centuries-old oaks, reached through a lovely succession of meadows ringed by stands of trees. This park was more formal in its layout at the southern end where York Terrace was, but the farther they rode, the wilder the landscape became and the fewer people they encountered. A fellow in a decidedly shabby-looking coat crossed their path, and a few minutes later they encountered another man smoking under a tree, and several young bucks were about.

Eventually Max turned to Emily. "I know you are a competent rider, but will you promise me to take a groom with you if ever you come riding here without me?"

Emily wrinkled her nose. This felt like the country to her, and there she had always managed to leave the grooms behind. But they were still in London, and it was nice to know Max worried for her. "If it will make you feel better, I'll take Thomas if you are busy."

Max reached across to take her hand and kissed it. "It most certainly will make me feel better."

The last of her annoyance at his request left her, and seeing a wide-open meadow ahead, Emily challenged, "Race you to the oak at the end." Before Max could respond, she urged Addy into a gallop and employed every ounce of energy she possessed to get to the tree first. She won by mere inches; still, it proved how capable a rider she was, just in case a reminder was needed.

Max reined in his stallion and smiled. His wife knew how to make a point. "She really does fly. Darling, I know you can ride better than most men, I just don't like how all these young bucks lust after you."

She laughed. "You have that in common with my father."

Sir Henry had once likened looking after Emily's safety to guarding a bag of flies in Max's hearing, but he didn't think it to his advantage to mention that fact, so he urged Caesar into a trot and stirred them toward home. It was his job to keep his wife safe, and he took that responsibility seriously.

Blissfully unaware of her husband's musings, Emily overtook Max, having spotted a fallen tree. There was nothing like the feeling of flying over an obstacle on horseback. She lined them up to jump the tree and prompted Addy into a gallop.

Max's heart did an unpleasant little somersault seeing Emily head for the hurdle, but he refrained from telling her to stop. This was Emily; she rode like the wind and had a seat like no other. He of all people would not disappoint her by doubting her ability to clear a fallen tree. But still, he held his breath until he saw her land safely on the other side, then followed her over.

"This park is so much more fun than Hyde Park." She beamed. "I shall ride here every day."

It was gratifying to know his wife liked the location he had chosen for their home, even if he now wished he had bothered to explore the park first. But maybe this was to be expected in a park that led to more rural areas. In the country a shabby coat would have gone unnoticed, since most farmers wore them.

They returned to the stable about an hour later, rubbed the horses dry, washed up, and ate their lunch under a willow tree in the garden. They took a turn about the garden and made plans what to plant where, then it was time to get changed for their visit with the earl.

WARTHON HOUSE WAS A LARGE Tudor structure on the Strand, close to Somerset House. It was a majestic brickwork building three stories tall, with a steep gabled roof featuring an impressive collection of chimneys. Sandstone casings surrounded the mulled windows, but despite there being a lot of them, they didn't seem to brighten the facade. Emily had seen the prominent building many times but had never wondered who the gloomy monstrosity belonged to. It was set back from the street, and the approach to it was cobbled with diamond-shaped stones to mirror the small panes of leaded glass in the windows. Alighting at the bottom of a large outside staircase leading to the entrance on the second floor, Emily noticed the Warthon coat of arms hewn into the sandstone above a water fountain. The stairs led up on either side and converged in a landing directly over the coat of arms at the center of the facade. From the landing the stairs continued up to the front entrance.

Max used the heavy iron door knocker shaped like a lion's head. Moments later, the door was opened by a sprightly middle-aged butler who greeted them with a deferential, "My lord, Your Ladyship." He led them down a stone-flagged and oak-paneled corridor to a salon at the back of the house. The butler knocked at a door to the left; straight ahead there was a paneled glass door overlooking the garden and the Thames beyond.

At the command from within to enter, the butler took three steps into the room and announced them. "Lord and Lady Didcomb, my lord."

From the depths of an armchair by the fire, the Earl of Warthon greeted them. "Come in, come in." To Emily in particular, he continued, "Please forgive me for not rising, my foot is still plaguing me."

Emily curtsied and then rushed to the old man's side to take his outstretched hand. "Oh, there is nothing to forgive. I'm just saddened to find you still suffering."

The earl patted her hand and indicated for her to take a seat on the sofa close to him. "Sit, my dear. Tea will be served directly and then Max can show you the gardens, if you are so inclined."

Max sat down next to her and nodded a greeting to his grandfather while Emily smiled winningly. "Ah, yes, I just noticed them. You are so lucky to have an unobstructed view of the Thames."

The old man made a face. "It comes at a heavy price; the house is damp. Hence the fire on a summer's day."

Max thought the old man was putting it on rather thick, but as long as he was cordial to Emily, he had no cause for complaint. Showing her the gardens would be a pleasant enough task. "It's a nice stroll down to the river. There is usually a pleasant breeze coming off it."

"I'll have to take your word for it, my boy. I haven't been able to traverse all those stairs in some time." Turning to Emily, he continued, "We used to take meals out on the first terrace when we came up for the parliamentary sessions. Max always liked it by the river and spent hours watching the ships go by."

Emily turned to Max and was about to comment, but he shook his head almost imperceptibly, reminding her of the earl's aversion to trade, so she merely said, "That sounds like fun. How old were you then?"

Max smiled his thanks for not mentioning his ships. "I came to live with my grandfather when I was twelve, and back then we came for every session of Parliament. My grandfather was very involved in politics."

The earl chuckled. "I still am. I just can't sit through all those endless debates anymore."

Max watched his grandfather warily. He had never seen him be this nice to a woman before. His own mother barely warranted a nod from the old tyrant. Was he acting? Or was he genuinely smitten with Emily? Max could hardly credit it and vowed to remain vigilant. The tea tray arrived and Warthon didn't object when Emily offered to pour tea for them. He even commented that tea tasted better prepared by a pretty woman and bestowed a smile on her. A real smile, one that lit up his eyes, not one of those grimaces he usually doled out. It was very confusing.

They spent a remarkably pleasant hour with the earl before he said he needed to close his eyes for a spell and sent them on their walk through the gardens. Max was astounded the earl had maintained his pleasant demeanor for this long, but he was grateful. He still didn't think he had his grandfather's approval, but it seemed he at least didn't object to Emily.

Emily waved the butler away when he came to offer her hat. The sun was low enough not to burn and they were in a private garden, so they walked through the back door the butler held open and onto the boxwood-framed terrace. There was a fountain at the center of it, feeding a pond on the second terrace, which in turn fed one on the third. There were rosebushes under the windows, and each terrace featured formal gardens in geometrical shapes, with boxwood-lined paths, but besides the roses there were few flowers. The only whimsy was provided by the droplets from the fountain catching the sunlight in a sparkling rainbow, while below, the Thames shimmered silver. It was a delightful prospect and as if they had stepped back in time. The location of Warthon House was far enough upriver not to have to worry about the pollution caused by the wharves and poverty, but the river was still busy. Small vessels sailed past, and others rowed passengers across.

"I used to love coming to London when I was a boy, but not because of the ships on the Thames. My mother would come to London whenever I wrote to her that we would be here, and we would meet every afternoon at a spot by the river she could reach via a public path."

Emily was astounded. "Did your mother not live with you?"

Max's face was grim. These were not happy memories, but perhaps Emily needed to know. "My mother was not welcome in the earl's house. When the earl took me to live with him after my father died at Waterloo, she stayed behind in the house my father had bought for us in Suffolk."

Leaning her head against him, Emily hugged his arm closer. She had never seen him so serious. "How awful. You lost your father and had to leave your mother behind. What did your grandfather have against her? She is a cousin to the Countess of Weld, is she not?"

"She is at that. But her father was a younger son and a curate, not to mention my father turned away from my grandfather when he objected to the marriage. The earl cut them off and didn't even send a condolence letter when my father fell. He had no use for us until my uncle, the heir, broke his neck in a hunting accident, which left only me to inherit the earldom. Then he simply drove up at my childhood home, told my nurse to pack my bags and my mother to say her goodbyes."

The face Emily turned up to him was full of concern. "How cruel. You must have been devastated."

Max stopped to caress her cheek. Her sympathy and understanding were a powerful antidote to the nightmare that had been his early teenage years. "He wanted to mold me in his image, and my mother would only have been in his way."

"That is no reason to separate you from her." Emily looked ready to march back up to the house and give the earl a piece of her mind.

"I know." Max smiled for Emily's benefit. "It wasn't all bad, though. I met Ben, and Jane came to visit several times a year, and when we were in London, I saw my mother almost every day." There was no point in burdening her with the horror of the beatings and the humiliations his grandfather had dished out before Max learned to hide his feelings as well as his intentions.

"At least you had that." Emily frowned. "It does make you wonder what changed his mind about me. He is positively charming to me now. Is he trying to avoid an estrangement?"

Patting her arm, Max smiled down at her. "He may well be. I'm the only heir, after all. In any case, I'm glad he seems to like you, but in my opinion, we would do well to remain vigilant."

She nodded solemnly. "I figured as much when you didn't want me to tell him about your ships. He has no idea how rich you are, does he?"

Max was so proud of her. She was not only beautiful and talented, she also had more than her fair share of intelligence. "He knows I am in trade and that Ben is my partner. But no, he has no idea I'm worth twice as much as the earldom."

She giggled. "Oh, I'm glad you told me, now I don't have to feel guilty about our beautiful house anymore. I'll do my best to spend a fair chunk of your fortune decorating it."

Max threw his head back and laughed. "You came with a fair fortune yourself."

Grinning, she rubbed his arm. "Indeed, I saw the contract. Fifty thousand, and if you don't make me happy you have to give it all to me and let me live wherever I want."

He was still laughing. "I have every intention to make you deliriously happy. At least as happy as you have already made me."

Emily stood on her tiptoes to kiss him. "I love you so, Max. And you make me happier than I ever thought I could be."

UP AT THE HOUSE, THE earl's curses reverberated off the venerated old walls as his valet changed the bindings on his foot. "Leave off, you old woman, the day's work is not done yet."

The long-suffering valet sighed and tied off the ends of the bandage. "Can I persuade you to drink some of the barley water?"

"Leave me and take that foul brew with you." The earl's face was mottled red with fury. The man was holding him up. Warthon barely waited for the door to click shut behind the valet before he heaved himself out of his chair and hobbled to the window. He had to see how far the banshee's claws were dug into his grandson.

They were strolling down the third terrace and she was hanging off his arm, her smiling face turned up to him. "There is no denying it, the girl is a beauty." The old man stared and shook his head, while Max threw his head back and laughed at something she had said. The earl had never seen his grandson laugh like that, so open and utterly carefree.

"And she has captivated him with all that sweetness and light." He sneered. "But does she know about your dark side?" The sneer broadened into an evil grin, a plan starting to form in his head. "Let's see what Little Miss Perfect will do when she finds out."

It was time to have a conference with Weld, but not in town where the walls had ears.

CHAPTER NINETEEN

ON THEIR RETURN TO WARTHON HOUSE, MAX and Emily were informed the earl was resting and, realizing their visit with the old gentleman was at an end, decided to return to their own, far more comfortable, abode. Once home, they ordered dinner to be served in their private sitting room abutting the bedroom and did what newlyweds do.

Emily loved her spacious, light-filled new home, and she adored her husband and the time they spent with each other, but she also missed her family. This was the first time in three years she had been away from her father's busy house, and she wanted to know how her siblings fared.

Max saw her restlessness at breakfast the next morning and inquired, "What is it, my love?"

She smiled brightly. "Nothing really, I just wonder how everyone at Cavendish Square is." Growing more wistful, she continued, "They are all sitting around the breakfast table in the yellow morning room right now, planning out the day ahead and probably talking all at once."

Reaching for her hand and giving it a comforting squeeze, Max suggested, "Maybe we should look in on them on our way to see my mother."

His reward was an exuberant Emily. "Oh yes, Max. Let's do that." She was already out of her chair. "Should we ride down? I know Danny would be tickled pink if you took him up in front of you. He so admires Caesar."

Smiling at her enthusiasm, Max considered. "Then we will have to come back here and change. My mother wouldn't care, but the Countess of Weld is a stickler for the right attire for each occasion."

"That makes no sense, my father's house is on the way to the Welds."
But Emily knew Max to be right about the countess. "Never mind then.
Let's take the open carriage, go visit your mama, and see my family on
the way back for lunch."

He held out his hand toward his wife. "Just what I was about to suggest. And why don't we invite your family here for Thursday, then Danny
can see the new stable too."

Emily laughed and took his arm. "That sounds like fun. Now all we
must do is invite Edgar and it will by my brother's ideal day."

Stroking the hand resting on his arm, Max mused. "That's an excellent notion. I haven't been in the office for a week and should check with
Ben all is well with the business. Let's invite them and he can update me
and bring any papers that might need signing."

"It seems I'm hosting my first luncheon." She beamed.

Half an hour later, Max helped his wife into the open carriage, admiring her very grown-up, dark-rose-colored raw silk morning
dress. Her poke bonnet was fashioned out of straw and decorated with
the finest cream-colored lace Max had ever seen. The overall effect was
striking. "You look splendid in this ensemble."

"You can thank Isabella for it, she designed it." Emily sat and
smoothed the silk over her knees. "I absolutely love it and am so glad I
can finally wear this color."

Giving her another appreciative look, Max settled next to her and
directed the driver to the Earl of Weld's residence on Hanover Square.
"Your stepmother is a remarkable woman. Your father told me she sells
her paintings in seven different galleries around the country."

"She had planned to live on her art before she fell in love with Papa."
Emily's voice was full of pride for Isabella. "I know several people who
have her work on their walls and have no idea it was painted by a woman.

Most of them would not have bought the art if they had known, yet they are very proud of their paintings. I do wonder how many writers and artists are in fact members of the fairer sex." Growing more thoughtful, she added, "It's a shame we have to hide behind male names to be taken seriously."

Max agreed with her in principle but didn't quite know what to say. "You don't hide behind a man's name when you perform."

That made her laugh. "Well, I can't, unless I don a disguise. But I'm not being paid for my performances, nor do I play in official venues."

"Would you want to be paid?" It was a strange concept, women wanting to be paid for their art, but he liked making money himself, so he could see the appeal.

"I don't need the money, obviously, but being paid for something you are good at proves your time and your skill is worth that amount to someone. It's better than a compliment, it's proof you are good. But if playing in the salons of society's grand ladies for the edification of their guests is good enough for the Dowager Duchess of Avon, then it will have to do for me."

She said it with a shrug, but there was so much vulnerability in her eyes, Max wondered if she felt insecure about her musical ability. Or perhaps she was shy about revealing these thoughts to him. "I think you are every bit as good a musician as one may find at the opera or in a concert hall. Perhaps you should establish your own musical salon and only ever invite the very best to perform with you. Over time your reward would be how sought-after the invitations would become. That would be proof of your skill, wouldn't it?"

They had just turned into Hanover Square and were slowing as they approached the Earl of Weld's residence. Emily smiled at her husband. "I'll bear that idea in mind when I furnish the big salon. The acoustics are certainly good enough."

The carriage halted and Max jumped out, then turned to help her out. "Lady Didcomb's Salon. I think I like it."

EMILY AND MAX WERE LED into a drawing room tastefully decorated in shades of cream and green, where they were almost immediately joined by Constance Warthon.

"What a lovely surprise. I was so hoping I would see you before I return home." Constance embraced her son and kissed Emily's cheek. "Come, have some tea with me, and you can tell me all about your plans."

Emily curtsied and smiled. "Good morning, Constance. What plans are you referring to?"

Constance laughed. "Max always has plans. Usually they have to do with ships and treasures from far-off places. Don't tell me he isn't taking you on a bridal tour?" She looked from one to the other, but Max shook his head and Emily just shrugged.

At this moment the Countess of Weld entered the scene and evidently had overheard the last exchange. "My goodness, no bridal tour? Come at least to Brighton with us." Turning to Emily, she added, "We go every year. Summer is so lovely on the south coast, and Brighton has lots of entertainments to offer."

"Your servant, my lady." Max bent over the countess's hand. "All our relatives attended the wedding, so there is no need for a bridal tour to introduce Emily to her new family. But I wouldn't mind going to Brighton for a while, if Emily wants to go." He looked at her to gauge her feelings on the matter.

"Oh, I love Brighton." Emily's eyes sparkled with the memory of swimming in the sea and her first proper luncheon party at the Royal Pavilion. But then she thought of their house and all the fun they would have furnishing it, not to mention the splendid bathtub in her dressing room. She sent her husband a sweltering look. "Perhaps not right away, though? I would like to get accustomed to living in my beautiful house first."

Max was instantly at her side and brought both her hands to his lips, gazing deep into her eyes. "Of course, my love. We will do whatever you would like best."

Emily near swooned at the heat in his eyes, and the two older ladies cooed at the couple in love. The countess was the first to recover. "Do come join us whenever you are ready for a change of scenery, we will be there all summer. Warthon said he is about to return as well. The earl came by this morning to say his goodbyes. He said he wrote you a missive, Max."

Max had not expected his grandfather to remain in the capital for long; it was, however, strange he would say goodbye to the Welds but not to him. But then he realized the earl probably went to the house in Burton Street. He nodded. "Indeed." He would send someone to retrieve the note once they were at Sir Henry's.

Turning to his mother, he asked, "Will you be joining us in Brighton?"

Constance was taken aback for a second, then smiled. "Oh no, Max, darling. I'm going back home and you two can come visit me whenever you want." But to Emily it seemed a shadow had passed across Constance's countenance at the thought of going to Brighton. Given the Earl of Warthon had taken Max away from her when he had become the sole heir at the age of twelve, there was most likely some old hurt there.

The countess weighed in. "You know your mother; she can't stay away from the Orwell River and all those birds for long."

At the mention of the river, Emily asked, "You live by the Orwell? My father's ancestral estate is in Norfolk, and we travel through Ipswich when we go there. The river is beautiful."

"It's even more beautiful further down, closer to Folkstone," Constance enthused. "The reeds are a nesting area for herons, wrens, kingfishers, and all kinds of other birds. I just love it there."

"I would like to see that. I love all animals. Particularly horses, but all animals." Emily was in her element now, charmed by the idea of bird-watching with her mother-in-law.

Lady Weld, on the other hand, wrinkled her nose. "The marshes are a miserable place in summer when it's humid and every biting insect in the kingdom seems to congregate there. Come to Brighton and then visit your mother in September when the sea breeze blows inland and cools things off." She stood and shook out her skirts. "Time for me to see to packing up my summer wardrobe. Constance, why don't you stay in town for a few days longer so you can spend more time with the children."

Constance was surprised by her cousin's uncharacteristic generosity. "Oh, indeed, that would be lovely, Amalia. Thank you."

The countess took her leave, and as soon as she had departed and they could hear her retreating footsteps in the corridor, Emily turned to Max. "Can I tell your mother?"

Max didn't have to ask to what she was referring. "Go ahead, my love."

Excitedly moving closer to her mother-in-law, Emily whispered, "Max wanted to keep it a secret from his grandfather for now, but he bought us the most beautiful house on York Terrace, virtually in Regent's Park. It's marvelous. We can ride out into the park right from the back door. Would you like to come for lunch with us tomorrow? I'm planning to invite my family too."

"Oh goodness, yes, I would love to come." Constance sent her son an assessing look. She knew as well as he did what the earl was capable of and had a good idea why her son hid things from him. "Well, that ex-plains the lack of a bridal tour." Turning back to Emily, she added, "Has he left the decorating to you?"

Emily gasped. "Oh dear, I forgot. I must organize a sofa or two so people can sit in the drawing room."

"Or we could spread blankets in the garden and have a picnic," Max suggested.

"That might be the best idea. I don't even know what color I want in the drawing room yet," Emily confided to both.

Constance just laughed. "A picnic on the lawn sounds perfect to me."

They spent another pleasant quarter hour, then bid Max's mother goodbye and made their way to Sir Henry's house, from where Max sent his groom to retrieve his mail from Burton Street.

As Emily invited her mother-in-law to their new house, the Countess of Weld slipped into her husband's book room and closed the door behind her quietly.

"I did what I could to lure them to Brighton. The rest is up to Warthon."

Her husband looked up from his papers and grunted. "Well done." He evidently expected her to depart, but the countess settled on a chair in front of the desk.

Lady Weld focused her gaze on her wringing hands and took a deep breath. "For what it's worth, Edwin, I think Warthon is making a huge mistake." Emboldened by her own nerve to voice her opinion in her husband's hearing, she added, "The children love each other; any fool can see that."

The Earl of Weld's ice-cold eyes settled on his wife. "Only a fool would think becoming the next Countess of Warthon has anything to do with love. Bloodlines and legitimacy are the only things that count. Kindly leave the thinking to your betters, madam." Then he returned his attention to his papers, while the countess fled the room as fast as she could.

THE NEWLYWEDS WERE GREETED ENTHUSIASTICALLY by Emily's parents and instantly invited to join the family for luncheon. Grossmama, who was also present, declared herself delighted at the opportunity to spend some time with her great-granddaughter before her return to Avon the following day.

When Emily protested her removal, Grossmama took both her hands. "Oh, *Liebchen*, you are married now, you have a husband to look after you, and to entertain. It is June and you know how I hate the heat in the city." She drew her great-granddaughter closer and smiled conspiratorially. "You and Max are most welcome to come visit once you are settled into your new life."

"I will miss you, Grossmama. You haven't even seen my house yet," Emily complained.

A mischievous little grin appeared on the old lady's face. "Aha, there you are wrong. I saw the house before Max even showed you."

Emily gasped. "Really? Max said you advised him on the piano, but he never mentioned you chose the piano specifically for the room."

"We had such fun sneaking around to get the right piano for your drawing room." The old lady laughed. "By the way, I meant to tell you: use silk for the furnishings, no velvets. Silks will keep that marvelous acoustic alive."

"Thank you, Grossmama. I did wonder what effect soft furnishings will have."

They settled down to a family lunch in the breakfast room, with all the windows open to the garden. The invitation to picnic at Emily's new residence was communicated, along with the fact that Danny would be allowed to take a turn with Max on Caesar, eliciting an excited whoop from her brother.

During lunch, a footman discreetly handed Max several letters, which he briefly sorted, then slipped into his pocket, but not before Sir Henry noticed. "You are still getting your mail at your old address?"

Max nodded. "I intend to keep the house as my business address. But we went to see my grandfather for tea yesterday and he seemed positively smitten with Emily, so there may be no need for further sneaking around. This morning, while visiting my mother, we heard Warthon informed the Earl of Weld, before we arrived, he was to depart London today and that he sent me a missive."

"So you sent for it. If you like, you can use my desk after lunch," Henry offered.

"Thank you, sir. I would appreciate it."

"Do call me Henry, we are family now." Henry smiled.

Max's answering smile was warm. "And you must call me Max." He truly liked his father-in-law.

Henry refilled Max's wine glass from the carafe on the table. "Let's drink to that and then let's see what your grandfather has to say."

Max felt so much better he wouldn't have to decipher his grandfather's intentions all by himself. All that talk in the countess's salon of spending the summer in Brighton, innocent as it seemed, had made him nervous. Of course, he would have to take his wife to see the castle one day, but that didn't mean it had to be right away. He would have to go to Warthon for the Knights' anniversary in July, and given the nature of the celebrations connected with the event, he hoped his wife would be nowhere near then.

Max followed his father-in-law to his library, but in the end, his grandfather's missive just read:

Max,
The damp by the river is not doing me any good, I'm going back to Warthon. Bring your wife for a visit there, if you like.
Warthon

It wasn't much of an invitation as invitations went, but given his grandfather's past opposition to the match, it was akin to a miracle. And it made Max's hair stand up at the back of his neck. He handed the missive to Henry. "What do you make of it?"

"Brief and to the point. Is that your grandfather's idea of an invitation or a command?"

Max chuckled darkly. "Both, I suspect."

"Hm. So you feel you have to take her?" It was a rhetorical question really. Warthon was the earl and the head of Max's family, not to mention they wanted his goodwill for Emily's sake.

"He would see it as an insult if I don't, so yes." So much for keeping Emily well away from Warthon.

Henry confirmed Max's assessment. "Then you should go in the not-too-distant future. He made the effort to attend the wedding, it would seem he expects obedience in return." Handing the missive back, Henry poured them both a brandy.

Hearing excited voices in the garden, Max stepped to the back window and watched Emily play with her brother on the lawn. She had discarded her hat, and her hair was starting to escape its coiffure, but somehow that made her even more radiant. "Indeed. But something tells me it's not a good idea," he said quietly.

Max's worry put Henry on edge. "Are you expected to stay at the castle?"

Mulling the issue over, Max brightened. "Normally I would, but I could use the earl's former aversion to the match as a reason to book rooms in a hotel. Besides, my wife will want to attend entertainments in Brighton."

Henry nodded, much relieved. "The Waterfront is very good, and Emily knows it; stay there and go to the castle for morning tea. Less chance for mischief."

Taking the glass Henry held out for him, Max continued, "And it won't take much to entice Ben to Brighton, his father is still employed at the castle. Lady Jane's parents are already on their way there, and the countess always stays in town."

"An extended family gathering in Brighton," Henry mused as he joined Max by the window. "I'm sure I could persuade my wife to take a trip to Brighton for a fortnight toward the end of the month, but then, I'm afraid I have business in the north." He considered his son's antics with a smile. "I'm sure Danny would relish an adventure by the sea."

Both men watched Danny chase Emily around the garden until she used a tree to turn on Danny and started to chase him, making a monster face with her hands raised overhead, ready to pounce on her brother. Danny fled, screeching with delight.

"I'm afraid you married a hoyden," Henry remarked.

Max laughed. "A delightfully uninhibited one." To himself he thought his wife was never more beautiful than when she was flushed with physical exertion, and he wondered how long before he could make excuses and take her home. "The end of the month suits me. We still have decisions to make regarding the furnishing of the house."

"So I hear. And the hoyden must plan a picnic for tomorrow. You best take her home." Henry was pleased with how happy his daughter was, and the extent to which her new husband sought his counsel. He led his son-in-law through the music room into the garden. "Danny, say goodbye to your sister."

"Aww, not yet. I want to be the monster next," came the instant complaint.

"You can play monsters all afternoon tomorrow, remember? Besides, I need you to come and help me persuade Mama to take a trip to the ocean."

That got Danny's attention. He ran across the lawn to his father. "Where are we going?"

"To Brighton. They have a pier there, and bathing machines."

Max's and Emily's eyes met over the heads of father and son, and Emily grinned. "I suppose we are all going to Brighton."

CHAPTER TWENTY

BY THE TIME THE YOUNG COUPLE'S FRIENDS
and family arrived for the inaugural picnic the following day, Max felt
much better about the prospect of taking Emily to Warthon Castle.
Ben had already promised his mother-in-law they would join them for
a month, which would no doubt delight Ben's father as well. All that remained to be done was to choose furniture and fabrics for the house, and
craftsmen to do the job while they were away. To that end, Emily took
Isabella aside and asked her what colors she would recommend in the
drawing room as well as the two formal salons toward the front of the
house. The enormous dining room already had basic furnishings and had
recently been painted. It would do, and Emily figured she could manage
the guest bedrooms by herself.

Isabella was impressed with the beauty and spaciousness of the
house, and in particular the drawing room. She turned in a slow circle in
the middle of the lovely, sun-filled room while Danny and Edgar chased
each other around, testing the famed acoustics with their war cries. "You
certainly don't need mirrors above the mantels in this room."

Giggling, Emily tapped out a few dance steps. "No, we could hold a
ball in here, couldn't we?"

"No doubt." Isabella ran an admiring finger over the molding separating the walls into panels. "This is exquisite work. Not just the ceiling,
the walls too. I would leave the molding brilliant white and paint the
walls a pale jade green to reflect the outside. Then find wall sconces that
match the molding and place them to either side of all the doors and in
between each window, also on either side of the fireplaces. Above the

mantels you could hang two large oil landscapes: something mythical perhaps. And I think marble busts of your favorite composers would look wonderful placed along the wall between the two doors into the corridor."

"Only two paintings?" Emily was skeptical.

Isabella nodded slowly. "Yes, big ones of unrivaled quality. They need to be bigger than the fireplaces themselves, and they need to complement each other. The room is so big, you need focal points. Right now, you have the windows and the ceiling. The paintings will pull the room together, and the marble busts will keep this side light and airy."

The two boys raced out into the garden while Emily considered what her stepmother had suggested. "Oh, I see what you are doing. Then we can have a formal seating area around the fireplace closer to the piano, and in the corner by the entrance to the book room we can have some gaming tables."

Isabella checked Henry was on hand to supervise the boys before she continued. "Just so. I would put a chaise longue by the far window so you can rest and read, and an informal seating area with truly comfortable armchairs by the far fireplace. You can use the cherrywood furniture for the formal area."

"What color do you think for the curtains and the upholstery?"

"The same color as the walls for the curtains, but several shades darker. The cherrywood sofas and chairs would look lovely covered in a green-and-white-striped silk. For the informal area I would choose leather, and for your chaise longue, cream velvet."

Emily could see it all in her mind's eye. "Goodness, it will be grand and cozy all at the same time. Will you come with me tomorrow and choose fabrics?"

Isabella's eyes sparkled. She was in her element where aesthetics were concerned, and for her stepdaughter to seek her opinion was gratifying. "With pleasure, dear. We could also have a look at the gallery on the Strand. He had some wonderful oils in the back room last time I went."

"Then we should take Max." Emily chuckled. "I very much doubt he will want to choose fabrics, but paintings, yes." Emily thought for a moment. "Perhaps he would want his ships to be painted. Do you know anyone?"

Her stepmother's eyes went round. "Ships, plural?"

Emily grinned from ear to ear. "Ships, plural."

A sly smile crossed Isabella's lovely face. "Perhaps we should look for a Constable or two for the smaller salons. And a Turner for your magnificent foyer."

A huge grin split Emily's face. "Oh, yes, one of the large seascapes to go on the wall above the staircase. It gets marvelous light from the glass dome overhead." Ideas were racing through Emily's brain now.

"A large mahogany sideboard and mirror on the opposite side so ladies can check their appearance before they are shown in." Isabella evidently was having fun, but their creative brainstorming was interrupted by the arrival of Constance Warthon.

Both Emily and Isabella curtsied to the older woman, and Emily stepped forward. "Welcome to our home, Constance." Turning to Isabella, she continued, "You have met my stepmother, Lady March."

Constance smiled and offered her hand. "Oh yes, we met at the wedding." The two women shook hands, then Constance turned to have a look at the room around her. "This house is simply marvelous. You will have so much fun decorating it."

Turning in a slow circle, Emily imagined the drawing room all furnished with the things they had talked about. "Indeed, Isabella and I were just discussing what to do with this room."

Through the large windows they could see the two small boys playing under the watchful eye of Sir Henry while Ben and Lady Jane were settled on the blankets under the willow tree, Jane leaning in to say something to Ben that made him laugh.

Seeing Constance's eyes light up at the sight of the boys, Emily gestured toward the open French doors. "Shall we join the others in the garden? Lunch will be served shortly. Later, Max and I will take the boys up on our horses and go see the ducks in the lake."

"That sounds lovely. Do the rest of us walk to the pond?" Constance inquired.

Isabella took in the garden and park from the top step. "I intend to. It's a most pleasant walk."

Emily warned, "Don't tell Danny and Edgar about the ducks yet or none of us will get to eat any bread with our lunch."

The two mothers laughed, while Emily sought out her butler to tell him all their guests had arrived and he could start serving.

The whole company ate a delicious lunch on their picnic blankets, then enjoyed a delightful jaunt into the park. Later, Emily played Mozart for them all, the two boys sitting either side of her on the bench, mesmerized by her clever fingers. They rounded out the afternoon with a tour through the house and parted the best of friends, Isabella and Emily planning to meet the following day.

CHOOSING FURNITURE AND FABRICS TURNED out to be rather tedious, but with Isabella's help they made short work of it. They also found two marvelous landscapes for the drawing room, one depicting an ancient chapel in a shady glade, the other a brook scampering from rock to rock through an oak forest. Both had an element of enchantment about them. Max bought both paintings and ordered them framed in gold frames, but refused to set foot in another shop thereafter, so Isabella and Emily set out on their own. Emily was determined to get the basics for all the downstairs rooms organized and hire the craftsmen before they left for Brighton. Max had secured them a suite at the Waterfront Hotel, and they were to stay a whole month. Emily supposed that would be enough time for her to forge a relationship with Max's grandfather. After all, he had responded favorably to her during their visit to Warthon House. Her father and his family were to join them for the first two weeks, and the Sedons would be staying with Jane's mother, who rented a house for the Brighton season. Emily positively looked forward to a month by the sea.

AND SO IT WAS THAT ten days after the picnic on the lawn at York Terrace, Max and Emily arrived in Brighton in a curricle, ahead of the coach transporting their servants and luggage. Thomas and a groom brought up the rear, riding Addy and Caesar. The Waterfront was as comfortable as Emily remembered and the view just as mesmerizing. Outside, a cloudless sky stretched to the horizon, where it met the silvery-blue shimmering sea.

Sir Henry had arrived the day before, but he and Isabella had yet to return from today's painting expedition, so Emily and Max inspected their suite and ordered dinner for them all.

With the sun about an hour from setting, the couple decided on a walk to the end of the pier. They strolled arm in arm down the promenade, watching the attendants pull the bathing machines out of the water onto the pebble beach and lead their horses home for the day. There were still swimmers in the ocean, and farther out to sea a couple of fishing boats were heading back to the little harbor some ways down the beach.

Emily nodded to the bathing machines. "We should rent one of those for tomorrow. Isabella and I had so much fun swimming in the sea the summer my father met her." Emily smiled at the memory of their days at the beach.

Max had no trouble imagining Emily as a sea nymph gliding through the waves but had to ask, "I take it you can swim?"

She laughed. "Of course. Bertie taught me well."

Drawing her a little closer, Max steered them onto the pier. "I imagine the boys would love it too. Do you think they will let them into the cabin, or do we have to teach them how to swim first?"

"Well, you don't have to be able to swim to go sea-bathing, that is the point of the attendant. They even dunk you in and then drag you back into the bathing cabin if you want."

Emily's description brought to mind the image of a drowned rat. Max wondered who voluntarily submitted to such treatment. "I suppose that makes sense. I've never used one before."

She laughed again. From his horrified expression, Emily assumed Max would not be making use of a bathing machine any time soon. "Able men who can swim have to get into the water from boats farther out, to spare us gentle flowers the sight of you."

Joining in her laughter, Max pulled her to the left side of the pier to admire the white cliffs glowing pink in the setting sun. It was hard to imagine a more beautiful place, or a more perfect love. They and the world seemed in harmony.

He pressed a kiss to her temple as she admired the pink cliffs. "Have I told you today how much I love you?"

Emily leaned into him and teased, "This morning when you made love to me. But I never tire of hearing it, my love."

"I love you, I love you, I love you," he whispered in her ear, making sure his breath tickled just the right spot to make her squirm a little.

Just then a breeze whipped her skirt around his legs and made her shiver. With the sun sinking into the ocean, the temperature sank with it. Max wrapped his arm tightly around his wife's waist, and together they headed back along the pier to the promenade and the shelter of the hotel.

Back at the Waterfront the March family had just arrived, and after the ladies had freshened up and dressed for dinner, they ate in a private dining room overlooking the beach. The evening passed companionably as twilight passed into night. No one cared for the usual ceremony of separating after dinner, so moonlight danced merrily on the waves as they shared dessert and cognac. The only sign of tension was Max's insistence to notify the earl of their arrival before they made any plans for the coming day. To that end he wrote a missive, and had it delivered before he and Emily retired to their suite.

CHAPTER TWENTY-ONE

EMILY SLEPT SOUNDLY TO THE LULLABY OF THE waves and awoke to Max kissing that delicious spot behind her ear. Languidly stretching her neck to give him more access, she pushed her derriere into his morning erection. Emily loved waking up like this, wrapped in her lover's arms, feeling wanted, desired, and loved. Max's hand traveled over her belly to caress her thighs, then between her legs, where tingles were beginning to radiate outward. All the while his member pulsed against her bottom as if asking permission to enter. With a great sigh of contentment, Emily hooked her leg backward over his hip and was immediately rewarded when his fingers slipped through the already slick folds and into her channel to collect more of her nectar to spread all around her sex and especially the little nub that brought her so much pleasure. Next, Emily felt Max's cock enter her from behind and thrust up. She cried out at the sudden invasion but braced herself against the bedpost and pushed back so he could thrust deeper with the next stroke.

Max, delighted with his wife's response, buried himself in her luscious heat to the hilt and savored the feeling for a moment before he set a bracing rhythm while his fingers stroked her stiff little clitoris to bring them both to orgasm. He loved their bouts of early-morning loving. Being with Emily, his wife, was so different from the sexual encounters he had enjoyed at the club. He didn't think they could even be compared. He loved Emily with a fierceness that surprised him and only seemed to increase with every day he spent with her, every night he loved her physically. His very soul was bound to her.

Once their breathing had calmed somewhat, Emily turned to face

Max and wrapped her arms and legs around him in a powerful embrace. "I love you beyond all measure. Fiercely, madly." She ran her nose against his and gently kissed his lips. "Tenderly."

He hummed his pleasure into her hair. "And I love you. Deeply, with everything I am, everything I have."

The soul-deep kiss he bestowed on her thrilled her to her core. This was true happiness; this was home.

They lingered in bed for a while, kissing and caressing each other idly until they could hear breakfast being laid out in the next room. Emily bounded out of bed to use the chamber pot behind the screen while Max washed by the basin. Once he was done, they traded places and a few minutes later they went to eat their breakfast wrapped in their dressing gowns.

The cozy sitting room faced the beach, and their meal had been laid out by the open window so they could enjoy the view. Emily poured coffee for Max, while Max poured tea for her, then he spooned eggs onto her plate from one platter, while she filled his with bacon and mushrooms from another. Their eyes sparkling at the little morning ritual, they settled down to eat, holding hands across the table.

Into this idyll a knock sounded, and Max's man, Menton, entered carrying a small silver server. "This just came for you, sir."

Not one to put off the inevitable, Max took the missive, broke the seal, and read, then handed it to his wife. Emily was struck by how brief it was.

I shall expect you both for tea at four.
Warthon

"He is a man of few words who is accustomed to being obeyed, I take it." She smiled at Max over the coffeepot.

"You don't know how right you are." Max did not return her smile.

He could not shake the feeling something terrible was about to befall them.

AFTER CONFERRING WITH SIR HENRY on their morning walk along the bluffs, and armed with a dinner invitation from the Countess of Weld, who had lost no time welcoming them to Brighton, Max and Emily set off for their tea with the earl. They crossed the drawbridge into the courtyard of Warthon Castle punctually at four o'clock. Emily had opted for the closed carriage due to the ominous thunderclouds on the horizon, and Max couldn't help seeing them as prophetic.

Aware of his apprehension, Emily did her best to lighten the mood. "Oh darling, don't worry so much. Don't you know thunderclouds are a requirement when visiting such a thoroughly Gothic-looking castle?" She craned her neck to look up the facade to the parapet. "Goodness, this is beyond Gothic, it's positively medieval."

"And a complete fraud." Max chuckled, and the sound reassured Emily. "It was built in the late sixteenth century. The interior is entirely Tudor."

"See, it looks a lot scarier than it actually is—just like your grandfather."

They halted outside the imposing carved-stone entrance to the castle. Max knew better than to underestimate his grandfather's capacity for cruelty but hid his worry by jumping down from the carriage. He would just have to shield her from whatever the earl might throw at them. By the time he turned to help her out of the carriage, he had his features firmly under control. She looked like summer personified in an azure-blue gown a shade darker than her eyes, an exquisitely worked shawl of blond lace draped over her arms, and that marvelous straw hat with the blond lace ribbons. But the most alluring thing about her was still her smile. How he loved that smile. So full of love for him and just a hint of mischief.

Max threaded her hand through his arm and led her up the stairs. They could make it through tea, they had done it before.

The ancient rheumy-eyed butler who opened the door to them greeted Max with affection, putting Emily further at ease as she entered this house her husband seemed to loathe so much. When she had met him in London, the earl had not been even half as unpleasant as everyone had made him out to be; it stood to reason his house wasn't all that bad either. The old butler insisted on announcing them, so they progressed at a snail's pace through the oak-paneled foyer, under the carved staircase, and down a gloomy corridor to large oaken double doors, giving Emily plenty of time to look around. The foyer had been nice and airy despite the excessive wood paneling, due to an enormous window taking up most of the upper part of the wall into the courtyard. The Warthon coat of arms rendered in stained glass decorated the window and added red and gold to the flagstones on the floor. Emily liked the entryway, but the corridor was decidedly gloomy.

They stopped outside the carved oak door, and the butler used all his remaining strength to open the heavy portal before he croaked out, "Lord and Lady Didcomb, my lord."

Across the cavernous room, the earl waved them in. "Ah, there they are."

This room did have two windows with pointy Gothic arches, but they did little to dispel the gloom within. Emily could make out two men sitting by the enormous fireplace, but the earl spoke again. "Come on in, children. Weld was just leaving. I hear he is hosting you for dinner."

Max felt an apprehensive prickle at the back of his head. Not in all the twelve years he had lived as the heir in this house did his grandfather call him *child*. "Indeed, Lady Weld sent over an invitation as soon as she heard we had arrived in town. Will you be attending?"

The earl waved the suggestion away. "No, far too much hubbub for me, but I'm sure your wife will enjoy the company."

They had arrived in front of the two earls, and Max bent to kiss his grandfather's cheek. "I hope I find you well, sir."

"My leg is not paining me as much, if that is what you mean."

Emily sank into a respectful curtsy when Warthon turned his attention to her. "I'm glad to hear it, sir. How do you do?"

Warthon gave her his best smile. "Very well, thank you. Now that I'm looking at your lovely face again." And turning to the Earl of Weld, he added, "She really is a beauty, isn't she?"

"A true beauty, from head to toes," Weld agreed.

Emily blushed prettily and thanked both men for their compliments, while her husband fumed silently. He would thank them to keep their covetous eyes off his wife and their licentious thoughts to themselves. He knew how these two treated women. He was glad when a footman brought in the tea tray and Warthon indicated for them to be seated on the sofa facing the fireplace.

While they consumed their tea cakes, Emily remarked, "The country around here is lovely. Do you have a favorite ride to recommend?"

Warthon smiled at her. "So, you ride, then?"

"I like nothing better, except for playing the piano."

Weld nodded. "You should have her play for you some time. She is as good as Ruth Redwick."

Emily blushed. It was so much more meaningful to be complimented on her skill rather than her person; however, she couldn't allow that remark. "No one is as good as Grossmama, but I thank you."

The Earl of Weld rose and smiled down on her. "Well, the countess insisted on the piano being tuned this morning, so I hope you will play for us."

Emily inclined her head graciously. She didn't particularly like the Earl of Weld or the way he looked at her, but he and the countess had tried to get to know her, and Max seemed like a son to them. "It will be my pleasure."

"I look forward to tonight, then." With a satisfied nod, Weld bowed briefly to the men in the room. "Warthon. Didcomb." He turned to let himself out.

"Can't say I know much about music." Warthon cackled, watching his friend leave, then turned to Max. "But you should show her the ride through the south meadows. And there is a charming ride going up further into the hills."

Max nodded. "I was planning on taking Emily along the meadow path tomorrow, but the view across Brighton to the sea from the hills is remarkable. If the weather is good, maybe we will ride up there."

"I'm sure we can find you suitable mounts, just let Sedon know."

Max bowed his thanks. "No need, sir. We brought our riding horses."

"Ah, in that case the ride up into the hills might be too much for your wife, if you are coming all the way from Brighton."

Max had intended to give away as little as possible about his wife but couldn't help himself. He beamed with pride as he answered, "I doubt it. She frequently leaves me behind."

The earl shot Emily a calculating look. "You don't say. So, you really are a horsewoman. Good for you, my girl."

Emily smiled and offered to make him another cup of tea, but he declined and rang to have the tray removed. Once the servant had retreated, he pulled an intricately inlaid wooden box from behind his armchair. A much smaller, dark blue velvet-covered box sat on top, but the earl put it in his lap and set the large box on a table between his chair and the sofa where Emily sat.

"Since you are married to my grandson and heir now, I thought you should have a look at the jewels the Countess of Warthon will be entrusted with." The earl opened the box, and Emily caught her breath. On the very top layer lay a diadem fit for a medieval queen. One large sapphire sat in the center, surrounded by a spray of smaller diamonds gathered in the shape of waves which tapered in size toward the back of the circlet. Smaller sapphires were placed at the center of each wave.

"Goodness, it's beautiful."

The earl watched Emily from underneath hooded eyes, and Max wondered at the purpose of this exhibition. Had Emily truly charmed the old man? Was he truly willing to accept her and the fact she would be wearing the coronet, or was this a ruse? But if it was a ruse, to what end? They were wed, in front of God and high society. Perhaps Emily had the right of it, and he simply needed to trust all would be well.

Warthon explained, "This is the original coronet placed upon the first Countess of Warthon's head on the day her husband was made an earl for his service to his Tudor king." He flicked open a hinge and pulled the box up and out in both directions to reveal seven layers of velvet beds on each side, housing a marvelous collection of jewels.

Emily had peeked into her great-grandmother's jewelry drawer and had admired the even grander jewels her Aunt Hortense wore to official occasions, but this collection rivaled those treasures. There was a necklace, a brooch, and earrings to go with the coronet on the tray immediately below, and a stunning set of emeralds was housed in the corresponding tray on the other side. A string of pearls that seemed even longer than Grossmama's and a pearl choker with a cameo in the middle occupied the next layer, together with matching earrings and bracelets. A marvelous ruby necklace winked from the third tier of the box, and a diamond set with a tiara and several other sets occupied the other compartments. Endless diamond-encrusted brooches and bracelets sat on a velvet bed on the very bottom. It was a treasure to be sure, but Emily found there was too much of it to really see any of it. "It's fortunate there is so little light back here, I might be blinded."

Max chuckled, and the earl barked a laugh. "Not impressed by baubles, eh? Well, I hope you like my present nonetheless."

"Oh?" Emily looked at the earl rather than the treasure. "A present? What for?"

The earl pulled the layers of the box together, hooked the latch, and closed the box before he pulled the small blue box from his lap and handed it to Emily. "The treasure is for the countess, but this is my wedding present to you. They were my wife's, and I thought they would suit you."

Emily reverently took the box. "Thank you, my lord, how thoughtful. I'm honored to receive something that has meaning to your family." She gave him her very best smile and turned to Max, beaming. This had to mean his grandfather accepted her and their marriage. They could relax, Max could stop fretting. Opening the clasp, she held it so he would see the contents too.

And then she looked, and the contents inspired an appreciative, "Oh, *schön*."

On a light blue satin bed rested a truly beautiful pair of diamond and aquamarine earrings. The large, pale blue, rose-cut aquamarine teardrops sparkled in a gold setting and were surrounded by a continuous row of small diamonds. The pendant dangled from a French hook decorated with a gold flower, each petal studded with a diamond, and in between balanced a tiny branch with a diamond-clustered leaf on each side.

Emily took the earrings off their satin bed to admire the perfect balance and ease of movement. What a marvelous sight they would be when they caught the light of a hundred candles in a ballroom. The stones, being of superior color, clarity, and cut, sparkled with an internal fire even in the limited light of the cavernous drawing room. Emily sighed happily, then met the earl's eyes. "These are lovely! Thank you."

Max took one out of her hand and dangled it into the light from the window. "They will look splendid on you." He held it against her ear.

"And they match your outfit today."

"Try them on," Warthon encouraged.

It wasn't in Emily's nature to be coy. She looked around, and spying a mirror above a side table closer to the window, she slid the hooks of her pearl earbobs out of her lobes and handed them to Max. Fitting the earl's splendid gift in their place, she wandered over to the mirror.

Max watched Emily blindly thread the earrings into her lobes as she slowly crossed the room. It was such a feminine, intimate thing to do in the middle of his grandfather's drawing room, he felt the need to shield her from his gaze, so he followed behind her, blocking the earl's view.

Having completed her task, she let her hands fall to her sides and took in the effect of the earrings in the mirror. "My dress is the wrong shade of blue, but they are truly wonderful. Do you think they suit me?"

Max stepped behind her, his hands resting lightly on her shoulders. "I do."

The Earl of Warthon watched his grandson admire his wife in the mirror and congratulated himself on a job well done. The earrings were certainly the best the last countess's private collection had to offer, and the girl wore them well. Sir Henry's daughter was undeniably beautiful and his stupid grandson undeniably in love with her. Ruth Redwick, the Dowager Duchess of Avon, was right about that, but that didn't mean he had to accept this travesty. He had survived losing the love of his life, and so would Max. In fact, it might finally make the man of him he had brought him up to be.

When Emily, Lady Didcomb for the time being, rushed back from admiring herself to thank him, he smiled at her pretty curtsy and accepted her kiss to his cheek, then told them to go and have fun so he could rest his weary bones. He was certain the girl would trust him now. All that remained was to look for signs Max had had his fill of her. And if that failed—well, the earl had ideas.

CHAPTER TWENTY-TWO

THE GIFT HIS GRANDFATHER HAD BESTOWED ON his bride gave Max some peace of mind. Being painfully familiar with his grandfather's tightfisted nature, he thought it highly unlikely he would make such a present had he not accepted their union. He was further encouraged when Sir Henry agreed with him, even though Henry remained concerned his daughter may trust too easily. But since Max had no plans to leave her side or take any unnecessary risks with his wife, there was no need to worry. They would enjoy their summer by the sea, and he would remain alert.

They were all gathered in the Countess of Weld's drawing room, listening to Emily play a Mozart sonata. As her fingers flew over the keys and she swayed with the music, the light from the chandelier overhead caught in the myriad facets of the earrings the earl had given her.

Isabella leaned close to Max. "The aquamarines are stunning, especially with that dark blue organza she's wearing. Do you think they mean your grandfather has accepted her into your family?"

"I certainly hope so. My grandfather is not a generous man, and the jeweler on Main Street assured me the earrings were worth more than the house his premises are located in."

Isabella smiled at the thought of Max checking on the value of the gift to gauge his grandfather's sincerity, but privately worried the costly present could also be seen as a way to buy trust or affection. No matter, they would remain vigilant.

AT THE BACK OF THE room, the Countess of Weld smiled at her

husband. "I suppose Warthon is as smitten with the child as we all are."

"You would be wrong. Now hold your tongue," Weld growled.

The countess looked at her husband in dismay. How anyone could plot to destroy a happiness such as she saw in Max and Emily was beyond her. She grew even more concerned when her husband commanded her to write a somewhat alarming note addressed to Ben, then another to Sir Henry. Neither missive made any sense at all, but Weld placed them both in his breast pocket before he bid her a good night.

THE NEXT DAY DAWNED SUNNY and warm, so the family decided to rent a bathing machine and spend the day on the beach. The Thursday following, Max and Emily had the hotel pack them a picnic and ordered their horses saddled for their excursion up into the downs. It was a marvelous ride through verdant meadows and an oak forest to the top of a hill overlooking the town, the white cliffs to the east, and the ocean beyond. The air was so clear, Emily almost thought she could see the bench on the highest cliff on her father's estate east of Brighton, where they had once admired the sunset. But surely that had to be a fancy. Back then, it had taken more than two hours by carriage to get from Brighton to Charmely. What they could most definitely see from up there, however, was the whole of Brighton with all the Pavilion's exotic turrets and cupolas. Hove was farther along the bluffs, and Warthon Castle, square and gray and gloomy, below them on the right.

They could also see some ruined Gothic arches less than a mile south of the castle. "What's that?" Emily asked, pointing.

"The Abbey," Max answered, his expression somewhat reticent.

"Looks interesting. Can we go there, or will your grandfather mind?"

"No, he doesn't. It's a rather popular destination for walkers. The meadow path leads there anyway, so we can look if you like."

Emily shot him a sharp look. "You don't seem enthused at the prospect."

Drawing her close, Max sighed. "Do you remember me telling you about the secret society my grandfather and I belong to? Well, the abbey is a meeting place for the society, and I'm not proud of some of the things I've done there."

"Ah, your nefarious past." She wrapped her arms around his waist and grinned up at him. "What kind of things?"

"Good Lord, Emily. I can't tell you that, you are my wife." He rubbed the back of his neck.

"Yes, you can. Come on, out with it, what did you do there?"

There was steel in her voice now, and he knew her well enough to know she wouldn't stop until he told her, or she would find out through her father and his sneaky friend. He literally squirmed but relented. "I used to bring girls from the club there and have them do things for the members to watch." He blushed furiously. It really wasn't the kind of thing one should be telling one's wife.

Emily, not taking any of this club nonsense too seriously, laughed. "Goodness, you look like a guilty schoolboy."

"I rather feel like one."

She sobered and tried her best to make him look up. "Max, you promised me you wouldn't do anything with the girls again, and that is good enough for me. Most men have a past, or so Papa and Allen tell me. The only difference here is that I know about yours." Lifting his chin so he would meet her eyes, she continued, "I love you with my eyes open."

He finally looked at her and pulled her into a tight embrace, rocking her from side to side. "You are amazing, Emily Warthon. I hope to never disappoint you, my love."

Emily kissed him then and pulled him down into the grass, where they made love. Later they rode home holding hands across the gap between their horses.

THE ADVENTURES BY THE SEA continued and so did the teatime visits to Warthon Castle, all cordial if not exactly loving. Coming via a different route every time, Emily soon knew how to get to the castle from Brighton and along the sea from Hove. Riding every morning, she discovered each jumpable fence and learned which meadow was being grazed by sheep and which had just been cut for hay. She knew which roads got muddy on rainy days and how long it took to walk to the castle. In short, she was getting to know the area and the earl's land.

Their little group conversed and played and rode during the day and danced in the evenings, and all the while time flew with nothing to cloud their enjoyment. By the first week of July, when Henry and his family had to depart for their annual visit to Isabella's parents, Max felt sufficiently secure in his grandfather's goodwill toward his bride and their union that he decided they should remain in Brighton until after the Knights' anniversary on the seventeenth of the month. It was less than a fortnight away, and Emily was not ready to leave the entertainments of this charming seaside town behind just yet. Besides, London would be miserably hot, not to mention there were still craftsmen working in their house. So, they waved goodbye to her family and remained where they were.

Ben was the only one to voice any concern, but Max explained that with her family out of town, he felt uneasy leaving Emily alone in the capital when he had to come to Warthon for the Knights' gathering. In London she would be unprotected for two days, whereas he had to leave her for only one evening if they stayed in Brighton. In the end, Max asked Ben to spend the evening of the anniversary dinner with Emily to make sure no mischief could possibly befall her. Ben readily agreed, and they planned another picnic out in the meadows. It seemed simply too beautiful a summer for anything to go wrong.

IN THE DAYS BEFORE THE gathering, guests started to arrive at

Warthon Castle, many of them choosing to lodge in Brighton. Max explained to Emily that due to the nature of the anniversary and the strict rules governing the Knights, the castle was off limits to the women associated with the society on this day.

Lady Jane, asked discreetly by Emily during one of their informal lunches, confirmed the restrictive rule. "Good Lord, don't remind me. I tried for years to get them to let me be part of it, but it remains an antiquated club for old men." She clucked her tongue dismissively. "Take my advice, don't waste your time on it."

Emily couldn't quite obey; it was all so very mysterious. But then she met a few of the gentlemen who had taken lodgings in Brighton to attend the dinner and concluded she wasn't missing anything. She straight-out laughed when Max told her Ben, who was not invited either, would dine with her and guard her while he was away. What did Max think could possibly befall her in a respectable hotel in a fashionable English seaside resort? But since she liked Ben a great deal, she had no objections. Emily's only concern was Jane might not want to share her husband for the evening.

Jane, however, reassured her. "Never fear, Emily. When you have been married above three years, an evening alone is a treat."

"Goodness, is that what I have to look forward to?" Emily laughed along with her new friend. Lady Jane was bright, possessed of a cutting tongue, and Emily liked her very much. Nonetheless, Emily refrained from telling Jane she would be counting the seconds till Max was at her side again and couldn't conceive of a time or circumstance when that might change.

MAX KISSED EMILY GOODBYE AROUND seven o'clock, promising to be back well before midnight. "I'm sorry about this evening. I would much rather spend it with you, my love, but I do business with a lot of the new members." He lifted her hand to his mouth and kissed her wedding ring. "I shall miss you."

"I'll miss you too, darling. But Ben will keep me company." She smiled but suddenly felt like if she let go, she might never see him again. It was silly, of course. Trying to dispel the strange feeling, she smoothed the silver-gray velvet lapels of his midnight-blue dinner jacket, then looped her arms around his neck. Emily pulled him down to kiss him deeply, uncaring of Ben in the room. "Hurry back to me."

Hugging her to him, Max breathed her in. "I will." Then, turning to Ben, he took him by the arm and pulled him into the corridor so Emily couldn't hear him. "I'll do my best to come home before the display starts. I'm sure everything will be fine, but I'm glad you are here. Thank you."

"Of course. Go take care of our investors." He thumped Max on the back, then shooed him away.

Max alighted from his carriage in the castle's courtyard half an hour later, noting he was not the first to arrive. A footman admitted him, but no sooner had he stepped into the foyer than the Earl of Weld hailed him from the doorway of a private sitting room to the right. "Didcomb, we have a problem."

Max could hear angry voices and stepped into the room to find his grandfather berating a red-faced young man. "What the hell do you mean you can't handle three women? What in blazes have you and Jennings been doing for the past three months?" Turning accusing eyes on Weld and Max, he continued, "He was supposed to train him!"

"Where is Jennings?" Max asked.

"On his deathbed, apparently," the earl raged.

Weld supplied quietly, "His man says he lost his breakfast this morning and hasn't been able to keep anything down since. He looks as weak as a kitten and was unable to stand when I looked in on him a short time ago."

"Beresford will have to do it by himself, then." Max shrugged.

"I can't," the young man wailed. "I get shy when people look at me and then I go…"

Warthon looked disgusted. "We wasted our time on a limp cock?"

The young lord was miserable. "Only when I'm performing all alone and everyone is looking at me."

Max rolled his eyes. "The girls will help you; they know how to put on a show."

"What if they laugh at me?" Beresford seemed close to tears.

Grabbing Max's hand, the old man rasped, "You will have to help the whelp."

"Absolutely not." Max was shocked his grandfather would even suggest it.

"Don't go all missish on me just because you're married," Warthon thundered. "These are traditions going back to the twelfth century."

"Respectfully, the answer is no, sir."

"There was a time you wanted to be the dungeon master," the old man reminded him bitterly.

"That was a long time ago." Max felt as if he were in a nightmare. He knew he was heading for a cliff but couldn't stop moving toward it. "I informed you and Jennings three months ago I would no longer take part in the displays. I gave Emily my word."

"Oh balderdash, she would never know."

"But I would," Max said quietly. He didn't think anyone had heard him, but young Beresford looked at him pleadingly. So, Max addressed himself to Beresford. "If you are involved in the act with others, you are able to perform, correct?"

The young man nodded, his blond curls settling on his brow, similar in style and color to Max's.

"Have two of the girls pleasure each other and watch them till you are ready."

Beresford brightened. "And I could spank the third, then fuck her."

"There, you see, you just have to get creative." Perhaps they could work this out.

"That will not do, boy," Warthon snarled. "Have you forgotten what we are celebrating with this anniversary?"

Max shrugged, but his eyes were grim. This smacked of a setup. He turned to Weld. "Which room is Jennings in?"

"The green room on the third floor."

Max turned on his heel and went to talk to the dungeon master himself.

MAX FOUND THE MAN IN question heaving over a bucket, halfway falling out of his bed. "What on earth is going on, Jennings?" The room smelled foul.

Jennings groaned and leaned back into the cushions, perspiration beading on his upper lip. He wiped his mouth with a wet cloth before he opened his eyes. "I felt fine this morning, then after breakfast this started." He raised his hand in apology. "I know you don't want to do it anymore, but I can barely stand to take a piss, and Beresford has stage fright."

"So I hear."

"Can't you just have one of the girls give you a suck? It would make the kid feel better. He is good once he gets going."

"I told you I gave my wife my word." More than anything in this world, Max wanted to be true to Emily, to be worthy of her.

"I know, but this is an emergency. This is the only of our ceremonies that requires a display to celebrate. That or a claiming."

Max shook his head. "What about the claiming, the ritual one? Who was chosen to perform it this year? Maybe he could keep Beresford company?"

Jennings pulled a face. "Sinclair."

Max sighed. The lecherous octogenarian was certainly capable of enjoying his "virgin," but having him there for the entire display would be a challenge. Still, it was something to work with.

Jennings started to look deathly pale around his mouth again before he bent forward and retched into the bucket once more. There was no help to be had there. One thing was certain, Max would leave right after dinner to avoid his grandfather's demands.

On the way to the private salon, Max instructed a footman to place a comfortable armchair in the nave of the abbey and sent a missive to Lord Sinclair to tell him he would have the honor of watching the entire display from the altar. When Max reentered the salon, all three men were sitting in brooding silence.

Max addressed his grandfather first. "I will not be taking part in the display. However, Jennings and I have come up with a plan." Rotating toward Beresford, he continued. "Start the display with the virgin sacrifice, so Sinclair will be there with you, and he will be the one to perform first."

Beresford sighed with relief. "That will work. Sinclair never has a problem. Thank you."

Keeping his face neutral, Max turned back to his grandfather, who was exchanging a look with Weld. "Will that do, sir?"

Warthon made a dismissive gesture, displeasure oozing from his every pore. "It will have to." He rose, leaning heavily on his ivory cane. "I best go greet my guests."

CHAPTER TWENTY-THREE

BEN AND EMILY HAD A LOVELY DINNER IN THE public dining room of the hotel, went for a stroll on the beach afterwards to watch the sun sink into the ocean, and finally settled down to port and tea in the sitting room of Max and Emily's suite. The last light was bleeding into night, and Emily was starting to expect Max to walk through the door. But it wasn't Max who knocked a few minutes before ten o'clock; rather, it was a hotel page with a message for Ben. Ben took the missive, wondering why his mother-in-law would write to him here, and broke the Weld seal.

Ben,
Please hurry back, Edgar has taken ill.
Amalia

"How strange. He was peacefully sleeping when I left."

Emily looked at him with concern. "Anything amiss with Edgar?"

Ben handed her the note. "I hope Max gets back soon. He said he would try to leave Warthon as soon as he could after dinner."

"Ben, there really is no need for you to stay with me." She smiled and pressed the missive back into his hand. "I'm perfectly safe and your family needs you."

"I promised Max I would stay with you." Ben was clearly conflicted.

"And you did. Max will be back any minute now, so there is no need to worry about me." Emily wondered, not for the first time, why the two men thought she couldn't be left alone for an evening.

Gratefully nodding, Ben cautioned, "Stay here until Max gets back. I'm sure it's nothing serious, but I do want to check on Edgar."

Emily shooed him out. "Of course you do. Now go."

Sketching her a brief bow, Ben rushed out of the suite. It was hard to think with worry for his child coursing through him. He jumped down the stairs three at the time and ran all the way to his mother-in-law's rented townhouse a few streets over.

The perfectly unruffled butler appeared from the bowels of the house when Ben crashed through the front door and hollered, "Has the doctor been called?"

"Not to my knowledge, sir." The butler gave him a quizzical look, and Ben's heart sank.

"Where is the countess?"

"The countess retired about an hour ago."

Something was most definitely wrong. "Have her maid rouse her. I'm going to check on my son." He ran up the stairs but paused on the landing. "And have my horse saddled."

Ben didn't stop for anything else until he reached the nursery where Edgar was sleeping, completely untroubled by the woes of the world. What the devil was going on? Gently closing the door, Ben marched toward the countess's chambers one floor down. Before he could knock, however, his wife stepped out of their room farther down the corridor and demanded, "What is going on? I heard you ask for a horse?"

"Nothing good, I fear." He briefly pulled Jane to him, in need of reassurance. "I need to talk to your mother." He handed her the missive and knocked on his mother-in-law's door. At Jane's sharp inhale he held her closer. "Edgar is peacefully sleeping."

The Countess of Weld opened the door and frowned at her daughter and son-in-law. "What is the meaning of this? Martha said it was urgent."

Jane handed her the missive. "Why did you send this to Ben at the

Waterfront?"

Lady Weld took one look at the note, blanched, and backed into her sitting room to the closest chair. "Your father and Warthon are up to mischief." She let her hand with the note drop and swallowed hard before meeting Ben's eyes. "He had me write this several weeks ago, and I had hoped it was just one of his cruel jokes." Her lips pinched miserably. "There is more to it, isn't there."

"I'm afraid so. Lady Didcomb is unattended and likely to trust Weld." Ben was already on his way down the corridor.

Jane and the countess could hear his horse being brought around, then the sound of him galloping off in the direction of the Waterfront Hotel. Jane was the first to move. "Watch over Edgar. I'm going to the hotel."

EMILY POURED HERSELF ANOTHER CUP of tea and rang for Suzie. If she was to wait alone for Max's return, she might as well be comfortable. But when the door opened mere moments later, it wasn't Suzie but the Earl of Weld who strode into the room.

"Good evening, my dear."

Emily scrambled to her feet and curtsied. "My lord. What brings you here at this time of night?"

The earl bent over her hand and smiled in a fatherly fashion. "Max asked me to look in on you and see if you would like to join him at Warthon Castle."

"Oh?" Emily felt a frisson of unease—what could hold Max there for so long he would send for her? And why not send a note? But they had spent a lot of time in the company of the Welds these last few weeks, so she had no reason to mistrust the man. "I thought tonight's affair was for gentlemen only?"

The Earl of Weld chuckled. "You are right, of course. But Warthon needs Max longer than your husband had anticipated. The male-only dinner is over, so you are welcome to join him now."

Emily was torn between wanting to go to Max and the feeling something wasn't right. And then she remembered. "My lord, Ben received a message from your wife that Edgar has taken ill. Please don't worry about taking me to the castle, Max will be back soon enough."

Weld shook his head. "You are very considerate, my dear. But there is no need. My wife's messenger found me on the road. The doctor has already arrived and it's nothing but a summer cold." He smiled that fatherly smile again. "Come, get your coat, and I'll take you there."

Ben's father-in-law had never been quite this nice to her before. The man adored Edgar but looked down on Ben, so why would Max trust him to bring her to the castle? Was Max in trouble and Weld was the only messenger available? Emily supposed she would never find out if she didn't go with him. Her decision made, she strode to her bedchamber to get her hooded cloak. It got cold by the sea at night. She briefly wondered what was keeping Suzie but decided against ringing for her again and went with Weld.

THE EARL OF WELD TRAVELED with two outriders holding lamps lighting the way, so they made it to the gates of the estate within half an hour. But from there they turned left toward the chapel rather than to the castle. Realizing their direction, Emily inquired, "Isn't Max at the castle?"

"No, my dear. The festivities have moved on. You are in for a treat: not many get to see where we hold our amusements."

There was something about the man Emily couldn't like, but they were here now, and she was curious. The next moment, the castle came into view, and she forgot all about the odd glint in Weld's eyes. "Oh, how lovely." The whole castle was lit up with hundreds of torches along the high walls and around the parapet.

Weld chuckled his patronizing chuckle again. "Indeed. Warthon certainly made an effort for this year's anniversary. Wait till you see the ruins."

Emily wondered if he meant the abbey, but then the chapel came into view on the other side of the carriage, and it was every bit as magical as the castle. The structure was illuminated from within, all the stained glass glowing in the night. In addition, torches lit the facade and the sides of the small church. They came to a halt in front of it.

"We are going through the chapel. There is a tunnel that leads right to the ruins."

By this time Emily was thoroughly caught up in the adventure of it all and made no objection when the earl helped her out of the carriage and a footman held the main door for them both. They walked through the chapel and to a small portal at the back of the altar. Emily had to duck her head to get through, but on the other side the tunnel was tall enough to allow her to stand and walk upright.

Weld was right behind her and urged her forward to a set of stairs about twenty yards in. "The stairs go through the hill and to the abbey."

The tunnel and stairs were well lit with more torches. They made their way up through the inside of the hill, and all the way Emily's anticipation and unease increased in equal measure. But since Weld was at her back, she could only go forward, so she walked up the packed earth steps until they came to a cobbled chamber roughly double the width of the tunnel, and from there an extremely narrow flagstone staircase wound upward inside a sandstone structure, most likely the abbey. She could hear the strangest noises from above and through the wall to her right. It almost sounded like flesh slapping and grunting. And was that a woman moaning?

She turned wide eyes to Weld and whispered, "What in the world is that?"

The man just grinned and put his hand on her elbow to urge her forward. "You will see in a moment."

Suddenly, everything about this felt wrong.

But her apprehension did not lessen her compulsion to see who made such noises, what elicited such a chorus of male appreciation as she could hear coming from behind a rough wooden door with big, hammered iron hinges at the top of the stairs. However, when she gained the landing and reached out to lift the crude handle, Weld steered her to the left and up another circling staircase. "No, my lady, you will join the earl on his private level."

Was it her imagination or had the *my lady* held a certain amount of mockery? "Where is Lord Didcomb?"

"You will see him in a moment."

Fear snaked its way around Emily's heart, but it was too late to turn around, so she lifted her skirts to continue up the stairs. The strange fleshy noises grew louder as the open door to a mezzanine came into view. This level seemed empty until she stepped closer to the banister. Weld was right behind her. Too close. He was breathing hard, whether from climbing the stairs or excitement, she couldn't tell, but it made her uncomfortable. And then she saw the Earl of Warthon on the other side of the balcony. There was an oval opening ringed by a solid sandstone banister between them. A slow smile full of wicked anticipation spread across Warthon's hard face as she acknowledged him with a curtsy. The genuine amusement in his eyes when he indicated for her to look below chilled her to the bone.

Emily, apprehension throbbing in her chest, stepped closer to the banister and looked over the edge, down into the abbey. The mezzanine below them came into view first, where men bent over the edge to get a better look at the spectacle below, murmuring and grunting and making lewd comments she couldn't quite make out over the droning in her ears.

Far down below, on the floor of the abbey, there was a blond man…

A blond man in a blue jacket and shiny black boots, like Max's.

Good Lord, it had to be Max.

Emily's hand flew to her mouth to stop the gasp as she tried to process what she was seeing.

A naked woman was spread across the altar stone, and another man, a very old man, was noisily pumping himself into her. Her head disappeared right in front of the blond man, Max, her husband. His back was turned to her, his head bowed slightly so she couldn't see his face, but she recognized the distinctive lapels on his jacket. He was pushing his member down the woman's throat, his hips undulating back and forth as he focused on the woman.

Emily couldn't tear her eyes from him, from the disgusting, awful display. From his beautiful, treacherous, beloved form. From the movement in the woman's throat where he was pushing his member, the same member he had made love to her with this very morning. She could feel pieces of herself dying as she watched. And she could feel Warthon's venomous eyes on her. He had planned this. This was his doing, she knew it, but that didn't lessen the pain ripping through her. Max traced his thumb along the woman's throat, and Emily couldn't hold the keening wail of despair in her throat any longer. She shut her eyes to the awful sight as the sound of her own misery filled her head.

For a long moment there was nothing else, then an evil cackle came from the old man opposite Emily. "You didn't know this side of him, did you, girl?"

Her eyes snapped open to face Warthon, hurt coursing through her. It obviously showed, because the earl chuckled.

"Oh."

The patronizing sound made Emily clench her teeth so hard they ached.

Warthon made a dismissive gesture and taunted, "You best get used to it; he will never change."

Emily had the distinct feeling he didn't want her to get used to any-thing. The menace in Warthon's eyes was a clear and present danger.

Below, Emily could hear someone, most likely Max, running out of the church, and she knew she had to get away before he could find a way to stop her. She turned and shoved Weld out of the way to get to the stairs. He grunted and reached out to grab her, but Max's hateful grand-father commanded, "Let her go."

His triumphant laughter followed her as she flew down the stairs and through the tunnel with only one goal in mind: to flee this awful place. To get away from here, from the hate-filled maniac above, from Max, from her love for him, from her hurt, from the pain that seemed to be ripping her apart. From the images burned into her brain.

She ran and ran and ran.

MAX CAME TO GRADUALLY. HIS head felt numb, as if he'd had far too much to drink. What had happened? He opened his eyes to discover he was lying on a sofa in the private salon at the castle, and he was cold. Looking down on himself, he discovered he was missing his coat, waist-coat, and boots.

"Son of a bitch." With the vicious curse on his lips, he shot to his feet and out the door. The clock in the entrance hall showed him it was twenty-three minutes past eleven. Good Lord, more than an hour had passed. More than enough time for treachery.

Max stormed out of the castle, intent on throwing himself on a horse and getting to Emily as fast as he could. There was light in the stable, evidence the guests had not departed yet, but before Max could call for a horse to be saddled, the quiet summer night was rent by such a howl of despair, it stopped the heartbeat in Max's chest.

Emily.

What was the bastard doing to her?

His heart restarted and began to hammer a frantic beat.

The sound had come from the abbey.

The coolness of the night air reminded Max of his missing garments, and comprehension dawned. He had to get to her.

Protect her.

Get her away from this awful place.

He had crossed the drawbridge and was running toward the chapel in his stocking feet before he knew what he was doing.

EMILY RAN OUT OF THE tunnel and through the chapel that had seemed so magical before. She pushed the door open with the full force of her horror, and there she ran into Ben pulling his horse to a stop and jumping out of the saddle.

"Give me your horse." Emily didn't wait for a response, took the reins and swung herself astride into the saddle.

"Don't let her leave!" Max's desperate voice came from behind her. "Emily, please."

Ben grabbed for the halter.

She made the horse dance out of his reach. "Please let me go, Ben. I can't. Please."

Something in her face made him step back, and Emily rode into the night without a backwards glance.

"NO!"

She could hear the despair in Max's voice, but it didn't matter, she couldn't consider him at this moment. All she could think of was to get away.

CHAPTER TWENTY-FOUR

MAX RAN, SLIPPED, AND STUMBLED, WATCHING Emily ride away at a full gallop. What had she seen? What did she think he had done! And why was there no horse anywhere? He came to a stop next to Ben when he saw Emily turn and jump a gate rather than take the road. "Oh God, she's going to break her neck."

"What the hell happened?" Ben's angry voice broke the spell.

"I need a horse, go after her." Max had already turned toward the stables, and Ben ran to catch up. "Whatever she saw, it wasn't me doing it. I have to tell her."

"Let her go. She is in no state to listen to you." Ben turned to a footman to order him to go to the stables and have His Lordship's carriage readied.

"She is in no state to be left on her own," Max was shouting in agitation as the footman overtook them.

"That may be true, so let's follow her in the carriage, and not too close."

Max couldn't believe his ears. "Didn't you just see her jump a gate in the dark?"

"Yes, Max, I saw. And if you follow her on horseback, she will ride faster. Merlin knows every blade of grass around here, so it's safest if you let her go for now."

There was no denying Ben was right, both about his horse and about Emily. Max stopped and bent over, bracing his hands to his knees, suddenly feeling dizzy. "Oh God, Ben. What have I done bringing her here?"

His friend put a steadying hand under Max's elbow and guided him toward the drawbridge. "Let's get you away from here first, then you can tell me what exactly happened." He checked the chapel entrance over his shoulder. "I don't doubt the two earls are on their way to come gloat."

"I knew he was up to something, why didn't I trust my instincts?" Max wailed.

"Come, not here."

"And why were you not with her?"

Ben cringed. "My father-in-law tricked me into leaving. I'm so sorry."

"Probably thought he could drive a wedge between us whilst he was conspiring." Max growled. "The vile cads!"

From the direction of the chapel an evil cackle floated toward them on the breeze. "Good riddance to the hussy. You will thank me soon enough, boy."

Fury like he had never felt before coursed through Max. "You are the bastard, not her. How could you?" he bellowed, not caring that half the Knights bore witness. "You will die alone, and I hope you do it soon." Max felt such rage and hatred toward the despicable excuse for a human being that was his grandfather. He would not speak to him again, that much he knew.

"Not here," Ben urged, applying his considerable strength to pull Max toward his chaise. "Don't play into his game."

"What do you mean, play into his game? You don't even know what he did to Emily, to me. I'll kill the mean old rotter."

"Hush your mouth, Max. Think of your wife."

"I'm thinking of Emily. What do you think I'm thinking of? But yes, we need to go."

They had reached the drawbridge where the path from the chapel merged into the road to the gate. Max's carriage had just rumbled across, and his footman jumped down to open the door.

"To the Waterfront, as fast as you can," Max commanded as he got in.

Ben jumped in and sat across from Max. At least they were away from the evil old man and Ben's dastardly father-in-law. Max could barely draw breath he was so angry at Warthon, and himself. God only knew what Emily was going through.

Would she let him explain?

Would she believe him?

Would she ever be able to forgive him?

EMILY HAD NO IDEA HOW she got to Brighton. She could barely see enough through the torrent of tears to direct her horse to the hotel. Thomas was at the back door, thank God. She slid off the saddle into his arms, and he guided her upstairs to their suite.

"What happened, Miss Emily? My lady?" Thomas asked gently.

"I need to get away from here, Thomas." She couldn't stay here, where Max would come looking for her.

"Suzie, pack my things." She said it to the room as she walked in, but it was Jane who stood from the armchair by the fire.

"What did those stupid old men do?" Jane demanded.

"They broke my heart," Emily whispered as she collapsed on the carpet. She was at the end of her strength but simply could not stay where Max would find her. She couldn't see him, not yet, not tonight. She was grateful when Thomas took charge.

"I'll hire a coach and bring it to the back door. I know a place we can go."

Looking up at her trusted servant and friend, Emily nodded. "As fast as you can. Lord Didcomb will be here soon." Turning toward the bedchamber, she encountered Suzie's worried gaze. "Bring the purse, please, Suzie. And then pack our things. Don't worry about the big trunk, just take what we need."

Suzie nodded and hurried to get the purse. Emily handed the whole heavy pouch to Thomas but held on to his hand. "Make sure His Lordship won't be able to follow us."

Thomas nodded grimly.

"And hurry."

"I'll have it downstairs in twenty minutes."

Suzie was already packing in the other room, so Emily sagged back onto the carpet.

Jane sank to her knees in front of Emily. "Here, drink," she said, handing Emily a glass of brandy.

Taking a sip, Emily let the brandy burn down her throat and took a deep breath. "What will I do?"

Jane shook her head. That was for Emily and Max to figure out. "I have a fair idea what they made Max do. And then they forced you to watch?" When Emily nodded, she continued, "If it hadn't been for Ben and Max, I would have been part of one of these displays myself. My own father would have done that to me."

Emily physically jolted. "Are you saying the woman was forced?" The thought was so abhorrent she ran her hands helplessly over her stomach. She would never have suspected it of Max, but right now she had no idea who he was.

Jane blushed, appalled she had been so dreadfully misunderstood. "No, good Lord, no. Well, I would have been forced, but on any other occasion they bring in professionals." She took both Emily's hands and waited for the younger woman to meet her gaze. "Please know Max only did what he thought he had to do, and I know for a fact he did not plan on doing whatever you saw him do before he left this evening. They forced him into it. Warthon and my father."

Relief pulsed through Emily. At least the man she loved was not a rapist, but still, how could he? After what he had promised her.

Taking a swig of her brandy, Jane growled. "They fooled us all, the vile old brutes."

"Max warned me not to trust Warthon, but I thought he liked me." Emily sobbed helplessly. "I can't face him, Jane. I just can't face Max, not yet. It was awful."

Jane looked like she wanted to cry along with her. She rubbed up and down Emily's arms. "I understand. You need time. Drink your brandy and then help your maid with the packing. I'll go down to the lobby and hold Max off. Send word to me whenever you have arrived where you are going, so I know you are safe and can tell Max as much." She pulled a handkerchief out of her sleeve and dried Emily's tears. "Can you stand? I better get downstairs."

"Thank you," was all Emily could muster. Helping each other stand, the two women embraced, then Jane grabbed her cloak and left.

Energized by the hope she might make it out of Brighton without having to face Max, Emily went to shove the contents of the dressing table into her portmanteau. A short while later, a coach could be heard pulling up outside the back door. She and Suzie grabbed what they could and ran downstairs.

THE CARRIAGE HAD BARELY COME to a halt outside the Waterfront before Max jumped out and ran up the stairs to the foyer, but that was as far as he got. Jane, arms crossed in front of her and with a mighty scowl on her face, blocked his path to the stairs. "You can't go up there right now, she is far too overwrought."

"Out of my way, Jane. You don't know what happened. I need to see her, explain." Max had to stop, a suspicious hitch to his voice. "You don't understand, I love her. I can't lose her."

"That's precisely why you need to leave her be right now." Jane remained firm.

"You saw her? How is she?"

"Hurt beyond measure. And angry. You need to give her time."

"But I need to explain."

Ben came up behind them. It was late and the foyer mostly empty, but Max was in his shirtsleeves, his socks ripped to shreds around his feet, and the desk clerk was listening with interest. Ben opened the door to one of the private salons, and finding it empty, pulled his friend and his wife in there.

"No need to make this whole affair public."

Max looked around as if just noticing where they were. "Thank you. But I need to go see my wife."

Ben studied Jane, who now stood guard by the door, and had the sudden feeling she was hiding something; something that would hurt Max. He came up beside her and linked his arm into hers firmly to draw her away from the door. "Yes, Max. I think the time has come to see how Emily fares."

Jane shook her head wildly at her husband but said nothing. Max threw her a suspicious look, then ran out and up the stairs as fast as he could. Ben and Jane followed, picking up their pace to a run when Max's wail of despair reverberated through the hallway.

"She's gone."

So much for keeping things quiet.

Max knelt on the carpet in the same spot where Emily had collapsed earlier. He was clutching a chemise that must have fallen out of Emily's luggage in her haste to get away. Through the open door into the bedroom the signs of hurried packing were evident. A lovely pink-and-silver evening dress was carelessly thrown over the chaise at the end of the bed, and a single slipper had found its way under the dressing table next to the box containing the priceless aquamarine earrings the earl had given her. Max staggered over and flung the box viciously against the wall. It broke, and the lovely earrings flew in opposite directions, skittering under furniture. "I should have known he would never accept her. Should have known he would never make her such a costly present if it wasn't meant as a payoff."

Ben grabbed Max by the shoulders. "She didn't take them. She didn't take the payoff. I'm sure she knows the earl was behind whatever she saw."

Max let himself be led to a chair in the sitting room and accepted the brandy Jane handed him. "Perhaps it's time you told us what exactly Emily saw. She was beside herself, Max."

Max turned miserable eyes to his childhood friend. "Warthon betrayed us both."

Jane rolled her eyes. "That much is clear. What did Emily see?"

Max growled and locked eyes with Ben.

Ben shrugged. "Just say it. Jane knows more about the Knights than any other woman alive. She has no illusions left to be shattered."

Letting his head drop into his hands, Max spoke in a quiet monotone. "She most likely saw Beresford fuck one of the girls."

All color drained out of Jane's face. "Beresford? But why?"

"He was wearing my jacket, waistcoat, and boots."

"And he resembles you," Jane said miserably.

"I was wondering earlier why he had let his hair grow longer. I was drugged and they took my clothes." Now that Max said it out loud, he wanted to kill his grandfather all over again.

"Good Lord," Jane breathed. "I'm so sorry, Max."

Ben pressed his lips together, intent on getting the rest of the story. "How did this all come about?"

Max raked his fingers through his hair, trying to piece it all together in his own mind. "Jennings took ill, possibly poisoned by my grandfather. And that idiot Beresford has stage fright."

"The hell he does." Ben looked furious now. "Jennings had nothing but good things to say about him when I talked to him before we left London."

Disgust turned Max's stomach. "The stupid weasel. He must have known for a while he was to be Warthon's instrument. They put on a very convincing show to make me take part, but when I refused and told them how to run the display without me, Beresford seemed grateful and Warthon agreed to it. I should have left and returned to Emily right then and there." There was nothing Max could do about it now. Whether he had been in the abbey or not, his wife believed she had seen him doing despicable things to another woman, and now she was gone. He pulled himself off the floor. "I must find her. Who knows what else my monster of a grandfather has planned for her?"

Ben couldn't deny that was a concern. "You and Jane see if any of your servants or the hotel staff know anything. I'll go to the stables and make inquiries there."

Nodding, Max pulled the cord to summon his man. "Yes, please. And, Ben, thank you."

MAX'S MAN WAS ABLE TO tell him that Emily had left attended by her maid and her man Thomas, a fact that gave Max some measure of comfort. At least she wasn't out there in the dark night all by herself. A closer look at their room revealed she had taken all her regular clothing and the purse of money he had placed in his dresser, so she had at least enough funds to get to London. He thought it likely she would go to her father's house. All her evening attire was still there. She had run away from him and taken nothing he had given her. It was utterly depressing.

Jane was the first to return. "She is no longer in Brighton."

"How do you know?" Max was staring out the window unseeing, just barely keeping himself together.

"Emily was seen getting into a coach by the back door mere minutes before you arrived at the front. She is in a traveling coach, and her man was riding her dappled gray. I sent out pages to all the other hostelries in town and she has not checked in anywhere else, I'm certain of it."

For once, Max was glad of Jane's managing ways. It had not occurred to him to check all the other hotels and inns. "Did anyone see in which direction she went?"

"No, I'm hoping Ben will find that out." She put her arm around his waist. "She will come back, Max. She needs time to think, to come to terms with what she saw."

Max leaned into her, accepted her embrace, and sighed. "I don't know. To her mind I did exactly what she was most afraid of. She was adamant she could only marry me if I was ready to be true to her, and as far as she is concerned, I wasn't. She thinks I betrayed her, betrayed her trust, our love."

"Did she know about the club?"

Max only nodded.

"Warthon most likely found out about that and decided to exploit her fear. But Max, she loves you, and one doesn't throw away love like yours because of one incident, no matter how spectacularly bad. She will also realize that it was your grandfather's doing, even if she remains convinced it was you in the abbey. She will realize you are a victim just as much as she is, and eventually she will want answers."

A sob escaped him, and it was such a miserable sound, he could only shake his head. "I wish she were here to berate me. It couldn't be worse than this."

Jane guided him to the sofa and made him sit. "I know you are worried…" She didn't get any further, as her husband entered, and Max lurched toward him.

"Did you find her?"

Ben shook his head. "I'm sorry. All I could find out is that her man hired a coach and four. He must have paid the driver extra, because no one in the stables knew where they were going. They took back streets out of town, but the proprietor of the pub along the North Steyne saw a coach turn into the London Road around the time they would have departed Brighton."

"So, she is going to London?" Max's tone was almost hopeful.

"It looks that way, but maybe that's what they want us to think. She could turn off toward Reading later."

"Oh, for heaven's sake, Ben. What do you mean?"

Ben paused for a moment. He had given this thought while he tore up the town for information. "Max, I know all you can think of is getting to Emily so you can explain to her that it wasn't you she saw. But you can't, and right now you need to let your grandfather think he won. You know he is watching somehow."

Max looked at his friend in open-mouthed astonishment. "I can't find my wife, Ben."

"Yes, and I have been very thorough. We can't find her. But think of it this way: if we can't find her, then Warthon won't either, and as long as he thinks he has won, she is safe. He could do far worse to her if he thought his ploy hadn't worked."

That had occurred to Max too, but he wouldn't allow it to paralyze him and keep him from finding his wife. He couldn't. "So, you think I should simply sit still and wait for her to come back to me? She won't. She thinks I did exactly what I promised her I wouldn't if she married me. As far as she is concerned, I didn't just betray her with another woman, I broke my promise to her. I couldn't have hurt her more if I'd tried." Max sank his head into his hands, spearing his fingers through his already disheveled locks. "I can't bear it, Ben. She is all alone and hurt."

"I know." Ben sat next to his friend and patted his shoulder. "But she is not alone, she has Suzie and Thomas with her, and for now, she is safe."

CHAPTER TWENTY-FIVE

THEY MADE GOOD TIME TO THE TOP OF THE Downs. Turning east from there, they reached Charmely around one o'clock in the morning. Suzie and Thomas half-carried their distraught mistress into the house, where the sleepy but concerned housekeeper, Mrs. Bennett, took over. Knowing Mrs. Bennett had a broad motherly streak, Thomas returned to the coach driver and instructed him to go back to the London Road out of Brighton. He was to continue to London, changing horses regularly. Anyone following from Brighton should think the entire party had driven through the night to get to London. Thomas gave the driver a hurriedly scribbled note to deliver to Cavendish Square before he urged the man to get on the road. He hoped fervently Lord Didcomb would assume Addy had been put up somewhere for the night when he learned she was no longer being ridden alongside the coach.

Having done everything he could think of to afford his mistress the time she so obviously needed to gather herself, Thomas went to rub down her horse and then found himself a bed. Tomorrow he would see what else could be done, but first he would get out of Suzie what His bloody Lordship had done to upset their young mistress so much.

EMILY WOKE TO THE SOUND of the ocean, and for a brief moment couldn't remember the events of the night before. She stretched and reached for Max, and as her fingers skimmed over the cold, untouched linen, the whole living nightmare came flooding back. He had engaged in a sexual act with one of the women he had promised he would never touch again, and he had done so in front of other men. Mortification threatened to overwhelm her as she wondered how many of those men watching had attended their wedding. Did they know Warthon had arranged it all to humiliate her? To drive her away? Had they known of Warthon's plans? Weld must have, but for how long? The duplicitous knave.

Pummeling her pillow, Emily shrieked with helpless rage. How could she have walked right into their trap? Why had she not seen the signs of Warthon's treachery? Surely there had been signs. But Jane had said Max had not planned on this, so perhaps he hadn't seen the signs either. He had been suspicious, though; that was why he had asked Ben to stay with her.

But then, why, oh why had he done what she saw him do?

She didn't even have a word for what he and the other man had done; it had looked so depraved to share a woman like that.

Then she dissolved into pitiful tears once again, because Max had betrayed her. And if she had not seen him, then she would not know, but he would still have betrayed her and she simply didn't know what would be worse: to know, or to carry on in ignorance. It would have rotted their love from the inside because he would still have known, and that would surely affect him over time.

Warthon was beyond the pale. A rare bastard, her father would call him. How she wanted Papa at this moment. But if she went to Papa, he would make decisions for her. He would most likely raise heaven and hell to annul her marriage, and she had a sneaking suspicion that was exactly what Warthon wanted. And if that had been the aim, she would be damned if she played into Warthon's hands.

She had to think.

And she did her best thinking on horseback.

After ringing for Suzie, Emily opened the portmanteau holding her dresses and pulled out her dark blue riding habit. In their haste they probably left the matching hat behind, but she preferred to ride without one anyway.

"Good morning, my lady." Suzie entered, bearing a tray with hot chocolate, by the smell of it.

"Help me into my habit, Suz."

Encouraged by the fact Emily was up and no longer crying, Suzie put the tray down and came to help her mistress. Riding stays were laced, stockings pulled on, and buttons done up before they realized Emily only had the shoes she had arrived in. In the clothes press, Suzie found an old pair of riding boots which miraculously still fit, coaxing an almost-smile from Emily. But when Suzie poured her a cup of chocolate, Emily waved it away. "You have it, I'll have something when I get back."

Emily walked out of the room and headed down the stairs, but not even the prospect of a ride could bring forth her usual enthusiasm. It was as if all joy had been drained out of her, as if she were sleepwalking through the day.

Suzie, meanwhile, stepped to the window, the cup still in her hand, and watched her mistress walk across the stable yard below. She heaved a great sigh and addressed herself to the cup in her hand. "I could kill His bloody Lordship."

THOMAS HELPED HIS MISTRESS INTO the saddle and tightened the belt. "I wish you would let me come with you, my lady."

"There is no need, Thomas. I'll not stray from my father's land." Emily watched Thomas double-check every buckle on Addy's tack, obviously nervous to let her go alone. He had been her friend since she was twelve years old, and she needed her friends to make it through this mess. She reached down to touch his shoulder. "Thomas, I'm in trouble and I need to think."

Thomas smiled up ruefully. "And you think best on Addy."

Emily didn't quite manage to smile back, but she nodded. "Yes."

Stepping back, he bowed and watched Emily ride out onto the path parallel to the cliffs. As long as she stayed on Addy's back, he told himself, she wasn't likely to throw herself over said cliffs. She loved that horse too much.

THOMAS FOUND SUZIE IN THE kitchen, sharing the leftover chocolate with Mrs. Bennett. Knowing he loved the bittersweet delicacy, Suzie handed him her cup. "She didn't even want her hot chocolate."

"I know, she's in a terrible state. Do you know what happened?"

"I suspect the old earl, and that Lord Weld. It was his burly brute who waylaid me with endless questions in the kitchen last night, and by the time I got up to the suite she was gone."

Thomas nodded. "I figured it would be something like that, you would have been with her otherwise. Something is off about this whole thing. Do you know what Lord Didcomb did?"

"That's what I would like to know," Mrs. Bennett chimed in. "The poor mite doesn't look like herself at all. She is a newlywed; she should be happy."

Suzie and Thomas sighed simultaneously. "They are."

"Deliriously happy."

"At least they were until last night," Suzie clarified. "Before Lord Didcomb left, they embraced, and he promised her he would be back from his dinner up at the castle before midnight. Mr. Sedon was to stay with her, and he took her down to dinner. It was a bit odd that His Lordship had asked his friend to stay with her. Do you think he suspected treachery?"

"Or he knew he was about to do something bad and wanted to keep it from her," Thomas speculated darkly.

"No, I don't think so. I was there when Mrs. Sedon came. She was worried her father and the Earl of Warthon were doing something to them both."

Thomas finished the last of the chocolate and set down the cup by the sink. "She would know. Mr. Sedon's man told me how hard it was for them with her father when they first got married." He scratched the back of his neck; he wasn't a gossip normally. "Did Miss Emily say anything about what happened?"

"Her Ladyship," Suzie corrected pointedly. "She was really upset and kept saying she had to get away before he came home—talking about Lord Didcomb. Then later in the carriage she sobbed that he had broken his promise not to do anything with those women again." Pointing at Thomas with a sudden intake of breath, Suzie continued, "Do you remember that day we took her to Mr. Strathem to find out more about that club His Lordship owns? I bet it has something to do with that, and the old earl set one of those girls on Lord Didcomb and made sure our poor lady saw. Do you think we should send for Mr. Strathem?"

"Suzie, that's brilliant. But I think she might want Eliza Strathem. I'll send a note to them." Then, turning to Mrs. Bennett, Thomas inquired, "When are you sending supplies up to London next?"

"I have cheese, honey, and elder wine to send up with the summer hay. It's not due yet, and I was going to preserve pears first, but we can send the cart tomorrow if you don't want to use the normal post."

Thomas rubbed his thumb over the cleft in his chin. "The post will be faster. Can we send one of the boys to ride to the next posting inn along the London Road this afternoon? I want to avoid running into Lord Didcomb."

"Yeah, don't want him knowing where she is till she's ready to see him," Suzie added, glad there was someone they could ask for help without going to Sir Henry. She felt sure her mistress would have gone straight to her father if she wanted him involved.

WHILE HER SERVANTS COMPOSED A letter to the Strathems

in Chelsea, Emily urged Addy into a gallop along the cliffs to clear her head. Ever since she had seen the look on Warthon's face and then Max down below, she had felt as if her breath had remained stuck in her lungs, and her blood glugged along her veins half frozen. No wonder her brain was unable to think clearly. She loved Max, her tattered heart beat for him, but right now she needed to function without him. She had a notion both their lives depended on it. The gallop made her breathe more deeply and warmed her blood until her body felt more like her own. By the time she got to the overlook where the steep cliffs abruptly descended toward Brighton, she felt more able to gather her thoughts.

Emily reined in her mare and studied the town below. Seven deliriously happy weeks had passed since her wedding, but that one spectacularly bad night threatened to destroy it all. Her love, her marriage, her future, it all depended on what she did next. All depended on her ability to think herself out of this mess, to look beyond her hurt. But the hurt racked across her with angry claws as it reached inside and squeezed the breath out of her once again. This time, however, she didn't allow herself to fall into it.

Emily slid off Addy, secured the reins to the saddle so the horse wouldn't get tangled in them while she nibbled at the short grass, and stepped closer to the edge of the cliff where the trail ended. It was a magnificent overlook. Her eyes traveled across the landscape to where Warthon Castle was nestled into the hills in the distance. By now Warthon would know she had left. Was he congratulating himself on the success of his scheme? Had it been his aim to drive her away? Or had he hoped to cow her by letting her see the power he had over Max? No, that wasn't it. He had no need for such a demonstration; she was no threat to him. No, when she had fled in horror, she had heard his cackle, had seen the gloating eyes just before she had turned to run. He had enjoyed her pain. She had done exactly what he had wanted, and he expected her to keep running to her father.

It suddenly became clear to Emily: the Earl of Warthon wanted the hurt to reach Papa. He was the ultimate target. Inflicting pain on Max and Emily was just the weapon he used to get to Sir Henry. Papa had warned her. Max had warned her. But neither could have saved her from the cunning old man. He had never had any thought of accepting her. Grossmama's letter had only served to make it clear to him he couldn't stop the wedding, so he had come up with a plan to hurt her and Papa another way. Even when Warthon had shown her the countess's jewels, he had looked at Max when he had talked about wearing the coronet. He had meant Max, not her. Max was the one to wear the coronet. Stupid child she was, she had seen and heard only what she wanted to. Warthon intended the jewels in that box to go to another woman, not her. She would never be countess if he had anything to do with it. He expected her to run to her father and for Papa to protect her by annulling the marriage. But there could be no annulment if she couldn't be found. And no, she couldn't go to Papa. Not yet at least. She refused to do what Warthon wanted her to do.

Lady Jane had helped her to get away, and now that Emily looked at it in the clear light of day, it was entirely possible Jane's father would have foreseen her actions. Jane thought to spare them further devious interference from the old men, but she had inadvertently kept Max from explaining himself to Emily. Max had come after her at the abbey, had been desperate for her to listen, but she had been in a deluge of pain, betrayal, and unfathomable hurt. She had not been able to hear what Max had to say, not then.

With her legs somewhat unstable, Emily sank down into a cross-legged sitting position. She still believed that Max desired her, that he loved her and didn't want any other woman. Last night in the abbey his body had not looked enraptured like he did when they made love. His shoulders had been tense; his movements had had none of his usual languid grace. Something had happened to make him do what he did. Warthon had somehow bullied or tricked him.

Max had been truly wretched when he came after her. That had been despair in his voice. It hadn't been the guilty bleating of someone who had been caught; she had heard anguish. It had echoed so perfectly the way she felt. He loved her, there was no possibility she was wrong about that. But it was clear now Warthon wanted her gone, so perhaps it was for the best she had not gone back to hear Max out. For now, she needed to stay hidden. Warthon was ruthless and vile—who knew what he might do to her, or Max, to remove her permanently from his grandson's life.

Did that mean she wanted to go back to Max? Could she? Could she ever trust him again? Did she want to allow the part of him that had been in another woman's mouth back into her body? Probably not. At least not for as long as Max was willing to engage with his grandfather. Good Lord, the image of it was seared into her mind's eye, could never be unseen. But was it fair to make him choose between her and his grandfather? And would that guard against Warthon's interference? Not likely, given the length to which the earl had gone to get rid of her. What a mess! What a damnable mess.

And then the hurt of Max's betrayal curled around her again. Could she forgive him? That was a much harder question and one she couldn't answer yet. It might depend on his answers to her questions, but those she could not ask without seeing him. And the best she could do for them both for now was to remain where she was and let the earl think he had won.

She was crying again. Being separated from Max felt wrong, like a nightmare she was desperate to wake from, but at the same time afraid of waking from, because this pain in her heart might be the last connection she had to Max. Her love, her heart, her marriage might not be repairable.

Addy moved closer to cover Emily's hair and face in horsey kisses until Emily stood so she could hug her. "I know, Addy, you still love me, and you always will. But you know he is my everything. Being without him is like living without my heart." Another torrent of tears streamed down Emily's face, running into the horse's fur, mixing with the sweat on Addy's shoulder. Emily took strength from Addy as she looked back to Brighton, wondering if Max was still down there or if he had followed the breadcrumbs Thomas had laid back to London. She hoped fervently Max hadn't gone back to the castle. What would she do if Warthon still held power over him even after what he had done to her, to them?

"Enough, Emily," she admonished herself. "He loves you and he went searching for you. All you have to do is be careful not to be discovered, stay out of the earl's way, and make some inquiries." Resolutely wiping the tears off her face, she took the reins, circled Addy around the hillside so she stood a good foot higher than the horse, and swung herself back into the saddle. "You are the daughter of a decorated spy to the crown; this old cretin cannot scare you off."

She felt a little lighter when she rode into the stable yard an hour later. Her head and her heart were still in a jumble, but at least she could breathe again. Warthon, not Max, had done this to them, and that meant there was hope for them.

CHAPTER TWENTY-SIX

THEY WERE ON A MAD DASH TO LONDON. IT AP-
peared once Emily had left Brighton, neither she nor her man Thomas
had bothered to conceal where the coach was going. Almost every inn
from Brighton to London reported a sighting of her coach last night.
However, it did not become evident why they had not tried to conceal
their destination until Max stood in the foyer of her father's house on
Cavendish Square.

"My wife arrived here this morning with her maid and footman. I
need to see her." Max was trying to step around the housekeeper to get to
the music room, Emily's favorite place in the house.

"Miss Em...Lady Didcomb is not here, sir." Mrs. Tibbit tried her
best not to wring her hands. "And I haven't seen Thomas or Suzie since
they left this house with you on your wedding day."

Max could well see the old family retainer was less than pleased with
him. Emily's safety and happiness was his responsibility, and she evidently knew something of how miserably he had failed on that score. "But the
coach drove all the way to London and was seen turning into the square."
He was no longer trying to get past the woman.

"A coach did arrive here this morning, but Her Ladyship wasn't in it."

"Where did the driver go?"

"I wouldn't know, sir."

It felt like his last tether to Emily had been cut and the sheer enormi-
ty of what had happened the night before was about to overwhelm Max.
The whole foyer seemed to tilt and sway before his eyes, the black and
white checkerboard tiles of the floor coming closer. Someone, probably

Ben, grabbed his arm and led him to the stairs, where he lowered himself onto the third step, holding tight to the banister.

"Stay there, I'll get you some water," Ben commanded.

The strong hand under Max's arm disappeared, and Mrs. Tibbit's worried face swam into view. "The coachman just stopped to bring this." She pulled a folded but unsealed piece of paper out of her apron pocket and placed it into Max's slack hand.

Trying his best to focus, he opened the short letter. Thomas must have written it; the hand was unfamiliar and masculine.

Dear Mrs. Tibbit,

Something happened this night and our Lady Didcomb has need of privacy, away from everyone. She is safe and both Suzie and I are with her, so no one needs to worry about her. I sent the coach to London to make sure no one would follow us. Please do not be alarmed and give my regards to Sir Henry. I will write again should we need anything.

Kind regards,

Thomas

"Our Thomas is a capable lad, and Suzie is devoted to her mistress," the housekeeper said kindly.

"I know they are." Max handed the missive back to her. "But I need to explain something to her. Beg her forgiveness." What on earth was he going to do now? "Do you know where Sir Henry is?"

"He went to his estate in Norfolk."

Max dreaded telling his father-in-law what had happened, but at the same time he longed for his counsel. "When do you expect him back?"

"Not till Thursday next week. He is going from Norfolk back to Gloucestershire, where Lady March has taken the children on a visit with her family."

Good Lord, he couldn't wait that long. If he couldn't find his wife to make things right, he needed someone he could trust to help him confront his grandfather. Perhaps it would be best to make sure this could never happen again before he talked to Emily. But confronting his grandfather was something he couldn't do alone. The old man still held too much power over him, damn him. "Do you have their direction?"

Mrs. Tibbit almost sighed with relief to be able to do something for the poor miserable young man. "Sure do. Baron Chancellor's estate near Bilbury. But Sir Henry won't be there for a while yet. He never stays more than one night with my lady's family."

Taking the glass of water Ben placed in his hand, Max drank the whole in one gulp. Mayhap he should have thought to drink something before now. "So, he won't be there till Tuesday." She nodded and he handed the empty glass to her. "Thank you, Mrs. Tibbit."

Turning to Ben with a weary nod, Max admitted, "I feel better for the water. And knowing Emily is at least safe." He took his friend's outstretched hand and let Ben help him to his feet. "I'll go to Bilbury on Monday. I need to talk to Sir Henry. He needs to know what happened, and he might know where Emily is."

"That makes sense. You would miss him in Norfolk. It's Friday and Sir Henry will probably set out for Gloucestershire on Sunday." Ben regarded Max for a moment before he inquired, "I need to go back to Brighton to keep an eye on the two earls in case they plan something else, correct?"

"Please, yes. I must see to things here, and the devil only knows what those two will do next." Max was suddenly utterly exhausted and so very glad his friend was by his side. "Let's stay at Burton Street tonight. I don't think I can face the other house just yet."

It wasn't very far to the Burton Street Mews, but tired and despondent as they were, it felt like an age. When they were finally in Max's study, surrounded by models of ships and locomotives and all they had built over the past six years, Ben turned to Max. "I'm so sorry I stopped you from going after her at the chapel. I never thought you wouldn't get a chance to explain."

Meeting his eyes, Max sat heavily into his favorite Queen Anne chair. "No, Ben, you were right. Her safety must come first, then as well as now. If I had succeeded in stopping and explaining myself to her, my grandfather would be plotting worse right now. But I so hate that she is hurting." Pressing his fist to his mouth, his eyes bleak, Max explained, "The things she must have seen, Ben. It was far too easy for my grandfather to manipulate me into thinking I was the paranoid one. I should have left the moment he tried to involve me in the display. I knew it was a trap, and still I stayed, in deference to Warthon and the Knights' traditions. No, Ben, I need to confront the old bastard and distance myself from him and the Knights so they can never again come between me and Emily, can never again be used to hurt her. This hold he has on me needs to be broken so I can be true to her."

Max's eyes brimmed with emotion. "I love Emily. And it's a miracle I can love after the schooling I got from the earl. Love is stronger than his whips, and I'm so very glad it is, but I must be worthy before I seek her understanding and forgiveness."

Fully aware of how monumental this break from the Knights would be for his friend, Ben filled two crystal tumblers with brandy and handed one to Max. "I'm so glad you see that now. Love is more important than anything, worth anything. Besides, you don't need the Knights." He gestured to the room around them. "You built all this without their help, without your grandfather's help. In fact, without his knowledge. You built this company despite the old men and their antiquated ideas." And silently Ben acknowledged this utter disaster may just be the making of his friend. Emily was the making of him. She was strong and wild enough to hold his interest for a lifetime. Ben raised his glass in a silent toast and

Max answered in kind.

"I wish I could have understood this without Emily getting hurt." A sad smile curved Max's lips. "She is my heart, my love, my everything, and I might never see her again. And still, I can't regret loving her."

BEN LEFT FOR BRIGHTON EARLY in the morning, and Max felt the loss of his company keenly. Lingering over his morning coffee in what had been his bachelor residence, he allowed himself a few minutes to indulge his anxieties. What if he couldn't extricate himself from the Knights? What if Sir Henry refused to help him after Max had hurt his daughter? What if his grandfather laughed at his decision, belittled him like he always did, demanded he bow to tradition and history? What if that still mattered to Max?

Enough of the fretting. He wasn't a cowed twelve-year-old any longer, and his grandfather was nowhere near as large or frightening. He stood and crossed the narrow hallway to his office. Knowing the twenty-two members of his London club who had been present at the Knights' dinner would be arriving back in town in the next two days, he sent out requests to attend a meeting in the club on Sunday. Max vowed it would be his last time in that house and hoped one of the men at the meeting would take on ownership of the club, dependent on the approval of the women who worked and lived there.

No one had ever left the Knights, at least no one in living memory, so Max supposed the only thing he could do was inform his grandfather he would not be attending any more of their meetings. He also hoped he wouldn't be confronting the earl by himself. It was good to have a plan, but much was uncertain.

What was not in question was his need to go home, the home he had started to make with Emily. Not only did he need to pack for his trip to the West Country, but it was also, he felt sure, the place Emily would send word once she was ready to see him. How he hoped she would allow him to see her, to explain, to apologize, to love her.

Max called for Caesar and headed to York Terrace, thinking of the day he had found the house and then gone to the dowager duchess to help him find the right piano for Emily. Circling to the back of the terrace, the first time he had shown Emily the house came flooding back. He remembered her excitement over the new stables and being able to ride straight into the park as if they lived in the country. Max recalled her amazement at the bathtub in her dressing room, and the flush of pleasure on her face the day she had consulted Lady March about decorating the drawing room. Dismounting by the back gate, he led Caesar through the tall barn doors into the cool shade of the stable. He waved away the groom, took the saddle off, and divested the horse of his bridle.

"You will be missing Addy too, won't you?"

The big stallion rubbed his forehead on Max's shoulder and followed his master to his stall. Max filled his box with fresh hay and bolted the lower part of the Dutch door. Caesar rumbled a nicker at him before devoting himself to his hay, so Max stepped into Addy's stall and caught his breath. It was as if Emily had just been here. He could hear her delighted laugh as she had spun on the spot in this space and declared it perfect for Addy. For some reason he could smell her scent—tuberose and something earthier. It was so dear and unexpected, his emotions welled. He closed his eyes to hold back the tears and hold on to the sense of her presence as he leaned against the wall, letting himself slide to the floor. Rubbing the part of his chest that hurt more than he ever thought it could, he prayed they would find each other again. And then he remembered what she had said that first day. She had said if they were ever parted, this would be where he could find her, and it gave him a measure of comfort that he could feel her presence in this room he had built for her mare.

He imagined Emily on Addy and knew he should have stopped his journey to London the moment the innkeepers no longer reported the dappled gray pureblood. She was nowhere near London, but that didn't tell him anything new, brought him no closer to finding her. It only confirmed she had been determined to get away from him. But she had Addy with her, and that had to be a comfort to her. Max stayed in Addy's stall for a while longer before he braved the house, which would surely reverberate with her voice. Eventually he would have to go to their bedchamber. Would the sheets still smell of her? He shook his head at such a fancy; of course the sheets would have been laundered.

As MAX ROAMED THROUGH THEIR house, finding corners where he could still catch an echo of his wife's scent, Emily ambled aimlessly through Charmely, trying to avoid lunch. Mrs. Bennett had literally stood over her during breakfast to make sure she dunked her strips of toast into her soft-boiled egg and ate them. The housekeeper was a dear woman, but Emily couldn't go through that again. She had spent the morning repeatedly, incessantly playing the first movement of Beethoven's Sonata no. 8 in C Minor. An exercise in frustration and futility, trapping her in her own world of sound. Without Max the emotionality of the piece was ugly rather than passionate and left her feeling as if she were wandering directionless in a barren landscape. So, at the sound of the lunch gong, she stabbed a variation of discordant hideousness into the ivory keys and left the piano vibrating in protest.

Never in all her life had Emily felt so emotionally drained, so devoid of all joy, so utterly despondent. Not even music could lift her spirit. Her true love had betrayed her. The world looked gray and food tasted like ash. She missed Max so much her whole body ached with it, but no matter, she had to carry on.

Emily stepped outside so she at least wouldn't have to smell the pea soup and fresh baked bread. Mrs. Bennett meant well, but Emily couldn't, she just couldn't. The image of Max with his member in the faceless woman's mouth, her breasts bouncing with the other man's thrusts; Emily couldn't put that memory aside. And all the men who knew he had done it! Warthon had been most thorough in his zeal to destroy them. And still she had to try to find a way back to Max, because she loved him, and she couldn't let the old bastard win.

Taking a deep breath to calm her fractured breathing, Emily squeezed her eyes shut in an attempt to banish the scene haunting her. It was useless; that night was firmly lodged in her brain, but at least the sea smelled briny and fresh and raw.

The flower meadow in front of the house had been recently harvested. Only a few poppies spread coquelicot cheer along the low stone wall separating the meadow from the sheep grazing between the farmable land and the cliffs. Her feet as heavy as her soul, Emily directed her steps to those precious specks of color in the otherwise gray day. It was unlikely the sun would break through the clouds and fog, and the moisture was making the air clammy and uncomfortable. At least the day suited her mood, but it did nothing to stop the questions swirling in her troubled mind. How could one human being make her so miserable when there were millions of them on this earth? It seemed to her only one of them mattered, and she had failed to matter equally to him. It always came back to that. Why had he not cared enough for her to say no? Would she ever matter more than the earl and that stupid fusty society with its barbaric rituals?

She knelt next to the wall and addressed herself to the cheerfully nodding poppies. "What should I do? You seem peaceful and happy with your lot, what is your secret?" The poppies kept nodding at each other in the sea breeze. "You talk to each other? Well yes, I suppose that is good advice. But how can I talk to him when I'm all at sixes and sevens? I'm so torn. How can I tell him how I feel when I'm still so very upset with him?"

Angrily wiping the new tears from her face, Emily thought a letter might be a good idea. "At least that way I won't fall into his arms before I have a chance to tell him all the things he needs to know. If I do that nothing will change. But how can I get a letter to him? The earl most likely has him watched. Oh, why does that man have such power over him?"

But that was a question for another time. Right now she needed to find a way to communicate with Max that wouldn't give away where she was. And then she remembered the day Max had shown her the new stable he had built for her. She had told him he would be able to find her in Addy's stall, should ever they be separated. Maybe Thomas could sneak into the stable and leave a letter for Max there, once she had made up her mind what to say to him. Oh, but what to say and how?

CHAPTER TWENTY-SEVEN

EMILY CRUMPLED UP ANOTHER ATTEMPT AT committing her feelings to paper, adding one more crushed ball to the collection covering her father's study floor. Writing this letter was an impossible task. It was Saturday, and after a thunderstorm the night before, the weather had cleared, but the storm inside her continued to rage. Whenever she managed to collect her thoughts enough to form an intelligible sentence, those awful images came flooding back, and then it all seemed pointless and hopeless. She thought she had worked it all out, but she simply didn't know what had happened that night, what had made Max do what he did. There was even a part of her that hoped it hadn't been Max, against the evidence of her own eyes. She suspected it had all been orchestrated by the earl to drive her away, but could he really have fooled her like that? And what if Max had always planned to do those things and the earl had only taken advantage of Max's proclivities? And what if Ben had been with her so Max could blithely do those things without her finding out? She didn't really believe that, but what if it was the truth and she was blinded by her love for Max?

In all this confusion, the clip-clop of horses and the sound of carriage wheels coming down the drive reached her ears. Emily fervently hoped her faithful servants hadn't summoned her father. She wanted to run into his arms and have him fix her problems, make her feel loved and safe, and call her "poppet." But she was not ready for his "I told you so." And she certainly didn't want to have to defend Max to him, which she would have to do if it was Papa rattling into the stable yard.

However, there was no use in sticking her head in the sand. If it was her father, she might as well enjoy the shelter of his arms before she had to explain everything to him. Emily picked her way through the letter graveyard on the floor and tucked a stray strand of hair behind her ear on the way to the back door. But when she stepped out into the sunny stable yard, it wasn't her father but Allen and Eliza who rushed toward her, enfolding her in their loving arms.

"Darling, we were so worried about you," Eliza cried, squeezing her tight.

"We came as soon as we heard, sweet pea," Allen added.

Emily collapsed into their arms, dissolving into tears once again. "Eliza, Uncle Allen, I'm so very happy to see you both." She hiccupped. "But how did you hear?"

Allen grinned down at her tear-streaked face. "Thomas thought you in need of a knight in shining armor to help you slay dragons, so here I am, reporting for duty, my sword-arm ready."

"I'm so glad you are here." Emily attempted to smile through her tears. "Oh, but it's all so confusing, I don't even know which dragon to slay." Emily allowed herself to be held for a spell before she stepped back, aware they were in the stable yard with the coach driver looking on, and an unfamiliar woman standing next to the carriage. Emily hid her face in Allen's lapel. "Did she come with you?"

"She did." Allen indicated the woman. "This is Marie. Marie, this is Lady Didcomb."

The woman curtsied deeply. "My lady."

"Why don't you find the kitchen, Marie," Allen suggested. "We will call you when we are ready."

The young woman nodded without looking up, and Emily concluded she was a servant.

Smiling, Allen took Emily's elbow, and helped Eliza up the steps with his other hand. "We come with news. But let's get Eliza to a sofa first and ring for tea and toast." He indicated Eliza with his head. "Carriage rides are not her favorite activity at the moment."

Forgetting her own situation for the first time in three days, Emily gasped. "Oh, my goodness, how could I forget? And you came all this way to help me. How are you feeling? How is the babe?" She was holding Eliza's hands now, urging her into the house.

"The babe is just a tadpole for now, and I'm well, just tired." Eliza smiled gently, rubbing her almost imperceptibly rounded abdomen.

Mrs. Bennett came rushing toward them in the hallway, so Emily turned to her. "Mrs. Bennett, I think you know Mr. Strathem, and this is his wife. She is in a delicate condition and needs to rest. Also, we need tea and cakes and sandwiches."

Eliza shook her head vigorously. "No, no cakes and such for me. Just toast, please, and dry. Everything seems to make me bilious at present," she added with an apologetic smile.

"But I would love a sandwich, or perhaps a hunk of your most excellent cheddar, Mrs. Bennett," Allen chimed in.

"Of course, Mr. and Mrs. Strathem." Mrs. Bennett indicated the open door down the hall. "You just settle in the drawing room, and I'll bring tea, and by the time you've had something to eat I'll have your rooms ready for you." With that the stalwart housekeeper disappeared in the direction of the kitchen, leaving it to Emily to lead her friends to the drawing room.

Eliza settled on the sofa in the light-filled room overlooking the cliffs and the ocean beyond, letting out an appreciative sigh. "I'm so glad we are here at last. The jostling was really getting to me." Allen urged her to put her feet up and moved chairs for Emily and himself so they could all sit close together before he closed the door.

Emily could no longer contain her curiosity. "You said you had news?"

It was Eliza who answered. "Indeed, we do, darling. But maybe we should wait for the tea tray. The information is rather sensitive, and you might not want the servants to hear. From Thomas's letter we assume you haven't told him what happened."

Emily's face crumpled as she realized she had not told anyone what she had seen. In three long days she had not been able to unsee the image, and in all this time she had not unburdened herself. No wonder she had felt so desperately lonely. Thank the heavens her friends were here.

Emily was glad when Mrs. Bennett bustled into the room with the tea tray just then, and as soon as she closed the drawing room door behind herself, Emily turned to her friend. "Oh, Eliza, it was horrible."

Emily collapsed into the chair closest to Eliza. "Max had to attend a dinner for the Knights at the castle. Women were not allowed, so Ben Sedon stayed with me. You see, Max was worried, and I thought he was being silly. And now I don't know if he planned to do that thing all along and just didn't want me to see." She shook her head as if to clear it. "The earl had been kind to us all summer, even Papa thought the danger had passed, so I thought all was well." It was difficult to get the words out past her constricting throat. "In any case, it was getting close to the time Max had said he would be back, and I was starting to truly miss him." A blush tinted her pale cheeks, but Eliza clasping her hand encouraged her to continue. "An urgent note from the Countess of Weld was delivered saying that Edgar was ill, so I encouraged Ben to go. But I think it was Lord Weld who tricked Ben. Weld came shortly after Ben had left and told me Max wanted me to come to the castle. Only he took me to the ruined abbey by Warthon Castle, and Max…" Her voice broke and Allen handed her a handkerchief.

In barely a whisper, she continued. "We went through a tunnel and then up endless stairs. I heard the noises long before I got to the gallery overlooking the altar." She swallowed convulsively at the memory. "Oh God, the men who watched it all. They were on a mezzanine below where

Weld had led me. And there were two other women, far below where…" Max did something…" Emily was about to die of shame, but she had to tell this to get it out of her head. She fixed her eyes on the carpet between them and whispered, "He had his male part in the mouth of a woman laid out on the altar while another man was having relations with her." Good God, had she really just said that out loud? She squeezed her eyes shut briefly and continued, "The earl was there, on the same gallery as me, and laughed when he saw my face." That mean laugh still reverberated in her head.

Her desperate eyes found Allen's. "Before we wed, Max promised me he wouldn't touch those women again. He promised me and I trusted him."

"So, you haven't spoken to Max since this happened?" Allen asked.

Eliza rubbed Emily's shoulder, her expression troubled. "I'm so sorry, darling. How awful it must have been."

Pressing the handkerchief to her eyes, Emily murmured, "I was so hurt, so utterly shocked, I couldn't breathe! It was too much, so I ran. All I knew was that I had to get away. Max followed me, but I couldn't look at him. I just couldn't. I got on a horse, and somehow, I got to Brighton." She dragged in a shuddering breath. "The rest Thomas probably told you."

Allen pulled Emily into his arms. "I'm so sorry, sweet. But darling, take heart. I don't believe he did what you think he did. The news we have makes a lot more sense now. We obviously had no idea what the Earl of Warthon is capable of." Prying the handkerchief out of her hand, he dried Emily's eyes.

Emily sniffled. "Just tell me your news. I know what I saw, but I don't know any of the why. It's all so very confusing."

Allen exchanged a look with Eliza, who nodded her encouragement.

"You remember the girl from the club I asked about His Lordship?" When Emily nodded, Allen continued, "She arrived at our house not a half hour after we had read Thomas's letter. She was completely beside herself, afraid for Lord Didcomb, and also for you."

Sitting up a little straighter, Emily's brow furrowed. "Why would she be afraid for him, or me?"

Allen held her hand tightly. "You see, she was there."

Emily's free hand flew to her mouth, visions of the woman on the altar assaulting her, and tried to scoot away from Allen.

"No, sweet pea, hear me out. What she has to say will make things clearer."

"That woman! You brought her here?" Emily's eyes were wild.

"Yes, Emily. You need to hear what she has to say." He paused until Emily nodded, although the stiff set of her shoulders remained.

"Marie is the girl your father sent me to find at the club three years ago. She was mistreated by the earl, and Didcomb helped her to get away. He took her to London and offered her a choice, a position in his club or a reference to get work as a maid. She opted to stay in the club. That's how she ended up at the abbey that night. Will you talk to her?"

Emily's eyes were huge. She swallowed down the bile in her throat and squared her shoulders. She had wanted answers; here was her chance. "Yes."

"Good. I'll go get her." Allen patted her hand before quitting the room. He returned soon after, ushering in the woman they had left in the yard earlier. She kneaded her hands, her arms close to her sides, and kept her eyes to the ground.

"You are Marie?" Emily asked tentatively.

"Yes, ma'am."

"What do you have to tell me?"

Marie finally raised her gaze, her green eyes entreating. "It wasn't him, Lady Didcomb." She was pretty, with curly blond hair and a pleasing figure, but her dove-gray dress was exceedingly ordinary. Emily would have taken her for an upper servant had they met in the street.

Emily's brow furrowed. "What do you mean?"

The young woman took a deep breath. "What you saw in the abbey, it wasn't Lord Didcomb. I had to come tell you. You see, he treats us well, he does. When he left the club because he found you, we girls were all excited for him. His Lordship is a good man, he deserves love after what he suffered from the earl."

Still looking suspicious, Emily nodded. "He did suffer. Warthon separated him from his mother when he was twelve." Curiosity got the better of Emily. "What happened?"

Encouraged, Marie told her story. "I don't like going to the castle, the earl scares the living daylights out of me. He's a spiteful old menace and he's got more power than what's good for one person." The expression in her eyes left no doubt the earl truly frightened her. "This is a bad business, my lady. I worry for Lord Didcomb, and for you. You see, after you left that night, Lord Didcomb cursed his grandfather for what he's done to you, and him. He told the earl he'd not see him again and wished for him to die alone. Shouting it, he was. And so loud we heard him all the way at the abbey."

Emily vaguely remembered shouting behind her, but in her state it had only spurred her to ride faster. She wondered if Max truly intended never to see his grandfather again.

Marie continued, "I knew the earl was up to no good. Lord Jennings, who is the dungeon master and responsible for the displays, got sick to his stomach right after breakfast that day, so he wasn't around. Lord Didcomb had told him to train a new partner months ago when he told us all he wasn't coming to the club no more, and Jennings did. Lord Beresford was doing the displays with him, and he seemed to be enjoying himself. The earl knew too."

Emily held up a hand to stop her. "So are you saying Lord Didcomb was forced into this situation? Why did you say that it wasn't him in the abbey?"

"No, my lady, he wasn't at the abbey." She turned pleading eyes to Allen. "Lord, I'm not telling this right."

Allen squeezed Emily's hand. "Patience, my dear. Let her tell it her way."

Emily held his gaze for a moment, then let out a slow breath. "I apologize, Marie. Please continue."

Twisting her reticule in her lap, Marie pressed on. "The first I knew there was trouble was right before the big dinner. That's when Lord Didcomb came to us girls and told us Beresford was feeling insecure about doing the display by himself, so Lord Sinclair would be part of it from the beginning. I knew something wasn't right, because Beresford had never had no trouble before, but I couldn't say nothing with him standing right there. I didn't see Lord Didcomb again, but when Beresford came to perform in the display, he was wearing His Lordship's jacket and waistcoat. I thought it was odd, but when I heard a woman scream above and Beresford never even looked up, that was mighty strange. He kept his head down, while one of the earl's footmen ran out of the abbey. Then, when I heard Lord Didcomb curse his grandfather way down by the chapel, I figured the earl had done something awful to you both."

There was absolute silence for a long moment while Emily stared at Marie and tried to fit these new facts into all she had seen. A sob escaped her, but there was joy in her eyes. "It wasn't him. The scene I witnessed, it wasn't Max."

"No, it wasn't." Allen smiled. "I didn't know who Marie had heard scream, but if you combine her report and yours, it becomes clear Warthon tricked you into thinking Max was betraying you."

"Then what did he do to make Max give the other man his coat? This Beresford was wearing his boots, too, I recognized them." Emily swallowed hard, her eyes flashing. "The vile, despicable wretch of a decrepit old earl. God, I hate him."

"You and me both, my lady. He is evil," Marie agreed.

"Thank you so much for telling me. I truly appreciate it. If there is ever anything I can do for you, please come to me." Emily reached out to shake Marie's hand.

A shy smile brightened the young woman's face. "His Lordship has been good to me. I had to do what I could."

Eliza, who had been listening intently, rose to tug the bellpull. "I'm so glad you came with us, Marie. As agreed, our coach will take you back to London. Will you be all right there?"

"Yes, ma'am. One of the other girls is covering for me. I best get back, though."

Mrs. Bennett appeared and informed Marie that the coach was already waiting for her, with a picnic basket in it.

"Thank you, Mr. and Mrs. Strathem." Marie inclined her head to them, then curtsied to Emily. "Best of luck, my lady."

The three friends watched her as she strode out of the room with a spring in her step.

"It was brave of her to come tell me." Emily paced the length of the room. "God, how I despise Warthon."

Allen's lips twitched at her vehemence. It seemed Emily was prepared to fight for her love. "Indeed. It seems the old goat orchestrated the lot. He is devious and cannot be trusted under any circumstances."

"I know. I could see in his eyes how much he wanted to hurt me, that's why I came here." An idea started to form in Emily's mind. "And if I want to be able to trust my husband ever again, I must sever the ties between him and his grandfather forever. Words spoken in anger won't be enough, it has to be a complete break. But if his mother couldn't do that, what hope do I have? Max also seems very focused on the Knights." The corners of her mouth pulled down in distaste.

"I don't think his mother had a choice but to let the earl have his heir. Didcomb was just a boy and his father deceased. He is a grown man now, and you are his wife. I have seen the way he looks at you. He loves you, he can make that choice."

"But he should make it freely."

"That would be ideal."

Emily wandered over to the window. It hadn't been Max. She was still reeling with relief. Blowing her nose noisily, Emily contemplated her next move. She wasn't ready to see him, not yet. There was still too much unsettled, too much danger. But she could write to him, to let him know she knew he had not betrayed her. Emily turned to her guests. "May I leave you in Mrs. Bennett's capable hands? I need to think."

Allen waved her away, and Eliza stood to embrace her. "Of course, darling." She smiled encouragingly. "Don't mind us, Mrs. Bennett is capable indeed."

Allen closed the door behind Emily and returned to his wife.

"The poor child." Eliza laid her head on Allen's shoulder, seeking the comfort of his arms. "I wish Henry was here. I have a feeling this won't be resolved until he confronts the earl and finds out why that man hates him so."

Allen rubbed her lower back, which he knew to be sore from the long drive. "I'm so glad Marie could tell her it wasn't Didcomb she saw."

"Me too. Can you imagine?"

THE OCEAN WAS CALM, THE sun tinting the endless expanse sapphire and turquoise. No whitecaps raced toward the beach, no waves ceaselessly crashed into the cliffs. As Emily sat and breathed the briny air, everything calmed inside her. Max had not deceived her. He had not done the things she had seen. And that meant the blame for the events of that horrid night fell to Warthon alone. Well, and Weld, but mostly Warthon. The knowledge brought a lightness to her heart. There was still Warthon to deal with, and Max's attachment to the Knights, but Emily felt hopeful for the first time since that night. A night that felt like it had happened an age ago. She was still unsure how to proceed, but she believed a way could be found.

Suddenly restless, Emily swung her legs over and hopped off the wall to return to the house. It was time to write to Max.

CHAPTER TWENTY-EIGHT

MAX HAUNTED HIS GREAT BIG EMPTY TOWN-house like a ghost. As he had assumed, all the sheets had been laundered, but in the back of one of Emily's drawers he found a crunched-up fichu still fragrant with the essence of Emily—a heady mixture of horse, hay, tuberose, and exuberant exertion. Max slept with his cheek and nose buried in it and forbade the servants to enter the bedchamber to prevent the precious smell from being washed away. Whenever he felt particularly low, he returned to his treasure, seeking evidence Emily, his wife, was real. He needed the reminder he had not just been rudely awakened from a magical dream. He was indeed married to the most wonderful woman this side of heaven. Her smell was inspiration to do all he could to become worthy of her.

But for now, there was nothing he could do but wait, checking the mail for signs of her hand. He also called on her friends, but all of them seemed to have fled the summer heat and stench of the city. So, he spent hours in Addy's stall, soothed by the remaining echo of Emily's voice and the hope he would indeed find her there.

On Sunday morning, before the meeting to announce his withdrawal from the Knights, Max went for a ride in Regent's Park after a fitful night's sleep. He was on his gelding, since he planned to ride Caesar the first twenty miles toward Oxford as soon as his business with the club was concluded that night. The stallion had superior endurance and would allow him to make good time to Bilbury the following day. Max planned to stay in an inn in Bilbury and present himself at the Baron Chancellor's estate on Tuesday morning. He didn't dare think beyond that point but hoped his father-in-law would at least tell him where to look for Emily. He couldn't stand the thought of Emily thinking he had betrayed her. How hurt she must be.

The cool early morning breeze soothed him somewhat, but the memory of Emily racing down these trails made him miss her even more. At times, the pain of his separation from her threatened to overwhelm him, but the hope of finding her soon drove him on. It urged him to visit all the places where her memory clung like morning mist.

As the morning sun rose golden and oblivious above the verdant oak trees, Max directed his gelding to the new stable to offer another heartfelt mea culpa to Addy's empty stall.

Both halves of the Dutch door into Addy's domain had been left open, so Max wandered in, his heart heavy. It had been four days since he had held Emily. Four days since he had been happy, had felt whole. Four miserable days stretching into an eternity.

The morning sun slanted through the easterly window, throwing a bright set of four squares against the lower half of the wall next to the door. Max only noticed it because the window was so very bright and his mood so very dark, but as he looked at the sunlit squares on the wall, he noticed a corner was shadowed by a much smaller rectangle. His eyes snapped up to the window and, looking closer, he recognized the rectangle as a letter set on the sill. Propelled by hope, he rushed across the straw-strewn floor to snatch the missive up and bring it to his nose. Sun-warmed tuberose: Emily! His name in her hand on the front confirmed two things: it was indeed penned by his beloved wife, and the letter had been hand-delivered since there was no address. No seal adorned the red wax to give her location away. Still, she had written to him. His heart pounded like a stampede of galloping hooves as he pressed the precious communication to his heart and strode for the house and the privacy of his book room.

Once safely at his desk with the door closed and the butler informed not to disturb him, he examined the letter once more. He turned it this way and that, smelled it again. Tuberose and a hint of the sea. Was she still in Brighton? He laid the letter carefully before him and breathed deep, hope and trepidation robbing him of his wits. At length, he summoned his courage, severed the seal with his knife, and flattened the single sheet before him.

The way the paper was filled by Emily's hand said a lot about her state of mind. His name was a quarter way down the length of the letter, but a postscript filled in the top. Additional sentences had been squeezed into the margins and the script grew smaller and more cramped together toward the bottom of the page.

Oh God, he just wanted to hold her, stroke her back until she was calm and tell her all would be well, that he would never again allow anyone or anything to come between them. He wanted to tell his wife he loved her more than all the trappings of his wealth and privilege, that he would give it all up for her, but the first words below his name were *I can't see you yet*, so he did the only thing he could do for her: he read her words.

Max,

I can't see you yet, but you should know that I'm safe and in a place where Warthon can't reach me. Mr. and Mrs. Strathem are with me and brought with them a woman named Marie, who was at the abbey that awful night. Thanks to her, I now know that you did not betray me, and that soothes my heart. Her account makes it clear we both were tricked and betrayed by the earl. Warthon had help from Weld, and the despicable earls separated me from Ben and tricked me into coming to the abbey. I'm sure Ben told you that side of the story.

I still don't know what happened to you, but at least I know you were not in the abbey when I saw someone who looked like you do despicable things to one of the women there. There are still so many questions. How did this man, Beresford, come to wear your clothes? Where had you come from when I heard you outside the chapel? And why, if you had concerns about my safety, did you go to the dinner at all?

I do not know what kind of pressure Warthon put on you. I also have no idea what kind of upbringing you had in his house for him to have such power over you, but those are things for you to contemplate. It is excruciating not to be with you, but Warthon is a danger to us both. He is your grandfather, and you are his heir, therefore you may not want to sever all ties with him, but I must avoid the earl at all costs. He will hurt me again and use me to hurt you as well as my father. I would go and ask him myself why he hates us so much, but I know that would be folly and he wouldn't answer me. His disdain for me and all women was made abundantly clear.

I won't pretend I'm not hurt by the events of that horrible night. Warthon's machinations were very effective in that respect. I desperately miss you, but until we can at least ascertain how to protect ourselves from Warthon, we best let him think he has succeeded in driving me away.

Your loving wife,

Emily

PS: I heard you cursed your grandfather and told him you would not return to Warthon for as long as he lives, but perhaps we—you, me, and my father—should confront him together. We cannot allow him to destroy us, to let him win.

Max's hands shook when he set the page back onto his desk. The thought of Emily in despair, seeing all those depraved things, wrenched his gut and made him curse Warthon all over again. To be separated from her, not able to comfort her, was agony. But at least Marie had told her it had not been him at the abbey. He sat up as the weight lifted off his shoulders, but then shivered at the danger she was still in. Why had he not seen this coming? Emily was right, he had been too weak to walk away from Warthon and the Knights. The independence he had believed he had gained from his grandfather and his perverted traditions had been nothing but an illusion. The earl had played him for a fool and hurt the love of his life. It was time Max broke with it all and became his own man.

Max carefully folded the letter and slipped it into his waistcoat pocket, right over his heart. He then pulled a sheet of paper from the top drawer and sharpened his quill while he thought. Eventually, he dipped his pen.

My beloved Emily,

I am desolate at the hurt I have unwittingly caused you. I love you with all my heart and am glad your friends brought Marie to you. I'm beyond relieved you know it was not me in the abbey, but I should have kept you safe from Warthon. After all, I know what he is capable of. It is no excuse, but I myself was betrayed by my grandfather in a way only his twisted mind could conceive of. He outwitted and drugged me, and you were hurt due to my stupidity. Forgive me, please.

I wish I were with you so I could hold you and tell you all will be well. You will never know how desperately lonely I am without you. I knew I loved you before this happened, but now that you are gone, all I can think of is how to secure your safety from my despicable grandfather so we can be together once more. Nothing else matters.

To this end, I am meeting all the men who were present at the dinner, to tell them I will be leaving both the club and the Knights. I do not want this part of my birthright. It was used by my grandfather to hurt you and is therefore forever tainted. After the meeting I'm to journey to Bilbury to meet your father. I must tell him all and ask him for help in confronting my grandfather. You are right, we must know what Warthon has against him, or the earl will hurt us again, and that, my love, I cannot allow.

I promise you, I will try to be a better man for you, and I will never cease trying.

I miss you with every fiber of my being and hope you will let me see you soon.

Your loving husband,

Max

He folded his letter and sealed it with wax, but refrained from using his seal. This was between him and his beloved; no title or privilege had any place here. Carrying the letter to the stable, he stood it on the windowsill, on the other side from where her letter had been, hoping whoever had brought Emily's letter would carry his back to her.

With his hope renewed by Emily's message, every action Max took that day gained urgency. He was doing these things for Emily and their future life together. He handed over the clubhouse's keys and deed to the women who lived there and made his intentions clear to his peers. Max felt the significance of fulfilling the promise recorded in his letter to Emily, and walking away from the house and the organization he had thought he would lead one day, he felt remarkably lighter. Not until this moment had he realized what a burden the Knights had become to him.

Winding his way out of the busy metropolis and finally giving Caesar his head on the open road, Max began to think of all he had to tell Sir Henry. He knew his father-in-law was his best hope to sort this mess out once and for all.

THE WAIT FOR MAX'S REPLY proved excruciating, but when Thomas finally handed her his letter on Monday afternoon, Emily cried happy tears over it until it was barely legible. Allen and Eliza were in Brighton to find out what they could about Warthon and Weld, so Emily sat alone under the walnut tree in the walled garden at the back of the house and let her emotions flow freely. She missed him so, it was almost a taste in her mouth, a misery only he could alleviate.

It was good to know Max missed her too.

Turning to his letter once more, it was truly encouraging to read his promise to hand over the club and leave the horrid Knights. He even seemed ready to declare independence from Warthon. It was all Emily had hoped for. He was willing to make sacrifices and changes to keep her out of harm's way, when he could simply have ordered her to come back to him. He was her husband, and he had every legal right to demand such a thing. But Max wanted her love and her safety. He was willing to take her side.

According to his letter, Max was on his way to Bilbury, where Isabella was staying with her parents. That meant someone, probably Mrs. Tibbit, had given him her father's itinerary and he knew when Sir Henry was to arrive at the Chancellor estate. Emily had not gone to her Papa for her own good reasons but didn't doubt her father's willingness to confront Warthon. Now that she knew Max was not to blame, she felt sure Papa would be eager to help them. He would accompany Max and they would arrive in Brighton before the end of the week.

But their arrival had to be monitored; she needed to be there when the confrontation between her father and the Earl of Warthon took place. Emily was done with men keeping things from her. Never again would she trust anyone to do anything that affected her happiness without her knowledge. Everyone had assumed the Earl of Warthon was reconciled to their marriage when he attended the ceremony, but no one had told her what the problem was in the first place, nor what made them think the problem had disappeared. Of course, she had made her own optimistic assumptions, but never again. She needed to hear firsthand what had caused the old man to treat her with such hateful malice. After all, there was no need for anyone to sugarcoat anything for her benefit; the devious old man had used his own grandson to hurt her. It was clear Warthon's objection was based on more than her illegitimacy, and she needed to know what made him hate her and her father so. She also knew neither her father nor Max would take her along, fearing for her safety. Neither could they be trusted to tell her the whole truth if they found it out, and that she could not abide. She would be there herself.

Ben Sedon might understand, and he was in a position to help her. He knew the castle inside and out, might even know of a place from where she could listen and observe without being seen. The only problem was going to Brighton. She had no desire to give Warthon another opportunity to hurt her.

Fortunately, she didn't have to go to Brighton: she could ask Allen to talk to Ben. Likely, Ben would recognize Allen from the wedding, so they could simply meet as acquaintances in the street. With a decision made, and emotionally exhausted, Emily leaned back against the cushions she had thrown under the walnut tree and promptly fell asleep.

Her dreams were full of the sneering earl torturing Max and laughing when she tried to free him, but in the old man's eyes, she could also see that he was afraid of her. Emily awoke with a start, the knowledge that she had power over Warthon because of Max's love for her still firmly in her mind.

The position of the sun announced it to be late afternoon. Voices were coming from the house, and then Allen and Eliza stepped out into the garden, a footman and Mrs. Bennett following them with a laden tea tray.

"Emily, my dear. Guess who we had lunch with down in Brighton?" Allen pulled her up from the ground as the servants set the garden table for afternoon tea.

"I don't think Max could have made it to Brighton yet, so who?"

"Max? Did you hear from him?" Eliza inquired, instantly interested.

"Yes, Thomas brought back a letter from him, but he went to Bilbury to enlist Papa's help. Who did you meet?" Emily hated guessing games, so she glared at Allen to get on with it.

Allen knew he was teasing her too much and relented. "Max's friend, Ben Sedon. He went to London with Max, looking for you last week. Max is in a right state, according to him." He rubbed a comforting hand over Emily's shoulders. "Anyway, Max sent Ben back down here to keep an eye on Warthon and Weld, to make sure they don't go after you again. Max is concerned his grandfather may not be done with his revenge, whatever it is for."

Emily plopped down into one of the wrought-iron chairs and took a cup of tea from Eliza. "Yes, that has occurred to me too. I think he is waiting for my father. Papa is the ultimate target." She took a sip, then looked from Allen to Eliza. "I think I was just a tool to cow Max with and hurt my father. What the earl underestimated is the love between Max and me. However, he is right about my father; Papa will go to confront Warthon, and that's exactly what Warthon wants. The earl wants to hurt him, and he evidently doesn't care who he uses to do that or who else gets hurt in the process. I, we, need to find out why and how far he will go."

Allen raised his cup to her. "Bravo, that is about the long and short of it. Ben reports both earls are smug and satisfied at present, but there is a distinct air of anticipation about them. They are waiting for something, probably Henry's arrival." Allen took a hearty bite of his cheese-filled pastry before he continued. "Mr. Sedon reports his father-in-law is now staying at the castle, which he says is not unusual but should mean he has no further need of his countess or Ben to deceive anyone."

"Good, then Ben can be our lookout." Having an appetite for the first time in days, Emily answered around bites of cheese and buttered country bread. "Can you contrive another meeting with Ben? I estimate Max and Papa will arrive on Thursday or Friday, and I want to know when they do. Allen, I know they won't let me come with them to confront the earl, but I must be there, I must hear for myself why the earl did what he did, why he hates Papa and me so much." When Allen started to shake his head, knowing full well what Henry would say to that, Emily's beseeching eyes turned to Eliza.

"You know the men are not going to tell me all, and I have already been on the receiving end of the earl's cruelty. I need to know, Eliza. It is not right to leave me in the dark. All I'm asking is for you to ask Ben if he knows a back way into the castle so I can witness the meeting for myself. It will most likely take place in the large drawing room. It's a cavernous room with lots of dark corners. There must be a place where I could conceal myself. I know it's dangerous and I will stay hidden if I can, but I must know." Her voice broke on the last word, and her hand holding the thick slice of bread sank back to her plate.

Eliza shot Allen a quelling glance and patted Emily's hand. "I do agree, you do need to know. This affects you, your life, and your happiness. But we need to make sure you can be there safely. We will go back to Brighton tomorrow. Mr. Sedon already knows we will be at the pier at eleven o'clock in the morning, and he is to meet us there." When Allen gave her an almost imperceptible nod of acquiescence, Eliza's tone changed. "He very much wanted to know how you are, Emily, and if he can come to see you. The poor man feels terrible for both you and Max, and the role he inadvertently played in the whole debacle."

Emily turned her eager face from one to the other. "Oh, please ask him if he knows of a place." Sobering, she added, "And tell him I don't blame him for what happened. The two despicable earls are to blame for it all, and they need to be stopped if any of us are to continue our lives in peace."

Considering the two women in front of him, Allen sighed. They were both strong, capable women, and why shouldn't Emily be allowed to help shape her own destiny? However, he had one condition. "Granted, Emily has a point. We will find out if there is a way to get you into the castle unseen and if you can be in the room and remain hidden. I will be with you and will protect you, but you will have to promise me to do as I say. But under no circumstance"—he turned to his wife at that point—"and I mean under no circumstance, are you, Eliza, to enter the castle."

Looking mutinous, Eliza opened her mouth to speak, but Allen laid his hand on her belly. "No, love, not this time. You and the babe will stay here."

Eliza braided her fingers with Allen's over her belly and smiled. "Oh darling, I do love how protective you are of me and the babe, but I can hardly sit around for nine months and do nothing. I will be fine."

Emily's face softened, seeing the love between her friends. "No, Eliza, Allen is right. You must think of the babe. It will put all our minds at ease for you to stay here and keep things ready for when we return. Don't soldiers have a duty to keep their base secure?"

"Indeed, they do." Allen winked. "Eliza, light of my life, will you stay and be our quartermaster? Please?" He kept smiling but held his breath.

Seeing the worry in her husband's eyes and aware of the new life within her, Eliza relented. "I suppose between you, Henry, Didcomb, and Mr. Sedon you will be able to keep the poppet safe from one crazy, old earl."

CHAPTER TWENTY-NINE

"I NEED YOUR HELP." THE PLEA FLEW OUT OF Max's mouth the moment Henry entered the room, but explaining why he needed that help was frankly harrowing. Max made several attempts to begin telling his dreadful tale of betrayal but had yet to find the right words.

Sir Henry, in the meantime, settled himself in a comfortable chair and waited patiently for his son-in-law to get to the point. But when Max took yet another deep breath, only to sink dejectedly into one of the voluminous leather wing-back chairs in Baron Chancellor's cozy study, Henry figured it might be easier to get the story from Emily. "Where is my daughter?"

"That's just it, I can't find her."

Truly alarmed now, Henry sat up straight. "What do you mean? What happened?"

Realizing his doddering had caused Sir Henry to fear for his daughter, Max assured, "She is safe, that much I know." He ran nervous fingers through his disheveled hair. "She wrote to me and told me she was safe, but I don't know where she is. You see, my grandfather was far more devious than either of us ever dreamed. He tried his best to manipulate me into doing something I had sworn to Emily I would never do again."

Henry held up a hand to stop Max, his face full of apprehension. "Are you speaking of a sexual display?"

"Yes." Max's eyes were full of remorse but also respect. "I should have known you would know about them."

Sighing, Henry motioned for his son-in-law to continue.

Max rushed on, needing to get it all out in the open. "When I refused, Warthon had me drugged, took my clothing, and had another blond man take my place, and then he tricked Emily into witnessing it. Needless to say, she was angry, hurt, and just wanted to get away. She fled before I had a chance to explain, and now I can't find her."

Henry growled his displeasure. "Is anyone with her?"

"Yes, Thomas and her maid, Suzie. We lost them somewhere between Brighton and London. The coach they hired went to London and delivered a note to your housekeeper there, but they were not in the coach." Now that he was standing in front of Sir Henry, trying to explain the mess he had made, Max had trouble communicating all the pertinent facts. "Oh, and she writes Mr. and Mrs. Strathem are with her."

Henry let out a big sigh of relief. So, Emily was either with Allen and Eliza in Chelsea, or they might be holed up at Charmely, his estate on the south coast. Either way, Emily was in good hands. Much calmer now, Henry went to pour them both a brandy. "You better explain."

Noting Henry's changing demeanor, Max also calmed somewhat, took another deep breath, and pulled Emily's letter out of his waistcoat pocket. "I think you better read this."

Recognizing his daughter's hand, Henry took the missive, but it took him a while to decipher the rather chaotic letter. He growled in rage several times, but when he came to the postscript, he hummed his approval. Then he abruptly stood, went to the door, and shouted for someone named William before he turned to Max. "Maximilian Warthon, I want to thrash you for what you let happen to Emily, but apparently she still loves you, so I'll leave the thrashing to her. We are leaving for Brighton in half an hour. I presume you have everything you need with you?"

Max only had time to nod before Henry left the room to arrange their departure and rearrange his family's travel plans. As much as Max had hated having to reveal his role in this debacle, he was relieved beyond measure to have his father-in-law's support in facing his grandfather. For the first time in days, he felt able to breathe, could see a future. A future free from Warthon. A future with Emily. But first they had to beard the dragon in his lair.

EMILY WAS SO IMPATIENT TO find out if Ben could get her into the castle, she walked all the way to the gate to await Allen and Eliza's return. It was a beautiful, warm afternoon, and secure in Max's love once again, she could appreciate the splendor all around her. The downs rose gently to her right, the ocean sparkled blue and brilliant to her left, and the sky stretched azure and cloudless to the horizon. She had found one of Isabella's wide-brimmed painting hats in a back salon and enjoyed the unobstructed view of the fields around her and the breeze it allowed to caress the nape of her neck. It took less than half an hour to walk to the gate, but the driveway was bordered by long-stemmed daisies, allium, a few cornflowers, and the occasional poppy, inviting Emily to pick a bouquet for the dinner table.

It was so good to have Allen and Eliza with her, even if they took their sweet time coming back from Brighton. They were friends she could rely on, friends who helped her navigate this crisis and who understood her need to be part of this fight for her life. Emily had collected an enormous armful of flowers by the time their gig came into view. Waving her arm overhead, she waited for them to turn into the drive and stop next to her.

"Can Ben get me into the castle?"

Allen laughed as he moved into the middle, transferred the reins to his left hand, and reached his right down to help her climb in. "Yes, sweet pea, he has an idea. But first let's get Eliza to the house."

Emily leaned over Allen to greet Eliza. "Are you well?"

"I am." Eliza smiled at her impossibly lovely and impatient friend.

"The jostling is much less of a problem in the open carriage, but we had a rather rich lunch."

Emily had witnessed two pregnancies with her stepmother and nodded wisely. "I'm sure Mrs. Bennett has mint tea. Do you think that would help?"

"Oh, yes, that sounds heavenly."

With that settled, Emily focused her attention on Allen once again. "So, what did he say?"

Allen looked to Eliza for guidance, but she only motioned for him to tell Emily, so he did. "Apparently, the drawbridge into the castle is not watched and can't be overlooked from the main living rooms, so it's relatively easy to get in. Mr. Sedon's father, as the stable master, is in charge of the courtyard as well as the stables, and there is a covered walkway from the stables into the kitchen so the staff can get back and forth in inclement weather. Your Ben says the kitchens are a labyrinth in themselves with hiding places aplenty. From one of the cupboards there, a secret passage leads to the back of the big fireplace in the hall. Mr. Sedon said you would know where that was. Evidently, it's the earl's favorite room and the one he receives visitors in."

Emily's face was flushed with excitement. "That's the room I called the main drawing room. Perfect, the earl has a favorite chair right in front of that fireplace. But doesn't Warthon know about the passage? Are there not likely to be guards?"

"No, Sedon says only he and Max know about it. They found the entrance when they were boys. Apparently Didcomb had frequent need to hide from the earl, who doled out savage canings at the least provocation. The secret passage was completely blocked by cobwebs when they first stumbled upon it, and it is the only place where the earl never found them."

Laying her hands against her flushed cheeks, Emily took a fortifying breath. Her heart went out to the boy Max had been, separated from his mother and seeking refuge from beatings in a spider-infested tunnel. She would be there for him. "Good, now I just have to find out when I have to be in the hiding place and find a way for Ben to show me how to get into it."

"The ever-helpful Mr. Sedon had an idea about that too. He is keeping an eye on the Waterfront Hotel, where at least Max will be staying since he still has his clothing and his valet there. Ben will visit with Max, give him his report on the movements of the despicable earls, and find out when he and your father plan to confront Warthon. Then he will send us a message and we will get to the gatehouse well in advance. We will hide within, and Mr. Sedon will pick us up there. Depending on whether Max wants him to come into the meeting with the earl or not, Sedon will get us in and stay with us, or leave us in the tunnel and then meet Max."

"Sounds like a perfectly reasonable plan," Emily approved. "But how will he get a message to us? I thought we agreed not to tell him where I am just yet."

"It's all arranged. He will send the message to the Golden Stag, just past the turnoff leading here. We will send one of the stable lads there to wait for it. Additionally, there is a back road leading to the Warthon estate through the downs from here, so no one watching from Brighton will be any the wiser. We just need a dark cloak for you." Allen winked at her as he directed the horse over the hill into the stable yard, pleased with the developments of the day.

Emily couldn't help herself; it was all so cloak-and-dagger, she giggled. "Thank you. I do not look forward to more dealings with the earl, but planning this is fun. All this passively being devastated over things that were done to me is not how I want to cope with life."

Both Allen and Eliza could only nod in agreement. Emily's melancholia when they had first arrived had been palpable. It was good to see her youthful enthusiasm break through. She would need it to deal with her treacherous in-law.

THE FIRST TWO DAYS OF their ride from Bilbury to Brighton had been silent and tense. But on the evening of the second day, Henry ordered their dinner to a private room in the inn where they broke their journey for the night. He then proceeded to get the entire story of this sorry mess out of Max, down to the last detail of the earl's deception, beginning at the wedding and ending with how Warthon had tricked Emily into witnessing the display. He wanted to know who might have known, how much they knew, and which footman had drugged Max. No detail was too small, Sir Henry wanted to know it all.

Max, grateful for an opportunity to unburden himself, told his father-in-law everything he knew and offered his theories on the events he had not been present at himself. After that night, the two men rode in companionable silence, both clear on what had to be done and looking grimly forward to it.

WEDNESDAY AND THURSDAY PASSED PLEASANTLY enough at Charmely with the weather sunny and warm. They went riding in the mornings and spent afternoons in the garden. Feeling more herself, Emily returned to the piano with renewed vigor, filling the house with music whenever they were indoors. The household noted with relief the melodies were no longer morose, although Emily still preferred dramatic pieces. She missed Max desperately and her emotions still roiled within her, but she was no longer confused as to what she wanted. She wanted her life with Max, and she would fight for it. The days trickled by easily, but as Friday evening turned to night without any word from Ben, Emily grew first quiet and then impatient. Worry started to creep in when they still had not heard by Saturday morning. She knew her father and she knew horses, and so she calculated they should have arrived in Brighton. The thing she didn't know was when they had left Bilbury. Even so, surely they should have arrived by now.

Breakfast was a subdued affair, and no one wanted to go for a ride or engage in any activity that would take them away from the house. What if they missed the messenger and then missed their chance to get into the hiding place? What if Warthon had lookouts and decided to face down Sir Henry in Brighton? Emily spent an hour in the stables, grooming Addy, but even that couldn't calm her. She was just about to send Thomas to check on the stable boy at the Golden Stag when the boy himself came galloping into the yard. Allen and Eliza appeared at the back door, their faces as expectant as Emily's.

The boy waved the message overhead, not sure who to deliver it to as they all converged on him. Emily reached him first and immediately slid a finger under the paper flap to break the wafer. She read while Allen and Eliza did the same over her shoulder.

Dear friends,

I am glad to report Max has arrived, and has come to free himself from his grandfather's influence once and for all. He and Sir Henry arrived late last night and are currently resting at the Waterfront Hotel. I saw them this morning for breakfast, and they plan to be at Warthon Castle at four in the afternoon, the traditional time for the earl to receive visitors. Because my father-in-law is now staying with Warthon and will be present at the confrontation, Max has asked me to join them. They are resolved to end this entire debacle today, and the underhanded way Weld tried to drive a wedge between Max and myself is part of this. We are to make ourselves independent of both earls.

As far as your plans to observe the meeting from the secret passage are concerned, I need you to meet me at three o'clock at the gatehouse so your path won't cross with Max's or Sir Henry's, both of whom would surely object to your presence.

I'm quite sure Max would never speak to me again if anything should happen to you, Emily, so please stay hidden no matter what is said. The earl is dangerous, we all know that now. Even more so since Weld will also be attending.

Your humble servant,

Ben Sedon

"There we have it." Allen grunted. "You and I, sweet pea, will be leaving here at one o'clock. That should give us ample time."

Eliza met Emily's expectant gaze and stepped into her role as quartermaster. "Right, that gives us two hours to prepare. Emily, please go and have Suzie braid your hair and pin it up. Best to keep it out of the way."

Fingering her loose twist and realizing how close it was to disintegrating, Emily turned toward the house. "I suppose you are right. Do you have a gun I could borrow? Mine is in London."

"Absolutely not," was Allen's immediate response.

Eliza could see the mutiny in Emily's eyes, so she explained, "I know you are a crack shot, but you have never handled a gun in a tense situation such as this. Your nerves can make the gun in your hand more dangerous to you than to anyone else."

"I will be right beside you with my entire arsenal of weapons," Allen reassured further.

Presented with the opinion of two experienced agents, Emily didn't think any argument she could present would sway them. "I suppose."

"Remember, you are only there to observe," Eliza cautioned. "Leave the confronting to Max and Henry. Ben will also be present, and Allen will be there as backup, if needed. You remain hidden."

The expression on Eliza's face was so fierce, Emily couldn't resist needling her a little. "Oh my, Eliza, you will be a stern mama." With that she swept into the house calling for Suzie, while Allen and Eliza exchanged speaking glances.

"Are you sure you don't want me to come along?" Eliza remarked.

Allen glared at her. The last thing he needed was to have to worry about two unpredictable women. "Quite sure."

CHAPTER THIRTY

THE SUNDIAL ON THE STABLE WALL INDICATED one o'clock when Allen and Emily set out on their way to Warthon Castle. Emily suspected Allen's dark leather suit concealed secret pockets and halters for guns, knives, and other instruments of the spying trade. She had known since childhood that her father and her adopted uncles were engaged in secret activities in service of the crown, but she had never been so very grateful for it. Allen was, aside from her father, the most capable person to have beside her for this task.

Eliza had relented and attached a knife to Emily's garter "just in case." The folds of Emily's dark blue riding habit hid it even when in the saddle, but the feel of it pressed to her thigh gave her confidence. She wasn't a spy by any stretch of the imagination, but she had been raised by one and she was determined to make her father proud. Her eyes were shaded by the short brim of a dark blue cap, which also hid most of her shiny blond hair. The most conspicuous thing about her appearance was her beloved dappled gray Arabian horse.

As soon as they turned out of the gate and into the country lane snaking along the downs toward their destination, Emily nudged Addy into a light gallop. Their journey passed without incident, and they arrived at the gatehouse marking the boundary to the Warthon estate fifteen minutes prior to the appointed time. As it always did during the day, the gate stood wide open, and through the trees they observed a shepherd leading his herd of sheep to the meadows surrounding the castle. Tethering their horses in a small, secluded clearing along the estate wall, Allen and Emily assured themselves the animals could not be seen from the gate or the castle, then let themselves into the gatehouse.

The inside of the structure was surprisingly neat, with a wooden table and chairs set along the back wall. But Allen and Emily didn't even have time to sit before they heard a horse approaching at speed. Moments later Ben Sedon came into view.

At the site of Max's best friend, Emily almost burst into tears as the reality she would be encountering Max today hit her with a force she hadn't expected. They would be in the same room, whether he knew she was there or not. She would see him, hear his voice, feel his presence. The longing for him almost overwhelmed her.

Outside, Ben tied his reins to a metal ring before he looked around to make sure there was no one else around. Eventually he looked through the window, and upon seeing them, stepped into the gatehouse, unaware of the turmoil his very presence caused Emily.

She straightened her spine and greeted her husband's best friend. "Hello, Ben."

Ben took both Emily's hands and squeezed. "It's so good to see you, to know that you are well. I am so very sorry for everything that has happened since we parted on that dreadful night."

Emily swallowed heavily but returned the squeeze of Ben's fingers. "It's good to see you too. How is Max?"

"He was in a state when we didn't find you in London, but he seems much better now. He is resolved to free himself from everything to do with Warthon."

"So he said in his letter. But I need to hear it for myself."

Ben nodded to Allen. "Mr. Strathem told me, and I think you are right. There has been more than enough deception for you and Max to overcome. This all must come out into the open. Just please stay hidden, the earl is dangerous. The last man who got in the way of his plans he simply shot in the head."

Emily exchanged a look with Allen. "I do hope Papa is armed."

Reassuringly patting her arm, Allen nodded. "Your father would never walk into a hostile situation unarmed. Besides, he was present when the earl shot the man who had kidnapped Isabella. He knows who he is dealing with, he just doesn't know the why."

"None of us do, that's the problem. But we should get going." Ben glanced left and right at the door and retrieved his horse. "I'll ride ahead to make sure the courtyard is clear before you enter. Simply walk through the meadow and over the drawbridge. Only the butler's pantry looks out over the drawbridge entrance to the yard, and the butler is old and shortsighted. Stay inside the gate until I signal you." He mounted and cantered toward the castle.

Allen offered Emily his arm and they promenaded through the meadow as if on a country walk. Leaning closer, he joked, "We should have brought one of Mr. Twill's guidebooks."

"Oh, Papa mentioned them. They were all designed to keep adventurous souls away from the abbey at night, if I remember rightly." Emily shook her head. "I should have heeded their warning."

"Come now, sweet pea, this is no time for self-flagellation. We are about to untangle this mess and then you can figure out your life without ever having to worry about the dratted abbey again." Allen squeezed her hand on his arm as they walked through the sheep-dotted meadow.

They made it across the drawbridge without incident, but as they stepped through the gate, and then through the carriage-sized corridor leading into the courtyard of the castle, they noticed Ben listening in on a conversation between a footman and the stable master. Ben was turned half toward them, and when he noted their arrival, he subtly lifted his left hand in a staying motion. Allen smoothly pulled Emily back into the shadows of the sandstone building.

The stables were to the left, directly opposite the front door of the castle, and in that space was all the activity. But the cobbled expanse of the yard also extended to the right of the gate and around the near flank of the main building. That part of the yard was deserted; however, it was overlooked by several gothic windows.

"So much for best-laid plans," Allen muttered under his breath, keeping a sharp eye on Ben, who was turning his back to them and pointing into the empty part of the yard.

Emily indicated her head in the same direction. "I think he is pointing toward the small wooden door at the end on this side of the castle."

At that moment a groom led out a saddled horse, and the footman turned to him and away from Emily and Allen.

"I think you are right," Allen agreed. They strode briskly toward the small door, where at least the other men in the courtyard wouldn't be able to see them. They made it across just before the mounted groom clattered over the cobbles of the yard and then the wood of the drawbridge. Pressing themselves to the wall next to the three sandstone steps leading to the side door, both breathed a sigh of relief when the man continued without looking back.

Emily scurried up the steps to try the door. "Damnation, it's locked. How will we get in?"

"Patience, sweet pea, subterfuge takes time," Allen whispered. "Ben will open the door for us, or I'll pick it. Either way, we can't go further without him. We don't know where the entrance to the passage is."

Emily tried her best to tame her restless hands. "All these windows make me nervous. I don't know what rooms are on this side."

Allen kept himself flat against the wall, making discovery from anyone inside less likely. "Let's hope it's a succession of unused salons. The view certainly isn't very appealing."

It was true, there was nothing of interest to look at in this part of the courtyard, just cobbles and wall. "All it takes is a maid looking out while she is cleaning and thinking we are burglars."

Thankfully there was no need to speculate any longer. A bolt was drawn and then the door opened from the inside. Ben waved them in, a finger on his lips. Once he had pulled the door shut behind them, he whispered, "I had hoped to bring you in through the stables, but the earl's footman was there sending a message for Warthon and ordering the carriage for later."

"What was the message?" Allen inquired.

"All I could find out is that the earl plans to dine at the Waterfront this evening. I suppose he found out Max and Sir Henry have arrived and wants to do some taunting." He laid his finger on his lips again as they heard footsteps on the bare floors. Pointing at the wooden planks beneath their feet, he mimed tiptoeing, and once the footsteps had retreated, led them toward the foyer. As quietly and swiftly as they could, they crossed the expanse of the entrance hall and followed a labyrinth of servants' corridors toward the kitchens, but just before they got to the bustling hub, Ben opened a panel door to the right and motioned them inside. The dust on the cabinet surfaces convinced Emily the room was unused, so once they were enclosed within, she relaxed a fraction. Ben went to one of the large cupboards, opened the five-foot door, and stepped inside. A press of his finger in the upper right-hand corner of the back wall made the wall silently slide to the side, revealing the passage beyond.

"Go to the end of this passage where it makes a left turn," Ben whispered. "From there you will be able to see the opening to the fireplace about twenty-five feet further in. There is no fire in the grate, so your view will be unobstructed, and you will be able to get through into the room if it should become necessary, but be careful." Turning to Emily, he continued, "Please stay hidden, for my sake as much as your own."

Ben lit a candle and set it into a tiny alcove just inside the passage. "Don't take the candle closer, it could give you away." He stepped back out and handed Emily into the passage. "I better go meet Max and your father."

Emily nodded, waited for Allen to get in beside her, and felt her way along the narrow passage.

Counting sixteen steps before she reached the left turn, Emily could hear voices from beyond the strip of light at the end of the tunnel as soon as she turned into it. She quietly inched forward until she stood close to the narrow opening. Allen was right behind her, his presence reassuring. From where they stood, they could see only the back wall of the enormous fireplace in the earl's hall, but Warthon's voice was clear and rather close. Emily imagined him sitting in his favorite chair by the hearth.

"I don't believe they have found the chit yet, but her father might know where she is. Why else would Didcomb go to him?"

"That seems a reasonable assumption." Weld's voice sounded farther away, but still easy to understand. Emily decided not to risk looking just yet; she could picture the hateful old men well enough.

"The bloody cheek of them," Warthon seethed. "Riding into Brighton, bold as brass, and stopping at the best hotel. Not much of a spy, is he? If he didn't want to rouse my ire, he should have been more discreet. Should have worked out what he has done by now too. Well, I'll rattle their cage."

There was a pause, then Warthon added as if to himself: "I'll make sure I'm there when they find her, and then...an eye for an eye, a child for a child."

Emily and Allen looked at each other, stunned. What could the vile creature mean?

"Does Max know what your grievance with Sir Henry is?"

Emily held her breath, dying to find out herself.

"That's none of his business," Warthon snapped. "He should have simply obeyed."

"Granted, but aren't you taking it a bit far? You already got your revenge. I don't even know what you have against March, his father was one of us."

"Ha, I don't expect you to be able to work that out, you never were all that bright."

"I beg your pardon?" Weld sounded affronted.

"Oh, come now, you and I are friends because you never pretend to be smarter than me. You know your limitations."

There was a long pause during which Emily had to press a hand to her mouth to stop a snort from escaping. Warthon certainly knew how to deliver a set-down. Weld deserved it.

"March is a fool to come here. He should know I want to see his face when I take her from him."

All mirth fled Emily's being. She had known it to be imperative to get herself away from the earl, but it was still shocking to hear him threaten her life. Her gaze met Allen's in the gloom, and she knew he felt the same.

"I thought we were just going to dinner." Weld sounded confused.

"We are. I want to see how they suffer." A cruel laugh accompanied the statement.

"Are you not worried Didcomb will remain stubborn if you taunt him now?"

"He had his chance." Warthon was angry again. "First he marries the chit against my will, and then, when I get rid of her, he runs after her instead of submitting to me." The old man was spitting bile now. "I can still get it up. I have a good mind to take Jennings's daughter off his hands and beget myself a new heir."

Emily was stunned. Max was his grandson, had the man no feelings at all?

"Good Lord, she is seventeen." Even Weld sounded disturbed by the notion.

"Right age to breed."

Angry tears escaped down Emily's cheeks. Warthon's malice was relentless.

Allen pulled her close and breathed, "Don't mind him."

Emily rested against Allen for a time, but the sound of a handbell pulled them back to the two earls. A few seconds passed before the door opened.

"You rang, my lord?"

"Fetch the tea tray."

"Right away, sir."

The servant departed, but moments later the door opened again.

"YOU HAVE SOME GALL, BOY, to bring that man into my house." Warthon's walking stick was accusingly pointed in Sir Henry's direction, making Max shiver with the memory of the pain that gesture used to herald.

The old man's eyes snapped from his grandson to Henry, and there was no mistaking the hatred in them. Henry took a sharp breath at the visceral feeling of malice assaulting him but stayed quiet. He was there to provoke a reaction from the man so Didcomb could extract the reason for all this animosity, and it was working.

"I wouldn't have had to consult him if you had seen fit to tell me what you have against him and his daughter," Max goaded. "Now once and for all, what has Sir Henry done to you that is so heinous it justifies destroying my happiness?"

"He killed my son!" Warthon thundered, his chest heaving, his eyes bulging as he rose out of his chair. An apoplexy seemed imminent as he shouted, "He killed my boy, the last connection I had to my Eugenia."

Henry met Max's gaze, lifting his shoulders, utterly mystified. "I was at Waterloo, but to my knowledge I wasn't stationed anywhere near your son."

Max was equally as baffled. "Who is Eugenia?"

"Not him," the earl spat contemptuously, referring to Max's father. "Lord Astor, my only son with the woman I loved."

"Astor was your son?" Henry was dumbstruck. As far as he or anyone else knew, Astor had been the fourth son of the Duke of Elridge, and the French spy Henry had pursued for years. "But I didn't kill him."

Warthon, beet red with agitation, accused, "You did as surely as I stand here. You were the one to lead the chase after him all over the Continent. You were the one to put a flea in Wellington's ear about a traitor selling military secrets to the French. You hounded him even after the war was over; and you were the one who couldn't just let it go. You are the reason Fairly was in that chamber to pull the trigger. You killed him." His finger was still accusingly pointed at Henry when he let himself sink back into his chair.

"Astor was the traitor the French called De Sade Anglaise. I'm certain of it," Henry asserted. Robert had killed the swine in his own dungeon, where he had been torturing the woman who would later become Robert's viscountess.

The Earl of Warthon's eyes sparkled with fanatical pride. "He believed we should join forces with Napoleon and be part of his grand vision of a united Europe under one emperor. He was a hero, not a traitor, and you killed him for it."

An odd sense of déjà vu settled over Henry. The spark of madness in the old man's eyes was exactly like the look he had seen in Astor's as he had stood in that awful underground room, trying to kill Eliza with a bullwhip while telling Henry he should be one of the Knights. They were indeed father and son. A hush settled over the room as the shock of the revelation descended upon everyone who heard it.

"Hold on just a moment." Weld was perhaps the most confused of them all. "You set a cuckoo in Elridge's nest, and that cuckoo was Astor?"

Warthon nodded.

"That at least explains why Elridge severed ties with us," Weld muttered to himself.

"It also explains why Elridge didn't mourn his son," Henry added. He had always wondered at the duke's response to his son's demise. Elridge barely attended Astor's funeral and then went back to his life as if nothing had happened. It had squashed all questions as to the peer's involvement, after Henry had unmasked Astor as the traitor who had sold English military secrets to the French, but it had also seemed singularly unfeeling.

Weld shook his head as if questioning what he was hearing. "But how the hell did all that happen?"

Warthon sighed, abruptly shifting into a contemplative singsong, yet his eyes held cunning. "It was a rather common tragedy. Eugenia and Elridge were engaged from the cradle, and I didn't meet her until her betrothal ball on her seventeenth birthday. I would have given anything to run off with her, but I was already married, and my countess had just presented me with an heir, so there was nothing I could do." The old man stared at a miniature on the mantel that Max had always assumed was of his grandmother. "I came back here and licked my wounds. The countess presented me with a second son and then died shortly after. I didn't see Eugenia again until a decade later, after she had already given Elridge four children, three of them sons. What was between us was undeniable and we found ourselves spending every minute possible in each other's company. Those were the happiest eighteen months of my life. Until she died bearing me Astor." A tenderness crossed his face neither Max nor Henry would have believed he was capable of. "I invented all kinds of reasons to cross paths with my son, and a fine man he turned out to be. We thought the same, believed in the same things, and shared so much. He was truly my son in every sense of the word and a worthy successor as the leader of the Knights."

The revelation that Astor had been Warthon's son was strange enough, but the tragic love story was beginning to cloy on Henry. Astor had been a monster. Henry and his men had cornered him in his sex dungeon where he had been in the process of torturing an innocent young woman. It had been Viscount Fairly who had put a bullet in his brain, not Henry. It was true Henry had led the charge, and it had been Eliza, his mistress at the time, who had uncovered the connection between the traitor and the lord, but still, something felt off about the earl's convoluted tale. Warthon had everyone's attention on the story, but the picture he painted of his son was so disparate to the man Henry had known Astor to be, it was disturbing.

Henry was about to say something to that effect, when the old man, whose hand had been slipping behind the armrest of his chair, raised it.

"Gun!"

The single word rent through the air. Henry recognized Emily's voice but couldn't tell where it came from. But, forewarned, he expected the earl to point the gun at him and reached for his own. Instead, an evil smile crossed Warthon's face.

The Earl of Warthon turned to the fireplace triumphantly. "A bastard for a bastard, and you get to watch, March."

Max moved like lightning. "No"—was all he had time for as he threw himself into the fireplace. The two gunshots went off almost simultaneously, and then the earl crashed to the floor, Henry's bullet buried in his black heart.

CHAPTER THIRTY-ONE

"MAX!"

Emily gasped in horror. The scene had unfolded with agonizing slowness. She had seen the gun in Warthon's hand and must have cried out, because he turned to her with an evil leer, raising the gun. Then Max's body had been between her and the gun. She had heard the shot and seen the jerk in Max's body before he crashed into the back wall of the fireplace. Now he lay motionless.

She desperately scrambled to his side. "Max, can you hear me? Max." Trying to turn his crumpled, limp body, a sob escaped her. "Max, please don't leave me."

Weld's shocked voice came from somewhere in the room. "He must have gone mad; he killed his own heir."

Emily wanted to scream at the man not to say Max was dead, but all she could get out was: "Papa, help me."

Allen was already at her side, feeling for a pulse. He gave her an encouraging smile when he found one. "I think he knocked himself out when he flew against the wall."

There was so much blood, it was all over his coat, on his chest and his sleeve. Emily's heart hammered so fast she could barely hear anything for the rushing blood in her head and the worry shaking her whole body. She couldn't lose him now.

The door crashed open, and several people summoned by the gunshots entered the room. Sir Henry took command. "Send for the doctor. Both the earl and Lord Didcomb have been shot. Mr. Sedon, help get Lord Didcomb out of the fireplace."

Ben helped Allen get Max to the closest sofa and got his coat and waistcoat off while Emily searched his head for damage. She found blood and a hefty lump on the back of his head, but the spreading red stains were even worse on the white linen of his shirt. She couldn't look away.

"Damnation." Allen growled before he ripped the shirt down the front to see what damage the bullet had done. There was a bleeding hole the size of a halfpenny between the collarbone and Max's pectoral muscle, but it was shallow. Emily could see the metal of the bullet just below the level of the skin, with blood pulsing all around it. Frighteningly, there was more blood pulsing on Max's forearm.

"What the devil?" Allen must have seen it too and ripped the right sleeve of the shirt up to the armpit. The whole forearm close to the elbow was thickly smeared with blood. Whipping it away with the ruined shirtsleeve, Allen uncovered two bleeding holes. With nimble fingers he began to prod each hole, then felt the bones in Max's arm.

"How bad is it?" Emily asked, trying to control the shaking of her voice.

Allen smiled reassuringly. "Your Max is a very lucky man. The bullet went through the fleshy part of his forearm before it lodged in his chest. It needs to come out, and we need to stop the bleeding, but I suspect there are no organs or bones damaged."

The sober assessment did much to calm Emily, but she was still shaking.

Allen pointed to a bit of blood in Max's hair. "Did you find a lump on his head?"

"Yes, it is as you said."

Ben wrapped Max's coat tightly around his arm to stanch the blood. "Did someone go for the doctor? It would spare him a lot if we could get the bullet out before he wakes up."

The footman who had been in the courtyard earlier answered, "I just sent a messenger. He is not far."

Emily's mind whirled. Max was losing blood. The bullet needed to come out and all three wounds would need stitches, that much she knew. But then what? Could he be moved? All Emily could think of was getting Max away from this awful place. Out of the corner of her eye she could see Warthon's unmoving body, and the horror of that was almost more than she could bear. Her father, who had been checking the earl for signs of life, stepped close to her and put a calming hand on her shoulder. She raised worried eyes to his. "Is he dead?"

"Yes," was his simple answer.

Relief flooded Emily. Max was free of the horrid man and his influence. But what might that mean for her father? She couldn't think of that now. Max was at death's door because of her. He had protected her with his very body; what greater proof of his love could there be? "I want to take him back to Charmely, keep him away from all this."

"That might be best, but we can't move him until the bullet is out," Allen advised.

Ben agreed. "Some of the staff are very loyal to the old earl, so I do think it's best to take Max away from here."

"Point taken." Henry turned to Weld. "Do you know who the Justice of the Peace is?"

"Warthon was, and since Max is now Warthon, it's him, unless he wants to appoint someone else." Weld was rambling. "But I have seniority right now, so if we summon the constable from Brighton, I can tell him Warthon told us all a crazy story about a man who has been dead six years and then shot his heir. Thank God you were here and could put a stop to it."

Henry took the shaking arm of the Earl of Weld and guided him out of the room. "That is an excellent idea." He motioned for the footman. "Can you find us another salon where we could meet with the constable? Also send for the man and bring us some brandy. I believe Lord Weld needs to rest."

"That's most kind of you, March. I am a bit shaken." Weld let himself be led out of the room where the late Earl of Warthon still lay crumpled on the floor. Sir Henry had pulled the lids over his dead eyes earlier, and a servant had laid a blanket over him, but his malevolence still cast a pall over the room.

Ben grumbled under his breath, "My dear father-in-law certainly knows when to hang his flag into the prevailing wind."

Allen chuckled. "It works in our favor. Help me get Didcomb onto that table over there and take his shirt off. There should be enough light there for the doctor to work in." The table in question was on the other side of the room under the triple arch of the Gothic window.

They laid Max on the table, with a sheet under his torso and a cushion under his head. Emily cleaned the wound on Max's head and was washing down his shoulder and arm with brandy when the messenger returned with the news the doctor was detained at a difficult birth and wouldn't be able to attend Max for some time yet.

Emily couldn't stand the thought of waiting and in her agitation pulled her knife from its halter on her leg and started cutting bandages from clean linen. The longer the bullet remained in Max, the more damage it was liable to do. She turned to Allen. "Can you do it?"

Studying the hole the bullet had left in Max's shoulder, Allen sighed. "I would rather not. I'm not a great surgeon. I think we should stitch the wounds in his arms, though."

Ben cleared his throat. "My father has dug out a few bullets in his time. He sets bones too."

"Go get him," Emily and Allen said at the same time. Emily added, "I would rather we got it out before he wakes."

"Just what I was thinking."

While they waited, Allen carefully closed the holes in Max's arms with several stiches each while Emily held the arm still. Max started to twitch when Allen put the flame- and brandy-sterilized needle through Max's skin for the last time, confirming that time was of the essence.

It took a while for the stable master to arrive, but when he did, his shirtsleeves were already rolled up and his hands looked freshly scrubbed. Emily trusted him immediately. "Mr. Sedon, could you please help us? The doctor is detained."

Ben's father, a man on the cusp of fifty, tall and brawny with silver shot through his dark hair, nodded. "Ay, so I heard." He handed a slim blade and a pair of long-nosed tweezers to his son. "Rinse those in brandy."

Sedon the elder took less than a minute to extract the bullet, but it took the combined strength of Emily, Allen, and Ben to hold down the now delirious and thrashing Max while the stable master closed the wound, stitching with a sure hand.

Moments later, while they dressed his wounds with pads of soft lawn and bandage strips, Max came to. Emily was in the middle of securing his injured arm tightly to his torso with yet another bandage to keep the arm still and didn't notice right away that he was conscious.

MAX STIRRED AND GROANED, HIS hand going to his aching head before he opened his eyes. The pounding in his skull was nothing he had ever experienced before, and it took a moment for his vision to clear.

Finally, Max's gaze landed on Emily's hale form, as she worked to make him more comfortable, and a sob of relief broke out of him. "Thank God."

Emily jumped with joy at the sound of his voice. Laying her hand on his cheek, her voice was full of loving concern. "Are you in a lot of pain?"

Turning his head so he could press a kiss into the palm of her hand, he groaned at the agony the movement caused in his head and shoulder. Breathing heavily through the pain, he whispered, "I'm so sorry, love. Are you well?"

"I'm fine, Max, but you got between me and that gun. We had to dig a bullet out of you and stitch the wounds closed."

Mr. Sedon leaned in to check Max's eyes, then nodded to Ben.

Max remained focused on Emily. "I couldn't let him hurt you again."

Lifting his shoulders, Ben put a glass to Max's lips. "Drink this, it will help."

Sipping the offered liquid, Max fixed his friend with desperate eyes. "Get Emily away from here. Warthon wants her dead. I saw it in his eyes." He shuddered at the memory, then groaned again.

Taking his uninjured hand, Emily braced to break the news to Max. "Darling, I'm so sorry, but your grandfather is dead."

Max closed his eyes for a moment, a wave of relief washing over him. But then he remembered all the times he had thought he had gotten away from the monster, only to be trapped by him again. "Ben, God only knows what orders he left, get Emily to somewhere safe."

"Relax, my friend," Ben soothed. "We will get you both away from here. The earl can't hurt you now."

Max gave a jerky nod and focused on Emily once more. "Please don't leave again."

Pressing her lips gently to Max's forehead, Emily felt a tear slip down her cheek. "No, love, I'm coming with you."

Max let out a sound between a sigh and a sob and lost consciousness again.

"What did you give him?" Emily inquired, gently stroking a blond curl off Max's brow.

"Brandy with a few drops of my father's special mixture. It will make him sleep and help with pain and swelling." Ben handed her a small flask. "Give him three drops three times a day in water, or nine drops in brandy to make him sleep."

Allen took the flask and opened it to smell the contents. "Is there laudanum in it?"

"I put some laudanum into the draught I just gave him, but this is just arnica, valerian root, lavender, rosemary, peppermint, and cloves."

Handing the flask back to Emily, Allen rubbed the back of his neck. "Good. Laudanum has its place, but it can do more damage than good. Don't give him any more if you can avoid it, Emily. Although, the doctor is sure to prescribe it when he comes to check on Max," he growled.

THE NEXT TIME MAX WOKE he was in a coach. His eyelids were too heavy to lift, but the warm softness beneath his head smelled like Emily, so he let himself drift back to sleep.

THEY HAD MADE IT TO Charmely and settled Max in bed by the time the doctor arrived. Since Max was conscious for the visit, the doctor could confirm the bump on Max's head had not resulted in a concussion. The physician checked all the wounds and declared himself very pleased with Mr. Sedon's work but remained concerned about Max's multiple injuries. A week in bed was recommended and a diet of easily digestible food. And sleep. Sleep, sleep, sleep. Max remained fever-free, so Emily could somewhat relax and finally agreed to let Thomas and Max's man-servant, Menton, sit with him while she slept and saw to their horses. Sir Henry had brought Caesar up from Brighton and Emily took it upon herself to exercise him and Addy together. Eliza kept all tasks involved in tending Max well organized. Allen, always more comfortable with action, went to Brighton to help Henry and Lord Weld with the investigation into the death of the earl. The whole affair was a tragic, tangled mess of an accident, as far as the law was concerned. There was nothing left to do but arrange Warthon's funeral.

MAX WOKE TO THE WARMTH of sunlight on his face, and when he opened his eyes, the light blinded him. However, his head no longer pounded. Someone bent over him, and the shadow it cast allowed his eyes to adjust and focus.

"You are awake, my lord." His man's excited voice stated the obvious, but all Max noted in the unfamiliar sun-filled chamber was Emily's absence. He could remember her at the castle, after he had been shot. When he had awoken in the coach, she had been his cushion, her smell more soothing than whatever they had given him to make him sleep. At some point she had fed him soup, he recalled that, and then she had been asleep in a chair by his bedside, but where was she now?

"Where is my wife, Menton?" His voice sounded foreign even to himself, hoarse from disuse. Water was being poured into a glass and then Menton held the glass to his lips. Max drank, inordinately grateful.

"The countess watched over you all night. She needed some fresh air this morning and went for a ride."

Max relaxed back into the cushions. She had not left again; he would see her soon.

The countess?

Christ, he had forgotten he was Warthon now. That would take some getting used to.

Lifting his hand to his face, he encountered several days of growth. "I would like to bathe and shave."

Menton looked unsure. "I'll shave you, sir. But the doctor said your wounds need to be kept dry for two weeks. I will consult Mrs. Strathem about bathing."

"Wounds, plural?"

"Yes, sir. Unfortunately, or perhaps fortunately, the bullet went through your arm before it embedded itself in your upper chest. You also injured your head in the fall, but all your wounds are healing well."

Contemplating this information, Max tried to pull himself into a sitting position. "How long have I been here?"

"Five days, my lord." The servant helped him sit up and stuffed cushions behind his back. "The doctor said you should sleep as much as possible, but you had the last of the sleeping draught last night. I shall bring you tea and something to eat."

"What time is it?" The sun was bright and seemed to be high in the sky.

"Just after eleven in the morning."

Early enough for breakfast, then. "Bring me some eggs and bacon, I'm hungry."

Menton smiled, evidently encouraged by his master's appetite. "I shall confer with Mrs. Strathem."

As soon as Menton departed, Max pulled back the covers to swing his legs over the side of the bed. Zounds, he did need a bath. There was nothing wrong with his legs, according to Menton's report, but he felt rather like a newborn foal as he made his way across the room. There was a lovely view of the cliffs and the ocean from one of the windows; the other overlooked the approach to the stable yard. Max didn't know where he was, but speculated it had to be somewhere to the east of Brighton. His room was airy and bright, with sage-green drapes and two velvet-covered armchairs in the same shade grouped around a table by the window. A comfortable-looking armchair he had observed Emily sleeping in was to the right of the bed, and an open door led to a dressing room. That's where he found the necessary.

He had just managed to relieve himself, and was contemplating how to put on his dressing gown with his arm strapped to his torso, when the door opened and Eliza Strathem walked in, followed by a matron with a huge tea tray. Menton brought up the rear.

"Ah, Lord Warthon, it's wonderful to see you up, but perhaps you would like to return to your bed to eat." Eliza Strathem turned away from him, while Menton helped him into the dressing gown. "No bacon, I'm afraid, but there are coddled eggs, toast, butter, and Mrs. Bennett's most excellent preserves. Later you can have a sitting bath, but you will have to take care not to wet your bandages."

Max wanted to object to all of it, but his legs were still weak, and he wanted to preserve his strength so he could talk to Emily once she returned. He wanted to be upright and dressed for that. He gave his assent and climbed back into bed.

"YES, I KNOW, CAESAR, YOU are a good horse. You miss him, too, don't you. Have patience, he will come see you as soon as he can." Emily rubbed the big stallion's powerful chest while he nickered and blew at her. Addy stood patiently on the other side of the stall door, waiting for her mistress to do the same for her. "We are all waiting for your master to get better." She ran her hand over Caesar's shoulder one last time before she took his halter off so he could go nibble on his fresh hay. But rather than turn to the treat, he whinnied and crowded Emily at the stall door. "Hey, what are you getting so excited about? I'm just going next door to see to Addy." She chuckled, but then heard another chuckle behind her.

"He might be excited to see me."

"Max." She turned with as much excitement as Caesar. "What are you doing out of bed?" His eyes held such longing as he took in her face, it drew her like a lodestone.

"Mrs. Strathem thought a little fresh air might be good for me." He smiled ruefully.

"So you decided to go to the stables?" She laughed, pointedly contemplating the dust dancing in a sunbeam coming through the closed window.

"That's where I hoped you would be." The smile spreading over Emily's face made Max weak in the knees. It felt like the sunlight after a week of unrelenting rain, like the answer to a prayer. He reached up to scratch Caesar's chin, needing something to do with his hand. A hand that ached with the need to touch her, to draw her into his arms. "Emily, I am so sorry for all the hurt I have caused you."

Swallowing the lump in her throat, Emily stroked Caesar's neck, feeling the same need to occupy her hands. "You didn't hurt me, your grandfather did."

"I should have known, should have kept you safe. And I should have left the Knights before we married."

"I agree with you on leaving the Knights, but your grandfather would have found another way to hurt me."

"How can I make it up to you?"

Her dimples made a brief appearance. "Taking a bullet for me should suffice as reparations."

Max flashed a grin, warmth flooding his eyes. "One of my finer moments."

Addy, growing impatient for her mistress's attention, brushed her lips up along her neck and face before she started to nibble on her hair. Emily curved her arm up around the horse's neck and scratched between her ears but didn't take her eyes off her husband. "I missed you so."

"And I you. I never knew how much I wanted you, needed you, loved you until you were no longer there." It was his turn to swallow hard. "Oh Emily, I was desolate without you." He stepped closer and reached out to touch her face.

She smiled and molded her cheek into his palm. "Before I knew it wasn't you, I was so afraid you had done those things because I wasn't enough for you."

That shocked him. "Oh, God, no. Don't ever think that." His eyes were dark with love and hurt and naked want as he stepped closer. "You are enough for me. You are all I want." He brushed the back of his fingers down her cheek. "I'm so sorry I failed to protect you from my grandfather's scheme. I promise I will never knowingly do anything that could hurt you ever again."

"I hurt you too, when I ran." Her eyes, full of love, searched his. "Forgive me."

"There is nothing to forgive, love. I'm just glad Warthon didn't succeed in breaking us apart and we can start anew without the pall of his ill will."

Sighing, she closed the gap between them. Her front touching his, her face turned up to him, the two horses rubbing their heads against their shoulders, pushing them closer to each other.

Max caressed her face, reading every beloved part of it with his fingertips. Then he stroked his uninjured hand over her hair and down her back, until he finally held her close, while the horses nudged them closer still. "It seems Addy and Caesar are keen on this reunion."

"It seems that way." Emily chuckled, snaking her arm around his neck on his uninjured side and standing on her tippy-toes to brush her lips over his. "I love you, Max. Life without you was miserable. Kiss me."

The words were like a benediction. The nightmare that had begun with the Knights' dinner was truly at an end. Max closed his eyes and leaned his face into hers. "And I love you. With everything I am." His lips found hers, kissing her with all the tenderness and passion a woman could wish for.

EPILOGUE

EMILY LEANED HER HEAD AGAINST HER HUS-
band's shoulder with a contented sigh. They both sat on the piano bench,
but while she faced the ivory keys, he faced into the room where their
friends were still gathered.

"Tired, darling?" Max leaned back to look at her face without dislodging her head.

She smiled, presented her lips for a kiss, and continued playing her
lullaby for their two-week-old son Marcus. "Dreadfully. I hope no one
will mind if I take a nap right here."

"Say the word and I'll throw them all out." He chuckled.

"I'd like to see you try." She laughed, then yawned, snuggling back
into his shoulder. "The babes are already asleep, and the older children
will have dinner with us. It will be fun."

It had already been a long and eventful day. Marcus's christening
at St. George's that morning had not only been early, but also incredibly well attended. Everyone was already in town for the season,
so the reception rooms on York Terrace had been filled to the brim
with well-wishers all day. Add to that a colicky baby and chronic lack
of sleep, and Emily's need for a nap was no surprise. Thankfully, the
crowds had departed, and now they were only surrounded by those
they loved.

Max placed a lingering kiss on the crown of Emily's head and
breathed in the fragrance of her hair. "We might have to hand-feed
your papa," he murmured and nodded to where Sir Henry reclined

in an armchair. The brand-new Lord Didcomb, securely tucked into the crook of his grandfather's arm, fought the weight of his eyelids. The baby girl on Sir Henry's other shoulder was already asleep. Henrietta Strathem was Henry's fourteenth godchild, and a decided favorite. Her proud mother, Eliza, occupied the sofa, resting against Allen and conversing with Isabella, while Max's mother shadowed Dorothea March. The toddler was determined to keep pace with her brother, Danny, and Edgar Sedon. The boys, however, had eyes only for the Honorable Charlotte Pemberton. At four years of age, Robert's daughter had all the magnetism and fire of a pirate queen, and as the oldest of the bunch assumed the role of leader. Currently, she ordered her pirates to board the chaise longue on the other side of the room and bring her the treasure, a demand that had Isabella, Jane, and Charlotte's mother, Stephanie, standing as one.

"Charlotte," cried the long-suffering Stephanie.

"Edgar, stop this very instant," ordered a resolute Jane.

"Danny, I'll thank you not to climb on your sister's furniture," Isabella admonished.

The three mothers shared looks full of humor, but it fell to Ben to enter the pirate fray and open the French window. "Last I checked, pirates don't operate in drawing rooms. Take the battles outside, please."

The three children looked at each other, then, with a rallying cry, threw themselves down the steps into the garden, followed by Dorothea and Max's indulgently smiling mother.

"I believe Mama is happiest with our band of cutthroats," Max murmured into Emily's ear.

"She is patiently waiting for a turn with the baby," his wife whispered back.

"Impossible, she has barely put Marcus down since he was born."

"She has been an enormous help." Emily stood and moved to the bell pull. "Let's have a quiet cup of tea while the kids are occupied."

"Excellent notion," seconded Henry as he stood with the two babies. Max took his son and together the two men settled the youngest members of the party into the armchair to nap. The piano bench was moved to the foot of the chair to prevent the babies from slipping to the ground before Henry and Max joined their wives on the sofas surrounding the fireplace.

His arm around Isabella's shoulder, Henry surveyed the assembled company with evident pleasure. "My friends, life has turned out rather well for all of us, hasn't it?"

Allen and Eliza leaned their heads together. "Indeed."

"It certainly has." Robert kissed Stephanie's hand.

Smiling, Max gathered Emily close. "Talking of friends, where is your cousin Bertie?"

"He left just after lunch, hoping to ride all the way to Oxford tonight," Emily supplied. "He has some exam he wanted to get out of the way so he can break early for summer. Bertie and his friend Lord Mallbury plan to dig a newfangled drainage system on the viscount's estate."

Henry chuckled. "Ah yes, I heard him complain Avon wouldn't let him try out the scheme on his soggy south pasture. I thought it rather a good idea."

"He was positively indignant about his father's lack of faith in him," Emily confirmed.

Max shook his head. "That's Avon's loss. Bertie has a good head on his shoulders when it comes to land management. If ever there was a man who needed his own land, it's Bertie."

Several heads nodded in quiet assent. Max was a welcome addition to their circle. Tea arrived and once served, conversation flowed freely once more. It was a rare occurrence for the entire group of friends to be together in one room, so they savored the moment. They had been through much together over the years and cared deeply for each other, and thus the friends remained in perfect solicitude in a tableau of harmony, a family of mind rather than blood.

THE END

ACKNOWLEDGMENTS

Writing the acknowledgments this time around feels like the end of an era. Not only is this the last book in *The Gentleman Spy Mysteries*, but during the writing of this book my son became an adult and finished high school, allowing me to dedicate more time to my craft. In short, I feel like I am finally free to be a writer, and it's a marvelous feeling.

But of course, a lot more than just writing goes into publishing a book. The first person I want to acknowledge is Michelle Halket at Central Avenue Publishing. Thank you for letting me tell this interconnected succession of stories my way; your continued support means the world to me. And let's not forget about the amazing cover you created for this book. You have outdone yourself with this one.

Many thanks to Molly Ringle for editing *The Spy's Daughter,* and indeed the entire series. The continuity of excellence you have provided has been a boon. Thank you for your attention to detail and all your suggestions, they have helped me become a better writer.

A huge thank you goes to my writer friends. Let me begin with my lovely friend Carmen Chancellor. I treasure our mutually supportive writerly lunches in our little corner at Leonor's. Every writer needs a cheerleader, and you are mine.

This book and the whole series might not exist without the encouragement from my Book Besties: Kelly Cain, Cathie Armstrong, Jamie McLachlan, and Amanda Linsmeier. Thank you for always being there when I need you; you truly are the best.

A special thank you to Kelly Cain for setting me straight once again, and to Amanda Linsmeier for all your excellent suggestions. You two are the best beta readers a writer could have. I have learned to trust you completely.

I also want to acknowledge my husband and son who share me with my stories. Thank you for understanding how important writing is to me.

Bianca M. Schwarz was born in Germany, spent her formative years in London, and now lives in Los Angeles with her husband and son. She has been telling stories all her life, but didn't hit her stride until she started writing books she would want to read for fun. *The Gentleman Spy Mysteries* are those books.

THE COMPLETE GENTLEMAN SPY MYSTERIES
ROMANCE, MYSTERY, & INTRIGUE IN REGENCY ENGLAND

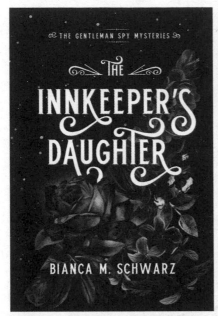

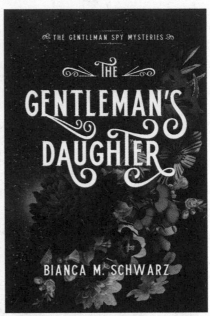

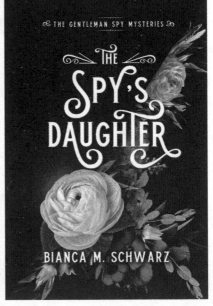

more romance from central avenue

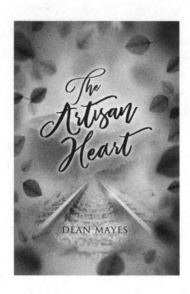

The Artisan Heart by Dean Mayes

Hayden Luschcombe is a brilliant paediatrician living in Adelaide with his wife Bernadette, an ambitious event planner.

When an act of betrayal coincides with a traumatic confrontation, Hayden flees to Walhalla, nestled in Australia's southern mountains, where he finds his childhood home falling apart. He stays, and begins to pick up the pieces of his life by fixing up the house his parents left behind.

A chance encounter with a precocious and deaf young girl introduces Hayden to Isabelle Sampi, a struggling artisan baker. While raising her daughter, and trying to resurrect a bakery, Isabelle has no time for matters of the heart. Yet the presence of the handsome doctor challenges her resolve.

As their attraction grows, and the past threatens their chance at happiness, both Hayden and Isabelle will have to confront long-buried truths if they are ever to embrace a future.

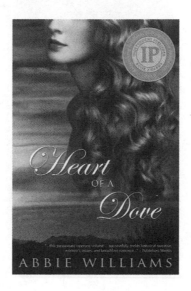

Heart of a Dove by Abbie Williams

The Civil War has ended, leaving the country with a gaping wound. Lorie Blake, a southern orphan sold into prostitution at fifteen, has carefully guarded her aching soul from the disgrace forced upon her every evening. Two years have passed, leaving her with little hope of anything more. Meanwhile, three men – longtime friends – and a young boy with a heart of gold are traveling northward, planning to rebuild their lives in the north and leave behind the horrors of their time as soldiers.

Fate, however, has plans of its own, causing their lives to collide in a river town whorehouse. Forced to flee, Lorie escapes and joins them on the journey north. But danger stalks them all in the form of a vindictive whorehouse madam and an ex-Union soldier, insane and bent on exacting revenge. At last, Lorie must come to terms with her past and devastating secrets that she cannot yet bear to reveal.

Heart of a Dove is the first book in a gripping, sweeping romantic saga of pain, unbearable choices, loss, and true love set against the backdrop of a scarred, post-Civil War America.

Summer at the Shore Leave Cafe by Abbie Williams

The last thing she expected was to fall in love.

Joelle Gordon is leaving Chicago and her cheating husband to head for her hometown of Landon, Minnesota. There, she returns to the Shore Leave Cafe, the lakeside diner the Davis women have run for decades. Joelle's family, including her three teenaged daughters, Camille, Tish, and Ruthann, is made up of strong women who have long believed in a curse upon them – a curse that robs them of the men they love.

This summer has plenty in store for Joelle. Finding herself confronted with the reality of single motherhood, the last thing she expects is gorgeous, passionate Blythe Tilson, a summer employee at Shore Leave, with an uncertain past. Can Joelle resist the temptation of a younger man, and does she dare to consider loving someone again, or will the Davis family curse prove all too true?

This first book in the sweeping Shore Leave Cafe Romance series is a story about heartbreak, blame, family, destiny, and the difficulties of returning home.